I0819223

SAFARI MURDER PARTY

SAFARI MURDER PARTY

RACHEL MOORE

BERKLEY
NEW YORK

BERKLEY
An imprint of Penguin Random House LLC
1745 Broadway, New York, NY 10019
penguinrandomhouse.com

Book design by Jenni Surasky
Interior art: Bamboo frame © StockSmartStart / Shutterstock
Title page art: Bamboo mat © Amphawan / AdobeStock
Organizational chart by Jenni Surasky

Library of Congress Cataloging-in-Publication Data

Names: Moore, Rachel (Rachel E.), author.
Title: Safari murder party / Rachel Moore.
Description: New York: Berkley, 2026.
Identifiers: LCCN 2025024226 (print) | LCCN 2025024227 (ebook) |
ISBN 9780593954539 (hardcover) | ISBN 9780593954546 (ebook)
Subjects: LCGFT: Thrillers (Fiction) | Detective and mystery fiction.
Classification: LCC PS3613.O5665 S24 2026 (print) |
LCC PS3613.O5665 (ebook) | DDC 813/.6—dc23/eng/20250528
LC record available at https://lccn.loc.gov/2025024226
LC ebook record available at https://lccn.loc.gov/2025024227

Printed in the United States of America
1st Printing

The authorized representative in the EU for product safety and compliance is Penguin Random House Ireland, Morrison Chambers, 32 Nassau Street, Dublin D02 YH68, Ireland, https://eu-contact.penguin.ie.

To anyone who swears they'll take PTO eventually:
Read this on vacation

The world is made up of two classes—the hunters and the hunted. Luckily, you and I are hunters.

—"The Most Dangerous Game,"

BY RICHARD CONNELL

DYER CARTWRIGHT
Chief Executive Officer

RAUL DIAZ
Chief Technology Officer

FLETCHER SPENCE
Executive Assistant

DEEPTI KAUR
Chief Financial Officer

MELV LEXINGTON
General Counsel

MOLLY BRADHAMPTON
People Team Lead

JET-SETTER MAGAZINE

JACKIE CALDERA
Editor in Chief

JOPLIN JENKS
Senior Designer

FORD JEPSON
Designer

SALES

THEO GROFF
VP of Sales

RICK EVANSTON
Sales Development Representative

OPAL MEENA
Sales Development Representative

SHEILA DAY
Sales Intern

MARKETING

DENIS BERTRAM
SVP of Marketing and Publicity

BRIAN DUNLAP
Paid Ads Specialist

BRIAN RUSSO
Paid Ads Specialist

SAFARI MURDER PARTY

PROLOGUE

Wilderness hummed around Fletcher as she fought to catch her breath. She'd grown begrudgingly used to its melody over the last few days—the whistle of hot wind through the reeds at the watering hole, the elephant trumpet in the distance, the frog song from the jungle thick.

Of all the people Fletcher thought she'd be here with, the last was Waylon.

Waylon, who had tried to sabotage her career when it had barely begun.

Waylon, who had every right to inherit the Cartwright legacy and none of the qualifications.

Waylon, who held a steak knife to her throat, the blade pinching her skin.

Something greedy burned in his gaze. A hunger. Like he'd been wanting to do this for a long time and only now got the chance.

"I want to trust you," he said, the steel scraping across her rapid pulse.

Breathing. Fletcher wasn't breathing. "Then trust me."

"But how do I know you won't betray me?"

"I could ask you the same thing." The last week flashed behind Fletcher's eyes. Sparkling cocktails served with gourmet meals. Handshake deals signed with blood. And now, a knife to her throat. Careful, she asked, "What do you need to convince you?"

His voice was low in her ear. "Tell me what you want, Spence, and I'll let you live."

Last month, she could have answered his question in a heartbeat. TSA PreCheck. An invitation to the company retreat. A byline in the travel magazine she'd sold her soul to. But that was before. Before she'd ever set foot on this patch of untamed land, and before there was a serrated edge against her esophagus.

He was asking the wrong question. She knew what she wanted.

What was she willing to do to get it?

1

Three Weeks Earlier

Fletcher could be dead, and she'd still see the safari when she closed her eyes.

The mock-up November issue of Cartwright Media's *Jet-Setter* magazine splayed across the workshop table in front of her, right next to a paper take-out box spilling with lo mein, and her phone, where some fraction of her consciousness watched her boss's little blue dot travel up Fifth Avenue. The rest of her attention was glued to the glossy photograph.

For the last half hour, she'd stared at the magazine. Something was off.

She stabbed her fork into the noodles, swirling them mindlessly until the bite was so big she had to unhinge her jaw to chew. "It's missing something."

"Add sriracha," Ford said from the other side of his desktop.

From here all she could see was a thin stripe of her coworker's bleached-blond hair, but she knew he was scrubbing through test shots from last week's luggage shoot in Bali, featuring a pair of mated toucans and what was being dubbed "the perfect weekender bag."

"Not Szechuan's," she said. "Page twenty-three."

If she'd been behind the camera, she would've framed the shot differently, angled the model forty-five degrees clockwise, and called out for more emotion. The centerfold spread—a spotlight on Southern Hemisphere wildlife experiences—should've popped. Instead, it was lopsided and top-heavy, guiding readers' eyes away from the page instead of toward it.

Pacing across the office, Fletcher swatted the magazine onto Ford's desk and pointed at the bald composition. The page was *literally* missing something. "Shouldn't there be something else in this third to balance it out?"

"By 'it,' do you mean the naked man holding a strategically placed tote bag next to a lion?"

"I'm serious," Fletcher said.

"That doesn't mean anything," Ford said. "You're Fletcher Spence. You're *always* serious."

Truthfully, she didn't want to hear his boss chew him out for not catching the framing error. But also she wouldn't say no if the editor in chief walked through the Design Lab doors and offered Fletcher a spot on her staff. (Her bank account could really use the promotion, too.)

"He looks displaced, off-center"—Fletcher's eyebrows raised when she grazed the lines cleaved against his hip bones. What came next disappeared off the bottom of the page—"delicious."

Ford flicked her hand away where it lingered. "Have you forgotten your farm-fresh boyfriend so quickly?"

Fletcher couldn't possibly roll her eyes far enough into her head. When work best friends became real-life best friends, there was always an uncomfortable overlap in professionalism. Even more so when the best friend in question was Ford Jepson, who had never once conceptualized personal privacy. They were purely platonic—Ford exclusively dated men with Guy Fieri goatees or people of any gender who could bench-press his body weight, and being that Fletcher was neither, her long-distance love life was frankly none of his concern.

She settled on saying, "Kent and I are fine."

"When's the last time you saw him?" Ford asked. "Phone sex can only sustain someone for so long."

She didn't bother informing him that she wasn't having phone sex at all because Kent said it made him feel vulnerable, which made Fletcher feel like a jar of homemade kombucha that needed a release. But when you've been with someone as long as Fletcher had been with Kent, that was totally normal, right?

Satisfied there wasn't any juicy gossip to squeeze out of her, Ford's eyebrows cinched as he reverted his focus to the photo and picked at his thumbnail. A terrible habit. Fletcher stopped destroying her nails cold turkey in high school when college applications and internship interviews came front and center. She needed to be pristine, right down to the cuticle.

Just like the November issue if Ford wanted to keep his job.

"You know I'm right," she said, looping her purse over her shoulder and chucking the dregs of her lo mein into the garbage. "Jackie will thank you."

"Will I?" A voice, bright as the midday sun, chimed behind her. "Spending lunch on my floor again, Fletcher?"

Jackie Caldera was known for three things: becoming *Jet-Setter*'s youngest editor in chief three years ago at a ripe thirty-nine; once beating the CEO's son at a company outing to Topgolf; and wearing a bold red swatch of Chanel lipstick every day without fail. This afternoon, it was smeared under her bottom lip, the aftermath of a lunch meeting with the C-suite at the new Nordic-Japanese fusion bistro in Hell's Kitchen.

Even slightly smudged, she was still the HBIC. Jackie commanded every room she walked into—especially the Art and Design Lab on the forty-third floor of Cartwright Media's Fifth Avenue office.

"On my way out," Fletcher said, her voice sliding easily back into its corporate-girl cadence as she propped the door open with her hip. "Don't worry about the centerfold bleed on page thirty. Ford's on it." She answered Ford's petrified look with a mouthed *You're welcome.* Stepping into the hall, she scooped her phone out of her purse at the exact moment it started ringing, crooning, "Good afternoon, Mr. Cartwright. How was your lunch?"

On the other end of the phone call, her boss's crackling tenor was cut off by sirens. Which meant he was outside the building. It'd give her plenty of time to get back upstairs into position. "You know I love Japanese whiskey, Miss Spence. Remind me what's on my calendar this afternoon?"

Fletcher jammed the elevator button for the penthouse. There was a *whoosh* on the other end of the line as Dyer must have stepped into the front lobby. Right on schedule.

"I canceled your afternoon appointment with Dr. Hawks like you asked, so all that's left is for you to finalize the guest list for the Lydell trip, and I'll send out invitations before the end of the day."

"It's on my desk," Dyer said.

"Fabulous." Fletcher prayed he didn't hear the hopeful way her words tipped upward.

She shimmied through the elevator doors the second they pried open. Walls of unstreaked glass showcased the Upper East Side sprawl, glittering windows teetering upon two-hundred-year-old streets. She didn't need to glance at her reflection to know how she looked: Her white polyester blouse was tucked into a T.J. Maxx pencil skirt, a pair of secondhand black heels clicked with every step, and her strawberry blonde hair was slicked into a low ponytail that draped over her shoulder. Absolutely no frizz. No wrinkles.

Weaving around a couple leather armchairs carefully positioned beneath a crystal chandelier, she headed for the frosted-glass door at the far end of the floor—Dyer's office. "Also, Jackie had a late-morning meeting with Melv Lexington, something about an ownership dispute, but it might be worth a debrief if you're up for it. It's her third meeting with Legal this month. Not sure where the holdup is."

Dyer hummed. "Send him up to me after my one o'clock. I need him to look over some paperwork before the trip."

"You don't have a one o'clock—" Fletcher was saying as she swung open the door.

Some things Fletcher had grown to expect to see when stepping into Dyer's office.

A display of the world's finest liquors, some with six-figure price tags.

A glass case housing a hand-carved ivory cane and the vintage Remington poaching weapon, both inherited from his grandfather: the publishing mogul who created the eponymous Cartwright Media in 1924 to catalog his world travels.

The first issue of *Jet-Setter*, framed in three-ply glass. Dusty and yellow, edges curled and ink faded. A snapshot of a hammock between two palms stamped with the same swirly retro lettering still used today.

But in all the years she'd been by Dyer's side, Fletcher had never walked into Dyer's office expecting to see *him*.

A coil of dread wormed its way into her stomach, but she pretended it didn't exist the same way she pretended to orgasm from penetration alone: quietly suffering. She plastered a forced smile on as fast as she could, but the man in the wingback chair definitely noticed her stunned expression.

There was no mistaking him. Wild blond curls, two inches over six feet tall with shoulders broad as the Hudson, and wrapped in a worn leather jacket. Waylon Cartwright sat at his father's desk with his fingers perched beneath his chin. The last person on planet Earth who was supposed to be here.

Waylon grinned, a wide flash of white teeth, and waved like he owned the place. He didn't, Fletcher was inclined to remind him. Not yet.

She pointed at his chest and sliced her hand across her throat. Message clear: *Get out.*

He crossed his arms flat against his worn white shirt and shrugged. His message was unfortunately also clear: *My dad signs your measly paycheck, so I'll do whatever I want, whenever I want, in whoever's office I want.*

Fletcher scowled, trying to ignore the metal taste in her mouth she got whenever he was around, as he kicked his feet onto Dyer's desk. God, she hated him.

"Miss Spence?" Dyer was saying on the other end of the phone line, and Fletcher snapped back to their conversation.

"Yes," she said quickly. "Yes, of course. I'll make sure Melv comes up."

"Good," Dyer said before brusquely hanging up. That usually meant he was exactly thirty-six seconds from the elevator door opening, which meant Fletcher had exactly thirty-six seconds to figure out what the hell was going on.

Fletcher *never* forgot a meeting.

And certainly not a meeting with Dyer's only son. Waylon hadn't stepped foot in the Cartwright Media offices in three years. She'd had the misfortune of meeting him only once before, but it was not a meeting easily forgotten—or forgiven.

She hated him. And he hated her right back.

"Fletcher Spence. Don't you ever get tired of cleaning up my dad's messes?" Waylon asked, one foot wagging back and forth. That desk cost more than Fletcher's whole apartment building—he had better not leave scuff marks on it.

"No," Fletcher said through gritted teeth, even if she really meant *yes*.

Yes, she wished she were downstairs, poring over upcoming editions of *Jet-Setter*.

Yes, she took this job only because being Dyer's executive assistant was as close as she could get to working for her dream magazine without a dazzling photography portfolio.

And yes, if she was going to bust her ass at work every day, it would be way, *way* better if she got to do it on photo shoots in far-off locations.

Not that she'd be saying *that* out loud to Waylon.

A mischievous gleam flared in his eye, like he knew exactly which buttons to press and had every intention of pressing them. "You know, you really ought to be at your desk to welcome guests when Dyer has an appointment."

Fletcher fought to keep her practiced composure. She'd rather get a colonoscopy wide-awake than admit he'd surprised her. "I don't come into your work and tell you how to pour lukewarm beer for kids with fake IDs, so feel free to keep your opinions to yourself."

If the tabloids were to be believed, Waylon spent the last three years slinging shots at some Brooklyn dive bar, role-playing middle class to spite his father. Mostly, Fletcher tried to forget he existed.

She spotted a pink sticky note underneath his boot—the Lydell guest list. When she tugged the pressboard folder the Post-it was attached to, it didn't budge, and neither did Waylon's paperweight of a foot. Three years, and he was still the jerkiest jerk to ever exist.

"Aren't you a pleasure to have in class," Waylon said—a statement instead of a question. He flipped a pen in the air and caught it. Settling in for the long haul. "You have a terrible bluff, by the way."

"Is that so?"

His blue eyes were asking for trouble. Everywhere they lingered, Fletcher turned hot. "It is so."

Her eyebrow raised in disbelief. Because despite him being an annoying wrinkle in her afternoon, she was objectively very, *very* good at her job. Exhibit A: Dyer was going to walk through the door in three, two, one . . .

"Did you find the approved guest list?" That voice could belong to only one person.

Her boss emitted the same chaotic neutral energy as Colonel Mustard. His sleek silver hair had been combed back so curls lined the base of his neck. Today, he wore a pressed navy suit paired with loafers Fletcher paid someone—using Dyer's pocketbook—to shine. Age curved his spine, but Dyer stood nearly eye to eye with Waylon once the younger kicked himself upright to shake his father's hand. The movement was stiff, unnatural.

As soon as Waylon moved, Fletcher snatched the guest list off the desk. Only barely did she refrain from waving it in Waylon's face like a checkered victory flag.

"Yes, sir. Got it right here," she answered Dyer's question.

The Lydell trip was the biggest Cartwright event of the year: a weeklong off-site on one of Dyer's private islands, a crescent-shaped sliver of land off the coast of Madagascar, where Dyer packed up the company's top performers to make deals and dole out promotions.

Fletcher had orchestrated everything perfectly. A perfectly scheduled itinerary, perfectly folded white cloth napkins in the shape of delicate swans, and a perfectly curated guest list that would include Fletcher's name squeezed in at the bottom. Her ticket to a new position at the company after three years.

Three years of seventy-hour weeks. Of counting emails instead of sheep and waking to nightmares of missed meetings. Of working twice as hard for half the recognition. She'd lost count of how many lunches she'd spent proofing upcoming issues over subpar takeout or how many Saturday mornings she'd filed expense reports in an empty office.

Fletcher deserved a spot. She'd earned it.

Maybe she should have waited before peeking, but she'd done so much waiting already. Skimming through the paperwork, she searched for her name among the candidates.

Then, she searched again.

A third time.

The list was only fourteen people long, so she would have seen her name. *Should* have seen her name. But there was no sign of Fletcher Spence.

She didn't make the cut.

"Sir, I—" But Fletcher's voice cracked, so she swallowed the words like the Zoloft she'd started taking since she accepted this position.

Even if it offered her negligibly more than a living wage, being Dyer's assistant had been her tether to New York City, the reason she'd managed not to be dragged back to Nebraska by only-daughter guilt and Kent's peer pressure. It was her foot in the door, a necessary stepping stone to her dream job.

She'd given it everything she had for years.

And in her place were two horrifying words:

Waylon Cartwright.

2

"He doesn't even *work* here," Fletcher was whining as she and Ford took the elevator downstairs that evening. Ordinarily, she had a strict no-shit-talking-at-work policy, but today was the exception. What did she have to lose?

"When have the rules ever mattered to people like him?" Ford asked. "He's hot, he's rich, he gets everything handed to him. I'm surprised he even showed his face here. I haven't seen him around the office since that night—"

"That we swore to never speak of?"

"—where absolutely nothing noteworthy occurred in a coat closet and no one nearly lost their job," Ford finished tightly.

"Exactly." Fletcher shook the memory out of her stiff shoulders as the elevator *ding*ed, doors opening. She'd rather fling herself off the Empire State Building than relive a single second from that night. Especially within earshot of her colleagues. "*Anyway*, aren't you at least a little bit bummed I'm not going to mail one of these beautifully thick cardstock envelopes to your apartment?"

Ford laughed. "You sending me one of those invitations would be the worst thing that ever happened to me."

"Worse than that time you drank a triple espresso before the production meeting?"

A pause. "Second-worst thing," he amended. "Point is, my PTO is already approved. My flights are booked. Slater from IT could accidentally delete InDesign off all our computers, and my Slack notifications would stay snoozed."

Fletcher groaned as they wove around the reception desk. "Do you have to go?"

Ford pivoted hard on the heels of his boots. Two firm palms planted on Fletcher's shoulders, and she tried not to wince, thinking of the creases. "I would sooner gouge out my eyes than spend a single extra second staring at those spreads. I cannot set my out-of-office autoresponder fast enough. Seychelles is calling, and I must answer."

"Your vacation doesn't start until halfway through the retreat. And Lydell is only a few miles away. If you'd gotten invited, you could still catch the tail end of your trip. Get a promotion *and* drink piña coladas off of someone's stomach."

Ford shook his head. "Nope. It's called boundaries. Say it with me. *Bound-a-ries*."

The thought of a week alone in the office should have thrilled Fletcher. Except she knew Dyer was going to call asking questions at odd hours. She had never touched her PTO because even if she wanted to take a day off, she couldn't. Dyer rang when he needed something—no matter what the calendar said.

"Taking some time off isn't a crime punishable by death, you know?" Had she said that out loud, or had Ford developed rapid-onset telepathic powers? "You don't have to kill yourself for this job. *Shouldn't*, even."

Fletcher mustered a small smile. "I've got to get home."

Ford caught up to her in a few quick strides. "Hey, I'm going out tonight, and you should join me."

"It's a Tuesday."

Ford's eyebrows wagged. "And?"

And, the worst part about not being invited to Lydell was that Fletcher still had to do all the prep work. There was catering to coordinate, itineraries to plan, clothes to launder.

In her purse, her phone started to chime. On instinct, she lurched for it, pursing her lips like, *See what I mean?*

But it wasn't Dyer's designated ringtone. This was worse.

"I've got to take this," she said with a sigh. *Sighing* wasn't as accurate as *deflating*. "Have fun tonight."

She regretted answering Kent's call almost immediately. One second, she was saying hello, and the next, a tractor engine whined at deafening decibels, a belt out of sync or the oil tank empty. She couldn't yank the speaker away from her ear fast enough.

"Sorry about that," Kent said once the whirring died. "Trying to get this combine back up and running so we can finish harvesting the Weinbach field. What's going on?"

"You called me, remember?" She didn't mean to sound short-fused, but the words came out like a live wire that he was foolish enough to grab onto.

When Kent was mad, he grunted. He was *such* a grunter. And apparently, it had been a long day at her family's farm where he spent his days helping out because here he was, grunting.

She could almost see him, hair grown too long, a grease stain on his white undershirt, lips turned downward. Teeth always clenched behind his jaw. He'd been handsome once, in a rough-edged brooding way. But, really, when you've been together since you were sixteen, did it really matter if you were attracted to them? A relationship in motion would stay in motion. Newton's fourth law.

Finally, once he was able to form full syllables again, he huffed, "I didn't know it was a crime to call my fiancée."

Fletcher pressed her lips into a pinstripe, a feeble attempt to leash her honest thoughts. Again. Every call had been like this lately. Measured words and muted frustrations. Days and weeks of her silencing his calls so that she didn't have to pretend she actually wanted to answer them. Days and weeks of him still calling, no matter what she said.

Or what she didn't.

Like, for instance, *Yes, I want to marry you!*

Pushing through the office's revolving doors, Fletcher imagined letting the tide of Manhattan sweep her away. Kent, however, was an anchor to the seafloor. She shoved out a breath, a long spool of white in the October evening. "We talked about that, Kent."

"I know you said you're not ready, but no one's ever really ready, are they?" Kent's voice strained against the words, feeling every inch of the thirteen hundred miles between them. Honestly, Fletcher couldn't tell if his bad mood was because of her or the broken combine header. Did she even care?

"I need to focus on my career right now. You know that." Now more than ever. Stupid invitations. Stupid Waylon.

Kent barked a laugh, grating. "Is that what you call making some billionaire's coffee every morning for pennies? A *career*?"

A blue post office box greeted her outside the office. Dyer would have never conceded to e-vites for a trip as prestigious as Lydell. So Fletcher stuffed and stamped and sealed all fifteen without a hint of dissent.

She could have taken the stack of envelopes to the company mailroom, but after the day she'd had, she couldn't wait to get home, swap into some pajamas, and crack open Lightroom to edit her recent camera roll in peace.

Waylon's invite was the only envelope left in Fletcher's hands. It should've been her name delicately penned on the envelope, her ticket to a weeklong getaway at Lydell Island where she could laugh and schmooze and come back to New York City with a suntan and a salary increase.

The envelope with that little red bead of wax like a bullet hole to her heart sank into the mail slot with cruel finality.

She shifted the phone to her other ear. "You mean a job at my dream company? Yeah, that's what I call it."

"You're working yourself to death for some lunatic who doesn't care about you," he said. "All I'm asking is for you to call home sometimes. Can you stop being so goddamn selfish for five minutes?"

Here it came. The same fight for the thousandth time, tonight of all nights. She wanted to yell, scream, cause a scene, but she didn't. Of course she didn't. Fletcher Spence didn't *cause scenes*. She planned things, fixed things, pretended things were fine.

Fletcher breathed through her nose. Apparently inhaling was the only human function she could manage while staying calm. "Kent, I—"

Something cracked in Kent's voice. A desperate plea. "It wouldn't be the end of the world if you took a break. I haven't seen you since July, you know?"

July when he proposed. July when she smiled and nodded in front of their extended families, ambushed at an Independence Day barbecue she agreed to attend only because the office was closed Friday and Monday and she could be there and back without taking personal time. July when she *swore* she wouldn't go back to Nebraska again until she had her first byline.

Fletcher turned down her block, each step kicking up crisp autumn leaves. The rest of the evening's commuters whizzed past, shuffling her back and forth, but it all felt like slow motion. Everything she wanted to say lodged halfway up her throat.

Her feet led her past prewar storefronts and walk-ups with rusting fire escapes. It was all so different from her family's parcel in the blink-and-you'd-miss-it town on the outskirts of Lincoln where she grew up, barefoot and wild on the farm. Back then, when she sprawled across the grass and daydreamed, she imagined soaring over the oceans with a scarf billowing in the wind like Amelia Earhart.

Then, when she was old enough to realize that she'd much prefer to fly in a plane that had a slightly lower chance of crash-landing to avoid getting eaten alive by coconut crabs, she rebuilt her vision board around traveling the globe with *Jet-Setter*.

As far as she could tell, Kent's globe ended at the Lincoln city limits. They were twenty-six years old. God forbid she wasn't ready to settle down, get married, pop out three kids, and adopt a golden retriever.

"What's going on with you?" Kent asked when she didn't respond. She could practically see him thoughtlessly swipe an oil-stained hand down his face, exasperated.

Bumping open the door of her entirely too-orange building, Fletcher groaned. If they weren't already fighting, they would be soon. "You know that company trip I've wanted to go on for the last three years? Dyer approved the guest list today, and I'm not on it."

Kent bristled like she knew he would. "I told you. He doesn't appreciate you. None of them do."

"That's not the point." Hot, angry tears welled in Fletcher's eyes, but she blinked them away as she hiked up and up and up toward her fifth-floor apartment.

"Like hell it isn't." Kent's drawl always exaggerated when he was frustrated. "You're killing yourself for this company that doesn't care a lick about you."

When she reached her door, something had been taped to it. Something that looked an awful lot like an eviction notice.

Which wouldn't make any sense because Fletcher had spent way too many nights eating Top Ramen and Haribo candy Girl Dinner so she could make rent for her to be evicted.

The all-caps, 140-point header begged to differ. Words like *30-day notice* and *occupancy* and *reconstruction* leaped off the page. A pit formed in Fletcher's gut when she reached the fine print.

Her rent-protected apartment was being converted into a commercial building.

A bitter tang coated her mouth. It was always a miracle she'd been able to afford this place without a roommate, but the real estate market was a certified shit show, and her measly 3 percent cost-of-living raises were a joke. No way was she going to find another apartment in her budget. Certainly not one close enough to answer Dyer's every beck and call.

"Fletcher?"

And if she couldn't find somewhere new to live, then what? Move in with Ford? Maybe. Bridge troll? Tempting. Tuck her tail between her legs and head back to Nebraska? Never.

"Hello?"

What she really, truly, *desperately* needed was a promotion. A new career track with actual growth potential. A photographer gig at *Jet-Setter*, working under Jackie. Why else had she spent the last three years lugging around her Canon and sneaking out while Dyer was in meetings to photograph the city, building her portfolio print by print?

"Fletcher!"

"What?"

Kent sighed so hard she could almost feel his exhale through the phone. "Come home, Fletch. You've got to quit letting people walk all over you."

The words came out before she could stop them, before she could worry about disappointing him or some version of herself who used to think she wanted this. "If I did that, then we'd have to break up."

"What are you talking about?"

"I can't do this anymore!" Her throat chafed, sore and rasped with emotion.

"Can't do what anymore?" Kent's voice shifted. Stern, like a parent lecturing a disobedient child.

"You. This. All of it!" she said. Then, sharper: "I don't want to come home, and I don't want to marry you, Kent."

She hung up before he could argue and somehow convince her to change her mind.

Fletcher crushed the eviction notice in her fist. She needed a drink. Stat.

After a couple rounds of Manhattans, Fletcher's thoughts had forsaken all margins and bled together into One Thought to Rule Them All: Figure out a way to get to Lydell Island.

Meanwhile, Ford "I have a second liver" Jepson's mission was to sweet-talk free drinks out of bartenders, and he was doing a great job. Perhaps *too* great of a job. Fletcher could already feel tomorrow's hangover forming at the back of her head.

"I still can't believe you actually dumped him," Ford said. His arm was slung around Fletcher's shoulders as they paced the Dumbo sidewalks toward their next destination, a bookstore-turned-bar called Subtext that Fletcher had seen all over Instagram.

After work, he'd changed from his Business Button-Up (white, untucked, satin) to his Party Button-Up (a short-sleeve patterned monstrosity he'd bothered to fasten only two buttons of). With his deep brown skin, bottle-blond hair, and arms polka-dotted with fine-line tattoos, he could always be mistaken as a cover model.

Fletcher's sensible heels and poly-blend blouse, on the other hand, would never qualify as couture.

"Me either," she muttered.

For longer than she'd been Dyer's Executive Assistant Fletcher, she'd been Kent Redburn's Girlfriend Fletcher. Always defined by someone else. She thought she'd feel freer, lighter, but instead she felt like a child's balloon caught in the rafters of a big-box store.

The bell above the door severed her thoughts as they entered Subtext.

Inside, a crackling fire staved off the October chill. Instead of walls, there were only bookshelves, packed with hand-me-down stories inked inside broken spines. Jazz filtered through the malty air, and for a moment, she assumed it was coming from someone's carefully curated Spotify playlist, but when she peered through an archway toward the back, there was a stage with a quartet playing.

It was sophisticated. Nuanced. Welcoming.

Exactly the last place she expected to see Waylon Cartwright.

"No way," she said, skidding to a halt.

"No way, what?"

Waylon was too busy flirting with a brunette at the bar to notice Fletcher gawking in the doorway. She'd come out to *forget* about him. Not stare at him while drowning her sorrows in bottom-shelf bourbon.

"Can we go?" she asked.

"Why?" Ford asked, oblivious. He either hadn't noticed the giant, egotistical elephant in the room or was choosing not to. "This place is amazing."

Precisely. Waylon was supposed to work at a grungy hole-in-the-wall overrun with rodents and roaches. Not the kind of place with craft cocktails and mood lighting.

Then, of course, Waylon glanced toward the door. His eyes slid away and then snapped right back, registering. His expression situated somewhere between grin and grimace. Like he was both irritated and intrigued at her appearance.

It took all her effort not to snarl in his general direction. Still, the thought of him watching her chicken out of a confrontation had Fletcher saying, "One drink."

Ford practically cheered. "I'll find us a table. Grab me another martini, extra olives?"

"How you eat those things, I'll never understand." The very thought made her queasy.

Her nuisance of a best friend batted his long lashes. "Pour moi?"

Kent's gruff tenor echoed through her mind, saying something about how when she wasn't working, Fletcher still put other people first. She shook it away. All her energy would be needed to avoid throwing up on Waylon when ordering their drinks. Fletcher sucked down a steadying breath and waded through the sea of tables toward the bar.

As soon as she approached, Waylon spun to meet her, like she'd snagged a trip wire. He'd traded this afternoon's leather jacket for a pressed button-down, the sleeves rolled up his forearms, but Waylon still wore the same slanted smile, the same smug confidence afforded to heirs apparent.

"Two Fletcher sightings in one day? To what god of misery do I owe the displeasure?"

All she did was scoot onto a barstool, but Fletcher's heart rioted like she was running for her life. "If I didn't know better, I'd think you were following me."

"Because I'm here? At *my* bar." His eyes were crystal blue beneath the low light. Too blue for his own good.

"Right."

Waylon sugared a glass rim, measured cognac, and slid a sidecar to the patron sitting next to Fletcher. "Did you need something?"

Wasting her breath talking to Waylon Cartwright was on the short list of things Fletcher had no desire to do, but it was a necessary evil. It had been three years since Waylon acknowledged the company—or Dyer—existed. Inviting him to Lydell made absolutely no sense, and Fletcher needed to know why.

Straightening her shoulders, she asked, "Have a nice chat with your dad this afternoon?"

"So, that's why you're still in your little receptionist outfit at"—he tossed a bottle of Tito's above his head and checked the silver-plated watch on his wrist while it spun—"nine forty-three p.m. You're here on business."

"First of all, I'm not a receptionist. And secondly, these are regular-people clothes."

"Regular people who are receptionists." A smirk crept onto his lips. Like he enjoyed this. Riling her up. His hands moved at light speed, swinging glass bottles with the same care he afforded to human emotions. (Which was to say: none.)

Fletcher simmered. "Not the point."

With a nudge, he sent a vodka cranberry sailing down the bar. "And thirdly?"

"A drink. Can I please order a drink?"

Fletcher peeked over her shoulder. In her absence, Ford resorted to flirting with a blond with biceps the size of Montana. When she turned back, Waylon was pouring amber whiskey into a cocktail glass.

Her nose wrinkled. "What is that?"

"The drink you wanted." Waylon plunked the coupe in front of her. "And seats are limited. Take your Manhattan and get back to doing my dad's dirty work."

How did *he* know *her* usual drink? "No, thanks. I want a martini. Extra olives."

Waylon's eyes narrowed, and suddenly Fletcher's skin felt too tight. His claim about her poker face from earlier rang in her ears. Was she smiling weird? She flattened her lips, but that felt wrong, too. What was a mouth supposed to do? Just sit there?

All he said was "Fine. Take this to Jepson, then. He'll drink anything."

While Waylon shook and shimmied enough gin and vermouth to sanitize a surgery wound, Fletcher tapped her nails against the counter. Irritation lanced down her spine. Had she learned nothing from *Jet-Setter*'s November proof? When interacting with an animal on their territory, it was best to appear nonthreatening.

Well, if Waylon were an animal, he'd be an apex predator, and Fletcher suddenly felt a little too much like a fawn. Wide-eyed and wobbly legged and definitely about to get eaten, exactly like she felt the first night she met him.

The most important part of her job was knowing every*thing* about every*one*. When the company hosted events, she was always right by Dyer's side, feeding him intel, because the head honcho of a century-old publishing magnate used his spare brain cells making decisions for global investing rather than remembering who couldn't eat shrimp without going anaphylactic. That was what Fletcher was for.

She knew that Cartwright's CFO Deepti Kaur couldn't swim but took two weeks of PTO to the Maldives every summer to lounge on the white sand. Naked, if you believed the rumors.

She knew that Denis Bertram, the SVP of Marketing and Publicity, took medical leave last month for emergency gallbladder surgery.

And, now, she knew that Waylon Cartwright was twenty-eight,

an Aries, and a former Merit Scholar who graduated summa cum laude from Oxford. He was a serial dater, a troublemaker, and a constant PR risk. But three years ago, Fletcher knew him only as a handsome stranger hiding in the coat check closet during the biggest Cartwright Media charity gala of the year. She could still smell the leather and suede, the spilled champagne.

Remembering that night made Fletcher want to throat-punch him.

On the inside.

On the outside, she twirled a strand of copper hair around her finger, trying her damnedest to look like she wasn't thinking about how three years ago she almost kissed him.

Waylon flipped the shaker bottle behind his back and caught it in time to pour into the triangle glass. He slid the martini toward her and then rested his elbows on the bar top, knuckles under his chin. "Why don't you tell me why you're really here, honey?"

"Why were you invited to Lydell instead of me?"

"How do you expect *me* to know that?" Waylon tensed, but his words came as cool as ever. "You've spent more time with my dad in the last three years than I have in my whole life."

"Exactly. Why would he even bother inviting you? At least I want to go to Lydell."

"No, you don't."

Fletcher's mouth hung open. "You're right. I don't want to. I *need* to."

"Again: no." Waylon shifted down the bar and started making a negroni for a woman with a striking resemblance to Fran Drescher, but Fletcher didn't budge. A splash of Campari, a king cube, and an orange-peel ribbon later, he picked up right where he left off. "And because I know you're thinking it, *no*, I can't convince him to add you to the guest list."

A glare.

"It's a *company* trip. You don't work there." Fletcher tried to take a sip of Ford's martini, but the olives' freaky little belly buttons made bile crawl up her throat, so she set the glass right back down. "What's your angle? Weasel your way back into Dyer's good graces? Take the CMO position? Embarrass me in front of the entire company and nearly get me fired—oh, wait. You already did that."

The way Waylon watched her made her mouth go dry. He wiped his hands on the towel tossed over his shoulder. "They'll skin you alive on Lydell."

"I have what it takes."

"Not if you have to ask to be invited."

Waylon was objectively attractive. Hard lines and sharp edges. Always just shy of clean-shaven, only enough scruff to make you wonder, *Is he doing this on purpose?* It wasn't a crime to be handsome.

It was, however, a crime to kill her boss's son, so Fletcher refrained from homicide even though the cocktail forks were right there.

"Excuse me?" Fletcher asked. It was the liquor in her system leaving her feeling off-kilter. Definitely not the hardened way Waylon looked at her.

"If you really want to go, you should do something about it. But you won't. You do what you're told, Spence. It makes you a good receptionist."

"I told you. I'm not a—"

"Cash or card?" He slid the receipt for both drinks toward her.

"Twenty-eight dollars?" Fletcher balked. "*Each?*"

Something dark flared in his eyes. "Drink up, buttercup."

Fletcher fixed her stare on him, tipped the martini to her lips, and gulped. She'd prove him wrong, even if it killed her.

3

Fletcher wasn't sure which hurt worse: the throbbing in her skull after a weeknight out or that Waylon was right about her.

She didn't sleep last night so much as she ruminated. Waylon's taunting echoed through her brain until the blue hours of the morning. When she finally dragged herself into the office, everything was exactly the same. She was still getting evicted, she and Kent were still broken up, and she still wasn't invited to Lydell.

Her booze-soaked vow weighed heavy on her mind.

Every time she'd tried to talk to Dyer about the invitations, the words died a slow, stammering death, somewhere between her clavicle and her uvula. She first tried that morning, a steaming mug of doctor-ordered reishi coffee in her hand. Then again after the Ops touch base where she'd copied forty-six thousand memos that all promptly ended up crushed and in the wastebin. Over and over and over, failing to find the right words as October's crisp oranges faded into November grays.

Finally, the Friday before the trip, Fletcher couldn't take it anymore. She jabbed her fork at her lo mein. *You do what you're told, Spence.* Another stab, twisting this time. *It makes you a good receptionist.*

Next to her, Ford eyed her violent fork. "You good?"

No, but Fletcher's mouth said, "Yes."

She had only two weeks left to figure out a new living situation, but the pile of rejected apartment applications in her inbox nauseated her. Or maybe that was lunch. Did she even *like* lo mein?

She and Ford had become friends shortly after she'd gotten hired. Turned out, the secret to making friends into adulthood was to body-slam into them, destroying a pistachio muffin in the process. He offered to buy her lunch to replace her sad, smashed pastry, and they'd been grabbing lunch together ever since. Sometimes Sweetgreen, sometimes dollar pizza from a place that also did pedicures, but most of the time they ended up with Szechuan's. Two orders of combination lo mein, his recommendation, and she'd never ordered anything else.

Was she predictable? A pushover?

Waylon burrowed in her head. Taunting her. Fletcher pinched her eyes closed, shutting down the thoughts.

The Design Lab door swung open, and Joplin, a pink-haired senior designer, walked in, headphones over her ears. Fletcher lowered her voice when she said, "I only have two weeks until my apartment gets makeover-montaged into a Saks, and every time I try to talk to Dyer about Lydell, I choke."

"I already said you could crash with me," Ford said.

"Yes, but have you considered that I actually *don't* want to hear you and—what was his name again?"

Ford's nails tapped his chin. "Ricky. I think."

"—Hear you and *Ricky, I Think* ravishing each other until day-break." Fletcher pushed her take-out box away from her, forehead sinking against the table.

"Then do something about it."

Fletcher lolled her head to one side. She scraped open her left eye-lid. "I'm out of somethings."

Ford leaned his head on the table to meet her eyes. Or eye, technically. "What are you talking about? You're Fletcher Spence. You could run this company in your sleep, and you're always one step ahead. If you can't figure out a way, no one can."

Fletcher scoffed. Then, like clockwork, Dyer rang, and she was dragged back to her desk. But a crop seed had been planted, and it took root the rest of the day. While she scanned expense reports, while she updated Dyer's calendar, while she organized meeting notes.

Which was how she ended up at LaGuardia at 6:07 the next morning in her best (okay, only) pumps. A vicious wind tore at the threads of her copper braid, and she braced her arms against her chest for warmth. Dyer's behemoth of a jet had been taxied over, but the team was nowhere to be found. None of this surprised Fletcher.

T-minus 87 seconds before the cars pulled in, twenty minutes to board and prepare the plane, and twenty-three hours in the air before the landing gear cranked out for arrival.

Maybe reciting the itinerary in her sleep could be Fletcher's party trick.

Assuming Dyer let her attend the party.

The headlights of three black SUVs sliced across the tarmac right on cue. Fletcher roped her thrifted Longchamp bag over the handle of her rolling suitcase, centering herself. Familiar figures climbed out of the cars, varying sizes of to-go lattes clutched in their hands, as shiny-vested worker bees migrated luggage onto the jet.

None of her coworkers dressed like they were going to a private island—all tailored blazers and starched shirts. Fletcher wasn't much better. Her pencil skirt was, like, 70 percent rayon and 100 percent overdressed for the Southern Hemisphere summer they were headed toward.

At the back of the pack, Dyer took slow, deliberate steps with the rest of the C-suite, their heads craned together conspiratorially. Today, he wore an ecru suit with a pale blue shirt, the top unbuttoned, and wing tip loafers. His grandfather's ivory cane tapped against the asphalt.

Fueled by caffeine and spite, Fletcher marched across the tarmac.

One flash of her Cartwright Media badge had been all it took to get access to their terminal. Turned out, there were a few perks to being Dyer Cartwright's right-hand woman. She was going to walk straight up to Dyer, and she was going to give him a piece of her—

"Miss Spence," he said casually. "Enjoying your morning?"

Fletcher's eyes widened, but she trained her voice to stay even. To sound like she definitely wasn't surprised at how *unsurprised* he was by her being here. "Yes, thank you. And you?"

"Delightful." He nudged his glasses back up his nose. The others finished boarding, leaving Dyer and Fletcher alone on the runway. "I don't recall extending you an invitation."

"Um, that's . . . true." Panic clenched Fletcher's heart. The whole speech she'd practiced about her infallible work ethic and devotion to the company? Vaporized from her memory.

Wreathed in dawn's muted gray and the flashing airport lights, Dyer's clip didn't slow on her behalf. "Why are you here?"

"To go to Lydell." She really shouldn't have pounded that Americano before she came over. The lights started to swim. Her pulse did laps around 100 bpm.

Dyer nodded. An acknowledgment more than a consideration. Fletcher had seen that look on his face plenty of times before.

Something about the familiarity settled Fletcher's stomach. This was part of her job. And even if the rest of Fletcher's life was falling apart, she could do her job. "In the three years I've been with Cartwright Media, I believe I've proven myself an invaluable asset to the team."

Nodding, Dyer didn't hesitate. "Most certainly."

She reached into her bag and snagged her Canon. "You know how much I love *Jet-Setter.* Taking photos for your grandfather's magazine is my dream. I'll do whatever it takes to prove I can join the staff. I'm a good assistant, but I could be a better photographer."

"That's where you're wrong," Dyer said.

"I'm sorry?"

"You're an *excellent* assistant. Have you considered I'm not ready to say goodbye to you?"

Well, no. She hadn't.

Dyer pivoted. The sudden severity of his stare stopped Fletcher in her tracks.

"I've got to give it to you. You've got gumption. I've always appreciated that about you, Miss Spence. You wouldn't have lasted a second at my company without it."

Her thoughts spun. Gumption was good, right? He wasn't firing her. Right?

"It's one of the many traits I look for in new hires. Tenacity. Determination."

Yes. *Yes.* Finally, she was being recognized.

Dyer stroked his chin. "Interesting indeed."

"I could take photos," she said, clutching her camera to her chest. "Document the trip. For my portfolio. You don't have to decide now—all I'm asking for is the chance."

"Oh, that . . ." A hum. His steel-enforced gaze trained on her camera. "I'm afraid that would be quite burdensome."

Before she could stop him, Dyer hooked his cane around Fletcher's camera and swatted it to the pavement. He dug his heel into the lens with a horrifying metallic crunch. Fletcher sucked down a single gasp, shock coiling at the base of her throat.

She reached for the body of the camera—thank god she packed a spare 55 mm lens—but Dyer's cane hammered down once more against the viewfinder. Again and again and again. Narrowly missing her fingers as she tried to salvage it. The razored edge of a glass shard pricked her thumb, one long slice down the pad. Copper stained her tongue as she sucked the blood away. Only then did the cane still.

"My dearest apologies," Dyer said insincerely as he loomed over her. "Perhaps I've overreacted."

No, Dyer Cartwright never overreacted. He calculated every move and countermove. A conductor for his own symphony, a grand master in his own game.

A hot flare of embarrassment slashed across her cheeks. Was everyone watching, faces pressed to their windows? She wouldn't cry. She *would not* cry. This was a test. A test she was determined to ace.

For months during college, she had set aside half her work-study paycheck to upgrade from her point-and-shoot to a real DSLR. And then Dyer hired her, and her hours were filled with scanning memos and making dinner reservations and coordinating travel, running around until her budget pumps left festering blisters on her heels.

But the dream never wavered—*Photo by Fletcher Spence*. Now the prospect of a byline had been reduced to a bludgeoned pulp.

Dyer crouched next to her, his arthritic knees popping on the way down. It did nothing to lessen the chill that crawled under Fletcher's skin, slithering around her skeleton, as he pressed the cane's ivory handle beneath her chin so that she had nowhere to look but at him.

"You play by my rules, Miss Spence, and you could have everything you've ever dreamed of." He stood. Smartened his suit jacket. As if everything was perfectly normal. "No photos on the island. I hope you understand."

"On the island?" The cogs in Fletcher's brain spun. Dyer vanished into the plane, but Fletcher stayed rooted right there on the tarmac, afraid that if she so much as flinched, he'd change his mind. "On the island. Lydell Island. *I'm going to Lydell Island.*"

Of course, by that point, she was talking to herself. The airport employees started glancing at her. *Pull it together, Fletch.*

She pinched her eyes shut and pulled in a long stream of air that smelled distinctly like jet fuel. And possibilities. Shania Twain's voice punctuated her thoughts with a swift "Let's go girls," and Fletcher rushed toward the boarding stairs before Dyer reneged on her invitation.

All eyes settled on her in the cabin. Her coworkers' hushed gossip fell silent. Rows of cream leather seats lined each side, each filled with a colleague. Suddenly, Fletcher was far too aware of the way her stomach clawed at the base of her esophagus like it needed somewhere to go.

Then an attendant guided a crystal flute brimming with something fizzy into her palm. Fletcher sipped and sipped, praying for liquid courage. As she paced down the aisle, every face was one she knew. The Cartwright Media org chart had been seared into her memory. Fletcher forced herself to smile, even if it meant biting her tongue.

The C-suite clustered together toward the front with Dyer at the helm. Next to him, the CTO, Raul Diaz, typed furiously on a laptop after acknowledging Fletcher's existence with a cursory glance. Deepti Kaur, the CFO, leaned over her briefcase to whisper something to Jackie Caldera, who peered up toward Fletcher and offered her a red-lipsticked grin.

Then there was Melv Lexington, the company's general counsel, dressed like he was caught halfway between running the New York marathon and breaking a case wide open—a three-piece suit paired with tortoiseshell glasses strapped to his head with a neon-green Croakie, skin tanned down to the dermis from hours jogging Hudson River Park.

Behind him, the Sales team took up the middle, flocking around their ringleader, Theo Groff. For as long as Fletcher had been at Cartwright Media, Theo had sulked around the office, eyes glimmering with greed. Several members of his team had been invited—and they all watched Fletcher, eagles hunting a field mouse.

"Look who showed up!" Rick Evanston had a gap-toothed grin and a knack for dropping things in front of women so that they'd pick it up for him. He was, unequivocally, an asshole, and Fletcher routinely daydreamed about volunteering him for the first manned mission to Mars.

Next to him, Opal Meena daubed lip gloss onto her full bottom lip. Over the last four years, she had easily become one of Cartwright Media's top-producing salespersons ever. "Oh, Fifi's here," she said before going straight back to lip-glossing.

Of all the things Fletcher'd been mistakenly called over the years, Fifi was hardly the worst.

Opal turned and asked the intern, Sheila Day, to hold her compact mirror. Sheila's job description literally included selecting call-holding music and doing lunch runs for the Sales team. How could she possibly be one of the company's top performers when she spent half her hours picking croutons off Opal's Caesar salad? But she was Dyer's niece, and a little nepotism went a long way.

The Marketing team was much less concerned with Fletcher's arrival. Two Paid Ads henchmen Fletcher knew best as Brian and Other Brian were in a heated debate about conversion rates, refereed by the SVP of Marketing and Publicity, Denis Bertram. Between rounds of bickering, Bertram patted his round, bald head with a silk handkerchief, sweat forming on his dark skin.

"Fletcher Spence."

Fletcher would deny under penalty of perjury the way her heart thumped around in her chest the minute Waylon spoke her name from the last row. It was purely adrenaline. A biological response to breathing the same air as someone she was clearly allergic to.

There was a tinge of bewilderment in Waylon's tone. To the untrained ear, he almost sounded impressed by her arrival. He wasn't. Surprised, certainly. Agitated, maybe. But impressed? No.

And across from him? The only empty seat.

Waylon kicked one ankle over the opposite knee, the picture of casual cool, but a muscle in his jaw strained like he barely refrained from sticking his tongue out at her. "A receptionist *and* a stowaway. Who knew you could be so multifaceted?"

Fletcher spared him the satisfaction of a response and melted into the buttery leather seat, becoming smaller and smaller as New York did the same outside the oval window.

Somewhere over the Atlantic, while blue surrounded them on all sides, even the caffeine and adrenaline couldn't keep Fletcher awake. Night navies yawned across the sky, and she dozed, off and on over Africa, until a particularly blinding ray of light seared her retinas. With half a mind to draw the shade down and roll over, she propped herself up on her elbow and peeked out the window.

Sleep was suddenly out of the question. They'd arrived.

Tucked between Port Louis and Réunion island, Lydell was a thin strip of land shaped like the tip of a French manicure. A steep mountain jutted up from the center, two ends curling down in spindles on either side. At its base, thick swatches of green coated the landscape, fading to dried-brown chaparral and sagebrush the farther the land extended from the peak. A swirling cerulean sea lapped at the craggy shoreline, clearer and bluer and deeper than any ocean Fletcher had ever known.

The landing strip eased into view, a short stretch of creased pavement at the center of the island in a clawed-out clearing among the forest.

Without warning, the plane's nose tipped, pitching toward the earth. Landing gear rattled underneath, and the wings leveled. As the wheels touched down, slowing the plane to a grinding halt, some of the tension eased out of Fletcher's shoulders.

Across the aisle, Waylon raised the last of his in-flight aperitif toward Fletcher and said, "Welcome to the wild."

The wild, apparently, had white-glove service.

As soon as they deplaned, a flurry of staff in crisp yellow shirts whisked them onto a flatbed safari truck with an arched canvas roof. Fletcher squeezed onto the last seat next to Sheila.

"Oh my god, Fifi, this is going to be—so!—much!—fun!" Sheila's voice was the human equivalent of a helium balloon. Spiraled blonde curls had been tied into a knot on her head with a handkerchief, but it did very little to keep them in place. "Opal told me last year she went zip-lining and snorkeling and—"

"What did I tell you about talking about me like I'm not here?" Opal asked from Sheila's other side. Her wide deep brown eyes hid behind a pair of pink bedazzled sunglasses that she somehow managed to make look couture. (Were they? Opal's commission was probably six times Fletcher's salary.) Peering around toward Fletcher,

Opal added, "Last year, I arrived as an associate and left as a team lead. Best week of my life."

Hope thrummed in Fletcher's chest, and her gaze landed on Jackie across the truck. Her first real photography publication was so close she could almost reach out and grab it.

The truck chugged into the jungle canopy, aiming down a narrow trail through the thicket. Instantly, the sun faded into a soupy green, determined to shine through the leafy mosaic. The air temperature plummeted enough to raise a chill on Fletcher's arms as they carved through the undergrowth.

Here, everything was salt and earth, iron and the scent of something indistinguishably sweet. Not a skyscraper or a streetlight or another soul in sight. A wind, ancient and all-knowing but graciously soft, kicked a few strands loose from Fletcher's braid, and they tickled the back of her neck—the way it felt when someone was watching you.

"Look! A monkey!" Sheila squealed.

Hanging from the vines, a primate swung through the jungle, all sleek black fur and impeccable upper-body strength. Then the monkey opened its mouth. Deep and guttural, the call shook through Fletcher, something primal coming alert inside of her.

The longer she looked, the more she noticed. Blinking yellow eyes stalked through the greenery. Vibrant birds flitted from one branch to the next—toucans and parrots and macaws. In a wide, murky river, an anaconda slithered.

"For some reason, I didn't expect so many wild animals," Fletcher said as diplomatically as she could, given the way her heart jostled around her ribs.

"Egbert Cartwright had them all imported," Theo chimed in. His collared Ralph Lauren shirt was an aggressively pastel plaid that did little for his ruddy complexion. "The electric fence keeps them away from the buildings, but out here, they can get pretty close."

"Doesn't this break endangered-animal protection laws or something?" Fletcher dared to ask.

Too eager, Theo answered, "It's a sovereign island. The rules are different when you're a Cartwright. You don't play by them—you make them."

"There's no place like Lydell," Dyer said with a twinkle in his eye.

Seeing her boss outside the office felt like bumping into your first-grade teacher at the supermarket. Here, the blue of Dyer's eyes grew sharper, his posture straighter. She'd always thought him synonymous with his penthouse office and steamed suit jackets, but the island brought out a different side of Dyer Cartwright entirely. Something wilder. Less predictable.

Fletcher tightened her grip on the railing as her stomach somersaulted. When the tree line broke, the high savanna unraveled before them. Windswept plains, covered in a tall-grass peach fuzz, stretched toward the cliffs.

Out here, the sweltering sun seemed less harsh somehow, as though it had been hung from the sky only to sweep across this scrap of land. Gauzy and bright, the sunlight cast spearing shadows behind everything it touched.

Acacia trees with their umbrella tops dotted the horizon, and the truck followed a grooved path across the untamed landscape. Giraffes plucked eucalyptus leaves straight from the branches. Zebras grazed in mesmerizing packs. Cheetahs raced through the grasses.

None of these species belonged to this Indian Ocean lava rock formation, but there they were. Chartered in by greed and curiosity, a bone-deep selfishness. Curated only for the Cartwrights' pleasure for over a century by Dyer and his father before him and *his* father before him. A cruel caricature of real wilderness.

Up ahead, her oblivious colleagues discussed quarterly OKRs and SLAs with the passion of fraternity brothers defending their fantasy football leagues. Completely unfazed by the zoo they'd entered.

"Let me check the conversion rate on our last web banner," Brian was saying. He had a swatch of dark hair, gelled out of his face, and thick-rimmed glasses nudged up his nose. His laptop teetered on his kneecaps.

Next to him, Raul's heavy brows furrowed. Words without functional meaning to Fletcher spilled from his lips—*cloud access point*, *authentication*, *encryption protocol*.

"What would we do without you?" Other Brian said with a relieved sigh, since evidently his web page had loaded.

"Come on, everyone. We aren't here to talk shop," Dyer said. His arm rested easily on the guardrail despite how bumpy their journey was.

Joplin, with her hot-pink pixie cut and watercolor tattoos trailing down her warm brown arms, hung halfway over the railing, watching the horizon pass. "No, we're here for the salt and tequila. Ain't that right, Bubbles?"

Bubbles? Fletcher scanned her coworkers' faces for anyone who could convincingly respond to *Bubbles*. Her eyes gravitated toward Sheila—arguably the bubbliest person here—when a deep baritone pulverized her every thought.

"More like whiskey and tobacco," Waylon said. "You still smoke cigars, Raul?"

Waylon was . . . *Bubbles*?

A light danced in the CTO's amber eyes as he glanced toward Dyer. "Only when there's good news."

It was subtle, a curled edge, but Dyer smiled.

The promise of opportunity.

A roar cut through the conversation. The driver jerked the truck left, and Fletcher clung to the guardrail as they skirted by a pack of lions. The pride male rose onto his haunches, sabered teeth snarling.

Holy *shit*.

Exhaust plumed as the truck raced off. A slow, hesitant laugh parted Fletcher's lips. She clamped a hand over her mouth to capture it, but adrenaline pulsed through her with every heartbeat. If she didn't laugh, she didn't know what she'd do.

"The welcoming committee," Dyer said, a smile splitting wide open across his face.

He laughed with her, and then Melv laughed, and then Jackie and Raul and Deepti, down and down the ranks until they were all hyenas howling.

An engine buzzed overhead as the plane shot back toward the airport in Madagascar where it would wait in the wings. Leaving them alone for the next seven days. No scheduled meetings, no Slack messages, no stapled memos.

Just a safari paradise.

4

Lydell Manor was less of a house and more of a private resort. A tunnel of veiny baobabs led to an arrangement of polished-stone buildings that were dreadfully out of place among the elephant grass. The strict lines of columns gave way to manicured gardens, and tropical florals filled the air with a heady scent Fletcher wished she could bottle and wear.

More yellow-shirted staff members ushered them through a pair of arched acacia doors. Fletcher forcibly closed her mouth when her jaw fell open.

Glossy parquet floors guided them into a foyer with a grand piano and a three-story ceiling, and in the center hung an antique ormolu and cut glass chandelier that cost Dyer a fortune at a Sotheby's auction. A sheet of accordioning glass paneled the far wall, and outside, there was an infinity pool with a swim-up bar, an outdoor sauna (as opposed to the indoor sauna) caged by climbing jasmine, and a pristine view of the savanna's endless horizon. Late sun dripped down the grasslands, gold and bloodred.

If Fletcher's camera weren't buried in a trash can in Queens, she'd frame the horizon with imperfect symmetry, balancing the stretched neck of a giraffe with the parasol of an acacia tree. The colors would be breathtaking, all silhouettes and stark contrast.

Somehow, none of that was as surprising as the heads.

Beasts watched their entry. Ferocious, teethed things with beady, lifeless eyes. The heads of the same kinds of animals stalking this stripe of land had been stuffed and transformed into decor. A lion, mouth wide and teeth sharp, perched above the main entrance. Twin elephants flanked either side of the open landing. Three gazelles danced down the hall.

Hunted. Poached. Hung on display.

"*This* is why they had all those animals imported?" Fletcher muttered under her breath.

Beside her, Opal peeled her sunglasses off her face. "I know, right? All the money in the world, and this is how he decorates? Personally, I'd go for something a little less on the nose. Hell of a way for him to blow off some steam, though, I guess."

Blow off some steam? Fletcher planned corporate retreats, not hunting parties.

Didn't she?

Nausea brewed behind her belly button as she and Opal joined the others up ahead. Everyone else seemed content to funnel inside the house without second-guessing the decor, no matter how unsettling.

"A tour, perhaps?" Dyer announced to the room. He leaned on his cane with one hand, and a crystal lowball glass had manifested in the other. Suddenly, he looked nothing like the Dyer she knew and more like an Evil Old Rich White Dude.

Oh, god. *Was* he an Evil Old Rich White Dude? The animal skulls would beg to agree.

"My pleasure. Follow me," one of the staff members called.

Fletcher knew the woman's voice from countless calls coordinating Dyer's trips to Lydell: Carlotta. Tightly woven braids had been balled into a knot on her head with a scarf looped around her ears. She smiled brightly and beckoned them down a corridor.

Everyone moved in packs. The C-suite led the way. Then, the Sales team huddled around Theo with Marketing tight on their heels and Molly from HR floating around between them. Trailing toward the back, Waylon kept whispering things to Joplin, who giggled in answer. The sound was chalkboard nails and teakettle whistles.

Short of elbowing through the crowd to find her usual spot at Dyer's right side, Fletcher didn't belong anywhere. Bertram and the Brians would bore her to death, joining Waylon's entourage was a nonstarter, and she'd sooner drown herself than get sucked into an impromptu Sales stand-up.

For a fraction of a second, Fletcher imagined easily slotting into step with Jackie, discussing next quarter's photoshoot locations and top stories. Only for a fraction of a second, though. Any longer and she would have gotten totally and utterly lost.

The manor was a maze of doorways and waxy floors and ivory walls. Massive framed canvases with vintage *Jet-Setter* covers mapped their route. The first door they passed opened to a home theater with a full-size projection screen, velvet seats, and so many speakers that the surround sound had surround sound.

The cigar lounge could have doubled as an armory. Glass cases lined the walls, each housing antique hunting gear. Canteens and compasses and a framed canvas map of the island. Another reminder this was a boys' club, first and foremost.

Next, there was a meditation room with a trickling fountain. Then, a room crusted from ceiling to floor in pink Himalayan salt with strategically placed wide brass Tibetan singing bowls. Completing the trifecta was a med spa where everything smelled like bergamot and ylang-ylang.

A left by the 1973 issue spat them out in the Michelin-worthy kitchen where staff members chopped ripe mangoes and seared steaks. Bowling alley, indoor swimming pool, wine cellar. Every turned corner revealed new luxuries.

Carlotta urged them up a staircase that could be described only as *sweeping*. And—oh, good. The taxidermied heads were back.

Each room had an associated animal mounted above its door, which felt exactly as cursed as it sounded. One by one, Carlotta doled out bronze room keys with tassels tied around the handle, like they were in a Wes Anderson movie. The first went to Other Brian, who triple-checked his pillows were polyester, *not* down, since he was allergic to feathers. Then Molly, who vanished beneath the detached head of a zebra. Fletcher estimated six minutes max until Rick got jealous of someone's much larger room and Opal put him in his place with a snide remark.

"It's a lot to take in, huh?" Jackie appeared next to Fletcher, sinking toward the back of the group. Her in-flight skincare did the Lord's work because her under-eyes practically glowed, despite the hours spent breathing recycled air.

Hopefully Fletcher's resting *Is my boss a maniac?* face hadn't been too obvious. She worried at the end of her braid, and then realizing the bad habit, snapped her hand back to her side. "It's different than I expected."

"That's Lydell for you. So . . . unpredictable." Something indiscernible glinted in Jackie's gaze. "Anything can happen here. Who knows? There might just be a job on my staff for you at the end of this."

"Are you—Are you serious? Jackie, that would be—"

A dream come true. The answer to keeping Fletcher in the city. Everything she ever wanted. Could it really be so easy?

Jackie beamed. "I'm sure we'll have the chance to chat logistics this week."

From the cloud Fletcher was floating on, she almost didn't notice the way the crowd dwindled, room assignments being called out, until she was one of the only ones left.

Down the hall, Rick whined, "Why is hers so much bigger than mine?"

On cue, Opal responded with a dry, "I thought size didn't matter, Richard."

Carlotta guided them onward, leaving the bickering Sales team behind. She handed Waylon his key. "You're here in the jaguar room, Mr. Cartwright."

"Thank you, Carlotta," he said. Frankly, Fletcher was surprised he had manners enough to do that.

It wasn't until Dyer pointed down the hall and said, "Executives will be in the east wing," that Fletcher realized she was standing there without a room key.

"Wait, sorry. Where should I sleep?" Fletcher hated the way her voice bobbed with uncertainty.

Bertram scoffed. "In the staff quarters where you belong."

Fletcher's spine stiffened. She balled her hands into fists to stop them from shaking. She refused to let the others see her rattled, even as she verged into maraca territory.

"Easy now, Bertram," Deepti interceded with a hand on the SVP's arm. "You know how much Dyer loves supporting charities."

Waylon hovered in the doorway. She didn't have to look at him to know he wore a smug, lopsided grin. Enjoying her humiliation, no doubt.

Fletcher pivoted toward Dyer. To what? Defend her?

While everyone else shared SOPs and KPIs and a hundred other three-letter acronyms, Fletcher measured success by the number of dinner reservations she planned and files she organized. But she had never been alone.

Dyer was always there, calling the shots. Giving every movement purpose. They were a team. He couldn't do his job unless she did hers. And now Dyer didn't acknowledge their comments at all, just fixed Fletcher with an even stare.

Ordinarily, she could interpret every minuscule motion of his facial muscles. Intrigue was a scratch of his chin. Disappointment in an arched eyebrow or a leftward gaze. A twitch in his cheek meant he wanted a reason to leave the conversation.

This expression was flat. Impassive. "Yes, of course. Not to be forgotten. Carlotta, please prepare linens for Miss Spence and have her luggage delivered to the capybara room."

Capybara? Everyone else got majestic animals, and she got a *rodent*? The world's largest rodent, but that hardly softened the blow. After Bertram's and Deepti's digs, it was hard not to take this as another undercut.

Then, worst of all, Fletcher looked up to find the rodent of the hour perched high above Dyer's head. Her room. Right next to Waylon's.

The prodigal son smirked. With each word glazed in faux niceties, he said, "Guess we'll be seeing a lot of each other, neighbor."

Fletcher squinted. "How lucky for you."

"Something wrong, Spence?" It wasn't only a question. It was a challenge.

Yes! She hated him, and they would have to share a wall, and the mere thought of it made her want to shoot knives out of her knuckles Wolverine-style and slash his obnoxious smug grin to a trillion pieces.

Fletcher said none of that. She smiled. Sweet and unbothered and perfectly collected. "No problem at all."

She ducked inside her room, closing the door just shy of slamming. *Keep your cool, Fletcher. He wants to get a rise out of you.*

Thankfully, the capybara room deserved its own postal code. She'd hardly even know he was on the other side of her walls.

Also thankfully, the capybara room was *not* rodent-themed.

Jute rug, vintage trunks arranged like nightstands, fan blades designed like palm fronds. But it was not without the usual Cartwright elegance: a crystal chandelier; an en suite bathroom with a Jacuzzi tub and a double vanity; silk jacquard curtains framing a massive window.

And the view. The *view.*

From this vantage, everything glittered in the golden light. She hauled open the windowpane, and below, there were courtyards dotted with bistro tables and dripping in bougainvillea. The east wing jutted out toward the savanna. Sunlight striped the grasses, sparkled against the sea beyond the salt-slicked cliffs. No beach with pristine sands. The steep drop fed into churning depths.

Lights had been strung up over the pool patio, and a string quartet bowed their heads, tuning their instruments to the perfect pitch. Silverware clattered and glasses clinked as dinner was being prepared. Fletcher's private-jet sashimi felt like lifetimes ago. (How was she ever supposed to be satisfied by economy-class miniature pretzels ever again?)

A few of her colleagues were already down there, their laughter bubbling up like prosecco fizz. As the sun sank lower, watercolor pastels gliding across the sky, Fletcher found herself among them.

Attendants floated around the fenced perimeter with silver platters touting smoked salmon tartare and caviar on rosemary crisps and hazelnut-crusted, chocolate-covered strawberries. Fletcher snagged a piece of fruit, savoring it even as juice dribbled down her lips.

She could definitely get used to this.

Fletcher dipped inside her pocket for her phone. If her time zone math proved accurate, Ford would be brunching with Ricky, I Think and have his phone silenced, but some light gloating was in order.

Made it to the promised land!

You'd hate it here

Is what I would say if I were a LIAR. This is the most beautiful place I've ever seen. I'm never leaving. You think anyone would notice if I didn't come back to the office next week?

After shamelessly triple texting, she hid her phone again, before Dyer could give it the DSLR treatment and smash it to pieces.

The team moved in predictable rhythms, and for the first time since landing on Lydell, Fletcher found her footing. The Brians were both hidden behind their laptops, content to track SEO performance despite being on vacation. Theo and Bertram joined the execs where they hovered around Dyer, no better than moths. Molly, Opal, and Sheila giggled into glasses of chilled wine. Waylon and Joplin lingered by the bar—the bartender handed Joplin something purple with a spear of fruit and a knuckle-deep amber swig to Waylon.

Waylon's voice drifted across the patio, saying, "And a Manhattan for Spence."

Fletcher's eyes sliced toward his.

On any other day, maybe Fletcher would have ignored his existence like she had for the last three years.

But today, after setting the Guinness World Record for Most Jet-Lagged Human Being, she couldn't stop herself from marching across the porcelain pavers until she was close enough to jab a finger at his chest.

"How?" she asked. His shirt was so soft. Was that bamboo cotton? Not the point.

His lashes were long, a dark blond. And they batted like he'd done absolutely nothing wrong. "How what?"

"How do you know my usual drink order?"

Waylon's head fell back with a laugh. "Do you know the first cocktail I learned to make?"

"I'm sure you're going to tell me against my will."

"A Manhattan," he answered himself.

"It's a classic." Fletcher crossed her arms.

"Exactly. And that's how I knew you'd order it. It's safe. It's predictable."

"It's *reliable*. The best judge of a bar is their Manhattan. There's nothing wrong with being pragmatic."

"It's barely a step up from a Jack and Coke. It was probably the first real cocktail you ever ordered because you wanted to impress someone. Everybody's had one, and they might even consider it their favorite. But you know what I think?"

He leaned perilously close to Fletcher. Close enough she could smell the single malt Scotch on his breath and the Tom Ford cologne on his neck. Not unlike the first time they met, but deeper somehow. Older. She'd say maturer, but that would be giving him far too much credit.

The next time he spoke, his voice trailed into a whisper. "I think people who order Manhattans are too afraid to ask for what they really want."

Fletcher gulped, a shiver skittering over her skin from his proximity. The air between them buzzed with electricity. Like a blow-dryer a little too close to a bathtub. She took a step back for good measure. "And I think you should lay off the armchair psychology. You made a guess."

"A damn good one."

The bartender reappeared with her Manhattan before Fletcher could find her words—or, at the very least, words that weren't expletives.

"May I?" Waylon asked the bartender, before reaching over the counter and retrieving a gold skewer with a plump green olive. When he tossed it at her, Fletcher reared back to dodge its slimy arc. Her drink sloshed, splashing onto her blouse, a dark stain blooming. "*That* was how I knew you didn't drink a dry martini."

"Okay, fine. I hate olives. They looked like eyeballs. Tiny, impaled eyeballs." Her shirt clung to her skin as liquor dripped between her boobs. Humiliating. Through her teeth, she said, "You're a menace."

"And you're on vacation," he said as he downed the last of his drink. "Ditch the receptionist's clothes."

"For the last time, I'm not a—" Fletcher stomped as he walked away. *Ugh!*

Waylon stretched his arms overhead, tugging his henley off in one clean motion to dive in the pool, and suddenly her eyes were magnetized. Warmth spread across the high points of her cheeks.

It wasn't like she didn't expect him to have a private trainer and an entire wardrobe of swishy exercise shorts. Someone with as much disposable generational wealth as he had shouldn't also have the gall to be hot. Like, abs in the double digits, bronzed-Adonis levels of hot.

Toned or not, it didn't change his status as the bane of her mortal existence. A splinter digging under her skin. The titular vermin in the Whac-A-Mole of her most indulgent dreams.

Seeing him here, surrounded by people she knew, people she worked with, sent jealous flares over the trenches of her heart. He looked like he *belonged*. Belonged in a way Fletcher never had, and maybe never would.

She was about to pull herself away, really she was, when something clamped down on her shoulder. The hand belonged to Molly, the People team lead, who had never once in her life been seen without a pressed pantsuit. Tonight included. (But was anyone reprimanding her for dressing appropriately? No.)

Like Fletcher's, Molly's hair was red. But unlike Fletcher's, Molly's nearly radioactive hue came from painstaking hours in the salon. Her roots had started to grow in, and Fletcher wondered if she noticed. Molly straightened the tote on her shoulder. Had she brought performance-review paperwork and boilerplate contracts, ready to sign?

"Truly the last person I ever expected to see on the Lydell trip," she said, and it took Fletcher a few blinks to realize Molly wasn't talking about her. Her mascara-rimmed gaze was fixed on Waylon's blond curls. "I haven't seen him at one of these things since he was still with—oh, what was her name? Tall, supermodel, perfect hair?"

It didn't matter that Molly had described every woman Waylon Cartwright had ever entertained. Fletcher knew.

"Eliza Shelton."

"That's right!" Molly let out a low whistle. "Hard to believe it's been three years."

Three peaceful, Waylon-less years since the Cartwright Media Annual Gala for Impact disaster, a night involving a shattered champagne tower, the camera flash of a front-page photo being taken, and a little-known coat-closet encounter where Fletcher and Waylon briefly became allies before vowing to share a mutual hatred.

Back then, the ladies' man with a fool's gold smile had a fiancée. A living human being had agreed to marry him. Presumably of her own free will.

They'd broken up shortly after the charity nightmare, but as Fletcher watched Waylon shake the water out of his curls like a shepherding dog post-bath, purposefully trying to soak Joplin, she pictured the younger, scruffier version of him she'd met. Drunk, hiding from his dad at the biggest party of the year, no sign of his betrothed in sight. One foot out the door before he'd even dumped her.

Waylon left a string of broken hearts behind him, and Eliza was just another casualty. Fletcher's heart ached for her with a pang of knowing guilt. It must have been a horrible kind of torture to be in love with someone who could never love you back the way you deserved.

"Heard it was a nasty break, but I can't say I wasn't jealous of the rock on her finger. Although, when you work like we do, who has time to settle down anyway?" Molly asked, a playful lilt to her voice.

"God, truly," Fletcher said. Her thumb trailed over the bare spot on her ring finger. The spot Kent wanted to fill. "I'll cheers to that."

Their glasses clinked, and Fletcher tipped what was left of her spilled Manhattan down the hatch. Whiskey had soaked all the way through her bra, tacky and cold. She needed to get changed, but she couldn't tear her gaze away from the pool's deep end.

Joplin barely had time to kick off her espadrilles before Waylon dragged her beneath the surface. She reemerged, tangling her limbs with Waylon's in a feeble attempt to dunk him underwater. The way their bodies pressed together . . .

Finally, Fletcher choked out, "I'm going to freshen up."

Back upstairs, she unzipped a fresh top from the packing cube dutifully labeled SHIRTS. (She was nothing if not meticulous.) This one was celery green with balloon sleeves tied in ribbons by her wrists. Better suited for the air-conditioned office rather than Lydell's sticky heat. But it would have to do.

"You're too afraid to go after what you really want, Fletcher," she mimicked Waylon's unsolicited advice.

Standing in just her sales-rack bra while rinsing the Scotch out of her blouse in the gold-plated sink, she let herself hate Waylon. She hated him for ruining her favorite shirt. For having everything he wanted in life handed to him on one of the staff members' silver platters. For never worrying about getting evicted. For his stupid, chiseled abs.

He must have known the effect he had on her, like a schoolboy pulling on a girl's pigtails, just to watch her get flustered.

And it was working. So, she also hated him for that.

Once the liquor had mostly been rinsed down the drain, Fletcher tossed her shirt over the shower's glass door. She blew a breath out through her mouth and situated the dry blouse over her shoulders. Dyer's promise cut through her spiral, and it straightened her spine: *You play by my rules, Miss Spence, and you could have everything you've ever dreamed of.*

The trouble with Cartwrights was that the rules were always changing, but with her jaw clenched so hard she'd definitely need a root canal when she was back in Manhattan, Fletcher nodded to herself in the mirror. Maybe everything with Dyer was a game, but, for once, she wasn't afraid to play.

Jackie had said there could be a spot for Fletcher on her staff. That was why she'd come here. She would do what it took to prove she belonged at *Jet-Setter*. Whatever the cost.

5

The first course had already been served by the time Fletcher made it down to dinner.

Violin melodies beckoned her toward the hidden grotto on the far side of the pool. Lit candles dotted her path. A light fixture had been hoisted into the air, woven from some variety of horns—impala? antelope?—and the centerpiece was an ebony-and-gold table with an arrangement of dahlias and eucalyptus.

A table set for fifteen.

Fletcher's heart plummeted. Another reminder that she hadn't been invited. That she didn't belong here.

Everyone else clinked their crystal flutes and sipped sparkling wines they were born knowing how to pronounce. All these things they intrinsically knew, Fletcher had to teach herself. Which fork was for salads and which was for the rest of your meal. What a hedge fund was. The art of summering in the Hamptons.

God forbid, Fletcher couldn't even tell impala horns from antelope horns.

At the opposite side of the table, Dyer wordlessly gestured with the serrated end of his knife. From the shadows, a server procured another armchair. Its golden legs scraped against the tiles with every agonizing inch. No one chewed. No one swallowed.

Eventually, the staff member shoved the chair at the end of the table, stuffing Fletcher between Sheila and Asshole Rick, right across from Waylon.

"Apologies," Fletcher said to the group bashfully as she sank into her seat.

Conversations whirled on without any regard to Fletcher's arrival, picking up right where they left off—without her.

Melv, Jackie, and Raul roundtabled about cloud-based document-management platforms. Bertram and the Brians chatted animatedly about the trademark logistics of incorporating a Taylor Swift lyric into a headline while Deepti and Opal traded keratin-treatment recommendations. An easy, familiar cadence. Rhythms they knew well.

Fletcher counted the steps to their dances. Melv would deadpan something unexpectedly funny, and Jackie would lift her lipstick-stained glass to salute. Right on cue, a French 75 tipped into the air.

Then, she overheard Brian mention a new email campaign idea and knew it was downhill from there. Other Brian, looking up from his untouched appetizer, would get so excited spit would start flying, and Bertram would lean away, a hand pressed to his distended belly as if to settle his churning disgust.

Fletcher's usual patterns didn't fit in here. Instead of gossiping over drinks and fine cuisine, she would normally be spending tonight in her apartment, head dangling off the sofa while *Sex and the City* autoplayed.

Ford would stop by, already buzzed off free drinks. He'd steal her Häagen-Dazs out of the freezer, and she'd let him. Before Carrie got back together with Mr. Big, he'd dart out the door, off to karaoke or trivia night. Then, a bit later, Kent would call, and she'd answer. He'd ask her to take him back, and she would.

That was on her for being a Type Nine Enneagram. Pleasing people made her good at her job. She made it look so easy: perfectly content to stuff envelopes and coordinate meetings and plan luncheons. Never a bad temper. Never a hair out place.

But being here, on this island, stabbing her fork into a peri-peri prawn and sipping sauvignon blanc with her pinky raised? Uncharted territory.

Across the table, Waylon sized her up. A blond curl dripped over his eyebrow, and his shirt stuck to him in wet patches from his evening splash. "So nice of you to finally join us, Spence." As if *he* wasn't the reason she had to go upstairs to change. "Don't worry, you still got the best view at the table."

Fletcher scowled. Simmered. "I've seen better."

Butting in obliviously, Sheila said, "Oh my god. No way. The views on this island are *insane*. Like, why have I never come here before?"

Waylon didn't take his eyes off Fletcher as he said, "Usually this is the kind of place you have to be invited to."

Before she could think better of it, Fletcher nudged Waylon's foot beneath the table with the pointed toe of her shoe. He dropped his knife in surprise, the sound ringing loudly over the small talk. Fletcher stifled her amusement as Dyer reprimanded him with a stiff glare.

"Luckily for Sheila," Fletcher said between bites, "her hard work is finally being recognized."

"And what hard work is that? Push any more unsuspecting victims into a champagne tower lately?" Waylon stepped on Fletcher's toe. He grinned, a cocky sidelong thing. If he scuffed her shoes, he was dead meat.

"I—*Sheila* was trying to stop you from getting her fired by causing a scene in front of that reporter. She didn't push you into it on purpose." Waylon winced as she retaliated with a swift kick to his shin. "It's not her fault you were drunk."

"I had three drinks. That hardly qualifies as inebriated."

"The cover of *People* would beg to differ."

Waylon caught one of Fletcher's ankles between his calves. She wiggled, but it was no use. The more she thrashed, the tighter his legs cinched.

Her glare said, *Cut it out.*

His answered, *You started it.*

"Is there something under there? What is going on?" Sheila asked, ducking her head beneath the table. Fletcher snapped her foot out of Waylon's death grip before they could get caught playing angry footsie.

She ignored the intern. Never once let her death stare leave Waylon's. "*Sheila* deserves to be here as much as everyone else."

"I have no idea what you two are talking about, and I've been quiet quitting for months." Sheila turned to her, fair cheeks pink from wine she was too young to legally drink in America. "But thanks, Fifi. I know the others disagree, but I'm glad you came back."

"Back?" Fletcher asked, stomach sinking.

"Honestly, when you were late to dinner, I thought maybe you'd called the jet to go home."

"Why would I do that?"

Sheila's expression grew doe-like. "Oh! I didn't mean it in a bad way. It's just . . ."

Bertram cleared his throat a couple seats down. "You have no business being here."

At that, her half of the table quieted. Churlish looks stretched toward Fletcher, and it took all her strength not to push her food around her plate, just to look busy. Waylon's gaze settled on her, heaviest of all. She braced for an *I told you so*, but he took another bite, his mouth too occupied with chewing to continue ridiculing her.

Bertram's beetle-black eyes inspected her. *Scrutinized* her. Searched for flaws he could extort. The disdain in his tone was palpable when he said, "You aren't a top performer. You are an assistant. There is no place for you here."

All Fletcher could do was blink. And stare. And blink some more.

This wasn't one of Waylon's underhanded jabs. There was no volley of insults, no silver-tongued back-and-forth. Waylon may have set the trap, but he didn't have to strike the killing blow. When she looked around, everyone's hands had frozen halfway to their mouths. Bertram had simply said what they were all thinking.

Fletcher hated to admit it, but on one hand, Bertram was right.

There was no denying she'd eked her way onto the island, hedging her bets and playing her only card at the right moment. A trick she'd learned from Dyer.

And on the other hand, Bertram had a stick so far up his ass it could scratch his brain.

He'd always been like this, stern and rule-following. He ran a tight ship on the Marketing team, constantly barking about higher conversion rates and keyword optimization. But he wasn't her boss, and he wasn't privy to her performance reviews.

He didn't know she'd worked seventy-hour weeks for the last three years without a single complaint. Or how she'd reshaped her life to accommodate Cartwright Media, bending but never breaking. She'd never once snitched on Theo for expensing a VR headset to "boost team productivity," or Joplin for making a private Slack channel called #shit-jackie-says, or Raul for giving Deepti a hickey at the company Christmas party while her husband grabbed drinks.

She'd stayed quiet then, but she couldn't stay quiet now.

Dyer and Jackie studied her from the head of the table, measuring her response. And Bertram watched her the way a kid with a magnifying glass watched an ant fry in the sunlight. Waiting to see her squirm.

"I'm as fortunate to be here as you are." Fletcher smoothed her lips into a congenial grin. It didn't reach her eyes. (Her eyes were molten-lava lasers.) "I'd never underestimate your expertise in your department, Denis. Don't underestimate mine."

With what could only be divine intervention, dishes streamed in through the double doors, pivoting everyone's attention. *Hallelujah.* Fletcher exhaled so thoroughly she blew out three tea lights that had to be relit by gloved waiters.

Each bite was more indulgent than the last. Biltong and fig salads, mango and lobster ceviche, kudu steaks in a truffle-and-brown-butter sauce. Fletcher must have died and gone to foodie heaven.

It was almost enough for her to ignore the whispers.

After the bowls of pear and ginger sorbet had been cleared, Dyer stood at the head of the table with a glass of imported whiskey in hand. He sagged a little heavier against his cane than normal, but his smile beamed as bright as ever. "I'm so glad to welcome you all to Lydell. You deserve a chance to unwind after your dedication to our publications this year."

A round of applause rose from the table.

"My grandfather's island has been a second home to me my whole life. It is where I married my sweet Tiff, and it is where I spread her ashes. As much as Lydell, she was also my safe place." Dyer's eyes went glassy, and Fletcher didn't dare fidget in her seat to glance at Waylon, afraid of what she'd find. Tiffany Cartwright had died long before Fletcher ever met the Cartwrights. "Tiff always said work brought out the best and the worst in me, and that who I become in my darkest moments defines how I will be remembered."

A kind of wet, heartbroken laugh filtered through his lips. Jackie reached over and squeezed the hand by Dyer's side. He glanced down at her, a gentleness in his gaze Fletcher recognized as grief.

"Wives really are right about everything, aren't they?" he said, raising a good-natured laugh. "We always loved coming here. On Lydell, we didn't have to worry about decorum. Here, we were free from expectations, as wild as the animals roaming the island's grasslands and jungles. Lydell Island is a world of its own."

Dyer looked straight toward Fletcher, and her smile moved into place on its own accord. For years, every time she'd seen Dyer, she'd pasted on this expression of cartoon excitement. Like there was nowhere else on earth she'd rather be than where he needed her. She wondered, vaguely, if she was as much of an anchor for him as he was for her.

"There is one more thing I forgot to mention," Dyer said. He let the silence linger for dramatic effect. Ever the showman. "This will be my last company trip to Lydell. It's time I announce my retirement."

The entire table gasped. Fletcher included.

No, no, no.

Her insides curdled like a glass of milk that had sat in the sun for too long. Wouldn't you mention to your executive assistant there would no longer be an executive for her to assist? Sure, they'd find a new CEO eventually, but Dyer *was* Cartwright Media. They were synonymous, no one without the other.

Sheila glanced at Fletcher over her shoulder, the question obvious in the intern's narrowed eyes. *Did you know?*

Heat flared up Fletcher's neck because no, no she had not. And she should have. It was her job to know. Had there been signs she'd missed?

"Who's taking over the company?" Deepti asked with a panicked edge.

Was *this* why Waylon had been invited? The heir, come to claim his father's throne? And, what? Fletcher was just expected to become his lapdog? To sit when he said *sit*, to stay when he said *stay*?

Shock gave way to something a little bit lighter. Maybe Dyer retiring could be exactly what she needed to leverage her move to *Jet-Setter*. Waylon would be happy to get rid of her.

"I've got all the details worked out." Dyer's glass lifted higher. "Tonight, we celebrate the legacies we inherit and what we choose to do with them. May you all choose wisely."

Melv stood next to him, clapping a compassionate hand on Dyer's shoulder. "This calls for a toast. To everything Dyer Cartwright's legacy has brought us, and everything yet to come."

And the table called out, "To Dyer!"

As the party lights extinguished and everyone wandered back inside, darkness clawed over Lydell. Fletcher leaned against her window and let herself feel small beneath the atlas of stars. The breeze stilled, and the grasses stopped rustling, and the night birds' evening songs quieted, as if the entire island knew change was coming, and there was nothing it could do but brace for impact.

Fletcher's face was wet when she woke up. Not from crying, though she considered it. Something stiff and dripping glided over the plane of her cheek, and her eyes snapped open as a giant purple tongue retreated. A slick of slime coated her cheek.

A giraffe grinned down at her like it enjoyed Frenching her and would happily do it again.

"Oh my god. Disgusting." She wiped the slobber off her face with the sleeve of her shirt. "At least ask for consent."

The giraffe culprit blinked down at her, its long neck craned inside her open window. Enviously long lashes, big black eyes—beautiful and mesmerizing, but not exactly good-morning-kiss material.

Wait.

A giraffe?

Fletcher untangled herself from her bedsheets and shooed the massive creature back outside with a hand pressed against its muzzle. As it retreated, she leaned out the window and pointed toward the drooping boughs of a nearby apricot tree, bloated with fruit.

"Look! Right there!" she called. As if the giraffe spoke English. "Plenty of food, just for you."

She could've sworn the animal winked at her before lolling its giant neck toward the fruit tree behind the outdoor sauna. It must have gone to the Asshole Rick School of Flirting. *Yuck.*

The savanna seemed to have crept closer overnight, like the tectonic plates themselves shifted with Dyer's retirement announcement. Her giraffe suitor must have stepped clean over the fence separating the patio from the wild, but that wasn't all. Vultures circled overhead, and just beyond the grounds, a pack of lions gnawed on a puddle of mangled red. Far too close for comfort.

An engine revved in the distance, more staff members heading up from their lodging at the jungle's heart, most likely. Fletcher's mouth started to water at the thought of a five-star breakfast as elaborate as last night's supper. Belgian waffles, eggs Benedict, bottomless mimosas.

For the first time in years she'd fallen asleep with her falsies still glued on. Not to mention the giraffe saliva caking into a hard crust. Hell would freeze over before she let her colleagues witness her in such a state of disarray.

Gripping the marble ledge of the bathroom countertop, Fletcher faced herself in the mirror. She was made of soft lines. Full cheeks, round lips, and carefully drawn eyebrows. All curves and no corners. Freckles, fading as NYC descended into overcast autumn, spread across her nose, pinpricks on a map. Already the Lydell sun had sketched redness onto the fair skin of her forehead and the peaks of her cheekbones.

Hundreds, if not thousands, of dollars of complimentary skincare products had been arranged on the bathroom counter. It put Fletcher's Neutrogena selection to shame. With a fistful of cleanser, she scrubbed her face until her skin pinked. She splashed her cheeks one last time, only to end up with very expensive suds in her eyes.

"Shit, shit, shit."

Fletcher reached blindly for a towel.

Oh, god. A towel.

She'd forgotten to grab one. New zits sprouted at the sheer thought of using the hand towel with all of its hand towel germs.

With her eyes pinched closed, Fletcher waddled toward the linen closet. Twisting the knob with skincare-slick hands proved harder than she'd expected, but when she finally pried the door open, her hand planted firmly against something warm and solid.

"Good morning to you, too."

A scream tore out of Fletcher's throat. Her eyes peeled open in terror—and then clamped shut in pain. The soapsuds burned so sharply it curled her spine.

She spun too quickly, slipped on a bath mat, and skidded back into the sink. Fletcher fumbled for something, anything, and her hands snagged on a bottle from her toiletries bag and brandished it like a sword.

"Are you trying to defend yourself with a bottle of hairspray?"

That voice. She recognized that voice.

Fletcher pried one eyelid up, a fraction of an inch, and winced against the sting. Waylon stood, shirtless, hands planted against his hips, and watched her half-feral survival instincts with a smirk.

She glanced at her weapon of choice. "Dry shampoo. Doesn't matter. Why are you standing in my closet?"

"I heard the water turn off. Thought I might hop in the shower."

"In my bathroom?" Fletcher shrilled.

"Don't you mean *our* bathroom?"

For the first time, Fletcher peered over his shoulder. Beyond him wasn't a set of shelves, stacked with rolled terry cloth. There was a bed, a dresser, nightstands. Bedroom things just like her bedroom things.

And between them, a jack-and-jill bathroom.

"Did you want to join me?" Waylon's photo belonged in the dictionary next to the definition for *smug son of a bitch*.

Fletcher would have rolled her eyes if she hadn't accidentally chemical peeled them. "I'd rather throw myself into an active volcano."

A hum vibrated in his chest. A hum that sounded a lot like he didn't believe her.

She opened her mouth, hoping something snarky manifested, but it simply hung there useless. Her thoughts tangled, a fly caught in a spider's web. Whenever he was near, she reverted to a twenty-three-year-old version of herself.

She stripped the towel from his arms and used it to wipe at her eyes as she stomped away, slamming the door behind her.

"You're welcome for the towel," he called.

His laugh, bright and clear, haunted her all the way downstairs.

The rest of the house was still, quiet save for the sound of an iPhone game chiming six inches from Sheila's face. The intern slumped on one of the microsuede sofas, body contorted into a horrible C shape that would give chiropractors nightmares.

"Morning," Fletcher offered half-heartedly as she smoothed her hand over the sofa's plush fabric. "Did I miss breakfast?"

"I don't think so," Sheila said. "No one's come out of the kitchen yet. Do you think I should sell my golden chicken to get a super-mega-blaster?"

"What? No. I don't care."

In the silence between sound effects, Fletcher listened for signs of life. The estate was missing the low-volume chatter it had yesterday before dinner when staff members fluttered between rooms. There was no popped champagne or crudités. No sweet smell of syrup or freshly brewed espresso.

Slowly, the others trickled downstairs. Joplin's pink curls were wrapped in a silk scarf, Opal still had her rollers in. Melv was fully dressed, his wing tip loafers clicking against the parquet floors. Did he sleep in chinos? It wouldn't surprise her.

Talk of sales-enablement campaigns and the ethicality of influencer marketing eventually drowned out the sounds of the waking safari. Both things Fletcher didn't have the headspace for before her first cup of coffee.

When the massive analog clock on the wall struck nine, Fletcher's stomach grumbled. Breakfast should be served by now. Did she spend all those hours curating the itinerary for nothing?

"Has anyone seen Dyer this morning?" she asked the room.

Most of the group was still bickering about margin percentages and hashtag uses. But most of the group wasn't responsible for knowing the CEO's schedule inside and out. For greeting him every morning after tai chi with a palm full of multivitamins recommended by his cardiologist. Had he remembered to pack enough?

See, *this* was why she should have always been invited.

"I'll go check on him quickly," she said to no one in particular. It wasn't like anyone was listening to her. Her role was always best performed on the sidelines. When she did her job right, she vanished entirely, an unseen force allowing operations to run smoothly for everyone else.

Following the vaulted ceilings down a hallway with a built-in saltwater aquarium, she found the executive suite situated at the far end of the east wing. Fletcher squeezed through the massive oak doors and latched them behind her.

Inside, there were pressed-linen curtains and handwoven rugs, a sitting area with a suede chesterfield sofa in front of a mammoth bookshelf stuffed with clothbound books, and a teak coffee table stacked with magazines from *Jet-Setter*'s backlog.

"Mr. Cartwright?" she called. All the lights were off. Maybe he was still asleep.

A set of double doors separated the bedroom from the lounge, one cracked open. Fletcher inched toward it on quiet feet.

"Dyer? Are you awake?"

No response.

Behind her, the door to the suite opened with a click, and Fletcher yelped in surprise. If Dyer wasn't awake before, he was now. Her heart thumped somewhere around her jugular as Waylon waltzed in, a loose cotton shirt half unbuttoned and his chest still damp.

"Sorry, I was—" She didn't need to explain herself to him. Besides, she freaked herself out for nothing. So why did her ribs feel too tight around her lungs? "What are you doing here?"

"My dad asked me to join him for coffee this morning," Waylon said, raising his hands next to his head in the picture of innocence. "Shouldn't I be asking *you* why you're in his suite? Unless you're sleeping with him. Do *not* tell me if you're sleeping with my father."

"Gross, no. I would never. I'm just trying to do my job."

Which. Ordinarily would have included knowing every minute of Dyer's calendar. It wasn't her imagination—something definitely wasn't right. The realization must have manifested on her face because Waylon's brows dipped, something like concern etching through them. *Like* concern, but decidedly *not* concern, obviously. This was Waylon Cartwright, after all.

The look left as fast as it came, being replaced easily by his usual pompous snark. "And we both know your job primarily involves skulking around."

"I do not *skulk*."

"Looks pretty skulky."

Fletcher barely swallowed an irritated groan. His dickwaddedness at least spurred her back into motion. She eased the bedroom doors apart, millimeters at first and then all at once.

Because Dyer wasn't there.

On the far side of the room, patio doors had been strewn wide open, their gauzy curtains floating in the breeze. The savanna sprawled beyond a bricked seating area, and beyond that, a boundless sea.

Pillows had been torn off the four-poster bed, the sheets strewn across the floor and stained red. Russet puddled on the hardwood. A few drops at a time. A trail, maybe, but Fletcher was no forensic scientist. She couldn't even look when she got her blood drawn.

A gasp caught halfway up her throat. "Dyer? Are you okay?"

"Dad?" Waylon asked, hovering behind her. The word sounded unnatural in his mouth, rusted over with disuse.

The room was empty.

Waylon pushed past Fletcher, practically shoving her out of the way. Tension rippled through the broad expanse of his chest. His mouth was fixed in a pinched line, indecipherable. "What happened?"

On the wall next to Dyer's bed hung an electronic panel—the kind that ordinarily controlled things like motorized curtains and thermostat temperatures. A little red light blinked. And blinked. And blinked.

Fletcher and Waylon gravitated toward it.

Fence disabled. Fence disabled. Fence disabled.

"Look," Waylon said, shifting.

Dyer's carved cane leaned against a bedside table. Hooked beneath its handle was a tiny silver drive and an envelope stamped with the company letterhead. Dyer's slanted penmanship crooked across the lines: *To my next of kin.*

"You don't think . . ." Fletcher started, but a roar snapped their attention outside.

The lions Fletcher had seen from her window were still working on this morning's kill. Only now, Fletcher noticed the trail of deep maroon marring the soil, the trampled way the grasses bent. Her knees gave out, and she sagged against the doorframe.

The pride male stretched his haunches before digging back into the meat. It stripped flesh from bone, blood staining its maw. Muscle tissue dripped from its chin. An entrail, an esophagus. Bite after gruesome bite.

Fletcher's heart seized. Her stomach bottomed out.

She wanted to look away but couldn't.

Because the lion reared with a growl, standing, and clamped in its mouth was a shock of silver hair belonging to the CEO's mauled head.

6

This was the most fucked-up all-hands Fletcher had ever attended.

Her screaming had scared off the pride, the last of them dragging Dyer's bloodied leg through the dirt. But all the horrified screeching had also drawn the rest of her coworkers into the suite. Because what they'd been really missing was a crowd.

Shock waves rocked through the rest of the employees, each in various stages of the grief cycle—Molly had a trembling hand pressed to her lips, Deepti sniffled into the pocket square she'd stolen out of Raul's suit jacket, and Melv started pacing, scrubbing the back of his sunburned neck.

"Someone call for help," Fletcher said, knowing full well that *someone* would be *her*. It was always her. But, for once, her phone was upstairs charging on the nightstand. A version of herself whose boss hadn't been eaten by lions might have been thankful for the work-life separation.

A familiar chime sounded next to Fletcher, and she dragged her eyes toward Sheila. The intern's phone was glued to the end of her nose. A rainfall of confetti flashed on-screen as Sheila beat another level in her game, and Fletcher batted the phone away.

"Seriously, Sheila?"

"What?" A hot-pink chewing gum bubble pressed through her lips, and she bit it until it popped. "I can't watch Netflix because my phone's being so sketchy right now."

Fletcher stripped the iPhone from Sheila's sparkly gel-manicured grip. She had Carlotta's direct line memorized. Her hands shook as she thumbed it in, but when she pressed the green call button, the phone didn't even ring.

The bars at the top vanished.

What the hell?

She pivoted toward Raul, but the CTO bolted around the corner, already retching. No way did he reach the toilet.

"Mine, too," Other Brian said, holding up his phone. Dismay painted his fair features.

Jackie nodded, her cell snug against her ear. "Nothing."

"Oh my god, we're *all* going to get eaten by lions," Joplin wailed.

"Does this mean we don't get promotions?" asked Asshole Rick.

It took twenty minutes and half a bottle of Xanax to herd everyone into the living room with the sunken conversation pit. This one, on the second floor, had a stone fireplace with a rifle strapped above the mantel, built-ins stacked with vintage books, and a U-shaped sofa with room for about thirty-seven perched on top of a bear-pelt rug. Cozy. Kind of.

Fletcher's back stuck to the leather cushions, hot and humid even this early in the day. Or maybe she sweated through her blouse.

That seemed justified. All things considered.

Waylon sat uncomfortably on the live-edge black oak coffee table, facing everyone else. Dyer's cane was perched against his thigh, and his fingers tapped a nervous rhythm against the ivory. It was the only sign of his frayed nerves. Everything else was a cold, unaffected shell. The most serious Waylon had ever looked.

"What are we supposed to do?" Joplin asked, wet with snot. She tugged a worried hand through her pink hair.

"How could this happen? *What* happened?" Molly asked. Mildly accusatory.

For a fraction of a second, Waylon's gaze found Fletcher's. She'd be lying to herself if she hadn't wondered the same thing. How had Dyer forgotten to lock his patio door? But it wasn't just that—the protective fence had been deliberately turned off.

This wasn't an accident.

And the note. No one wrote a note before *coincidentally* being eaten alive. He'd clearly intended for Waylon to be the one to discover his fate. Alone, presumably.

A nerve at Waylon's jaw twinged, stressed from the force of clenched teeth. As soon as he tore his line of sight away from Fletcher, she remembered how to breathe in a regular cadence. Being near him had her sympathetic nervous system on the fritz.

He tamped his father's cane against the ground, fingers paling around its handle. The room fell to attention.

"The only thing we know is that he's gone," Waylon said. The grit in his tone sent unsolicited shivers down Fletcher's back. Uncurling his fingers, Waylon cradled the USB drive in his palm, and the team forcibly ejected themselves from their couch cushions to get a better look. "And he left this."

Deepti frowned. "A flash drive?"

Raul's eyebrows shot up like he'd been Bat-Signaled. "Let's plug it in."

After producing a laptop from his bag, he inserted the drive and tinkered with the computer in chilling quiet. The *click*, *click*, *click* of indented keys.

Waylon smashed a button on a remote, and a projector screen descended from the center of the room, large enough to rival IMAX. Strangely, Fletcher wasn't in the mood for popcorn.

In a flash, Dyer's smiling face appeared on-screen. Cheeks round and skin flushed. Living.

"Wow," Jackie said. A bittersweet laugh parted her lips. "I didn't even know he knew how to film himself."

Bertram huffed, leaning back against the couch and adjusting the belt of his pants around his obtrusive stomach. "Always gets the last word, doesn't he?"

When Raul pressed play, the video started rolling, showing Dyer fiddling with his camera, straightening it so that he would be centered. All the air in the room evaporated. Goose bumps rose over every patch of exposed skin. Fletcher could hardly believe this man was gone, nothing more than a pile of half-eaten flesh. Her stomach Tilt-A-Whirled at the thought.

On-screen, Dyer cleared his throat. "Bit of a funny thing to do, filming a video like this. Is it still called filming these days? There's no film."

A laugh went up around the living room, soggy and vaguely mucus-y, but a laugh nonetheless. Dyer chuckled, too, like he'd anticipated the effect of his own charm. He could run a billion-dollar company, but he could barely work an iPhone camera. That was Dyer, for sure.

"By now, you all know what I know: Life is fleeting. Never is that more apparent than on Lydell Island. Time, as we've all learned, is precious, so I'll keep things brief." His features tightened, and Fletcher heard more than one coworker swallow anxiously. "I've been a dead man for months. In February, I started seeing a cardiologist. Dr. Hawks, awful man that he is, found a tumor growing around my heart."

Fletcher bit down on the inside of her cheek. All those missed appointments—the way Dyer kept asking her to reschedule. This whole time, she'd thought they were routine. Dr. Hawks had been trying to *save* him.

Waylon sucked in a breath too loud for the silent living room. Had he known?

Dyer smiled, and it was so familiar that Fletcher's own heart squeezed. Disbelief coursed through her veins. Yesterday had been the last time she'd ever see his mischievous grin in person, and she hadn't even *known* it was the last time. It felt unfathomable, his sudden departure. But here it was. Fathomed.

"There were treatment options. Procedures I could do. Surgeries to be had," he said. "Or I could come to Lydell, drink something a little extra stiff, and lie down in the bed I shared with my wife one last time, listening to the sounds of the wilderness we loved so much."

A gasp worked through the crowd. He had died the same way he had lived: according to his own rules.

"I've always known the company would go on without me. That's why this hard drive contains two items. This video, and my last will and testament."

Next to her, Molly inhaled shakily. Fletcher's breathing felt just as uneven. She picked a thread loose in her skirt, trying to keep the nausea at bay. It wasn't working. All she could think about were the taxidermied animals dotting the manor's halls. Would Dyer want to be embalmed and stuffed, put on display for the rest of eternity as immortal as he always felt? Were billionaires into that kind of thing?

It was a little too easy to imagine him taking up permanent real estate in his penthouse office, perched in the corner case with a Madame Tussauds smile.

Then she'd *really* beg to transfer to Design.

"Melv," Dyer said, peering to the side. It happened to be the side Melv *wasn't* sitting on, but it was a valiant effort. "You'll take the liberty of reading all the paperwork, I'm sure, but I'll cut to the chase. Everyone here knows there is only one remaining Cartwright."

Fletcher's eyes cut toward Waylon. She was certain she wasn't the only one who found her gaze drifting his way. The rightful heir. Not even Sheila—Waylon's mom's sister's daughter—was a Cartwright by blood.

Waylon leaned his elbows on his knees, rolling the heirloom cane in his hands. Barely even bothering to watch. Couldn't he at least have the decency to look interested in inheriting the entire Cartwright legacy?

A brief glint of affection splashed across Dyer's face—real, genuine—before vanishing behind his usual theatricality. "To my son, Waylon Cartwright, I leave Lydell Island, its animal inhabitants, as well as all of its structures and assets. It's what your mother would have wanted, and you know I've never trusted anyone more than Tiffany to protect what I love most."

Big surprise. Next, he'd inherit the yachts, the planes, and the Bora Bora home. Then, the Upper East Side penthouse, and the stocks and bonds. Cartwright Media and all affiliated assets. The whole kit and caboodle.

Dyer cleared his throat. "The rest I leave to fate."

Her colleagues inched forward in their seats, but Fletcher shrank back into her cushion, coiling her knees toward her chest. *To fate?* In all the years she'd known him, Dyer had never left anything to the whims of others.

When *Jet-Setter*'s Amsterdam issue spawned a national outcry about marijuana legalization, it coincided with Cartwright Media's lofty donation to a running politician whose platform miraculously aligned. When the board of directors feared stagnation, Dyer organized a last-minute meeting to absorb a smaller publication. When everyone else was exclusive to print, Dyer ushered *Jet-Setter* into the digital age.

He'd always navigated speed bumps with an innate charisma Fletcher often envied. But more than that, he didn't merely extricate himself from sticky situations. He'd orchestrated them entirely.

One hundred years of periodicals had been printed under this banner. What kind of leader would leave that up to *fate*?

Dyer stroked his chin in the video, leaving plenty of dead air for dramatic effect. He was sitting in his office. When had he filmed this? How had she missed it? The moment lasted entirely too long. Finally, he continued. "I've always heard publishing is a cutthroat business, and nowhere is that truer than on Lydell. I've gathered each of you here for a reason. For your tenacity. Your instincts. Your gumption."

The word flared through Fletcher like a flint strike.

"You'll need it to run Cartwright Media."

Murmurs turned to unashamed whispers. The Brians craned their heads together, chatting. Deepti blew her nose like an elephant trumpeting and then folded the handkerchief neatly in her lap, curiosity piqued.

"This is my will here. I'd like to read some of it for you." Dyer shuffled through some papers until he found a stack latched with a gold binder clip. "As of the announcement of this will, all invited guests on Lydell Island are eligible for the inheritance of the remaining assets, including ownership of Cartwright Media, all mutual funds managed by Dyer Cartwright, and domestic and international properties deeded to Dyer Cartwright."

"Eligible?" Asshole Rick asked. "Why eligible?"

Dyer, of course, didn't hear him.

Half the room turned to Melv, waiting for the lawyer to make sense of this completely nonsensical sentence. Melv was rapt with attention, literally on the edge of his seat.

"You may have noticed," Dyer continued, "the manor is a little quieter this morning. I've sent the staff off the island. All wireless connectivity and phone lines have been disabled and will remain offline for the next five days. What happens next is only between us."

Reaching beneath his desk, Dyer extracted his ivory cane, the same cane now in Waylon's hands.

"My grandfather carved this from the tusk of an elephant he'd killed here on a hunting trip. It's a depiction of the beasts found on Lydell. Vicious animals in a lawless land, but at the top—"

Past a winged vulture, elephant, zebra, giraffe, cheetah, and maned lion, Dyer unfurled his fist to reveal the grip, the double barrel of a shotgun.

"Us."

Time slowed down, seconds stretching into hours.

"Cartwright Media's next leader needs to be a fierce predator. Someone strong enough to survive in unforgiving landscapes. I've disabled the electric fence separating you from the wild. A rescue crew will arrive at the marina in five days, once you've had the chance to prove your grit and determination in this harsh environment."

Rescue crew? The room didn't spin—it lurched with bone-crushing centrifugal force. Someone shifted in their seat. Someone else coughed. Fletcher didn't see who because her eyes had gone tunnel-y. She was going to throw up and pass out, in that order.

On-screen, Dyer speared onward. Laughing like he hadn't sentenced them to death. Or, maybe, laughing because he knew he had. The former CEO of Cartwright Media laced his fingers beneath his chin.

"If you can survive here, you can certainly handle a board meeting.

However, only one guest will be able to take immediate ownership of my assets upon returning to the Cartwright Media offices in Manhattan. Choose wisely. All other guests must forfeit. This is what Lydell has always been: a hunting ground."

A smile. His last.

"Good luck. You'll need it."

7

Silence fell like a guillotine.

The video ended, stalling on a screenshot of Dyer reaching toward the camera, and no one moved to change it. Fletcher's fingers quivered, cortisol drumming through them. The rest of her went numb.

Retiring was one thing. Retiring meant Dyer would don a floppy sun hat, fly the coop to Florida, and live out the rest of his days as a snowbird. Conducting a company retreat to kill himself and maroon the guests with limited resources to see who would be the last one standing? That was something else entirely.

Fletcher couldn't look at any of the others—afraid of what she'd find in the darks of their eyes. Once, at a Lunch and Learn, Bertram bodychecked an associate to get the last serving of tiramisu. What would he do for a company with a multibillion-dollar valuation?

"What a nightmare," Molly howled, clearly in her own personal HR hellscape.

"He was always off, that Dyer," someone grouched very loudly. Probably Bertram.

"Did he say *if* we survive, we get the company?" Brian, or maybe Other Brian, asked, as if either one of them stood half a chance at lasting five days without Wi-Fi. "What does he mean, *if*?"

They had to be missing something. Fletcher's panic carved out Melv—a pinprick surrounded by webbed black. He was the attorney, the voice of reason. Used to courtroom squabbles and complicated paperwork, he'd be able to decipher the will's legalese. He'd make sense of this.

Steeling herself, Fletcher asked, "Melv, what exactly is going on? Is the will legitimate?"

Melv sighed like it took a tremendous effort. Poor guy had probably been looking forward to a day or two without culling through fine print. "Settle down, everybody. Let's take a look."

Between stretching his shirt collar and huffing impatiently, Melv managed to click a few buttons and pull the digital copy of the will up, still broadcasting onto the projector screen. Through the legal jargon, Fletcher could hardly decipher anything. Headers and subsections blurred together as Melv scrolled down the seemingly endless document.

"Section C, Section D . . . *Oh.*" Fletcher could practically hear the lump in Melv's throat. "Section E, subsection four. Survivorship will be determined on Lydell Island. Each invited guest is hereby considered a residuary beneficiary. This provision allows residuary beneficiaries to demonstrate leadership, resourcefulness, and confident decision-making in the kill-or-be-killed world of publishing."

He glanced at his audience, the sanity of which hinged on his next word. The skin between his brows creased.

Melv kept reading. "Assets are not to be divided between the residuary beneficiaries prior to return to the Cartwright Media Legal offices at 674 Fifth Avenue, 58th floor, New York, NY 10022, after my last departure to Lydell Island. At which point one sole beneficiary will herein receive the full reward, claiming ownership over all assets, including Cartwright Media, LLC, and its subsidiaries. In the event none of the residuary beneficiaries claim ownership in thirty days, assets will be divided by the acting chairman of the board."

Fletcher heard every word Melv spoke. And yet. *And yet.* None of the sounds out of his mouth registered. A stringy, suffocating silence unfolded as she suspected the rest of them tried to parse out the true meaning, too.

The engine they heard this morning? Dyer said he sent the staff members away, but now Fletcher realized it didn't just mean they wouldn't get turndown service. They were trapped. On an island filled with vicious creatures. Because her billionaire boss resigned them all to fight for his inheritance in some heinous display of late-capitalist greed. No staff, no cellular data, no security from the animals.

It wasn't just a matter of inheritance—but survival.

"So, that's it?" Sheila squeaked. Could she even spell *bequeathment*?

Melv's exhausted stare cut toward the intern. "No, there're sixty-six more pages. But that's the gist of it. At the end of the week, only one of us will become the proud new owner of Cartwright Media."

Deepti took to pacing. "So, now we're supposed to—what?—just pick someone to inherit the company? Obviously, I'm picking me."

At that, dissident voices roared around the room. No one believed they were any less deserving than the person sitting next to them. The Lydell guest list suddenly made a lot more sense—the C-suite's seniority, Melv's cool-tempered problem-solving, Molly's ability to successfully navigate company politics, and Joplin's creativity. Marketing and Sales were wild cards, but Fletcher had seen them all sacrifice something for the company. Skipped lunches, missed parties, late nights. Any one of them could argue their spot for the helm. But . . . stranding them in the Indian Ocean to work out the details? That was overkill, even for Dyer.

Melv quieted the room. "We have until the rescue crew comes to decide."

"Assuming any of us live that long," Jackie sulked.

Every head in the room swiveled toward her. Reproachful.

Jackie only shrugged. "Don't look at me. Dyer's the one who abandoned us here, and this island is teeming with predators on the hunt for easy prey. You heard the same will reading I did. If my options are kill or be killed, I know which one I'm choosing."

Fletcher's mind spun, a run-on sentence. *What on earth is going on* and *how do I get out of here* and *do all company retreats devolve into a ritualistic sacrifice?*

Waylon laughed. The humorless sound soaked up the room's lingering conversations.

Melv clasped his hands in front of him. "Something you'd like to share?"

Wiping beneath his eyes, Waylon mopped up unshed tears. "No. Please, go on. If you want to kill each other to entertain my dad's final fucked-up wishes, be my guest."

"No one is killing anyone," Raul countered. He leveled Jackie with a hard glance. "We can hold a civil discussion. It doesn't have to be anarchy."

"You heard Dyer. Lydell's a hunting ground. Always has been," Jackie said like it was obvious.

Joplin, the voice of the people, said, "You're talking about murder. Murder is illegal."

"That's enough, everyone. The will doesn't specify how the beneficiary is decided. But . . ." Melv's mouth flattened. "Nothing is illegal on Lydell."

Theo had said something similar in the truck. Fletcher hadn't thought it would matter so much. The truth of it settled over all fifteen of them, itchy and uncomfortable. Dyer had left them to determine the inheritance of the company by any means necessary.

But he couldn't have intended for anyone to die over it.

"This is ridiculous." Waylon shoved himself off the couch. "You're all pathetic, you know that? My dad's dead, and he's still finding ways to pull your puppet strings."

Unrattled, Melv said, "Waylon, please. I know you haven't been with the company for quite some time, but people's livelihoods are on the line."

"And people's lives," Jackie echoed.

Waylon's stare hardened. "You're right. I don't work at Cartwright Media now. I don't want to work at Cartwright Media ever. Do what you want, but leave me the hell out of it."

No one stopped him as he stormed out, vanishing down the hallway.

Joplin sniffled once. Twice. The harbinger of an ear-piercing wail. The sound was a fissure in the dam, holding back the grief, the fear, the fury inside the rest of them. Voices rose to the rafters, each one louder and more volatile than the next.

"Great. We're just supposed to sit around arguing about who becomes a billionaire while we wait for some crew to get us off this godforsaken island?" Opal sagged to the couch, exhausted by the thought alone.

Opposite her, Theo jerked upright. The poor man's skin stretched red and thin, like a balloon seconds away from popping. "Sounds like the lot of us will be dead by then."

Raul tugged him back to the cushions. "Hold on. No one is dying."

"Except Dyer," Molly brooded.

Asshole Rick butted forward. "And now we're all fucked."

For once in her life, Fletcher agreed with him. They were all totally, completely fucked.

"This is barbaric! No one is inheriting the company like this," Joplin tried. Her gaze wandered back to Melv, and Fletcher's followed. Waiting for him to step in. Waiting for him to say they were wrong.

"Someone has to," Rick said, woefully unhelpful.

Never mind, she still hated him.

"Stand down, Rick." Theo pushed himself off the sofa with a grunt. Paced toward Rick at the head of the room. "I'll meet with the rest of upper management, and we'll decide who takes over. This doesn't concern you."

Something contorted Rick's face, all wrinkled and puffy. His quick temper flared. "Sure it does. I'm as eligible as any of you to inherit the company. Why settle for taking your job when I could take over all of Cartwright Media?"

Theo stepped forward. Loafer to loafer. "Is that a threat?"

"Was it a threat when you nominated Opal for last quarter's commission bonus even though my sales were higher?" Asshole Rick bit back.

Across the room, where Opal had been poorly consoling Joplin, her head perked up. "Hey, I worked with higher-profile accounts. Leave me out of your pissing match."

Theo started, "Like me, Opal's a go-getter. You want something at this company, you've got to work for it. I eat, sleep, and breathe Cartwright Media, and I have for the last two decades. Why don't you—"

Melv moved between them, hands out to physically separate them. "Before anyone does something regrettable, why don't we all take fifteen? I'll take a closer look at this will, and we'll regroup."

Despite Melv's best efforts, the mention of a break only frayed everyone's nerves more. Telling someone to calm down was the quickest way to make them angrier. Tension ratcheted up until the air in the sitting room grew so helplessly thick, Fletcher felt like a stapler floating in a mound of green Jell-O.

Neither salesman budged. Melv's fingers strained against their chests.

"Gentlemen," Melv said, firmer this time and far too generous. "Maybe Waylon had the right idea. We could all take a minute to ourselves."

Theo turned to the room, eyes blazing and jaw set. "No, Jackie's right. Dyer knew what he was doing. This is *exactly* why he brought us here. If that old bastard wasn't already dead, I'd kill him myself."

Joplin cried harder at this.

It nearly drowned out Rick's moaning. "Dyer invited us *all*. Not just the execs. It's anyone's company."

In the center of the conversation pit, Theo's attention returned to Rick, still fuming. "You've never bothered showing any initiative before, Rick. I don't expect you to start today."

"Initiative?" Rick echoed. A dark sneer wiped across his lips. "Initiative?" He marched across the living room and stripped the rifle off the mantel. Melv reared in shock as Rick slammed the barrel against Theo's chest, the brittle rib cage, and the beating heart beneath. "How's this for initiative?"

It was Fletcher's own voice she heard shouting, "Stop!"

She lunged forward, the adrenaline in her system clearly mistaking her for some kind of hero. A gun like that was ornamental. It wouldn't be loaded. It was decor. Nothing worse. Nothing bad could—

Her hand reached Rick's shoulder a second too late.

The blast rang Fletcher's ears into oblivion. Her lungs choked on gunpowder.

Then, there was blood on her face.

Sticky. Hot. Metallic. Dripping onto her cheek, her chin, her chest.

Theo wilted. Barely alive. His eyes lowered to half-mast as a corsage of red sprouted at his breast pocket. Weak, he drooped against the seat cushions, a hand feebly coming to his chest.

"Rick, what have you done?" Fletcher shouted.

They had all kinds of corporate trainings—sexual harassment prevention, cybersecurity awareness, regulatory compliance—but no lesson on what the hell to do when one of them got shot through the heart.

The world didn't slow. Opal and Sheila hunched together in the corner, whispering. Bertram counseled the Brians with meaty hands on their shoulders. The rest formed an angry mob around Rick. Everyone hollered over one another, making it impossible to comprehend their words. Didn't anyone want to say goodbye?

Fletcher's body moved, desperate to do something. Fix something. Anything. She hefted one of the fur throws off the sofa even though it was about a million degrees outside. She had half a mind to hide under it, but instead pressed it firmly against Theo's chest, despite the queasy spinning the room was doing.

Theo looked up at her. She looked down at him. He was about to die, and there was nothing she could do. What was the right thing to say to a man like him on his deathbed? (Deathcouch?) She hadn't liked him all that much in life, but even he deserved . . . something.

It's okay was a blatant lie.

The Sales team will be nothing without you was equally untrue. They were feral creatures, clearly rabid enough to kill their own leader. And the company as a whole would easily chug on without him. If he'd died under ordinary circumstances, she would have sent condolence bouquets to the Groffs and forged Dyer's signature on the sympathy card.

As Theo writhed and sputtered, blood crusting his lips, she landed on something in the middle, the only honest thing she could think. "You gave everything you had to Cartwright Media. You were good at your job. You can rest now."

A sigh left Theo, like that was all the validation he needed for his eyes to glaze over. She was certain the moment he was gone. It didn't take long. The light dimmed in Theo's eyes, the wax of a candle dripping until there was nothing left.

That was when the *Holy shit I'm going to throw up all of my intestines* set in.

There was a finality to death she learned early—hogs on the farm, bacon in the skillet. But this? Theo was dead, and he wasn't orchestrated-my-own-demise dead, like Dyer.

He was shot-by-his-direct-report dead.

Murdered-in-cold-blood dead.

Dead dead dead.

The useless violence of it. Rick's blatant arrogance. His disrespect for the fragility of life. All Fletcher could do was suck down a half-formed gasp and wipe the stray tear trailing down her cheek.

Some desperate part of her wanted to believe it was a clever ruse. Her heart continued beating, a steady drum: *not real, not real, not real.*

But it was.

There was no saving Theo.

There was no saving any of them.

Fletcher's pulse throbbed in her throat, and sweat pilled on the back of her neck. Melv had read the fine print, and now Theo had a bullet hole through his chest. This entire house was filled to the brim with old hunting contraband. Who would be next?

No. *No.*

She stamped a towel on the grease fire of fear burning behind her ribs. Rick had always had a short fuse. He threw tantrums. He picked fights. No one *else* was going to hurt anyone. These were her coworkers. People she knew. People she'd scheduled team-building Central Park picnics with, roller rink retreats, and ax-throwing off-sites.

Well, on second thought, ax-throwing was not particularly comforting right now.

Fletcher peeled herself away from Theo's rapidly cooling body to see Raul land a punch square on Rick's jaw as if to knock some sense into him. The salesman staggered backward, but his sly smirk didn't flinch.

"Is that all you've got?"

"This isn't *Call of Duty*, asshole," Raul barked. Despair contorted his dark skin. "He's not going to respawn at the next checkpoint. You killed him. He's dead."

Rick wiped a smear of blood off his face with his cuff. "You heard Dyer. The hunt's already started, baby. I'm trying to inherit a fortune."

Raul's face scrunched up in disgust. "You're an animal."

Unfortunately, in his adrenaline-induced haze, Raul had clearly failed to bring Rick's familiar Remington into the equation. Rick cocked the barrel and pointed it toward Raul's chest. "You want to say that again?"

Cries went up. For the first time all morning, Fletcher was at least marginally convinced that everyone on this island hadn't lost their minds. Just Rick. (And she truthfully wasn't sure he'd ever actually *had* his.)

Deepti threw herself between Rick and Raul. The barrel pressed against the buttons on her blouse each time she breathed. One rasped command left her mouth. "Don't."

It was enough of a distraction for Brian to knock the gun out of Rick's hands. An awful clanging rang through the sitting room.

Finally, Rick seemed to notice the shift in the air. The breeze lifting strands of Fletcher's braid buzzed dangerously, tinged with the scent of iron. He wanted more blood to be shed, but it could easily be his next. They outnumbered him, twelve to one.

Both hands went up next to Rick's face. He took a hesitant step backward, then another. Waiting to trip the snare wire, caught in his own trap.

"You know what?" he said. A strand of greasy black hair slid over his forehead, and he brushed it away with his forearm. "I'll go. But you're no better than me. I came here for the career development like the rest of you. You think I'm an animal? Watch what you'll become."

The week had only just begun.

"Opal. Sheila. Come find me. Sales sticks together," Rick said, conveniently sidestepping the fact he'd just single-handedly executed the VP of Sales. He scooped the shotgun off the floor on his way out.

No one trailed after him. For a long moment, no one moved at all. When she heard the front doors open and close, Fletcher watched Rick through the wide windows, tracking his steps toward the garage. It didn't take long for an engine to rev. The tires of an ATV kicked up clouds of dust as Rick sped down the baobab-lined drive, spearing across the savanna.

At once, everyone exhaled.

It did little to settle Fletcher's stomach. One look around the room proved everyone else was thinking the same thing. Even if Rick was rotten to his core, he wasn't wrong.

Who could they trust when one of them could turn as fast as Rick turned on Theo? There was a multibillion-dollar inheritance on the line, and only one of them could claim it in the end.

8

Theo's blood stained Fletcher's hands. It must have soaked through the blanket she'd used to stanch his wound, but with all the dying and shouting, she hadn't noticed until she was standing alone in the conversation pit.

Well, alone-ish.

Technically, Theo's body was still there with her.

Everyone else had retreated, she imagined, to the far corners of the estate to develop a plan. Hopefully not a plan *of attack*, but Fletcher wasn't placing any bets. Ordinarily, she'd expect the Sales team to be day drunk in the pool while the marketers and execs took turns kissing Dyer's ass. But clearly, whatever screwed-up version of reality she'd been thrust into when she landed on Lydell wasn't one that operated how she expected.

The only other living person still downstairs was Melv, rustling around in the kitchen for god knew what. When she finally convinced her feet to move, she found him with his head in one of the cabinets.

"Did you really not know?" she asked, leaning against the frame of the kitchen doorway. The words clawed out of her, unwilling talons hooked in her chest. She didn't want the answer. But she needed it.

"That Evanston would blow a hole through Theo?" Melv asked, swiping a hand over his face as he stood. He righted himself with a copper pot he'd stuffed to the brim with fruit, ransacked from the fridge. For his thirtieth anniversary with the company last spring, she'd sent him a box of Harry & David pears. Good to know it was the right choice. "Of course not."

Fletcher shook her head. "About the will. What it was. What it meant."

"He asked me to finalize it last month." Melv met Fletcher's gaze, and it settled her stomach. Like even though she was very much an adult, there was comfort in having an Adultier Adult here to help. "He was dying. I tried to talk him out of this trip, but you know Dyer. He was—"

"Adamant?"

"A pain in my ass." Melv polished an apple with the hem of his shirt and took a thick bite. Chewing, he added, "The language in the will isn't explicit, but it is ironclad. How we choose his successor is up to us and us alone. Believe me, I didn't know he'd include that video and practically stick a shotgun in Rick's hand. I thought he just wanted us to settle the details away from the public eye."

Dyer trusted Melv implicitly. They'd worked together for so long, it was only natural. Melv kept Dyer out of trouble and protected the company fiercely. If even Melv couldn't talk Dyer out of stranding them on a secluded island, his mind must have really been made.

Beyond the walls of the estate, gun blasts erupted. Fletcher winced at the thought of whatever poor creature found itself at the mercy of Rick's shotgun. Hopefully it wasn't another colleague.

A grimace ghosted across Melv's face. "He won't last the week. Evanston always was too single-minded to lead."

The week. God, the reminder that no one would come looking for them for at least five days made Fletcher's skin all kinds of clammy.

"The rescue crew," Fletcher croaked. She cleared her throat, trying but failing to resecure her grip on her rapidly spiraling emotions. Nothing good ever came from crying on the job. "Who cares about the inheritance? All we have to do is make sure we're still around to be rescued. Then we can all go home."

"I wouldn't hold my breath hoping anyone else is thinking as altruistically. Anything could happen in five days. In the meantime, I plan on keeping to myself." Melv situated his stash of food on the counter. Something flickered in his gaze. "I suggest you do the same."

His hand dipped into his fruit vat and procured half of a plastic-wrapped papaya. A peace offering. The orange fruit stared at her long after Melv retreated down the hall, leaving Fletcher alone-ish again.

She started unwrapping the pity papaya but recoiled at the sight of her nails. Theo's blood had dried into russet flakes around her cuticles. Ruining her perfect manicure. Bite untaken, she dropped the produce. There needed to be a hot shower in her immediate future, or she couldn't be held responsible if she was the next employee to snap.

The air in the manor felt obtrusive. Her lungs strained against the lingering metallic tint, even with the windows open. Beyond them, the pool glistened in the midday sun. Compelling. But Fletcher craved the kind of whole-body scrub not suitable for the prying eyes of a flirty giraffe or a peeping colleague.

And, if she hiked all the way to her bedroom, there was no guarantee Waylon wouldn't barge in, demanding a turn in *their* shower.

As she paced the halls, trying to find somewhere to slip in and clean off, Fletcher could barely think past the blood pounding in her ears. Bertram had been right about one thing. She never should have come here.

The thought was a clarion bell and a death knell. Dyer hadn't invited her. Not by accident, and not because he didn't think she wasn't capable of greatness . . . but because he knew what he had planned for this trip. He curated the guest list, choosing only the most ambitious, the most starved for power. And he knew, whether he admitted it to himself or not, exactly what this week could become.

A massacre.

Suddenly, she wished she'd tagged along on more of her dad and Kent's hunting trips. They'd dressed themselves in tans and greens, packed the truck with a couple rifles and a case of Coors, and headed out before the first rooster crowed.

They'd be gone for hours, coming home with a truck full of birds to pluck or deer to skin. Their dinner plates would be full for weeks, the freezers stocked with game. But sitting at the table, while Fletcher pushed food around her plate, they'd talk about the animals that got away. The ones that were too fast, too hard to catch.

Brute force didn't always win.

She could survive this. She could make it through the week.

The med spa came up on her right. Exactly what she needed.

Fletcher slipped between the fogged glass doors into a tranquil lounge. Vases stuffed with pampas grass sat on polished glass end tables and woven rugs spread wide across the floor. Another door waited at the far end. She nudged through it.

Crisp lines of white tile fed toward procedural rooms with heaps of machinery—Hydrafacial machines, red-light therapy masks, a line of cryotherapy chambers. There, at the far end of the hall, stood yet another fogged door labeled MUD BATH SANCTUARY. Bingo.

Inside, she found three porcelain tubs, sparkling despite their intended use, and beyond them, a row of rainfall showers. She couldn't get undressed fast enough. Twisting the silver faucet, the water ran hot enough to scald. Fletcher didn't flinch when it burned.

She scrubbed her nail beds, desperate to remove the caked-on remnants of Theo's veins. Strings of eucalyptus hung from the showerhead, but not even aromatherapy could unravel the knot in her stomach.

She squeezed an exorbitant amount of Oribe shampoo into her hands because she'd earned it. Today, she'd lather, rinse, *and* repeat. If Dyer wanted to play his mind games, the least she could do was take advantage of his bougie shampoo.

The only way out of this mess was to get off the island and go home.

Except . . .

Fletcher tipped her head back with a frustrated sob. It wasn't like she had much of a home to go back to. Her eviction date crept closer with every passing day. A rightful promotion was the only hope she had of staying in the city. She was *not* crawling home to Kent with her dignity in shreds, even if it killed her. (And at this rate, it might.)

Where did that leave her? Casual homicide?

Dread raked down her spine as she watched Theo's blood swirl down the drain. Streaks of burgundy paled until they disappeared entirely. She was left with soapsuds, fragrant and cleansing.

She wouldn't kill, couldn't kill. Not even if it meant inheriting more money than God.

A sniffling cry cut through the med spa, and Fletcher slammed the faucet off. Her pulse pounded, heart banging around her chest. Someone was here. And Fletcher was naked.

She swiped one of the cotton towels and draped it around her chest. Poking her head past the curtain, she saw no one had wandered into the mud room yet, but a voice still chattered away—no, not a voice. Voices.

Hopping across the cold tile on wet feet, Fletcher aimed for the light switches. She doused herself in darkness and pressed a listening ear to the door. Muffled words got lost, drifting to the spa's high ceilings.

Adrenaline buzzed in every corner of Fletcher. Ordinarily, she'd touted herself excellent at crisis response. Her usual crises involved wrinkled cummerbunds before black-tie affairs or missing memos ahead of stakeholder meetings. Not power-hungry coworkers cut off from society. Her nervous system could hardly keep up.

"I don't know what Dyer expected to happen," one of the voices said, and Fletcher finally placed it. Joplin strode closer, her words growing louder with each step. "Rick's vendetta against Theo aside, it's not like the rest of us are going to start shooting each other." She'd been crying. Sniffling.

"Of course not," Jackie responded coolly.

Fletcher sank deeper into the shadows as their silhouettes edged into view. Their shapes blurred through the glass, but there was no mistaking Joplin's pink hair or Jackie's red lips. Vaguely, Fletcher wondered if they could see her, shivering and swaddled in terry cloth.

Joplin wiped beneath her nose, stalling entirely too close to the door for Fletcher's liking. "Waylon didn't say anything to me. Do you think he knew? We've always been close, but . . . not close enough for him to give me a heads-up that his dad was a psychopath?"

Whatever kind of wretched jealous thing reared its head inside Fletcher's chest was none of her business. So what? Waylon and Joplin had nicknames, and she'd climbed all over him in the pool—of course they were *close*.

Jackie laughed. "You needed this to convince you? This industry has always been vicious, and Dyer was the worst of them all."

A snorting sound followed. "Thanks for this. Talking about it with me, I mean. I feel like nothing makes any sense anymore."

"I didn't have much of a choice. I could hear your wailing three doors down."

"Sorry, I'm a Pisces," Joplin said, a little levity finding its way back into her voice.

The outline of Jackie's arm landed on Joplin's, guiding her back toward the front of the spa. Their voices drifted with them. "Rick's always had a few screws loose. There are smarter ways to accomplish what he wanted."

Wait . . .

What?

Fletcher should have moved. Should have spoken up. Should have told them that no one else had to die, but Jackie's words were a knife to her throat, forcing her silence.

Something crashed, then twinkled. A lot like a plate of metal instruments skittering across the floor.

Maybe . . . Joplin tripped?

Another bang proved that theory unlikely. Fletcher's stomach plummeted into kneecap territory as Joplin groaned, then yelped. A series of tinny beeps sounded, followed by a distinctly mechanical *thunk*. After that, everything quieted, save the clicking of tasteful heels and the latching of the med spa door.

Until the screaming started.

Fletcher eased open the door, praying the hinges wouldn't squeak. There was no telling what she'd find out there—and she didn't want to fall in the crosshairs. But the spa floor was empty, the lights dimmed. Only a flashing blue LED illuminated the hallway.

A flashing blue light that, admittedly, wasn't on before.

Fletcher tightened her towel and dared to go out into the main floor. The banging didn't stop, but as she neared the lights, the screaming became more coherent: "Jackie, you bitch!"

The closer Fletcher got, the more obvious the blue blinking light became. The cryotherapy chamber had been turned on. With Joplin inside. And the blue light? That would be the lock.

Fletcher skidded in front of the glass wall separating her from Joplin. The designer's eyes flared—hope quickly replacing fear. Fletcher hadn't been able to save Theo. But Joplin wasn't dead.

Yet.

Frost already lined her lashes. Blue tinted her lips.

"I'm going to get you out," Fletcher said, but it was hard to hear herself over Joplin's continued shrieking: "Hurry up! I'm going to kill Jackie!"

Perhaps some sense could be talked into Joplin when her skin wasn't at risk of turning black and chipping right off.

Fletcher pivoted toward the backlit screen controlling the chamber. A big blue lock icon floated in the middle, and every time Fletcher jammed the buttons, a robotic voice chimed, "Chamber is in use. Chamber is in use."

"I want it to *not* be in use," Fletcher said.

"Chamber is in use," the voice responded.

Come on. There had to be an emergency shutoff somewhere, right? Or maybe a power cord Fletcher could cut? But the chamber had been built inside the wall for a seamless finish. Sleek, sophisticated, and a complete safety hazard.

If she wanted to get Joplin out, she was going to have to break through the door.

Sparkling frost limned the glass's edge. The on-screen thermometer read -50 degrees Celsius. And dropping. Machines like this easily reached -130 degrees. They were meant to be microdosed, but the timer wasn't dwindling near fast enough. Instead of a matter of minutes, Jackie had set the timer for an hour, and the override wasn't responding.

Something heavy. She needed something heavy.

Scouring her surroundings, Fletcher searched for anything she could ram against the triple-paned door. As she pulled open drawers, there were Kybella syringes and single-blade razors.

"Holy fuck, what is taking so long?" Joplin bemoaned, a ch-ch-ch-chatter in her teeth with every word. The thermometer reading plummeted. No sign of stopping anytime soon.

Fletcher spun. Finally, her eyes locked onto the facial machine sitting neatly on a metal rolling cart. It had tentacle tubes protruding from every direction, but Fletcher wasn't particularly concerned with that. She grabbed the cart and pushed, feet kicking, until it smashed into the glass door.

A hairline fracture, if anything.

She tried again, this time getting a running start. Her towel threatened to slip down, so Fletcher clamped her elbows to her sides as the cart slammed against the cryo chamber. The impact jolted her backward, rattled her teeth.

"Maybe I can get someone to help." Desperation clawed through Fletcher's voice. "Waylon, I can get Waylon."

"Waylon?" Joplin's usual volume quickly waned.

"Yes, Waylon! You like Waylon! Bubbles, right?"

Joplin's teeth chattered. "Champagne. Long story."

"I'm going to get help, and I'll be right back, I promise."

In response, the designer's frigid body slumped against the glass, hands frozen to the door handle but unable to open it.

"Joplin? Joplin. Can you hear me?"

"Tell Waylon, I never liked Eliza. Tell him—" Joplin slurred, but Fletcher never found out what came next.

She recognized Joplin's absence the moment it came, the flame inside snuffing out in the cold, her eyes glazed and emptied.

And that made two.

Jackie killed Joplin.

Jackie, the editor in chief.

Or maybe she could be promoted to CMO. If CMO actually stood for Chief Murder Officer.

Which made two of Fletcher's current remaining colleagues known killers. The ratio of trustworthy people at Cartwright Media evaporated like water in the Sahara. The shock left Fletcher hollow.

She couldn't blink away Joplin's lifeless stare. No matter how many times she squeezed her eyes shut and pried them back open, she saw Joplin, frost-slicked and angry.

Fletcher had left her there. All things considered, Joplin would be preserved just fine. Maybe science would advance far enough they could thaw her out a hundred years from now, good as new. If Fletcher won the inheritance, she'd fund the initiative herself.

With Joplin gone, Fletcher's mission had only solidified. The sooner she got off this island, the better.

A deadly game had begun, and Fletcher refused to be responsible for taking someone's life. She'd never be able to live with the guilt. The blood on her hands would eat her away like hungry rust.

Ford's voice rang through her head: *You're always one step ahead.* There had to be another way off this island. Something that wouldn't require her to sit around waiting to be murdered for 120 hours until a rescue crew came.

Of course, it would be easier to escape if she weren't wearing this robe. She'd swiped one of the spa's mulberry silk robes after pointedly deciding to leave her clothes heaped on the med spa floor, stained as they were. Fresh, clean clothes, and she'd feel . . . well, not like a million bucks, but at least like her five-figure salary.

As she neared the yawning accordion doors to the patio, shouting halted Fletcher in her tracks.

"So, that's that? You're as bad as him," Raul was saying. Fury painted his face in shades of red.

Fletcher tiptoed toward the door and craned her neck around the edge, but she couldn't see who Raul was yelling at. Jackie, if she had to guess.

The other half of the conversation must have responded unkindly because Raul faltered backward, barely halting at the lip of the pool. "Don't do this," he begged. It wasn't a good look for him.

Meanwhile, Sheila stretched across one of the chaises, a silver reflector perched beneath her chin. Sunglasses had been tugged down over her eyes, and earbuds poked in her ears. Noise-canceling, presumably. Her head bobbed to an unheard beat.

The intern didn't notice the spit flying out of Raul's mouth. Didn't hear the crack of a pistol. Didn't smell the smoke or feel the splash of pool water lapping beneath her lounge chair as Raul rocked onto his heels, sinking into the deep end.

Fletcher bit into her cheek to keep from screaming.

The chlorinated water swirled red. Raul floated limply, linen suit jacket splaying around him as pool jets whirlpooled the CTO clockwise. Up Fletcher's throat climbed the sour taste of bile—her empty stomach didn't have much else to give.

She sagged against the doorframe. Three. Three of her colleagues dead in as many hours since she discovered Dyer was the lion lunch du jour. At this rate, Fletcher could forget about surviving the week. She'd be lucky to survive the day.

Beneath her, Fletcher's feet dragged her toward the staircase. Too slowly. As she passed the next breezeway, someone cornered her. Cold metal pressed to the nape of Fletcher's neck.

"Here's the thing, Fletcher." She recognized Jackie's voice immediately, and it was like slurping a Szechuan's lo mein noodle down the wrong pipe. "I don't need you trying to undo my handiwork. Joplin was taken care of."

Words came much more easily when the barrel of one of Dyer's death machines wasn't rammed up against her spinal cord, and Fletcher barely managed to mumble a stream of gibberish.

Jackie leaned in, spearmint breath hot against Fletcher's ear. "You can't tell me you really wanted Joplin to inherit the company. Not after everything you've worked for, everything you've done for Dyer all these years."

"Joplin was an amazing designer," Fletcher said, remarkably eloquent, given the circumstances.

The barrel nudged closer, metal growing warm. "But?"

Thoughts beyond *Oh my god, oh my god, oh my god* felt entirely out of reach. "But she had a habit of coming back from lunch late and lacked an attention to detail?"

A hint of a laugh worked itself into Jackie's voice. "I knew you'd understand."

She didn't. She *definitely* didn't.

"Joplin's dead, Jackie," Fletcher stammered. "You killed her."

"Of course I did. Leading isn't easy. You have to be precise. Ruthless. Women—competent, capable women—get overlooked constantly. Would a man second-guess doing whatever it takes to get ahead?" Fletcher needn't answer. A cloud of gunpowder, a puddle of blood, and Theo's lifeless body said it all. "No, he'd lie, cheat, kill."

A blade of horror twisted in Fletcher's stomach. Before she could say anything, the gunmetal peeled away from her sticky skin, and

Fletcher inhaled deep into her belly. There was no time to relax. Over her shoulder, Jackie's manicured hand pointed the pistol out the window.

Not toward Sheila. Not toward Raul's bloating body. Farther.

Fletcher traced its aim. Jackie's gun pointed straight toward Waylon, where he hiked back up from the island's edge. Bluestem grass swayed around him, and he veered away from the foaming mouth of the ocean, the cliffside drop into an endless blue, and back toward the west wing. Hell of a time for a hot-girl walk, if you asked Fletcher.

She didn't need to be a sharpshooter to know Jackie's bullet was poised to lodge itself in Waylon's heart. Was Jackie in the CIA before she joined Cartwright Media? The marines? (Neither, actually. Jackie was a by-product of the tech start-up quagmire. Much worse.) Regardless, the woman knew her way around a hostage situation, that was for sure.

Jackie circled in front of Fletcher, whose knees had gone totally gelatinous. She rapped a perfect red nail against the trigger, priming it. Fletcher's stomach lurched with each *tap, tap, tap.*

"I did what needed to be done. Someone has to take over Cartwright Media, and not even Dyer thought the miserable excuse of a man he called a son has what it takes to lead this company. That's why we're here." Viciousness slicked her mouth into a sneer. "Do you think asking for permission made me the youngest editor *Jet-Setter* has ever known? Or being nice? Or *smiling more*?"

Rhetorical questions, obviously.

"Rick's precious conscience didn't stop him from killing Theo. It won't stop any of them. I'm not letting anyone take what I've rightfully earned away from me. Not Theo's rabid pack of salespeople, not Dyer's arrogant son." Jackie turned, repositioning the silver barrel against Fletcher's sternum. "And certainly not you."

Fletcher's heart rammed against her ribs, trying to escape—the rest of her was sweat-slicked and slippery. She was going to die. She was going to die in this silk robe. Unless she thought of something very, very fast.

"I can help you," Fletcher said. More of a gasp, really.

Jackie's detached laugh did little to calm Fletcher's stomach. "Enlighten me."

"No one knew Dyer better than me." Each word chafed against Fletcher's throat. A plan formulated in foggy ideas behind all the adrenaline and unadulterated panic. "Not just Dyer. The whole team. Their routines, their habits, their"—a breath, a swallow—"*weaknesses*. Whatever you need, I can help you."

"Why should I trust you?" Jackie's trigger finger was getting a little too impatient.

The Rolodex in Fletcher's brain spun and spun. How many days had Fletcher spent daydreaming about working under her wing? Every cell in Jackie's body meant business. She wouldn't hesitate to kill Fletcher if it meant getting what she wanted—a woman in this industry couldn't afford to be forgiving. There were always ten more less qualified men waiting to take her place.

Which meant that if she saw Fletcher as her competition, she'd have no problem eliminating her.

"I don't want to take over the company." Jackie's grip on her gun didn't loosen. Fletcher barreled on: "Why waste your time hunting everyone down when the best way to ensure you win the inheritance is to make it back to Manhattan before anyone else? By the time the rescue crew comes, Cartwright Media will already be yours. I can help you."

There was so much filler in Jackie's face that her expressions were a little fuzzy, but Fletcher was pretty sure she recognized this one as confusion. "You? And what would you get out of this little arrangement?"

"All I want, all I've *ever* wanted, is to be a *Jet-Setter* photographer. Let me come with you. Let me join your staff."

Let me stay on your good side and out of your crosshairs.

Jackie hummed. Considering, but not convinced yet. "How do you propose we escape?"

Everything Fletcher cataloged about Lydell flashed through her mind. The trail through the jungle, the airplane hangar near the mountain, the crosshatched boat slips on the island's opposite edge. "There's a marina where Dyer stores his yachts. That's the only way off until the crew comes, but you'll need a boat key."

"And you can get it for me?"

"Yes," Fletcher said and prayed it was true.

Jackie hesitated. Her finger never left the trigger. "I'll head that way tomorrow morning and kill anyone who gets in my way in the meantime. Find me a getaway boat, and you won't be one of them. Meet me by the docks at noon on Wednesday—with the key—and I'll make sure you live to see your promotion."

"Yes. Okay, yes."

Jackie holstered the gun through the slack of her Gucci belt—not exactly stellar firearm-safety procedures—and took a step toward Dyer's wing, the shadows that lay in wait. Primed to disappear, at least until it was time to strike again. "Then we have a deal."

As she turned to leave, a smile flicked Jackie's lips upward, equal parts innocent and sinister. Like this was an ordinary afternoon chat and not the most macabre quid pro quo that has ever existed.

Fletcher, meanwhile, tried to remember how to get her lungs to function. How hard could it be to suck air in and spit it out? She braced herself against the doorframe until her blood oxygen levels returned to normal operating standards.

Two days. Forty-eight measly hours. That was all the time Fletcher had to find a boat key and make it to the other side of the island. Her best chance at getting off Lydell Island alive.

9

How Fletcher would get the boat key was a different question altogether.

At this rate, if one of her coworkers didn't kill her, starvation would. Her appetite hadn't reared its head all day, but she was officially running on fumes. Usually, her stomach could win Olympic gold in pretending iced coffee counted as food, but Lydell wouldn't go easy on her. She wouldn't be able to make it across the island if she didn't find something to eat. If she timed it right, she might be able to squeeze into the butler's pantry for shelf-stable rations while everyone else polished off the caviar and champagne.

Then, there was the unfortunate truth that Fletcher only vaguely knew where the marina was. Her responsibilities rarely extended to Lydell's borders. All the prep work and planning fell to Fletcher, but as groundskeeper, Carlotta executed each assignment and kept the island well-oiled. Not that she was going to admit that to Jackie. The last thing Fletcher wanted was to give her a reason to see her as disposable. She barely trusted Jackie as it was.

Plus, the ever-present mental tally of living coworkers was being whittled away.

Theo, Joplin, and Raul—gone. Every semireasonable person who had rightfully protested this madness was getting picked off one by one.

Which left Rick, parading around the savanna. Jackie with her silver pistol. Deepti and Bertram, the remnants of upper management. Sheila, blatantly unaware of her surroundings, and Opal probably not much better. The Brians and Molly and Melv.

Waylon, unfortunately.

Eleven. Twelve, counting herself.

She was so deep in thought she didn't notice her bedroom door had been flung open until she stood right there in front of it. Which was weird because she hadn't left it like that.

Her pace slowed to a creep, and Fletcher peeked her head around the jamb, only to rock back on her heels in shock. The door had been forced off its hinges, no finesse about it, and the Brians. Were. In. There.

They'd thrown half her belongings on the floor. What was the point of meticulously folding her clothes into the dresser if they were going to get trampled on by two yahoos who spent company time beefing with Reddit memelords?

As if sensing her proximity, Brian glanced over his shoulder, and Fletcher flattened herself against the wall. The hallway behind her was bald as a colophon margin. Nothing to duck behind, nothing to use to defend herself. If she stayed here, they'd see her, skin her alive, and use her hide as a new rug in the Paid Ads office.

Shit.

Hands smacked across Fletcher's mouth. The grip was so tight, she staggered backward, hitting something rock-solid.

Abs. Those were abs.

And it didn't take rocket science to know whose.

Fletcher dug her elbow into the torso, aiming toward a kidney or at least a ticklish spot. Anything to loosen Waylon's death grip. Nothing worked. He peeled her over the threshold into his bedroom and clicked the door shut behind them.

Blond curlicues dripped over his brow, fresh from his shower. The whole room still smelled like soap. No sooner than he set her down did he mime a zipper over his mouth and hers for good measure.

Fletcher unzipped her mouth with a frown. Hushed, she barked, "What are you doing? Leave me alone."

Waylon shook his head, his scowl deepening. In a series of poorly communicated charades, he wagged his fingers toward the bathroom, made binoculars of his fists, and then crossed his torso with a dramatic *X*.

Fletcher stared until she was certain he was finished, and then whisper-shouted, "Spit it out."

The hard cut of his sapphire eyes could draw blood. Still, he committed to the bit and mimed unzipping his lips before saying, "If you go in there right now, you're dead. Russo and Dunlap are looking for you."

The Brians' government names caught Fletcher off guard, but no more than Waylon saving her from waltzing in on their siege. Acting selflessly wasn't exactly in his repertoire.

Fletcher migrated toward the conjoined bathroom, nearly tripping over a room service platter with picked-at leftovers from what looked like a late-night snack. His room was double the size of hers with a duvet spilling over the side of the bed and a pile of dirty clothes in the corner. If she didn't know better, she could have believed the Paid Ads knuckleheads had already ransacked his room.

Waylon followed her, and when they reached Fletcher's door, they stacked over each other, pressing their ears to the seam.

"Are you sure this is the right room?" Other Brian asked.

Something *thunk*ed. Her suitcase, maybe? "Gotta be. Bertram said he saw the bitch come this way after talking with Molly last night. If we don't find out what she knows, we're next. She's got to have notes around here somewhere."

Fletcher bit on her lip to keep from gasping. For starters, she was *not* a bitch, thank you very much. Secondly, whatever information they thought they'd find here, they wouldn't. During her first year at Cartwright Media, Fletcher had relied heavily on a chunky white binder—five inches, three-ringed, and tabbed to her heart's content. Eventually, as she committed everything to memory, she stopped lugging it around. And thirdly, it was obvious Bertram didn't think she belonged here. That much he'd made readily apparent. Sending his goons after her was a new low.

The shuffling on the other side grew increasingly closer. Fletcher moved on instinct, shoving her hands against Waylon's chest and pushing him into the shower. The tiles were still slick from his last rinse, and their entry was, to put it politely, indelicate.

Her hands grappled for purchase, finding only fistfuls of him. Waylon caught her by the hip. When she looked up, they were entirely too close and her robe entirely too thin. The curve of her breasts pressed against his shirt, and underneath, he was all sinewed muscles and veins. His grip on her waist stiffened almost reflexively. A wet heat palmed at her belly.

They'd been like this once before. Close enough to kiss.

The door flung open, and whatever passed between them evaporated like steam from a sauna. Fletcher blinked her libido back into her body. Their proximity was for survival. Nothing more, nothing less.

Neither of them breathed as the Brians marched into the bathroom. It wasn't the world's most original hiding spot—or even a good one, considering the drawn curtain would do little to protect them. All either Brian had to do was so much as glance in their general direction, and they'd be found.

Waylon seemed to know it, too. His entire body tensed, muscles contracting. A predator ready to pounce.

Before anyone could make a move, footsteps sounded in the hallway. Distant, but closing in. Fletcher didn't need to see the Brians to know the glance they exchanged. The silent way they communicated. It wasn't until they'd left her room that Fletcher inhaled again. Even then, it was shallow.

Waylon extricated himself from the shower without another word, and Fletcher could hardly blame him. That wasn't the team-building exercise she thought she'd be joining this week. But as he wandered back toward his bedroom, her gaze wandered after him.

"There's one other thing," she said carefully. "Joplin's gone."

He backtracked, framed by his door to the bathroom. "Gone?"

"Dead."

Waylon didn't exactly move, but something shifted. Like his gravitational force changed, his knees shuddering against the weight. "Dead. How."

It was supposed to be a question, Fletcher wagered.

"Hypothermia."

"In this heat?" His grip on the doorframe tightened. Trying to hold himself up.

"Also, she said she never liked Eliza."

"She told you that?" Hoarse grief coated his words.

"I'm just the messenger. Don't—" Fletcher tried to say, but Waylon caught her by the arm and dragged her back into his room.

He hauled Fletcher toward the plush edge of his unmade bed, and she *thump*ed down onto the memory foam mattress.

"Don't kill me," she said.

"What part of *this* makes you think I'm the one trying to kill you?"

Waylon now stood approximately four feet away. Brows knitted together, hands empty by his sides. Somehow, being alone with him felt more dangerous than both Brians and Bertram combined.

"The part where people keep dying in gruesome manners."

"Is there an ungruesome way to die?" he asked. "Who did it?"

"Killed Joplin?" Fletcher asked.

She swallowed Jackie's name. The editor in chief offered her safe passage—or, at least, *safer* passage. But it wouldn't hurt to have a plan B.

A new idea percolated at the back of Fletcher's mind. Even if Dyer was crazy enough to strand the rest of them here, he wouldn't sacrifice his only son. He'd give Waylon an exit plan, an escape route.

One Fletcher desperately needed right now.

As much as she hated to admit it, she could use Waylon's help. She could handle a map herself, but if she was honest, she'd grown reliant on Manhattan's gridded streets. The Lydell wild wouldn't be so simple. Waylon would know where to look for the boat keys and how to navigate the island without getting eaten by animals.

Telling Waylon that Jackie flash froze the only person on the face of the planet who could call him Bubbles and live to see another day wouldn't win Fletcher any brownie points.

For this to work, Fletcher needed to go all in.

An alliance with Waylon. Fake, of course. Normally, the thought of coexisting with him was enough to break Fletcher out in hives. This, obviously, didn't qualify as normal. She'd never *actually* work with the likes of him. A womanizing know-it-all with a secret agenda Fletcher was certain existed? No way. At least with Jackie, she knew exactly who she was dealing with.

"I don't know" was how she answered his lingering question.

"Her body's in the med spa. Locked in one of the cryo chambers. Could've been an accident."

Waylon pinched the bridge of his nose. A string of expletives left his mouth. He started to pace. That was when Fletcher noticed the way his shoulders hiked, the way a vein in his neck strained.

Muttering, he said, "Why would my dad do this to us?"

"You really didn't know about any of this?"

He stopped pacing. "Of course I didn't."

"Well, some people think it's suspicious how you stayed away for so long and came back into Dyer's life in the nick of time."

"Some people," he said, "or you?"

"Both."

Probably.

Her, definitely.

Waylon scratched his fingers over his stubbled jaw. Thinking, processing. "And you didn't know because otherwise you never would have been so offended you didn't get an invitation."

"Very aware of the miscalculation I made, thanks." The sigh was excessive, but after the day she'd had, Fletcher earned the right to be a little overdramatic. "But I am sorry. About Joplin. Really. I know you two were close."

"The only reason she came on this trip was to get a title change, and now she's dead. God, what a disaster."

"You could say that again."

Agreeing with Waylon Cartwright had to be the first horseman of the apocalypse.

He knew it, too, because he asked, "Okay, what's going on?"

"I don't know what you mean."

"Like hell you don't, Spence. We both know you'd rather run yourself through a paper shredder than show me an ounce of human decency." He stepped closer, and Fletcher gripped her fingers into the mattress to keep from scooting back on instinct. "What are you up to?"

She could still feel the sharp bite of Jackie's pistol against her skin. Her only hope at surviving was to help a killer inherit an international publishing conglomerate. And she needed Waylon's help to do it.

He didn't need to know that part.

"What if I proposed a truce?"

His eyes narrowed.

"Between us."

Waylon gnawed on his next words. "What kind?"

"The kind where we don't stab each other in the back. Metaphorically or literally." She rose to her feet, coming to stand before him. "Think about it. If we work together, we could find a way off Lydell. You get one last 'fuck you' to your dad, and we both get out of here alive."

Tension built in the column of his neck. "I don't believe for a second Joplin's death was an accident. There's nothing anyone here wouldn't do to get my dad's money. I'm not going to be responsible for letting what happened to Joplin happen to you, too." Waylon's eyes roamed over her, following the line of her arms down to her toes, and all the way back up. Something ignited deep in her core. An embarrassed flush rushed to her cheeks. "If you want me to consider a truce, you need to get changed."

Fletcher dragged her hands to her hips, the silk smooth beneath them. Without her usual heels on, he towered over her. Still, she lifted her chin. "No one would ever accuse you of being responsible. Pretending to care about me isn't part of the truce."

The gleam in Waylon's eyes sharpened to a point. "That's fine, honey. Doesn't change the fact that I can't think straight knowing you're standing there with nothing on underneath that robe."

Blushing was no longer accurate enough to describe the redness blooming on Fletcher's face right now. Waylon Cartwright could *not* have this effect on her anymore if her plan was going to work. Like losing her virginity to Kent in the back seat of his dad's pickup truck instead of somewhere sweet or thoughtful, if she pretended it didn't happen, it would be like it never did.

She tugged her robe tighter as she stalked back toward her room. "Don't make me regret this."

Finding a new outfit in the wreckage the Brians left behind was a feat itself. They'd torn apart her closet, flipped her mattress, and flung open the minibar like she might have resorted to contorting herself like an acrobat next to the Diet Cokes and tiny bottles of rum to avoid them.

Aha! A hot-pink dress caught her eye. It was high necked but sleeveless, belted at the middle, and cropped right above her knees. Easier to move in than some of her skirts. Plain, but also *hot pink*. When she'd packed it, she was going for *capable and charismatic*, not *Shoot me, I'm right here!*

She slipped it over her head anyway. If she was going to die, she could at least do it in a dress that made her ass look good. It would have been the perfect Summer Friday attire if it weren't for this—annoying—zipper.

Fletcher groaned. With her arms corkscrewed behind her, she fought to shimmy the zipper up its track. *Plato's Closet, please don't fail me now.* She wrangled it over the bells of her hips, but it snagged again.

Another grunt. She was starting to sound like Kent.

"Are you being attacked?" Waylon called.

"Everything's fine!"

He appeared in her doorway and took a second to survey the landscape. She couldn't decide if he was appalled by the mess the

Marketing bros left or the lack of capybaras in their namesake room. "It doesn't sound fine."

"My dress, the dress. It's—" Deflating, Fletcher turned, showing her bare back. "Could you zip it the rest of the way? And never speak of this again?"

A smug laugh responded. Fletcher's heart beating harder with every inch of space that disappeared between them. Leftover adrenaline from the day running rampant through her veins. His hands found the small of her back, the delicate zipper left hanging there. A shiver coursed over Fletcher's skin as Waylon's knuckles grazed up her spine.

It was hard to think with him this close. She'd been with Kent so long she forgot the spark of someone else's touch. The way her skin could feel electric, and his a conduit.

"What do you think?"

"Pink suits you."

"About working together," Fletcher clarified, turning a new shade of pink herself. If she wasn't feeling murderous now, a few hours in his presence ought to do the trick.

Was it her imagination, or were his fingers trailing against her skin on purpose? His voice turned low, gravelly. "I'm not going back to Cartwright Media, Spence. Ever."

As soon as the zipper reached the nape of her neck, she spun to face him. Too close. She inched backward, making enough room to stick her hand out for a ceremonial shake.

"Working together *now*. Dyer left the island to you for a reason. You know Lydell better than anyone else here, and I know the other guests. Admit it. We'd make a good team. Just don't do that thing with your eyebrows."

"What thing?" His eyebrows *thing*ed harder. Scrunched with

confusion but curled with amusement. Verged on wagging. Altogether too much.

"That—*thing*. They have a mind of their own." She gestured widely in the vicinity of his face. "It's my one condition."

"Okay, Spence. I'll make sure my eyebrows don't offend your sensibilities."

Nothing about him *didn't* offend her sensibilities, but at least he shook her hand in agreement.

The feel of his calloused skin against hers left her momentarily speechless. Steady, strong. Rough but gentle. Some part of her wondered how it would feel for him to *unzip* her dress instead.

Appalled at the thought, Fletcher wrenched her hand away as fast as humanly possible. Whatever biology lesson her body was trying to teach her, she had neither the time nor patience for it. She was a woman with an agenda: gather supplies, find a map, steal a key.

"First things first," Fletcher said, composing herself. "You said you smoke cigars, right?"

10

The first time Fletcher saw the cigar lounge, she assumed there had been some primal lapse in judgment. A surge of testosterone responsible for the decor so tacky it bordered on outright offensive. As if Dyer had briefly been possessed by the spirit of Clayton from *Tarzan*.

Mahogany hutches housed hunting paraphernalia, none of it nearly as dusty as Fletcher, upon first glance, assumed it would have been. Velvet and leather furniture ringed a zebra-hide rug—head still attached. The kind of place that in Nebraska would be strictly off-limits to women and children during *Monday Night Football*.

Nestled in a quiet corner of the second floor, the lounge was blessedly vacant when they arrived, although the scent of tobacco and vetiver lingered.

"Cuban or Churchill?" Waylon asked, flicking a lighter between his fingers.

"Neither." Fletcher's head was already crammed inside one of the cabinets, scouring for anything that could keep them alive. Growing up on the farm wasn't enough to qualify her as the Girl Scouts type. And even if it had, there probably wasn't a badge for Not Getting Eaten by Lions.

"Panatela?"

"No, Waylon. I don't smoke." Fletcher cast a sidelong glance at the blond helplessly shuffling through the humidor. "Keep the lighter, though."

"Suit yourself." Waylon rolled a cigar between his fingertips, the flame curling its paper. He pocketed the lighter, which meant he was capable of following basic instructions. Good.

Fletcher tried to ignore the way he tucked the cigar between his lips, puffed once, and exhaled a perfect circle. Like a mob boss. Or Foghorn Leghorn. Perfect. Nothing sexy about Foghorn Leghorn.

"Will you start packing?" she asked, her nerves frayed like consigned denim. "I want to get out of here before someone else shows up."

"Of course."

"As in, of course you don't want to meet an untimely demise at the hand of someone making three times your annual salary so you'll quit messing around?"

Waylon's shadow blocked the light, and Fletcher reared out of the cabinet, clutching a pair of canteens close to her chest. Smoke sifted off his cigar, too close to the wick of an antique oil lamp for comfort.

"As in, of course Fletcher Spence already has a plan," he said.

"It's not a cardinal sin to be prepared," she huffed.

His eyebrow shifted upward. Antagonizing. "You prepared for this?"

"No, I just *am* prepared. Like how you just *are* the human embodiment of a migraine." Rolling her eyes, she thought she caught a glimpse of her frontal lobe on the way back. "But yes, I have a plan."

Half her motivation for coming to the cigar lounge was the

hand-drawn map of the island that hung framed above the fireplace. The faint initials in the corner looked like they might have belonged to Waylon's great-grandfather Egbert Cartwright himself. Scenery and structures had been etched in careful charcoal—structures that now legally belonged to Waylon.

At the northeastern corner sat the estate. Then there was the staff quarters, deep in the jungle dark. At the opposite edge, another building guarded the marina and its pen-scratched docks. Salvation in a scribbled line.

"These docks," she said as casually as she could. "You don't think the staff would have taken the boats there, do you?"

Waylon didn't budge from behind the growing stack of safari regalia—flare guns, ammo boxes, pith helmets. "Boat, singular."

Not ideal, but at least it wasn't: *Boat, zero.*

"And it's still there?"

That earned her a measured glance. Hesitant, if a touch suspicious. "Should be. Why?"

"That's our golden ticket." She offered a quiet note of consideration. A hum that said this was definitely her first time thinking it. "We get to the docks, grab the boat key, and we'll sail away. No need to wait for the rescue crew to arrive."

Easy, right?

Waylon's rogue eyebrow did that thing again, and Fletcher's heart trampolined around her chest—against her will, she might add. All he said was, "Sure."

"What do you mean *sure*? It's a great idea."

"No, yeah. A great idea that everyone else is also having right this second. It'll be a massacre down there."

It was Fletcher's turn to scrunch her face up. "It's a massacre *here*. At least at the marina it's a massacre with an escape route. I'd rather be there than be a sitting duck for the next five days while the rest of the team goes on a murder spree."

As if that were a totally normal sentence for her to say.

"And besides," she added, "the estate has *amenities*. Hot showers, cold plunges, toiletries that cost half my biweekly paycheck. Rick's the only one ignorant enough to leave the manor right now. Everyone else will wait for someone to make the first move."

That person had to be Fletcher.

Her agreement with Waylon went only as far as it needed to. As soon as she had the key in hand, she'd join Jackie on the boat and say goodbye to Lydell Island forever. But it wasn't like she was leaving Waylon to *die*. With those muscles? He'd fight his way through the week, no problem.

Marigold daylight sliced through the slatted windows and her thoughts. The afternoon was dwindling. Fast. If she couldn't get him on board soon, they'd be hiking across the island under cloak of night, and Fletcher wasn't super keen on meeting Lydell's nocturnal predators.

"Well, we have to do something," she said, marching back across the room to stand toe-to-toe with Waylon. Nothing riled him up like a challenge. "If you hate my plan so much, do you have any brilliant ideas?"

Waylon hauled a couple canvas backpacks onto the card table and shoveled supplies deep into their folds, including a change of clothes for each of them. "We're definitely not going straight to the marina."

Fletcher huffed so hard she coughed. And then tried to cover up her huff-cough with an agreeable smile, despite how her eyes watered. The Waylon histamines were growing stronger, and she didn't pack any Zyrtec.

"The key to the boat is in a lockbox," Waylon finally said, taking pity on her. Annoyance and amusement flitted behind his eyes. He enjoyed this, egging her on.

"And the lockbox is . . ."

"Locked."

"Right," Fletcher said. She cocked a hip against the table, hoping her disappointment looked store-brand, not the *I'm next in line for the cryotherapy chamber* variety. "But you know how to get *into* the lockbox?"

Waylon shrugged. "Carlotta always did it for us."

"Do you even hear yourself sometimes?"

Fletcher tried to grab the other backpack to claim it for herself, but Waylon slammed his hand down on the table, blocking her. "I get it. I'm a Cartwright. How long are you going to hold my last name against me?"

"When it stops being applicable! God forbid you're asked to be responsible for your own boat key."

Waylon's cheeks reddened with frustration. "She's the groundskeeper! She was keeping the grounds!"

"It's. A. Boat. It's not even on the ground."

Fletcher inhaled so steeply she felt it all the way in her toes. Smoothing out her dress, she grasped at any semblance of composure. Which, with Waylon's oversaturated blue eyes on her, was kind of like trying to fill a fax machine with rice paper.

"Point is," she said, forcibly moving Waylon's arm out of her way. It went limp by his side as she gained full control of her backpack. "Carlotta must have the master key, so we can get it and get off this godforsaken island."

And away from Waylon.

Forever.

Waylon looped a compass around his neck, the brass hitting his sternum. "Of course, let me call her— Oh, wait. She's gone."

"Her office isn't, though." Fletcher pointed toward the smudged building near the center of the map. "We'll head toward the staff building. If it's anywhere on the island, it has to be there."

She could feel their next steps solidifying in her mind, the satisfying click of fitting into place. The scaffolding gave her something to hold on to, a ladder to climb, a test to ace.

All she needed was the map.

Sourcing a cocktail napkin and a fountain pen she had to dab against her tongue a few times to convince to write, Fletcher started sketching. A curved line there. A sharp peak of the mountain here.

Waylon hovered over her shoulder. "Is now the time for arts and crafts?"

"I'm making a copy of the map so that we can actually find our way. It's not like we have Google Maps."

She was pretty sure he laughed at her. But then a pith helmet sank over her eyes. When she nudged the bill so that she could see again, it was just in time to watch Waylon grab a pair of hefty yellow binoculars.

"What are you—"

He swung them into the map's case.

Glass shattered, sparkling. Waylon reached his hand through the frame's new gaping hole and withdrew the canvas. Fletcher's eyes lingered on the scattered glass, the binoculars-size hole. Someone should clean up the mess. Waylon, in a utopian civilization. Her, in reality.

"Here." He plunked the map down in front of her. Smoke curled off the end of his cigar. It burned all the way to Fletcher's lungs.

Red laced his knuckles, grooves etched by the jagged case. Two blood splotches dripped near the volcano's peak. Another by the western shoreline. Three across the jungle. Fletcher's head spun with every new stain.

"You're—oh my god. Why would you do that?"

His unrelenting gaze bored into her. "You can't play it safe anymore, Spence. Safe'll get you killed. You've got to take what you want."

Waylon could give her all the fortune cookie wisdom he wanted. He was still *bleeding on the map*.

She scrolled up the canvas as fast as she could. Mostly to give herself something to do while he grabbed one of the monogrammed handkerchiefs—silk, dark green—and wrapped it around his knuckles, tying it with his teeth. No sooner than she'd stuffed the map into her backpack were they out the door. Her mental list wouldn't check itself off.

Whatever fear-fueled momentum propelled her through the day had long since worn off. They'd need food, something beyond the binoculars to defend themselves with, and camping gear. (Fletcher seriously debated whether or not they'd have room to pack their fabulously soft sheets.)

But the manor was a minefield. Navigating it without setting off one of her colleagues required expert precision.

One hallway blurred into the next. *Jet-Setter* editions touting Mediterranean escapes and South American adventures breadcrumbed toward the main entertaining areas. At an intersection, Fletcher took a right turn, bypassing the prep kitchen's swinging doors.

Waylon stopped stubbornly in the middle of the hall. "Kitchen's this way."

Fletcher kept walking. "I know."

"I can hear your stomach growling from here."

"Quit listening."

A series of formidable steps shuffled down the hall behind her until Waylon spun her around by the shoulder. With a nudge, he pushed her back toward the kitchen. "Did I hallucinate when you said *Next step, food*?"

"Exactly. Food." Fletcher ground her heels in until they stopped their death march. "Not *kitchen*. The kitchen is inevitably occupied."

Waylon's overtalkative eyebrows rose in question.

With a gulping inhale, Fletcher spelled it out for him: "Opal doesn't go anywhere without a secret joint. I saw her pull one out of her makeup bag after last quarter's sales strategy meeting. She's definitely in the kitchen. Munchies. Sheila's with her because Sheila will take free drugs from anyone. Plus, when Sheila finished suntanning this afternoon, she found Raul floating like Gatsby in the pool—"

"Raul's dead?"

"Raul's dead. Shot. Floating in the pool. Keep up. So, Opal would have offered her a hit to stop her from freaking out. Even though Sheila drives Opal crazy, Sales will stick together. They're pack people. Stronger with numbers. But Opal's ambitious, and with Theo gone, she'll use Sheila. Rick, too. They'll stock up and head out to find Rick by morning."

"What are you?" Waylon asked. "The salesperson whisperer?"

"I'm good at my job."

For the sake of her own satisfaction, Fletcher led Waylon closer to the kitchen doors, following the sound of crashing silverware, slamming cabinets, and an unmistakable nasally voice.

"So, I was telling Eric that Penelope said that Wendy told *her* that Jeremy's parties aren't any fun unless you do cocaine, and there I was, cocaine-less."

Through the open sliver, Fletcher spied Sheila's mile-high curls where she sat cross-legged on the counter. She stopped talking only long enough to plop a leftover slice of sushi in her mouth. Fletcher could practically taste the day-old tuna from where she was standing.

Next to her, Opal swung a chef's knife through a mango, the

blade *chunk*ing into a wooden cutting board. The sound startled Fletcher backward. "How do you even get yourself into these situations?"

Sheila shrugged. "I just tell people I'm a Cartwright. Works like a charm. Nobody cares what I do when I've got Uncle Dyer's money. Like, this one time in college, I told him I needed money because tuition increased, but I cashed the check, skipped finals, and went to Saint Bart's." Fletcher peeked back at Waylon, whose mouth twitched in irritation but not surprise. Apparently a little low-stakes familial fraud was par for the course. "One night, we drank so much rum—"

"Remind me to never ask you a question ever again. Hurry and finish packing so we can go find Rick."

The intern chewed. Swallowed. Said, "I could tell you about my spring break trip to Ibiza instead."

"Please don't."

Fletcher tuned their conversation out the second she felt Waylon's smoke-warm breath on her ear. He whispered, "Touché. Follow me."

Dyer Cartwright owned more wine than France.

The basement's wine cellar doubled as a tasting room, with damask wallpaper and several refinished oak tables surrounded by high-backed chairs. It was bigger than Fletcher's apartment in every dimension. She had half a mind to barricade the door and wait the week out down here, drunk on pinot.

If she thought for even a second that Jackie would forgive her cowardice and still hand her a promotion rather than killing her on the way to the rescue boat, she totally would have.

Instead, she plucked a hundred-year-old red off the shelf and uncorked it next to their growing stack of more reasonable hiking snacks—cured meats and salted nuts and dried fruit—just for good measure.

Anytime she thought working with Waylon could be congenial, he'd do something stupid, like wield a jar of olives like a medieval torture device. Or, when her head started to spin and she dreadfully admitted that she hadn't eaten anything since dinner last night, hand-feed her grapes. If *hand-feed* was code for *started bombarding her with green grapes like tiny fruit missiles*. Two hit her in the shoulder, and a third bounced off her pith helmet.

"Would you knock it off?" she barked.

His smile hooked at the corners.

Oh no.

Rapid-fire grapes shot at her, his wrist a semiautomatic rifle. They pelted her. *Bang, bang, bangbangbang*. That one definitely had the stems still attached.

Fletcher smacked her hands against the table, cheeks flaming so hot it could put Cheetos out of business. "What's the matter with you? Were you bullied at Stuyvesant or something?"

Waylon poked a grape in her open mouth. She froze in protest. The tips of his calloused fingers touched beneath her chin, lingering only enough that her jaw snapped shut.

When she was done chewing, she said, "You incense me."

He nudged a bunch of grapes across the table. "You'll get over it."

Had grapes always been this good? The only thing that would make it better was a side of more wet, old grapes. She poured the red wine into a stemmed glass (Dyer would never even *think* about owning stemless glasses) and, when she was done, Waylon drank right from the bottle.

Fletcher sipped. If only to ignore the way Waylon was watching her, a notch forming between his brows. She could see it in her peripheral vision—deepening with an unreadable emotion. (Assuming, of course, Waylon Cartwright had emotions at all.)

They hadn't spent this much time together, well, ever. And what time they had spent together previously was as enjoyable as a Pap smear. Neither of them knew what to do with the dead air. The only sound in the cellar was grape chomping and wine slurping.

Eventually, Waylon asked, "Did you like it? Working for my dad?"

Did. Past tense. Because she would never work for Dyer again.

Which made her suddenly entirely too aware of her own propensity for emotions.

"You don't have to do this."

"Do what?"

"*This*. Act like being around me doesn't make you want to donate both kidneys." At his look, she added: "You're right. You'd never be that selfless."

Waylon leaned his elbows onto the table, perched his chin on his knuckles. "Answer the question, Spence."

"Yeah, mostly," she said, throat sticky.

Dyer was a good boss and, she'd thought, a good man. At least until the will reading. And the camera smashing. And that wasn't even touching on the sheer number of glassy-eyed animals he'd been decorating the estate with.

He'd always been calculated but never cruel. Or had she simply neglected to see it?

The surly fuckboy action figure sitting across the table, baby blues searing into her like the hottest flame, certainly had Fletcher questioning if everything she believed to be true actually was.

Three years of unspoken tension pulsed between them. He'd lost some of his boyishness since then. Cheeks slimmed and scruffed.

Shoulders broader, biceps fuller. His blond curls as obnoxiously thick as ever, though, evidently immune to male-pattern baldness.

Fletcher had to clear her throat before saying, "Don't take this the wrong way, but why would your dad have you inherit the island if you hated him so much?"

"Probably the same reason he left us all here to die. To get the last laugh." Waylon split a grape between his teeth. "And what *right way* was I supposed to take that, exactly? You should know better than anyone how my father felt about me considering you're the reason he disinherited me in the first place."

Fletcher's wineglass halted halfway to her lips. *Disinherited?* She forced another gulp to hide her confused frown. "You were capable of that all on your own."

Waylon brought a hand over his heart. "Aw. You think I'm capable?"

This time, it was Fletcher's turn to throw a seedless grape. He dodged easily, never taking his gaze off hers.

Wouldn't she know if he'd been *disinherited*? After their first encounter, Fletcher had learned everything about the Cartwrights. She'd made sure of it. The level of research she'd done bordered on criminal.

Gun to her head, she could've recited the addresses of Dyer's sixteen international properties, including four purchased under three different shell companies. The numbers of five maître d's were burned into her speed dial in case she needed to call in an emergency lunch resy—not that she'd ever eaten anywhere that nice on her own dime. The entire Cartwright lineage had been seared into her brain, so she'd always be ready for a pop quiz.

Egbert Cartwright founded Cartwright Media in 1924, excited to share tales of his travels to Bali, then Cairo, then Bermuda. (Close call with the Triangle of it all.) Monthly issues sold like deep-fried Oreos at the Lincoln County Fair. Which was to say, a lot. Enough that when Wilmer Cartwright inherited the company in the '50s, the brand was invincible. Impervious to his rollicking around the city with bottomless pockets, as Fletcher quickly learned all Cartwrights were wont to do.

By the time Dyer took command, *Jet-Setter* was the leading travel periodical. Synonymous with extravagance and luxury, but still aspirational enough to convince flyover state farmers and their ruddy-cheeked daughters that a three-week European river tour was not only something they should want to do but *could*.

Each edition had thick, glossy pages with vibrant photographs of places Fletcher dreamed about. Cabanas with billowing linen curtains. Snowcapped Alpine villages. Historic palaces, quaint country homes, pastel buildings clinging to jagged coastlines.

She couldn't then—and still couldn't to this day—fathom how Waylon Cartwright could hate it so much.

Everything he had, he had because of *Jet-Setter*, and he'd walked away from it of his own volition.

All Fletcher had *Jet-Setter* to thank for was a chronic stress disorder and a growing ulcer her gastroenterologist nicknamed Steven the Anarchist. An ulcer that probably started growing on a bitterly cold December evening, navy and crisp and sparkling with a dusting of snow and strings of holiday lights.

Even an eight-thousand-square-foot wine cellar was too small of a space to share with someone who nearly ruined your life, accusing you of ruining theirs.

Of all the times she relived the gala in stress dreams and sleep terrors, she never considered what happened after security had dragged a sopping-wet Waylon out by the collar of his tuxedo jacket. Business went on as usual, and Waylon went off on his own.

"We should go," Fletcher said, adjusting her pith helmet. Oak barrels and velvet tapestries soaked up her voice. Somehow, it was still too loud. Her skin felt hive-y, her lungs too tight. She had to get out of here. Away from him.

Waylon hesitated, only a breath, before shaking off whatever lingered between them and dredging himself upright. "What's next on your master plan?"

"Get far away from this murder house and find somewhere safe to sleep."

"Lucky for you, the Cartwrights have a long history of glamping. We should have some sleeping bags in the observatory. I'll grab them, and you can take the food to the garage. I'll meet you there." Fletcher's face must have morphed against her will, because he refocused on her with a quizzical look. "What?"

She snapped back to attention. Her facial muscles aimed for some semblance of neutrality, like she hadn't spent the last six hours violently oscillating between daydreams of roasting Waylon on a spit and feeling his calloused palms on her waist, her hips, her thighs. The stress was seriously getting to her.

"Nothing," she said. "I just never thought I'd live to see the day Waylon Cartwright and I cooperated. Let alone the day you used the word 'glamping.'"

A darkness lingered in his gaze. Hate, or something stronger. Loathing?

All he said was "Lie low. If you aren't in the garage in thirty minutes, I'm leaving without you."

Whatever camaraderie had fermented between them in the wine cellar popped like prosecco bubbles the second they stepped back onto the first floor.

Waylon veered left without a word goodbye, off to the planetarium protruding off the eastern wing, where they stored camping equipment for dark-sky excursions. The kind Fletcher might have been excited to go on had this retreat been anything at all like she'd thought it would be.

Fletcher turned right. The straps of a canvas tote monogrammed with Tiffany's initials strained against a week's worth of rations. The garage wasn't far—she could totally camp out there until Waylon returned.

It was a good plan. Great, even.

Until she turned the corner and ran straight into Molly.

11

Also, Molly had a machete.

It was braced over her head, ready to strike. Her fiery hair had once been slicked into a ballerina bun, but loose ends freed themselves into a stark red mane. A fat smudge of maroon inked her cheek—lipstick, Fletcher hoped.

A feeble, Victorian waif of a hope. But still.

"It's just me!" Fletcher shrilled.

Momentum had taken hold of the machete. The blade sliced downward, snagging on the weave of the tote as Fletcher spun out of reach. A few clementines rolled out of her bag as she threw her arms up to shield her face.

"Me," she tried again. "Fletcher."

Her chest heaved with labored breaths. There wasn't any blood dripping off the machete blade, but that was Fletcher's only solace.

Molly's eyes stayed blank. Dark. Wild.

It took all Fletcher's strength not to race down the hall in a blind panic, but she vaguely remembered learning it was bad to run from predators. Weren't you supposed to punch sharks in the face? Was this a shark-punching situation?

No, surely some sense could be talked into Molly.

"Spence. Fletcher Spence. We had drinks together last night. You did my onboarding three years ago. That's pretty much the only real time we ever spent together, but I still don't think I deserve to get macheted."

Nothing. Maybe Molly had been possessed by Dyer's vengeful ghost. He was probably mad Fletcher forgot to instruct the staff to fold the towels like giraffes instead of swans. Come to think of it, he *hadn't* had the chance to ream her for using the breakfast napkins last night at dinner. A poltergeist-haunting-worthy offense in his book.

"Molly, the heat's gone to your head. Put the knife down. You don't have to do this."

Molly's glare said otherwise.

"Shut *up*!" Molly groaned as she reeled her sharpened knife back like a baseball bat. "I can't stand it anymore."

"Okay, sure. Shutting up." Fletcher ducked as the blade swung overhead. Maybe even trimmed a few hairs.

As calmly as she could, Fletcher inched down the hall, hands still framing her face to block Molly's next swing. Her shoestring budget did *not* have any extra room for an emergency rhinoplasty.

Except the thing about being nervous was that her mouth had a mind of its own.

"I'm great at shutting up. If you need someone to shut up, I'm your girl." A credenza rammed into Fletcher's spine. *Ow*. "Actually, I feel like that would make me great at HR. Do you need more help on the People team? I could put in a transfer request."

Molly's jaw unhinged, and a banshee-loud cry filled the hall. "I'm so *sick* of listening to you people yap if you aren't going to say anything interesting."

"I'm not yapping," Fletcher whispered, skidding down the hall to stay out of reach of Molly's blade. How far was the garage? She couldn't remember.

"Day in. Day out. All I hear is: *Molly, can you approve my PTO? Molly, does calling the custodian's facial hair a 'porn star mustache' count as sexual harassment? Molly, Slater from IT is purposefully clogging the thirty-ninth floor toilets. Again.*"

Slater from IT historically had unpredictable bowels and a penchant for vengeance. Fletcher wouldn't put it past him.

"If I have to listen to one more sob story about how Rick's fifth grandmother died in her sleep and he needs to take a week of bereavement, I'm going to build a time machine so that he never has a grandmother to begin with."

The tip of Molly's blade swung perilously close. Things were devolving faster than Fletcher'd hoped—her schedule hadn't included a Molly Meltdown until at least nine p.m. Unlike Sales, Marketing, and the C-suite, she didn't have a team to rely on. She'd gone totally rogue.

Fletcher needed something she could defend herself with. Desperately. Anything would be better than bruised produce.

"Russo and Dunlap are in their own little Brian echo chamber, where nothing is their fault, and I'm never approving them to be hiring managers because the last thing this godforsaken company needs is *more Brians*."

Retreating, Fletcher's hands spread wide behind her, searching for a weapon or an exit route or both. Of all the things she'd thought to prep for this week—the welcome gifts, the hors d'oeuvres menu, the cocktail hour playlist—she hadn't devoted every inch of the estate's floor plan to memory, and it was about to bite her in the ass. Or stab her in the neck.

"Hiring Sheila was a paperwork nightmare. But you." Molly's

stare was white-hot and fixed on Fletcher with the kind of intensity typically reserved for serial killers. "Little. Miss. Perfect."

Fletcher smiled. The habitual movement vanished when she realized Molly definitely hadn't meant it as a compliment. Steam practically poured out of her ears. Her face had gone as red as her hair—if one of their demented coworkers didn't kill her, an aneurysm might.

"Not once has anyone ever come to HR with a complaint against you. Don't you think that's a little weird?"

"Isn't that a good thing?"

Desperate, Fletcher jiggled the nearest door handle, the knob of the gazelle room. *Damn it.* Sheila must have used her one functioning brain cell to remember to lock it.

"You show up from the middle of nowhere, with all this small-town charm like you were plucked out of a fucking Hallmark movie, and Dyer was *obsessed* with you."

"But not in, like, a creepy way," Fletcher clarified. The hallway was running out. Soon, Molly would have her out in the open foyer. Nothing to hide behind, nothing to protect herself with.

"You're always early. You stay late. You've never even taken a sick day," Molly said. All the machete swashbuckling kept Fletcher from ruminating too hard. "Three years, and not a single cold?"

"This feels like a super weird thing to be mad about."

Molly snarled. *Snarled.*

Okay, plan B.

Peeling through her memory, Fletcher fought for every last scrap of information she knew about Molly Bradhampton: at thirty-four, she wasn't that much older than Fletcher. Single but wrote a Substack about her dating escapades. Fletcher could picture her catching an Uber outside the office doors, touching up her lip gloss in her front-facing camera. One time, Fletcher had glanced a Manhattan Plaza

Racquet Club card on her desk and a Lululemon duffel at her feet. That explained her killer backswing.

She was so wrapped up in her thoughts, she didn't notice Molly's machete winding up until the blade *thwack*ed against Fletcher's ridiculous pith helmet. Her eyes shot wide open, but Molly's narrowed with determination.

At this range, she couldn't fight her off. She needed to appeal to Molly's most primal sense. Gossip.

Before Molly could strike again, Fletcher asked, "What do people say about Waylon?"

"*Don't* get me started on Waylon," Molly said, but unlike Fletcher predicted, the machete arm didn't relax by her side, placated. If anything, the rumor mill only riled her up. "He was bad enough when he worked under Dyer, but he's been a nightmare since the whole Eliza fiasco. But you know that. You were there."

She . . . definitely wasn't. But Fletcher didn't have the bandwidth to unpack that. Right now, her body was too focused on not getting stabbed through the spleen. Molly's advances were getting harder and harder to defend. Every step brought a new frenzy.

"But do I miss the way he used to storm around the office in a testosterone tornado?" Molly fake retched for dramatic effect. "No. He deserved to get kicked out of the company as far as I'm concerned. *And* he knocked over Ferdinand."

"Ferdinand?"

"My ficus!"

"How dare he?" A woman's ficus was precious.

Molly's focus shifted. "Why? Are you . . . interested in him?"

Fletcher flinched backward, closer and closer to the foyer, where sunlight glinted off the ormolu chandelier, shooting little rainbows from the parquet floor to the catwalk balcony between wings.

Jacquard curtains draped around the windows, woven with threads of gold, and beyond that waited the flat expanse of wilderness.

Fletcher made a fast break for it, and the foyer opened around her. Something wavered in the corner of her eye, but when she pivoted, no one was there. Just the taxidermied lion with its polished white teeth and hollow eyes, overseeing everything?

There wasn't much to work with: a baby grand piano; a side table with neatly arranged vases of cut flowers and stacked coffee table books; a leather settee. But this was the estate's main artery—if she could shake Molly off her tracks, she could lose her in the halls.

"We're not finished here!" Molly shouted behind her.

Pounding footsteps grew louder. Every *thud* against the hardwoods ticked Fletcher's pulse up a notch. *Oh, god.* With a jolt, Fletcher lunged toward the curtains, burying herself in their pleats.

Buttery smooth fabric enveloped her. Sweat dripped down her neck, equal parts from blind fear and the sunlight beating against the window and cooking her alive. Carefully, Fletcher slipped her feet out of her pumps, blisters already forming on her heels. With the points of her shoes sticking out beyond the veil, Fletcher shimmied behind the curtains to the other side of the foyer.

This time, Molly acted exactly as Fletcher expected. In the seam between drapes, Fletcher watched the People team lead circle, searching for any trace of Fletcher. Sniffing the air for a hint of her vanilla perfume, even. When her eyes locked on Fletcher's empty heels, Molly grinned.

Without waiting, without thinking, Molly hacked at the fabric. "You think you're going to run away with Waylon and live happily ever after?" she raved, even though Fletcher never said anything even remotely like that.

Eventually, the machete ripped clean through the curtain.

Only then did Molly realize her mark was missing.

Quieter this time, closer this time, Molly said, "You think that because you spent every day at Dyer's side that you're better than the rest of us? That *you* deserve everything?"

Fletcher hitched a breath, and the pressure in the air doubled.

She stood totally, completely, utterly still. The only muscle moving in her body was the rapid cant of her heart, a sound so loud she was half certain Molly could hear. The woman's shadow moved toward her window. Time to fight back.

Somehow.

When Fletcher tried to make a break for it, her arms and legs tangled in the fabric. It swirled around her, twisted, strangled. She fought against the curtains, and the curtains fought back, all while Molly tried to shish-kebab her.

Once she finally ousted the curtains, her options for defense mechanisms were slim. For all Dyer's peculiar design tastes, Lydell Manor was seriously lacking in the Things That Double as Swords department. Unless.

Her eyes lifted.

Curtain rods were basically fencing sabers. Fletcher yanked on the drapes, but the pockets snagged on the beam. Molly was all too eager to take advantage of the hesitation.

With two fistfuls of fabric, Fletcher used all her weight, leaning into it. Finally, threads snapped, and the curtain rod clattered to the floor. She grabbed it with two hands, swinging it to block Molly's attack. The blade's impact reverberated through her bones, through her gritted teeth.

"You don't have to do this," Fletcher said. She pushed, digging in her heels, until Molly and her machete bounced back. "We bonded on the pool deck! I thought you were a girl's girl!"

Molly parried, the flat edge of the machete cold against Fletcher's arm. So close to drawing blood. "Bonded? I don't know anything about you. Every person at this company has a deep dark secret. But not Fletcher Spence."

"No way! I totally have dark secrets. Like, um, I still watch *Friends* reruns even though the jokes aged like two percent milk." The machete shattered an amber vase on Molly's rebound. "Sometimes when Sales asks me to print them reports I pretend the inkjet's low on toner." *Think, think, think.* Fletcher circled back for her heels, sliding her feet into each shoe as she hopped away from Molly's advances. "Oh, last year I used the company card to pay for a manicure before our big meeting with Condé Nast!"

Molly's eyes narrowed. "Your biggest secret is getting your cuticles trimmed?"

So what if she liked striving for perfection? Perfection was neat and tidy, a clearly defined box, and she knew the exact shape of the lines she needed to fit herself into to achieve it. Or at least *look* like she'd achieved it. Perfection had made her an undeniable asset to Dyer, to the company. A lifelong overachiever. An agreeable only daughter.

Perfect. In all ways except one.

Molly moved to swing again—if it came down to Fletcher spilling her guts or Molly spilling them for her, she was always going to choose the former.

"I spent ten years in a relationship with someone I didn't love," Fletcher blurted. Light glinted in Molly's gaze. Intrigued. *And* she'd stopped swinging her blade, which was a huge plus. "I almost married him."

For a moment, a little humanity snuck its way back into Molly's face. "Why didn't you?"

"It's what my parents wanted. It's what Kent wanted. It was what everyone wanted, except me. I wanted to stay in New York, join *Jet-Setter*, take photos all over the world. But I—" Fletcher gulped, squeezing her eyes shut. Admitting it to herself as much as to Molly, she whispered: "I wanted to kiss Waylon Cartwright."

Like she'd been struck, shame slashed through Fletcher's chest. Remnants of the electricity she'd felt in that stuffy coat closet, the spark of an emotion she hadn't felt with Kent in too long, even then.

What little residual kindness existed in Molly's heart must have shriveled up and died because her ordinarily bright eyes went dark. "You wanted to *kiss him*? I knew it. You never really cared about Ferdinand, traitor."

Fletcher's retreat came to a grinding halt. Her back flattened against the paneled wall. A roar ripped up Molly's throat, the machete arcing toward Fletcher.

This was how she died. Carved like a Butterball turkey.

Then someone sneezed. Milliseconds later, something red and fuzzy *zing*ed across the foyer—straight into Molly's neck. Lodged in the jugular region.

A silver dart with fringed red fletching shocked Molly's mouth into an open O. Her movement slowed, slowed, slowed as her hands came swinging down. Enough of a delay for Fletcher to roll out of the strike zone. The blade embedded itself into the wall, slicing through the wallpaper straight to the stud. Right where Fletcher's head had been.

From above, someone asked, "What did you *do*?"

Both Brians huddled against the walkway railing overlooking the foyer. She *knew* she'd seen something moving around up there. In Brian's hands? A tranquilizer gun. The kind that zookeepers would use to knock out an elephant. His index finger lingered on the trigger.

"Sorry. Allergies," Other Brian said, hushed.

"Don't you take medicine for that?" Brian hissed back.

Other Brian reached into his pocket for a wadded-up, already-used

Kleenex to mop up his nose. "My bad, man. I didn't mean to bump you."

Fletcher would have sworn Brian said, "Come on. Bertram will have our heads if she gets away."

Almost like he hadn't been aiming for Molly at all.

Intention didn't matter. A syringe the size of her forearm still jutted out of the side of Molly's neck, and the injection must have been taking hold quickly. Molly's left arm drooped to her side and dangled there. Her face followed suit, skin sagging drastically, like a botched Botox job.

The eye that wasn't fast asleep, rolling around in its socket, burned with rage. All of it was guided toward Fletcher, which felt a little unfair given she hadn't been the one to shoot her with a tranquilizer dart.

The real culprits raced down the staircase, flinging the gigantic gun around like Rambo wannabes.

Fletcher had to get out of there. Now.

Shooting out of the foyer, she aimed toward the executive suites. Molly pried the machete out of the wall and lurched after her. Or tried to. Her lopsided Frankenstein gait wasn't built for running. Everything after that happened in slow motion:

Molly's numb foot snagged on the embroidered drapery.

Her body sloped forward, falling—and falling—and falling.

The arm holding the machete hit the ground first. Blade up. Still clutched in her good hand.

And in the fraction of a second that followed, Molly crashed to the floor on top of it. The machete speared through her chest, ripping between rib bones. Fletcher couldn't look away fast enough.

There was a *squelch* and a *gasp* and a *wheeze*, a whole symphony of horrifying onomatopoeia. Black film edged the corners of Fletcher's vision, like she'd slapped a terrible Instagram filter over her eyes.

"Oh my god, Molly."

Molly, of course, didn't respond. She had a packed schedule of Bleeding Out on the Parquet Floor, followed shortly by Not Getting a Proper Burial Because Her Coworkers Were Lunatics.

And, unfortunately, Fletcher's calendar was also filled with back-to-back agenda items. First on the list was getting the hell away from the Brians.

12

Fletcher's only solace was how painfully clear it was that neither Brian actually knew how to operate a tranquilizer gun. They spent their days neck-deep in Google Analytics and their nights debating the ethics of tracking user data. It wasn't like they were actually going to—

Another red-fletched dart whizzed past her ear, missing her by just a hair, and embedded itself into a *Jet-Setter* cover from 1978 featuring a fair amount of corduroy and freed nipples. Fletcher jolted, eyes wide, and her gaze caught on Brian's as he barreled down the stairs.

"No, no, no. Hold on a second." She thrust her staff toward them. Forcing distance. "Whatever bullshit assignment Bertram gave you, you don't have to do it."

The curtain rod épée wasn't going to cut it. She needed something bigger, sharper.

She needed a . . .

Machete.

"We aren't trying to kill you," Other Brian said.

This was bad. So bad. "Oh yeah? Like you weren't trying to kill Molly?"

Brian scoffed. "We *weren't*. That was all her."

On the ground between them, Molly was heavy, limp, cold. Fletcher tried not to think about how quickly the air had left her lungs as she wedged her foot underneath Molly's stiff torso and rolled her onto her side. The blade had inserted itself beneath her sternum in the soft between bones.

Molly's blouse was ruined, stained the darkest red. Her head lolled, eyes fixed on the Brians, like even dead she could hold a mean grudge.

As Fletcher grabbed the knife's hilt, the outrageous amount of adrenaline in her body was the only thing that stopped her from truly registering the difficult way the blade slid out, slick with Molly's blood. One day, this fucked-up vacation would be a big black blur in her memory. Like getting a concussion and forgetting the crack of your skull against the pavement. Unreachable in the depths of her mind.

But, for now, it remained all too real.

Wielding the blade with both hands, Fletcher needed to put as much distance as possible between her and the Brians.

"Don't come near me," she ordered.

With one eye pinched tight and the other eye staring down the viewfinder of a nose scope, Brian said, "Bertram gave us explicit instructions to bring you to him. Alive."

They were nothing if not lemmings veering cliffside at Bertram's command.

In Manhattan, Fletcher would have zipped her lips into a pretty, polished smile and bit her tongue until it bled. Lydell Fletcher didn't. "Was that before or after he warmed your bottle?"

It almost felt good to say what she was thinking for once. It *definitely* felt good to see the mix of shock and outrage on the Brians' faces.

While they were busy snapping their jaws shut, Fletcher tested the weight of the blade in her palms. There was a reason why parents told their kids not to run with knives, and Molly was the evidence. Fletcher, however, didn't have much of a choice.

She took off sprinting, her bag of produce slamming against her hip with every step. The fruit was about to be bruised all to hell. Skidding around the corner, Fletcher made a fast break down the east wing. All she had to do was make it to the garage in one piece.

Another dart flew in her general direction. It missed—thank god for Brian's astigmatism and shaky hands—but shattered a hand-painted vase filled with pampas grass. Clay spewed through the hall. How much ammo did that thing have? Fletcher didn't want to stick around to find out.

The first door on the right opened up into a theater. Rows of red leather chairs descended toward a silver screen, and ruched velvet lined the walls. It even *smelled* like movie theater popcorn. Dim light from the wall sconces might be enough to conceal her from the Brians. She was willing to take the chance.

Fletcher leaped down the stairs and threw herself on the ground in the fifth row. Army crawling, she wiggled toward the middle seats. Arguably the best seats in the house. As a plus, the sconces barely touched this section, so she clung to the shadows.

"I told you she wouldn't come peacefully," Brian snarked under his breath as the theater door nudged open.

Their footsteps were dull, padded against the plush carpet. Without peeking her head over the recliners, it was nearly impossible for Fletcher to tell where exactly they were.

Other Brian's voice sounded closer when he said, "I still think the gun's a bit much. Bertram said she knows everything about everyone. She's an asset, not a threat."

Fletcher slithered forward, far too aware of the *swish* of acrylic-rayon fabric against the carpet. If she died because of this hot-pink dress, she'd haunt the clearance aisle for the rest of eternity.

"That's what makes her a threat, moron," Brian said. "Just help me look for her. There's, like, a thirty-six-point-eight percent chance she's in here. Choosing door number one is like pissing in the first urinal. Everyone thinks no one will use it, so they all use it."

"Whoa, reverse psychology," Other Brian said.

Fletcher had to get out of there before the boy math melted her brain and it started dripping down her earlobes. Braving a glance up, she caught a flash of Brian's dark hair as he crouched down to check the aisle a few rows up. Other Brian ran recon, pacing along the doorway.

Guarding the only way out.

Brian lurked down the staircase, only three rows up from Fletcher. The invisibility of women in the workplace unfortunately didn't make a difference here. Especially not wearing fuchsia. But she couldn't just lie there and wait for Brian to shoot her.

Contorting her body to reach into her tote bag asked a lot of Fletcher's elbows, but she managed to wrangle a handful of grapes into her fist and lobbed them toward the screen. They scattered, splatting.

A surprised noise came from the doorway. Other Brian asked, "What was that?"

"Don't just stand there," Brian barked. "Come help me look."

Fletcher waited until the Brians sped past her.

Then, thrusting herself upright, Fletcher made a break for the doorway. One of the Brians shouted after her, and their footsteps followed. As a decoy, she opened three doors in a row before backtracking to the second, barely squeezing behind it before the Paid Ads specialists appeared in the hall.

She pressed against the wall behind the door, willing herself invisible. Grooves met her fingertips. Where was she? The room was so dark, it was impossible to tell where she'd landed, but it smelled distinctly like cedar and lavender.

Laundry room? Sleep-study chamber? A portal to another dimension? Maybe one where her coworkers hadn't turned into sociopaths?

Through the crevice of the doorjamb, there was just enough space to see the Brians stalking in her direction. On tiptoes, they crept forward, and it occurred to Fletcher that no grown man should be reduced to tiptoeing unless under very specific circumstances, like avoiding lasers mid-heist or preserving the magic of Christmas for a small child.

The Brians' shadows loomed in the doorway, blocking some of the light from the hall. Fletcher sank deeper into the shadows. Behind her, a switch plate stabbed into her spine. Her elbow knocked against it, and the overhead lights flickered on.

"In here," Other Brian said.

Damn it.

They wedged the door wider, Fletcher caught behind it. Amber bulbs illuminated a sauna. The walls were ribbed with wooden paneling, and the air tinged with spruce and sweat. The sauna!

Contorting her body, Fletcher flipped another switch. A robotic voice chimed, "Sauna activated. Adding humidity." Steam swirled down from the ceiling, turning the air soupy and fogging up Brian's glasses. The perfect distraction.

Fletcher skirted around the door while their backs were turned and made it halfway into the hallway before a hand clamped around her arm. Other Brian reeled her toward him, the tiles beneath their feet slippery with condensation.

"Tell Bertram he's never receiving an Edible Arrangement ever again." Fletcher stretched her free arm to its full wingspan, and with the tips of her fingers, she dragged open a towel warmer. Snagging the top washcloth, she rubbed it against Other Brian's arm.

He yelped, trying to bat it away. Failing.

"What's going on over there?" Brian wiped the steam off his glasses lenses, just for them to fog up again. "I can't see anything."

Other Brian grunted, but Fletcher replied, "A little good old-fashioned team building."

She dug her elbow into his side, and when that wasn't enough, she flung the hot washcloth toward his face. His hands flew toward the towel, and Fletcher took that as her cue to escape.

Garage. She needed to get to the garage. Her timer was definitely running out. It was all too easy to think of Waylon in the front seat of a Land Rover, ringed fingers drumming against the steering wheel, biding his time until he could leave Fletcher for good. She couldn't let that happen.

The Brians were coming, their shouts echoing in the sauna, mad now. Fletcher looped back to the theater (*How's that for your 36.8 percent?*) and watched as the Brians spun circles in the hall before creeping into door number three.

Fletcher bolted. Rooms bled together as she raced through the halls. When they arrived at the manor, Fletcher had glimpsed the garage on the far end of the complex, doors facing the open wild. All she had to do was get there. The food bag thumped against her back with every step, and the hand that wasn't holding the machete's hilt kept the pith helmet attached to her head.

Behind her, the Brians wised up and sprinted after her, yelling, "This way!"

Desperate to throw them off her trail while avoiding any other close encounters, Fletcher envisioned each person's daily routines and mapped them to the estate.

Deepti could be counted on for partaking in any wellness fad promising to get rid of hip dips or buccal fat or whatever other ordinary bodily occurrence women were being shamed for these days. Without Raul, she'd be on the hunt for someone else to form a symbiotic relationship with.

Melv almost certainly jogged the perimeter, itching to get his daily steps in. Meanwhile, Bertram would be heads down, nursing a bourbon with a splash of milk like a Madison Avenue advertiser from the '60s. Which put him roughly in the vicinity of the conference rooms. Fletcher skipped that wing entirely.

In the afternoons, Jackie usually dipped out to meet with a personal trainer—and when Fletcher snuck past one of the workout studios, there was Jackie, strapped into a VR headset, bopping around the room with an aggressive assortment of mixed cardio moves.

Fletcher swerved past the gym and darted through a full-blown bowling alley, trying to lose the Brians while they slipped and slid on greased lanes. She lost track of them somewhere around the concert hall, but ran into them again as they each opened doors on opposite sides of a Roman-inspired bath.

And froze.

Floating in the saltwater tub was a twelve-foot crocodile that must have wandered in, taking advantage of the disengaged fences. Gold eyes, sharp teeth. Hungry.

Fletcher gulped, eyes meeting the Brians' as the crocodile growled, beastly head pivoting between them. Deciding who to attack first.

She slammed the door behind her and didn't stop running until she reached a gold-and-glass atrium, lush with tropical plants. Inside, a few wrought iron benches dotted the room. The kind of place that looked like its only purpose was for tea parties or clandestine meetings. Birdsong chirped from the palm fronds, a few parrots flitting from tree to tree.

The windows boasted an unimpeded view of the savanna. Grasses billowed in the wind. In the distance, a herd of zebras gathered, a mirage against the horizon. And at the far side of the room? A second arched door.

Salvation if she'd ever seen it. If she could make it outside, she could circle back to the garage from the exterior and avoid the Brians completely.

To catch her breath, she ducked behind a leafy palm with waxy leaves fanning toward the glass ceiling. Its trunk slanted into a beautifully manicured planter, spilling with plumeria and ginger lilies.

This was fine. Everything was going to be totally fine.

Or it was, until something splattered on the curve of Fletcher's shoulder.

Wet. Sticky.

Fletcher peeled her eyes upward, half expecting some medieval torture contraption dangling from the ceiling with one of her colleagues strapped to it.

An exhale. No ceiling fan murder devices here.

Instead, it was a giant blue bird. The macaw responsible flapped its wings, happily unaware that it had defecated on her shoulder. Just a bunch of birds, pissed off about being trapped inside the atrium glass.

She knew the feeling.

Helplessly, Fletcher straightened the hem of her dress. It did nothing to fix the vile white splotch on her shoulder, but didn't some people say that getting pooped on by a bird was good luck?

Just when her breathing returned to normal, a voice behind her whispered, "Bull's-eye."

Ice ran through Fletcher's veins, fear jolting down her spine. She pivoted on her heels, swinging her machete up, and her mouth opened to scream.

Waylon's sharp glare stopped her cold.

The knife fell and so did her heart rate. Three weeks ago, she would have laughed in the face of anyone who tried to tell her she'd feel any semblance of relief to see Waylon Cartwright.

"Good rule of thumb? Don't sneak up on someone holding a freaking machete," she hissed.

An extra duffel had been slung around Waylon's chest, half unzipped with silver, holographic fabric poking out. Glamping supplies, presumably. Their backpacks were gone—he must have stashed them in the garage already.

Slowly, Waylon's eyebrows cinched tighter. "Why do you have a machete?"

"One day, after tens of thousands of dollars in therapy, I'll tell you."

"What happened to lying low?" he asked, an edge to his voice.

"I *am* lying low." Now was seriously not the time for a lecture.

He cocked his head. "Just like how you were supposed to be meeting me in the garage twelve minutes ago?"

"Been a little busy." As if he couldn't tell based solely on the frizz fiasco happening beneath her helmet, Molly's blood caked on her dress, and the *totally relaxed* way her shoulders scraped against her earlobes. "I thought you said you were going to leave without me."

He huffed, a low grumble of a noise. "I still might."

Footsteps hammered down the hall, and Fletcher braced her hand against Waylon's stomach, nudging him behind the tree. "Get back. Bertram sent the Brians after me again."

"I don't think it'll take them long to find you."

Fletcher squinted. "Do you really think I'm so incompetent that I can't shake off *the Brians*?"

"No, I don't think it'll take long because you're leading them right to you." He tipped his chin downward, and Fletcher's gaze followed.

Blood trailed down the machete's silver blade. A pool of maroon had gathered at her heels. A few feet away, several garnet droplets welled on the tiles. And a few more, and a few more, and a few more. All the way to the atrium entrance where two moon-eyed marketers appeared, sniffing like bloodhounds.

"We have to get out of here," she whispered.

"No shit," Waylon said. The second Fletcher tried to get moving, he shook his head. "Can't go that way."

"The way toward the exit?" The arched doorway had *Safety Right This Way!* written all over it.

"Trust me. Deepti's naked in the solarium, doing god only knows what, and she does not want visitors." He pointed to his actively blackening eye socket as proof.

Of course. "Sunning."

"What?"

"That's what it's called. When you get naked and flash your—"

Birds frenzied as the atrium doors opened. The Brians were splitting up, each scoping out a side of the room, and the Brian with the tranquilizer gun was coming their way. It would take more than a parlor palm to hide Waylon's broad shoulders. As soon as Brian turned the corner around a fountain shaped like Egbert Cartwright riding a rhino, he had a clear shot.

"Run!" said Waylon.

Silver bullets zipped by them, each one closer than the last. She cast Waylon a glance that must have said, *If I get killed because I listened to you, you're dead to me* because he nodded and took a sharp left behind a trellis of climbing hibiscuses. Fletcher followed, breathing easier now that they were beyond the reach of Brian's nose scope.

The doorway spat them back out into the hall, birds flowing to the corridor ceiling and singing as their wings flapped. And Fletcher was . . . lost. A 1986 edition of *Jet-Setter* touting a huge perm and car phone stared back at her from the wall. Useless.

She was beginning to wonder if she'd already died. If hell was an endless mansion filled with coworkers she thought liked her but clearly never did.

"This way," Waylon urged.

As they ran, his hand found hers. Electricity sparked down her arm, everywhere his fingertips trailed. Before she could ask what he was doing, he pried open her palm and grabbed the machete's handle.

He slammed his foot down on the blade, cracking it, before chucking the whole thing into a picture gallery. The knife bit into the floors beneath a gilt-framed Monet.

"We could have used that," Fletcher said, not restraining the annoyance that came from the depths of her soul. Did the Cartwrights have no respect for personal property, or what?

"That was going to lead them right to us," he said as he pushed Fletcher forward, his hand fitting neatly against the small of her back.

Her legs fought each step. Their gelatinous consistency could last only a few more feet, the breakneck pace of the afternoon finally catching up to her. Ten minutes—*five* minutes, even. That was all the breather she needed. Fletcher dragged Waylon into the nearest room, a study.

Every inch of Lydell Manor was breathtaking, but this one took the cake. Bookshelves lined all four walls. Leather armchairs and suede chaises dotted the lounge, two billiards tables populated the center, and at the back sat a full-size bar. If Fletcher didn't know better, she'd think it was Waylon's inspiration for Subtext.

Once Waylon closed the door, barricading them inside, Fletcher slumped into the nearest seat. Strands of copper hair stuck to her forehead with sweat. She'd *never* broken a sweat at work before, but there were a lot of firsts happening on this retreat.

"Give me a second." It was almost a whimper. Her side ached like it'd been torn wide open and poorly stitched back together. Every breath burned her chest, her back, her throat. "Usually, the only running I do is running Dyer's errands."

Muffled down the hall, two sets of angry footsteps headed their way. Close and growing closer.

Only then did Fletcher truly take stock of their location. She'd been so wowed by the dark wood paneling and subtle grandeur, a welcome reprieve compared to the rest of the estate's garish decor, that she'd failed to realize the study didn't have any windows. Only one door, and the Brians aimed straight for it. A fireplace, ashes long cooled, but she lacked the upper-body strength to scale the chimney.

Which meant . . .

"We're trapped."

13

Correction: "We're trapped, and you're making a cocktail?"

Waylon ignored her and poured two fingers of liquor into a chilled glass. In one smooth movement, he whipped a pair of tongs from the counter and dipped into the freezer for an ice cube the size of Fletcher's fist.

"Now? You want to make a drink *now*?" Her whispers were growing angrier. Some of the strength had returned to her limbs, and she marched across the room to the bar. "What part of this sounds like a good idea?"

"The part where I'm thirsty, and you trust me."

Fletcher didn't have time to tell him that she'd sooner trust a middle schooler with heavy machinery than trust him because the door to the study slammed open. With remarkably fast reflexes, Waylon flung the ice cube across the library. It soared, smacking Brian in the chest as soon as he appeared in the doorway. The lump of ice splattered, and Brian wheezed, a hand resting on the sore spot beneath his breastbone.

Waylon pivoted toward Fletcher, a well-worn look of wry entertainment befalling his features. "Like I was saying."

Fletcher dove behind the bar as a silver bullet flew toward her. Through her teeth, she snarled, "If you get tranquilized, I'm drawing on your face in permanent marker."

The Brians had them well and truly cornered. Fletcher huddled next to the vodka and gin, working up the courage to sprint past Waylon, both Brians, and the tranquilizer gun. She'd survived the last three years just fine without Waylon. Forget their truce. The only thing he proved himself good for was a tension migraine.

Well, and he'd kept her from walking right into the Brians' hands as they pillaged her bedroom.

And he'd made sure that she ate something so she didn't go into a hanger-induced rage.

And, inexplicably, he hadn't driven off without her when he could have easily stranded her in the homicide fun house.

Huh.

Before she could make up her mind about ditching him, Waylon sidestepped so that he straddled her as he plucked a paring knife from the counter. Trapping her. Lap to face.

"What are you—"

Not trapping. Protecting her?

Every time she moved, he adjusted his stance, and her face grew increasingly close to thighs tucked inside black denim that must have been specifically tailored to his muscle definition. To get to her, the Brians would have to go through him. And there was . . . a *lot* of him.

When she craned her neck up to look at him, there was a plain-as-day view of his abdomen beneath the thin hem of his shirt—not that she wanted to see it. It was just there. Past it, she glimpsed the lopsided smile that manifested on his face, ever the easygoing barkeep.

"You want something to drink?" he asked the Brians.

"Oh, is this a peanut-free bar?" Other Brian asked before Brian backhanded him in the belly to tell him to shut up.

"Let us have her," Brian demanded. He stepped up to the bar, too close for Fletcher to see him, but she could hear the scrutinizing way his eyes narrowed. "Bertram isn't worried about you."

From this angle, Waylon's smile twisted sideways. Arrogant as usual. "Flattered, truly."

"But I am."

The air in the room shifted so dramatically that Fletcher peeked around Waylon's legs—and immediately wished she hadn't. Brian's ridiculous gun was inches away from Waylon's chest.

And Waylon had never looked calmer. Did this dude ever break a sweat?

"I'm glad you turned your back on this company," Brian spat. "You would have run the marketing program into the ground. I'm sure you're used to everyone kissing your ass, but I refuse."

"Unfortunate," Waylon said. "My ass is highly kissable."

The hand that wasn't on the trigger reached across the bar and clenched a fistful of Waylon's shirt. "You think I'm joking?"

At that, Waylon laughed. "No one would ever mistake you for funny, Russo."

Brian thrust himself over the bar, hand reaching toward Waylon's throat. Tranquilizer be damned. He moved like he wanted to watch the life sap from Waylon's fully conscious eyes.

Fletcher was on her feet before she could talk herself out of saving Waylon. Without the machete that would have been really freaking handy right about now, she settled for the next best thing and snagged a bottle of rum off the shelf. It was vacation, after all.

She smashed the bottle against the countertop, little shards of spilled glass scattering. Maybe she shouldn't have skipped the company outing to the Yankees game to make copies for the QBR. Her swing could use some help.

Other Brian was behind her without a moment's notice, his arms coiling around her center and dragging her away. Fletcher kicked, fighting for purchase.

"Hasn't anyone told you not to bring Captain Morgan to a gunfight?" he asked, so Fletcher rammed the sharp edge of her bottle into his thigh. With a pained howl, his grip faltered, hands flattening against his leg.

Waylon's skin grew increasingly red, but he landed a solid punch against Brian's jaw, and that was enough to convince the marketer to release his choke hold. As Brian's glasses soared off his face, Waylon made a fast break for the pool table, brandishing one of the cues like a naginata.

Too fast, Brian lunged toward Waylon. Fletcher couldn't have stopped it, but she saw it coming. The way Waylon had the cue reared, tip aimed too high. How the fur rug scooched beneath Brian's Corporate Hipster Reeboks, and he lost his footing. When the arc of his trajectory misfired, and the cue speared toward his face.

An animalistic scream ripped through Brian as Waylon and the cue staggered backward. On the end of the cue, poked through the middle, with a little, wiggly tadpole tail hanging off it was Brian's. Entire. Eyeball.

"See," Waylon said, greener than usual, "that looks nothing like an olive."

Fletcher gagged. Therapy was no longer going to be strong enough. She needed a lobotomy.

Blood gushed from Brian's head, but there must have been so much epinephrine coursing through his body that he hadn't seemed to notice yet. Through gritted teeth, he growled and pulled the tranquilizer's scope up to his face, pinching his eye closed to take aim.

Which didn't work. For obvious eyeless reasons.

Peeling his remaining eye back open, Brian bypassed the sight altogether and stalked across the room to press the gun against Fletcher's chest this time. She was no expert, but a tranquilizer dart directly to the heart sounded a lot like sure and sudden death.

Also, this close, his oozing eye hole made her seriously want to vomit.

"Get away from her." Waylon ditched the pool cue, squaring his shoulders for a fight.

Despite the blood pouring from his leg, Other Brian found the strength to waddle into Waylon's path. "Stop right there. We've got direct orders from the boss. She comes with us."

He pressed his hand against Waylon's chest, but Waylon flexed his fingers back until Other Brian pleaded for mercy with shallow breaths. Mercy Waylon gave him, whether he deserved it or not. Other Brian wilted, cradling his hand, and Waylon stepped over him. "Sorry if I wasn't clear. I said, get away from her."

"Come any closer, and I shoot," Brian seethed.

He pressed the gun tighter against Fletcher's chest. It would have been plenty to make a girl nauseated on its own, but combining that with trying to avoid looking at the way his eyelid flopped around aimlessly without an eyeball to protect really put the whammy on Fletcher's digestive system.

Thankfully, Waylon halted. She exhaled with gratitude. All he had to do was stop moving, and she was ready to sing his praises. The bar for men was so low.

"You really don't have to do this," Fletcher said to Brian's forehead. She couldn't convince herself to look into his eye. "You said it yourself. Bertram wanted me alive. If you kill me, why wouldn't he kill you two right after?"

Brian glared, uncompromising. "Because the team would never hit our CTR goals without us."

"News flash, buddy," Waylon said. "If you're gone, the company will just hire another naive new grad they can pay less and work more."

Other Brian, from his heap on the floor, whined, "That's not true. We're supposed to scale our team soon. I talked to Molly about it already."

"We came *here* to get promoted to hiring managers," Brian said.

"And how's that going for you?" Fletcher asked.

Brian crushed the tip of the gun against her sternum, hard enough to bruise. "That's enough out of both of you."

He was going to shoot her, that much was clear. Acting on instinct and shaky adrenaline, Fletcher pushed her palms flat against the barrel, straining against the metal to point it up and up and up. Brian's finger, heavy on the trigger, pulled.

The shot zipped toward the ceiling. Speared through the chandelier. Glass shattered around them, raining sparkling crystals. Lights twinkled. The chandelier swayed uneasily—a creak, a groan.

Then she saw it: the link the dart broke on its way up. A sliver of delicate chain, precariously near the top, had been severed. The light fixture didn't stand a chance.

Suddenly, something smacked into Fletcher's chest. Not something. Someone. Waylon. He tackled her, arms wrapping around her torso. Her pith helmet flew off, somewhere in the vicinity of the fireplace. But instead of slamming her head against the ground and smashing all of her bones beneath the wide expanse of his chest, Waylon pivoted mid-fall, rotating so that she landed on him.

For a second, maybe two, they stared at each other. Chests heaving. The smell of mint and tobacco on his breath, summer grape on hers. His eyes swirled the same shade as the seas around Lydell, like his birthright was etched into his DNA.

The kind of details a person noticed right before she got crushed to death by a light fixture. When time slowed down and your seconds stretched like saltwater taffy, capturing every last sweet memory.

Of course, Waylon would be hers. Irritating her into the afterlife.

The crash of the chandelier, crystals breaking into smithereens, brought Fletcher back to reality. One that did not and would not ever involve dissecting the color of Waylon's eyes, because she wasn't dead.

She wasn't dead. She was—

Touching Waylon. Everywhere. A knee slotting between his legs. His arms banding around her waist. Their hearts beating out of sync, their lungs out of rhythm.

The sudden knowledge of all the ways their bodies pressed together put Fletcher at serious risk of spontaneous combustion.

She heaved herself upright. Standing, she felt each step crunch with cut glass. A puddle of dark blood inched toward her heels. Dim without the chandelier, the room had lost its former charm. It took her vision a few blinks to adjust.

All that ornate crystal easily weighed a hundred pounds, and Brian hadn't moved in time. His body crumpled beneath the fixture, too still.

"Oh shit." Other Brian paled. Whether that was from the shock or the blood loss, Fletcher couldn't tell.

She and Waylon moved toward the door, but unfortunately, they'd been so distracted by trying not to die, neither of them noticed the commotion had drawn an audience.

"What do we have here?" Bertram's baritone drove a stake of dread through Fletcher's chest.

The SVP of Marketing waddled into the study, vision glazed red. He was a forty-eight-year-old unmarried marketing exec, but the way his face morphed with calibrated ire was more Trained Assassin than Big SEO Nerd. (Although his striped tie and boring button-down screamed *desk job.*)

Behind him stalked Deepti. Clothed, blessedly. Whatever alliance they'd struck, Fletcher doubted it would last any longer than Deepti's other flings. The CFO was nothing if not efficient. She got what she wanted and cut her losses.

Either way, Deepti planted her feet in front of the door, holding her ground and also a Taser.

Fletcher shot Waylon a look that was supposed to convey a general sense of dismay and exponentially growing panic, but he'd trained his gaze on Deepti and her pink stun gun as if trying to gauge how badly something bedazzled could hurt. (A lot, obviously.) It wasn't the kind of weapon Dyer would have lying around—it was the kind she'd stash in a leather purse. One she definitely knew how to wield in emergencies.

"We tried to stop them," Other Brian answered Bertram's lingering question pathetically, "but the chandelier . . . it fell."

"Disappointing," Bertram mused over Brian's lifeless shape as his protégé Wicked Witch of the Easted beneath the chandelier. "I hoped I'd be able to work with him for longer. Great ideas. Subpar execution."

He dipped inside a refrigerator, masqueraded behind two cabinet doors. Fished out a bowl of cleaned, tailless shrimp. Pink and slimy. Tossing a crustacean down the gullet, Bertram made a noise of satisfaction at the back of his throat. Out of the corner of her eye, Other Brian shrunk into himself, his stomach clawing toward his spine.

Bertram's beady eyes glanced between Waylon and Fletcher, Waylon and Fletcher. "I'll admit, I am surprised to see the two of you in cahoots," he said, pointing his half-eaten shrimp between them.

"We are not in cahoots!" she said. At the same time, Waylon groaned, "Cahoots? Really?"

The light from the fridge was blocked momentarily as Bertram reached back inside for a glass bottle filled with red. He shook some into a dish and swiped his next shrimp through it. Relishing the taste, he slurped all the sauce off the crustacean before biting into its flesh.

Across the room, Other Brian retched. Dragging himself off the floor, he limped toward the exit. "I'm sorry—I need to—" Another gag. "Get out."

"You don't like cocktail sauce?" Bertram asked, but he didn't wait for an answer. With two unstabbed legs, he moved much quicker than Other Brian. Bertram daubed the shrimp in his vat of ketchup and horseradish, dangling it before his direct report.

Fletcher started toward them, "No, he can't! He's—"

But it was too late. Bertram poked the sauce-drenched shellfish between Other Brian's pursed lips. His palm clamped over Other Brian's mouth, refusing to let him spit it out. Other Brian's hands found his throat, terror rearing in his eyes. Images of Other Brian's untouched prawn on last night's dinner plate shot through Fletcher's mind. Soon, his lips would swell, the skin stretched taut.

"Allergic," Fletcher said, deflating against the bar top.

Her brain was firing desperate neurons. Yes, Other Brian was responsible for aiding and abetting an attempted murder. And yes, that murder was supposed to be hers.

But she also knew there was an EpiPen in the emergency kit in the kitchen. She'd ordered one specifically for Other Brian and his overactive immune system.

She didn't want to sit here, helpless, and watch him die.

Waylon hurled toward Deepti, fist-fighting the Taser out of her grasp, but Fletcher couldn't move. Her body felt frozen and on fire at the same time. Her muscles seized with fear. She didn't register Betram reaching toward her until he had a vise grip on her shoulder.

A choking noise came from Other Brian's direction that Fletcher had to look away from—both for the preservation of her own sanity and because Betram's fist yanked her neck at an unsustainable angle. The joints in her spine popped, stretched, strained.

She bit down the begging whimper that threatened to spill out her mouth. Realistically, she'd be more than willing to grovel for her life, but she'd rather not have to.

Waylon pivoted his attention and tried to reach for her, but the marketer knotted his knuckles in her hair and said, "You want to watch her die? Take another step."

Tension rippled down Waylon's neck. "You know, I never was any good at doing what I'm told."

"No time to learn like the present," Bertram said, his words slurring with passion. "Fletcher and I are going to come to a little agreement. And if not, I'll have to get rid of her."

Waylon crept forward, testing the waters. "You won't."

Oh, thanks. Call his bluff when it was her life on the line.

Fletcher imagined Bertram's eyes narrowing as his grip pulled against her roots. "You don't believe me?"

"I believe you. I just won't let it happen."

He really had to stop vowing to protect her because it could too easily be misconstrued for kindness. Unfortunately, any heroism was short-lived. Deepti scooped her stun gun off the ground and jammed it into Waylon's back. He hit the floor with a *thunk* and a groan.

Fletcher had to figure this one out for herself.

Everything she knew about Bertram felt just out of reach. That could have something to do with the way her vertebrae sounded like a beloved breakfast cereal at the moment. *Think, Fletcher. Think.*

She knew his belly was putting too much pressure on the buttons of his collared shirt and that he should have invested some of his annual bonus in a cologne that didn't smell like a seventh-grade locker room. She knew he'd been in charge of the Marketing department for a handful of years, but he wanted more. They all wanted more. That was why they came here.

Calendar pages populated behind her eyes as his finger grip tightened. Meetings with Dyer, did he have any?

No.

No, the schedule had been empty for weeks. Bertram had barely been at work. His out-of-office autoresponder flashed through her brain. She'd seen him on the LaGuardia airstrip for the first time since . . .

Fletcher wound her elbow forward and thrust it into his abdomen. Right up against the still-soft stitches from his gallbladder surgery.

Bertram moaned, immediately releasing her, and Fletcher scrambled forward. She braced herself against the bar as the ache in her neck radiated down her shoulders, her rib cage. There was no time to be relieved. Wild fury lit in Bertram's dark brown eyes.

Waylon's arms quaked as he struggled off the parquet floor, and Deepti lurked behind him, all too ready to shock him again. Beyond him lay a very squished Brian and a very puffy Other Brian, both of them very, very dead.

Fletcher and Waylon would be next.

Then, the study's door swung open to an alarmed attorney, and Melv blinked unwittingly at the horror movie he'd walked into. "What the hell is happening here?"

His entrance was all the distraction Deepti needed to make the first move, lunging toward a weak-kneed Waylon. Electricity zapped. Before she could make contact with his skin, Waylon drove his elbow into the crook of Deepti's arm and pried the stun gun from her grasp. The Taser flew across the room, landing in a rum puddle with an igniting spark.

Flames burst, hot and hungry. With the amount of liquor in this room . . .

Waylon clearly had the same thought. He snatched Fletcher out of the fire's path as it snaked toward the bar. As soon as cinders hit the bottles, everything exploded in a blood-orange blast. Smoke cloaked the room quickly in a choking gray.

Deepti barged past Melv, whose horrified trance had lodged him squarely in the doorway. She raced down the hall and out of sight. Her movement jostled Melv back to himself. "Everyone, follow me."

"It's okay," Fletcher said, scratchy against the fumes. "The sprinklers should turn on soon."

Smoke detectors wailed and sprinklers ejected from the ceiling, but the omnipresent robotic voice that would cameo in all of Fletcher's future nightmares snarked: "Fire protection system deactivated. Sprinklers disabled."

"Never mind."

Thanks a lot, Dyer.

Melv and his marathon-running lungs were far more prepared for this than Fletcher and her expired-gym-membership lungs. His fast clip had Fletcher cursing her choice of heels.

"Do I even want to know what just happened in there?" he asked.

"No," Waylon and Fletcher answered in unison.

Smoke ribboned into the hall. Booze and burnt flesh were a terrible combo. When Fletcher glanced over her shoulder, Bertram's silhouette faded as the soot thickened.

"We lost Bertram and Deepti," she said between hacking coughs.

"Good," Waylon muttered.

A fair response given all the recent maiming and Tasing and asphyxiating. Unfortunately, Fletcher's overactive conscience failed to get the memo. "If the fire spreads . . ."

"I'll worry about the others," Melv coughed, already turning back. "You two get out while you can. Go. *Go!*"

How they ended up in the garage was a blur of adrenaline, from the chase and the warmth of Waylon's fingers against her skin in equal measure. The next thing Fletcher knew was the crank of the garage door opening, the nectar-sweet breeze lifting the loose hair off her neck but not strong enough to mask the scent of gasoline.

Someone had been here already.

An engine revved as the only Jeep speared across the grasslands. Jackie's silk scarf billowed behind her as she veered across the savanna, kicking up dust. Fletcher's countdown ticking, ticking, ticking.

Waylon snagged their backpacks from a cabinet he'd hid them in. He could have left without her, could have stranded her at the estate and stolen Carlotta's master key for himself. And instead, he . . . came back for her.

They started running as Lydell Manor burned. She couldn't help but think it wasn't just the estate on fire—it was her future going up in smoke.

But if Fletcher didn't get off this island, she wouldn't have a future at all.

14

Fletcher felt worse than she did after a brunch with bottomless mimosas.

She and Waylon cleared as much distance as they could, leaving the burning estate behind them in a titian blaze. Grass scratched at her bare legs as they ran. Images of the afternoon replayed over and over and over again in her head. Between the blood crusted on her knuckles and the stench of smoke on the wind, her stomach finally waved the white flag into the sagebrush.

Here, under the last drops of sun, while she puked her guts out to the soundtrack of the afternoon savanna with Waylon hovering nearby, she was resolutely certain this trip deserved the gold medal for All-Time Worst Company Retreat.

In the manor, fighting for her life, the panic had been staved off by all the sprinting and slicing and sword fighting. The safari seemed downright serene in comparison. But as the adrenaline faded, every horrifying reality sank in.

Fletcher uncapped a wine cellar Evian to splash her face and rinse out her mouth. Her body sagged against her bones, palms planted in the hard dirt while she willed the world to quit spinning.

"Come on, Wilderness Barbie, we can go—"

"Don't," Fletcher said. She couldn't decide exactly what she didn't want him to do. Come closer? Speak to her? Existing was pushing it.

"There's a river down a quarter mile or so if you want to go get cleaned up, and we can set up camp for the night."

The thought of washing at least three different people's blood off her skin felt like a privilege too luxurious to entertain without visual proof of said river. Especially since there had been no shortage of bathtubs at the manor they'd been forced to evacuate.

"I don't want to bathe in a river, Waylon." Her fuse had been chipped and chipped and chipped away all day long. "I don't want to sleep on the ground. I don't want to have to wonder if you or Rick or Sheila are going to slit my throat in the middle of the night. I *wanted* to curl up in the capybara room and fall asleep on one-thousand-thread-count sheets and wake up tomorrow morning to find out that this whole thing was just a jet lag–induced night terror. I *wanted* this trip to be normal, so I could network my way into a promotion, that way I could maybe actually be able to afford a place to live when I go back to the city. But I can't. Because all of this is real, and the manor just *caught on fire*."

"At least no one's chasing us."

While it was true—Fletcher had briefly spotted the remaining members of the C-suite and Sales darting in opposite directions away from the estate—she wasn't in the mood to hear it. Even after the certified shit show of an afternoon they'd had, Waylon managed to sound unaffected. One hand was shoved into his pants pocket, and the other wrapped around the strap of his camping bag. All his emotions zipped up nicely behind a Cool Guy Facade.

It spiked her blood pressure. *He* spiked her blood pressure.

"Me," Fletcher corrected. "Bertram was chasing *me*. Yet again, you get off scot-free because you're Waylon Cartwright and you made it exceptionally clear you don't want anything to do with this company."

"Brian did try to strangle me." Waylon speared onward, apparently content that Fletcher wasn't going to pass out—or content to leave her there anyway.

Aggravated, she tailed him. "In a fit of passion! Bertram's vendetta against me was totally premeditated. He thinks an ambitious woman who wants to climb the ranks is more dangerous than you, and you inherited the whole freaking island."

"And its structures," he said, bending back the grasses to carve a path forward. "Including the manor. So, when you think about it, I just took a major loss."

"Oh, I'm *so sorry* you'll have to rebuild a *wing* of the *mansion* on your *private island*. Thank god for generational wealth. I would have hated for you to face real hardships. You're half the reason we're in this mess anyway."

"Am I, now?"

It was hard to look as mad as she felt while bobbling on unsteady heels, ankles like a newborn calf. "*Yes*. This morning, there were sixteen of us. Now, half those people are gone, all because *your* dad got some evil, mutant bee in his bonnet that *Ratatouille*'d him into creating his own personal *Hunger Games*."

"It was probably a tracker jacker then, instead of a bee, huh?"

"What do you know about *The Hunger Games*? You probably rooted for the Capitol!"

Waylon peeked over his shoulder, smirking even as Fletcher scowled.

"I'm serious, Waylon. I mean, this is—this is—"

Verbalizing it made it harder to breathe. Made it real. Nothing about Lydell felt like it should exist anywhere near reality—not the juxtaposition of the estate's brocade curtains and grass cloth wallpapers, not the IRL *Zoo Tycoon* experience, and definitely not a truce with Waylon.

"A disaster," Waylon said as the banks of the river came into view.

Serpentine blues etched into the otherwise neutral landscape. At this bend, the water was shallow and glistened beneath the late-day glow, but it wound into the jungle, widening and deepening as it went.

Fletcher kicked off her shoes, sludgy river mud squidging between her toes. She stomped for good measure. "Do you have any idea what this trip meant for me? I get four, maybe five, hours of sleep each night because there's always insurance to file for the house in Amsterdam or emails to draft to the *Jet-Setter* Asia team. My salary's barely enough to keep my head above water, and what extra money I do have is spent on shitty twenty-eight-dollar Manhattans from your equally shitty bar just to pretend I have a social life. There is so much instant ramen in my body that if you cut me open, I'd bleed out Maruchan Roast Chicken flavor packets. And when I get back home—*if* I get back home—there won't be a home to go to. I'll have to get a job at the department store it gets bulldozed into and sleep in the employee lounge on some horrible leather sofa."

She couldn't help it. She started pacing. Frustration bubbled out of her.

"I came here so that maybe, just maybe, I could have the chance to do what I love at the magazine of my dreams. It was supposed to be different. Fun. A chance to actually participate, instead of looking in from the outside. I thought I'd wake up this morning and eat so much smoked salmon I'd get mercury poisoning. I thought I'd suntan and shmooze and sip my little drinks without worrying that assholes like you would judge me for having the same taste in drinks as a newly minted twenty-one-year-old fintech bro. Instead, I had to watch *my boss* get *eaten by lions* and send everyone into a feral rampage."

Fletcher gulped down a breath. When she finally had the wherewithal to look at Waylon, his lips flattened into a firm line. His Adam's apple bobbed once, then again. A tint of real emotion cracked through his usual veneer. Unwanted sympathy panged through Fletcher's chest.

"My boss got eaten by lions," she said again, quieter this time as the gravity of it settled. "But he was your dad. Waylon, I'm—"

"Don't say sorry." He shucked off the tote and his backpack. "It's fucked-up, but my dad would have loved this, and you know it."

She could have never imagined the horrors he was subjecting them to now, but Dyer Cartwright had always been a man with a mission. He always had the right cards in his hand and knew exactly when to play them.

Stranding his only son on an island with fourteen rabid employees with no time to grieve, no time to process, and forced to play a role in a game he didn't consent to wasn't the mark of a loving father. Waylon watched his dad get ripped to shreds by a pride of lions that had been imported solely to hunt for sport. There was nothing unfucked-up about that.

But that was Dyer. Entertainer extraordinaire. The life—and death—of the party.

"I'm not sorry for him," she said, daring a step closer. "I'm sorry for you."

Waylon's stare hardened. "I don't need Fletcher Spence to feel sorry for me. I'm used to my dad disappointing me. But you. You shouldn't even be here."

Oh.

Days since Waylon Douchebaggery Incidents: 0.

Fletcher shook off whatever residual Midwestern niceties threatened to dismantle her hard-earned career and crossed her arms. "I'm well aware of how you feel about my attendance. Believe me. Now, if you'll excuse me, I'm going to take off this sensory nightmare of a dress, clean every inch of my body, and pretend you aren't here."

His hand lashed out, wrapping around her wrist. "Fletcher, stop. I've been trying to tell you that you don't deserve to be here."

Fletcher blinked. Indignance reared in her chest. Spiked and ugly, like a porcupine wearing jeggings. "Wow. Got it."

"That's not—"

"No, I think it is." Fletcher shook herself loose.

"What I'm trying to say is that you don't deserve *this*. Not because you aren't smart enough or hardworking enough or talented enough, but because you are. Because this job, this company, *my dad* was always going to take everything you have and give nothing back." His gaze met hers, fierce and unyielding. Suddenly, she wasn't sure if she was hot from the sun or something else. "You deserve *better*."

A sharp laugh carved its way out. "Is that so?"

For once, Waylon's tough exterior faltered. His brow didn't furrow so much as it crinkled, scrunched together like a bag of Doritos crammed into the break room trash can. Fletcher didn't buy it for a second.

"What?" he asked.

He inched closer, but Fletcher waded deeper. Cool water lapped at her ankles, her calves. "Smart? Hardworking? I seem to recall you had a few other choice adjectives for me the first time we met. 'Pathetic.' 'Embarrassing.' Ring a bell?"

Tears welled in her eyes, and she wasn't sure how to stop them. Three years they'd been waiting to be shed. When she couldn't trust herself not to let them fall, she turned her back to Waylon and tried to get a fucking grip.

"You had a few for me, too. 'Entitled.' 'Arrogant,'" he said, close enough now for her to feel his presence at her back. Her pulse ratcheted faster as his fingers found the dress's zipper at the nape of her neck. "I've revisited that night in my head so many times I've lost count."

Not a single muscle in her body moved—not even her heart. She was definitely going to need a defibrillator. Just when she thought she glimpsed the pearly gates, the zipper's descent stalled below her shoulder blades, and Waylon's hands fell away.

Fletcher worked hard to commit important details to memory—Dyer's pill regimen, when to schedule deep cleans of the international properties, how to fix the fax machine on the sixtieth floor when it started death-rattling—but she didn't have to work hard to remember that night. It had been stamped on her prefrontal cortex, forcing her to recall it every time she spotted that unreturnable green dress at the back of her closet.

Not once did she imagine it haunted him the same way.

"I hated doing those events," he said. "Everyone's stressed, the expectations are so high, and nobody actually gives a shit about the charity. It's all for show. And I . . . Well, I'd been avoiding my dad, knowing I was going to get another mind-numbing lecture about what it means to be a Cartwright and how I was *tarnishing the company name* because I didn't want to take the CMO job he offered me. And then, this redheaded woman walked in."

Fletcher's jaw fastened itself shut, afraid to hear the tremble in her voice if she spoke.

"I could have punched whoever made her cry," he said.

"You didn't even know me then." And the unspoken: *You didn't know how much we'd hate each other.*

"I didn't. I was certain we'd never met. This was not the kind of woman easily forgotten. Once the tears stopped, you had this megawatt smile. Defiant and determined. I knew right then that you were too good for my dad and his precious company. Too eager to prove yourself. Cartwright Media would destroy you."

"You were wrong about me. I have what it takes to make it in this industry, and—this job was everything I'd ever wanted. You almost ruined it." Fletcher twisted to face him. A scalding cauldron of emotion churned in her stomach. Vulnerability, self-pity, outright rage. He'd seen her, understood her, and still tried to define her choices without her consent.

Waylon's face sank lower until it was in line with hers, lashes long and thick. This close, she could see his heartbeat in the veins of his neck, right below the sharp edge of the jaw softened by stubble. He cleared his throat and said, "And for that, I'm sorry. But you were wrong about me, too. You said I'd always be a Cartwright, but that night, my dad had Melv write up a no-contact agreement. As far as my dad was concerned, I wasn't a Cartwright anymore. Not until the diagnosis. It took dying for him to invite me back to Lydell. Back into his life at all. So, maybe we're even."

She didn't want to believe him, and she didn't want to be even. She wanted to stay mad at him for the rest of her life and then some, her skeletal middle finger flipped in the general direction of his coffin. But some traitorous part of her heart decalcified, the hard shell chipping off. A prickly feeling gathered in the cave of her chest.

For a moment, his apology hung unanswered in the air. She almost accepted it, but the rumble of an elephant stampede in the distance reminded them exactly where they were. And why.

Waylon said, "I think this is the part where you get undressed and pretend I'm not here."

He also decided now was a good time to take his shirt off. Objectively, it was easier to ignore his presence when she wasn't face-to-face with *that*. Sunlight dripped off the planes of his chest—way too tan for a New York November—and the sight of it puddled in Fletcher's core.

"You, um." Fletcher swallowed. "You also have to pretend that *I'm* not here. Equal opportunity and all that."

Something flared in Waylon's eyes. Like he could tell the way her heart rate kicked up and liked being responsible for it.

"As you wish."

And then he proceeded to drop his pants to his ankles with no regard for her presence at all. Fletcher should have, probably, maybe, turned away sooner than she did. But for a long second, she just stared at the gray elastic of Waylon's boxer briefs, the way they hugged his thighs, the length of him at the center.

What was she doing? That was *Waylon* she was eyeballing.

One nice comment wasn't enough to forgive him for the psychological damage he'd unknowingly inflicted for the last 1,155 days. She turned then and fought the urge to forcibly shake out her limbs. Reaching behind her, she found her zipper carefully positioned within reach. Right where he'd left it for her.

The river was cool against her skin as she waded up to her shoulders, and if she closed her eyes, she could almost imagine she wasn't ten feet from her dead boss's naked son. She floated, letting her skin wrinkle and the daylight drain. Today had been eight million years long, and she was glad to see its end.

A groan of relief parted her lips. Fletcher couldn't help it.

Behind her, in a plane of existence Fletcher was refusing to validate with her cognitive awareness, Waylon chuckled.

Fletcher didn't respond, but she did sink lower, blowing bubbles out of her nose.

"I think this is the first time I've ever seen you relax," he said, his voice distant.

Fletcher snorted. "What happened to ignoring each other? You aren't supposed to be seeing me at all."

"I could sense it in your aura."

"Didn't take you as a big aura guy."

A clipped laugh. "Joplin's responsible for that one."

Fletcher's stomach lurched with envy at her colleague's name, thinking about how they clung to each other in the pool, the nicknames, the way his name sounded in her mouth—

Bitter guilt clogged Fletcher's system. Joplin was *dead*. She couldn't be jealous of a dead woman. Regardless of whether or not that dead woman had a romantic history with Waylon.

Shaking off the thought, Fletcher waded toward the banks and scavenged around her backpack for something—anything—to use as a towel. Cocktail napkins from the wine cellar it was.

To his credit, Waylon kept the toned expanse of his back to her the whole time she clipped her bra and shimmied into the spare set of clothes she'd packed—a cream-and-black tweed skirt, a chambray shirt, and a slightly-more-practical-than-heels pair of slingback flats. She offered him the same decency when Waylon buttoned a short-sleeved linen shirt, forcibly paying as little attention as possible to the way the water sluiced through the curves of his biceps, followed the veins of his forearms.

Tragically, noticing Waylon was growing increasingly harder to avoid.

Beneath the umbrella canopy of an acacia tree, their glampsite came together quickly: twin temperature-regulating sleeping bags; silk pillowcases for memory foam pillows that sprung out of capsules; and a solar lantern with USB charging ports.

Fletcher plugged her phone in as she sank into the fleece folds of her sleeping bag, snug despite the evening wind picking up with the first clouds on the ink-dark horizon. Still no service. She fired off a string of messages to Ford anyway, just out of routine. Although they normally discussed the slope of Ariana Grande's ponytail or which vegetable best embodied them as a person, tonight's messages read:

THIS IS A SHIT SHOW

THE SHITTIEST OF SHOWS

I want to go home

If I squint really hard at the horizon, I'm pretty sure I see you taking body shots off a guy with a handlebar mustache in Seychelles. Hope you're having more fun than me.

BUT NOT TOO MUCH FUN

He would never read them. They'd sit, unsent on her phone with that annoying red exclamation point error forever. But she could pretend.

"I don't think those texts are ever reaching that boyfriend of yours," Waylon said as he knelt on his sleeping bag.

"I think Ford's out of my league." That earned an amused huff. "But no, um. Kent and I broke up."

Broke up didn't accurately reflect the way things ended. She was single—he was in denial. And, if she was honest, he had been for a good long while. Their relationship had been dead in the water for ages—months, years? She'd just been too scared to admit it.

For the last three weeks, she'd been pointedly ignoring his calls.

If she hadn't been so dead set on proving to everyone she belonged on this trip, it would have been too easy to fall back into their old patterns. The same routine of trying to please everyone except herself.

"I thought it was serious," Waylon said.

"It was for him." There was an itch at the base of her throat she couldn't stop scratching. Sourness cut through her chest. "Actually, we got in a fight because he tried to tell me not to come on this trip."

Waylon considered this. "Who among us hasn't tried to talk our girlfriends out of crashing an international company retreat turned cage fight?"

Fletcher hummed. "I didn't think you were the girlfriend type."

The moment snagged and unraveled. Finally, he said, "Not lately, I'm not."

"Not since Eliza?"

Waylon's guard bolted into place in an instant. Fletcher watched it happen, the suave, charismatic character he played so easily being shuttered inside hurricane windows. Something cold, distant took form instead.

Normally, she'd relish the chance to dig under his skin, festering there like a splinter. Under the first dust of stars, it didn't have the same effect.

"Kent wanted me to be his wife," she blurted. "We were high school sweethearts, and I guess he always thought moving to New York was a phase I needed to, I don't know, get out of my system. All he ever wanted was to get married in a little white chapel and drag me back to the same life I had growing up. A farm, a couple of well-oiled crop-dusting planes and combines, four kids, a hundred acres, and a tire swing."

She didn't know why she said it, except maybe it was easier to talk about Kent than the events of the last twenty-four hours. And if she and Waylon were going to keep up this tentative truce, being on speaking terms helped.

Waylon laughed, bright and alive once more. "Let me guess, that didn't fit in your five-year plan?"

"Ten-year, actually." She sucked down a couple steadying breaths to keep her stomach from rioting again. There was nothing *wrong* with little white chapels. But Fletcher had always been more of a *destination elopement with a hot air balloon send-off* girl herself. Kent never understood that. "Maybe I should've listened."

A sharp inhale. "To his marriage proposal?"

"To his insistence that this job is a soul-sucking whirlpool of depravity that will lead to nothing and no one."

Waylon's eyebrows did that infuriating thing. A breath *whoosh*ed out of him that said, *Well, was he wrong?*

After that, silence. She couldn't bear to look at Waylon, knowing he was looking back at her. Unsure of what he'd find.

Somewhere in the cloying darkness, an owl screeched, and the noise had Fletcher burrowing deeper into her sleeping bag.

"We should take turns keeping watch," Waylon said. A yawn tugged at the corners of his lips, but he didn't address it. "I'll go first."

"Oh my god. Do my ears deceive me? Does Waylon Cartwright have a plan?" Fletcher said, eyelids heavy.

The stars above them spun like snow globe glitter or a December night's first flurries. As sleep sunk its claws into her, Fletcher couldn't quite name the stir of warmth in her chest, but she knew that sleeping next to Waylon Cartwright was the safest she'd felt in years.

15

THREE YEARS EARLIER

Champagne bubbles fizzed as featherlight laughter drifted to the ballroom's ceiling. A jazz band filled any lulls in conversation, crooning nostalgic melodies. No one at the Cartwright Media Annual Gala for Impact had maimed themselves with an hors d'ouevre skewer, bored out of their skulls. Yet.

By all accounts, Fletcher should have been smiling.

She wasn't smiling.

As she wove through the crowd, there were approximately 120 seconds before she lost the battle against her tear ducts. Her boss, a media mogul named Dyer Cartwright, was deep in conversation with the editor in chief of *Travel + Leisure*. Or was it *Condé Nast Traveler*? She couldn't keep anyone straight. Every ultrawhite grin blurred together until Fletcher's stomach churned and her head throbbed. Regardless, the conversation would buy her at least a three-minute weep.

Either her vision was tunneling, or the guests were purposefully closing in on her, trying to incite a panic attack. Planning this event was the first big chance Dyer had offered her to prove herself. She'd extinguished approximately thirty-six hundred fires today, and the night had only just begun.

First, the hotel accidentally double-booked, so their ballroom had been mistakenly decorated for a bat mitzvah. Her fairy godmother was a Taskrabbit named Pietro who swapped the centerpieces in record time.

Then, the caterers accidentally served shellfish on the allergen-safe table. (The last thing Fletcher needed was someone dying at her event. Imagine the headlines: *Shrimp Cocktail Blunder Makes Executive Assistant Accessory to Murder.*)

To make matters worse, her speaker canceled. The bestselling author slash motivational speaker slash philanthropist she'd pulled every string to secure for tonight—gone. According to the email from her assistant, the author had "a last-minute conflict" but was "honored to be considered for the event" and "wishes Fletcher the best." Pretty words, but Fletcher knew the signs of a too-stressed assistant when she saw it. She was one.

But this, the email notification waiting to be opened on her phone . . .

Make that sixty seconds until Sobfest.

The music shifted into something slower. A swan song if Fletcher had ever heard one. She made it to the coat check closet before allowing herself to read the full email. At least there her hopes and dreams would shatter while surrounded by cashmere and microsuede.

The email was from a reporter. Here. Hoping to get a comment from someone at Cartwright Media about Dyer's party boy son—or, more specifically, Waylon Cartwright's recent whirlwind engagement to a supermodel. Dyer had been plenty forward about his intentions for tonight's press coverage and absolutely none of it was to revolve around his son's messy personal life out of fear of how it might tank the company's reputation.

Fletcher hadn't even met Waylon yet. He'd ghosted her every email, and he failed to RSVP to tonight's gala, but if reporters were snooping around, hoping to catch wind of something unsavory to print in Page Six, Dyer wouldn't be pleased.

The first tear seemed reluctant to fall despite Fletcher having the foresight to wear waterproof mascara tonight. Once it dribbled over her chin and onto her event binder, there was no stopping the downpour. Every exhausted, overworked cell in her body shuddered with the world's quietest cryfest.

"What's wrong?"

"Nothing's wrong!" she chirped before even fully registering where the voice had come from. The lie was a sticky knob of peanut butter in her throat. Where would she even start?

The tag on her dress had been digging into her skin for the better part of an hour, and she couldn't rip it out because then she wouldn't be able to return it tomorrow. She *had* to be able to return it tomorrow in order to afford rent. (The dress was a stunning emerald jacquard, but not stunning enough to lose the only studio apartment in her budget where she didn't have to room with rats.)

Her boyfriend had bailed. So not only was she completely underwater, she was also dateless. Kent was supposed to fly in from Nebraska this morning, their first time seeing each other since Fletcher moved to New York City after college graduation. They'd been together for seven years, ever since being paired for a lab in eleventh-grade chemistry class, and had gone to the same local university. Things were . . . *fine*. Long distance was always going to be an adjustment. She was going to visit him. He was going to visit her. But getting hired at Cartwright Media had thrown a wrench in her plans to fly out for the fall harvest, and now, it was two weeks before

Christmas and the biggest night of her career. She already knew he didn't approve of her job, but she thought at the very least he supported *her*. Deep down, she knew Kent thought New York City was only temporary. An inconvenient, expensive detour on the inevitable road trip to housewifedom.

And now . . . *this!* At any moment, she was certain Dyer would ask for her resignation letter. She'd been his executive assistant for three months—three months of dry cleaning and scheduling and event planning, all culminating in tonight. A night Fletcher could barely hold together.

A better question would be, What *wasn't* wrong?

More important, Who was asking it?

Fletcher blinked away the darkness of the coat closet and the surprise of someone else infringing upon *her* hiding spot. The someone in question came into focus. Nursing a splash of bourbon, a man in the night's black-tie attire stretched out across a velvet ottoman. Wool tux, calf-leather oxfords, but the collar of his shirt had been unbuttoned and the ribbons of his bow tie spilled down his neck. He sported a mess of blond curls, so carelessly tangled Fletcher wondered if he'd styled it that way on purpose.

Or, she thought, blushing, *perhaps someone had left him like that.* As if she couldn't get any more pitiful tonight, had her sad, wet sniffles interrupted a coat closet tryst?

Eyes narrowed, the man asked, "Nothing? Really?"

Fletcher knew he could smell her bullshit—it reeked of major disappointment and Eau de Unemployed. She exhaled. "Just grabbing my coat."

On her way out, forever. Dyer could find her resignation letter on his desk first thing Monday morning. See? Even an overachiever when she was utterly failing. That had to count for something.

The man stood, and despite her heels, he loomed over her. His lips pressed into an amused tilt. "Let me help."

"That won't be necessary," Fletcher said in a rush. Where was his date? Hiding between the racks of Burberry jackets and Max Mara coats? "You're here to have a good time."

When he stepped closer, Fletcher caught a whiff of whiskey and cologne. He reached toward her, and, paralyzed, Fletcher mapped the arc of his hand as his fingertips brushed over her neck. His touch traveled upward, tracing the path of an errant tear that had carved down her cheek, until he tucked a loose strand of curled copper hair behind Fletcher's ear.

Breathing, it seemed, was completely out of the question. She swore she didn't recognize him, but there was something familiar about the gleam in his blue gaze. Dangerous, almost. For a moment, all she could do was stare.

A slow smile spread across his face, and this close, Fletcher could see the flush of a few drinks splashing over his cheeks. "And you aren't here to have a good time?"

Fletcher's soggy laugh surprised even her. "No, not me."

"I take it you're not a party crasher?"

"Executive assistant."

Understanding washed over his expression as he took another sip. "Hell of a job, planning a party you don't even get to enjoy."

The right thing to say sat idly on her tongue, dissolving like a sugar cube. *I'm grateful to get to work at Cartwright Media.* Or *It's a wonderful opportunity to work with Dyer Cartwright.* Or *I love my job, I love my job, I love my job*—the same mantra she'd been reciting to herself the last ninety mornings, praying someday she'd actually believe it.

That was the thing: She *wanted* to love it. Working at Cartwright Media was her dream job. Although, she'd always imagined her days flying between shooting locations, traveling the world with a camera around her neck, and seeing her name printed next to dazzling photographs of far-off places in *Jet-Setter* magazine. Instead, she was micromanaging a billionaire CEO who had called her Francesca at least three times in as many weeks.

Which was probably why what she actually said was: "Hell of a job is right."

The man laughed. The sound was intoxicating. If it could be bottled, Fletcher would drink it forever. "That bad, huh?"

"It's not—"

His cheek twitched, holding back a knowing grin.

"Okay, it's the worst!" Fletcher admitted with a punch-drunk giggle. Tipsy by osmosis. "I want to move to a new department so I can be a . . . Don't laugh, okay, but I want to be a travel photographer. Except I'm stuck in this horrible assistant job. I try so hard to be perfect, but I'm hardly able to tread water. I can't keep anyone straight. There are about six too many Brians on the team. My boss barely knows my name. I'm so busy *I* barely even know my name."

She hadn't said it out loud to anyone before.

Not to Dyer, should he get it in his head that he'd be better off with a less ambitious assistant who was happy to spend her days schlepping paperwork and planning charity galas. Not Kent, who would love nothing more than to hear how miserable the city made her, how delightfully not cut out for the Big Apple she was, and use it as ammunition to reel her back to the farm. And she certainly didn't make a habit of telling handsome strangers in coat closets her innermost thoughts.

He didn't laugh or lower his eyes with pity. All he said was, "And what is your name?"

"Fletcher Spence."

His gaze softened. "You could do it, Fletcher Spence."

Fletcher's eyebrows shot toward her hairline. "Do what?"

"Move to a new department. Become a photographer. Get everything you want."

There was something so genuine in his words that she believed him. It warmed her up, head to toe, like she'd downed the last of his bourbon. Suddenly, she couldn't remember the last time someone truly believed in her.

Some magnetic pull dragged Fletcher deeper into the man's orbit. He smelled like liquor and leather, tobacco and pine. His hand rested on her hip. Not too low, but not too high. Steadying. For a fraction of a second, she wondered what it would be like to kiss him.

He read her thoughts like the morning paper. Leaning down, tilting his head, splitting his lips. A breath apart. Maybe less.

Before the first brush, Fletcher arched back and blurted, "Wait! I'm sorry. I—I have a boyfriend."

The man's head cocked, but he stepped away. Studying her. This time, when he laughed, it was a cold wind. Sheepishness instantly replaced by stinging nettles. "Right. Of course."

What had she been thinking? She *hadn't* been thinking. That was the problem. This job had reduced her brain to a fine pulp. "I can't do—whatever this is. I love him."

Didn't she?

"Kind of like how you love your job?"

"Excuse me?"

A challenge manifested in the square of the man's shoulders, the set of his jaw. "You're crying in a closet, working a job you hate, and where's he?"

Nebraska, Fletcher thought with a grimace, hating the pinch of bitterness. Her skin prickled beneath her rental dress where the man's touch had glanced. Her tone turned defensive as she said, "You don't know him, and you don't know me."

"Don't I?" he asked. "It all seems pretty straightforward."

"What are you even doing here?" Fletcher crossed her arms around her binder in a feeble attempt to hold herself together. *Flustered* was an understatement.

"What everyone does at these things. Kissing people's asses and donating heaps of money to charity."

"I mean, *here*. In coat check."

He drank his bourbon to the dregs. "Hiding from my father."

She looked at the man again, really looked at him.

Tall. Handsome in a scruffy, I-don't-care-what-you-think way. But, in this light, he had a hint of Dyer's angular jawline and an all-too-familiar sense of entitlement.

The realization hit her like a glass of spilled champagne. "You're Waylon Cartwright."

"Guilty." He raised his empty glass in mock salute.

Embarrassment flamed over Fletcher's skin. Embarrassment and something hotter, angrier. "*You're* Waylon Cartwright."

One of his eyebrows lifted. "I am."

"You have a fiancée. And reporters watching your every move. *And* you ignored my RSVP, so you shouldn't even be here. And this—this is the most important night of my life. If you ruin tonight, I'm going to get fired . . ." Fletcher inched backward. "I can't get fired."

She had to get away from him. Immediately. But instead of grabbing her coat to make a fast break for downtown, Fletcher leveled her shoulders, clutched her event binder tighter, and pivoted toward the ballroom. With a deep breath, she pushed through the double doors and dived back into the fray.

She couldn't walk away from Cartwright Media. Not now. Not before she finished what she came here to do. Not until she got a byline.

But Waylon—Waylon could ruin everything. If he told his father what she'd said, Dyer would have her in an exit interview faster than she could say *Dry cleaning only.* He'd sit her in a middle seat on a flight back to Nebraska before they finished serving the canapés.

That couldn't happen. This was her one chance. She had to make herself indispensable. She'd work twice as hard. Three times. She'd learn every name. Memorize every calendar. Nothing would stop her from proving to herself and everyone else that she had what it took to succeed at Cartwright Media. Who needed sleep? Or three meals a day? Not Fletcher Spence.

Whatever Cartwright Media needed her to be, she would become. Right now, that was an executive assistant. But there would come a day when a spot on the *Jet-Setter* staff would be hers.

"Maybe I was wrong about you." Waylon's voice trailed after her, and she really wished it wouldn't.

"Unsurprising, given we met ten minutes ago," Fletcher cut back through gritted teeth as Waylon sidled up next to her with sloppy steps. She ironed a smile to her mouth like it belonged there. Like she was completely and totally unbothered by Waylon's presence.

His arm slung around her shoulder. Much too convivial a gesture for someone he'd briefly met among pea coats and scarves. With a whisper pressed close against her ear, he said, "You're just like everybody else. Dying to be close to the Cartwrights. Satisfied to let my dad push you around, deciding your life for you. Too afraid to go after what you really want. It's pathetic. Embarrassing."

"And you're better? You get everything you want handed to you, whether you deserve it or not. You're exactly as entitled and arrogant as everyone says you are." Fletcher extricated herself from his grasp. Her momentary lapse of judgment in the coat closet dissipated beneath the ballroom lights. She had a boyfriend back home and a job to do.

A flash stopped Fletcher in her tracks. The reporter. Thankfully, the khaki-clad journalist was currently preoccupied snapping photos of chatting socialites, but with the scene Waylon was starting, it wouldn't take long for his lens to point their way.

With a sharp spin, Fletcher one-eighty'd right into Waylon's chest. She shoved her binder against the buttons of his twill shirt. "You can't go over there. You. *Really*. Cannot go over there."

Waylon smirked. "I'd like to see you stop me."

He didn't slow. So, Fletcher pushed him harder.

Right into the champagne tower.

Crystal flutes crashed around him as Waylon slammed against the table. Soaking wet in the wreckage, Waylon scowled up at her. Next to her, a camera flashed. Again and again. The reporter whispered into his phone. Tomorrow, she'd surely see this on the front page.

Waylon lifted his hand, like he expected her to help him out of the mess. She ignored it, crouching next to him. "I won't always be an executive assistant," Fletcher spat. "But you will always, *always* be a Cartwright."

To her surprise, he laughed. A laugh that seared into some hidden corner of her brain, only to slither out in the darkest nights to torment her. Harsh and biting as a winter wind.

Dyer didn't mention the gala the next day or the day after. He greeted her every morning with a smile, and eventually, she became Fletcher instead of Francesca. It wasn't a miracle that she'd excelled and impressed, molding herself into the perfect assistant. It was short nights and second espressos and sheer determination.

As weeks passed and the tabloids went to press, the headlines boasted news of Waylon crashing the party (literally), dumping his fiancée, and a slew of subsequent scandals, each further solidifying that he was exactly as scumbaggy as Fletcher expected. Waylon didn't come into the office, and she didn't go looking for him. As far as she was concerned, running into him again in this life or the next would be too soon.

None of that changed the fact that on that December night, Waylon had seen her for exactly who she was when it felt like no one saw Fletcher at all.

16

Waylon snored. Loudly enough Fletcher worried it would give their campsite away. Fletcher seriously considered jotting a note to herself to contact a specialist to prescribe him a CPAP machine.

She had been wide-awake since her watch shift started an hour ago. Then, it had still been night black, but now the day's first golden rays speared through the blue dawn. In the early-morning quiet, she did what she did best: prepared.

With the map from the cigar lounge spread out in front of her and the lantern turned to its lowest setting, she traced a path from the river's banks through the jungle.

The staff building had been buried so deep in the trees no guest would ever accidentally spot it. It wasn't enough to be waited on hand and foot. The Cartwrights wanted to believe help appeared out of thin air and vanished all the same.

Although . . .

Her gaze lingered on Waylon's sleeping form, the way his sleeping bag balled up with knees pulled toward his chest. Gut twisting, she'd really have to reckon with the knowledge that it hadn't just been her scarred by their first meeting. They'd both hurt each other.

Maybe not all Cartwrights were cut from the same cloth.

His apology cycled through her head, genuine-sounding enough. Would it be so bad to forgive him? It *had* all worked out, hadn't it?

She hadn't kissed him.

She hadn't been fired.

She . . . was stranded on a private island and being drained of her life force by mutant mosquitoes while keeping watch at four a.m. because their coworkers might pop out of the woodwork to prison-shank her with an elephant tusk.

On second thought, she could stay mad.

Something rustled in the grass a few yards down. Frankly, Fletcher was surprised she heard it at all with Waylon snoozing nearby. At the very least, she'd sign him up for a Breathe Right Subscribe & Save. No other woman should ever have to listen to this.

Folding up the map, Fletcher tucked it back into her backpack and looped her fingers around the lantern's handle. What kind of animal was on the prowl at this time? It was too late for nocturnal creatures but too early for daylight predators, a liminal space where nothing bad could happen to her.

Was what she told herself to keep her heart from anxiously palpitating.

The noise grew closer, standing the hair on the back of Fletcher's neck upright. She waited, crouched behind the brush, her flats sinking into the wet banks. Sticking. The patent leather was better suited for Manhattan sidewalks than muddy savannas. She nearly lost a slingback, grabbing both sides of her leg to give a good tug, and barely recovered before face-planting into the damp earth.

"I hate you, business casual dress code," Fletcher grumbled.

Then she saw the culprit. A tire track through the mud. Two jagged lines carved across the river's wide banks. A few feet over, the grasses bent at odd angles.

Or, rather, something bent *them*.

Fletcher brought the lantern up by her face, seriously regretting not grabbing something stabbier before venturing off to confront the noise. The reeds swayed, whatever it was gaining ground and fast.

Two blinking eyes reflected the lantern light. A scream speared out of Fletcher before she could swallow it down.

But it wasn't an unknown predator. Fletcher came face-to-face with Jackie.

And she looked . . . like hell.

The editor in chief Fletcher knew was gone, replaced by a woman mad.

Mud caked her face, nearly masking the dark wells beneath her eyes and the way her lipstick smudged like a Batman villain. Yesterday's mascara left freckles on her cheeks. Her silk blouse had been positively shredded, sleeves reduced to ribbons. A familiar striped tie wrapped around her forehead, a blood-splotched tail draping over her shoulder.

Melv may have made sure the others escaped the estate before smoke inhalation killed them, but Jackie had clearly made sure Bertram didn't make it any farther.

"What are you doing?" Fletcher asked. It came out harsher than she'd truly intended, but in her defense she'd slept on the ground for a few measly hours; yesterday was objectively the worst day of her life; and clearly Jackie intended to make today just as bad, because she aimed the barrel of her pistol at Fletcher's forehead.

"Where is it?" Jackie asked, little more than a hiss.

Her finger curled around the gun's trigger. The red polish on her index fingernail had split. Fletcher broke a light sweat, but she couldn't decide if it was from the gunmetal or the botched manicure.

She'd never seen Jackie so unmade. The longer they spent on the island, the wilder she became. They needed to get off Lydell before she lost herself entirely. Which meant Fletcher needed the boat key, but . . .

"I'm working on it," she answered.

Jackie scowled, a guttural rumble coming through gnashed teeth. Just what every woman wanted to hear with a gun pointed at her skull. "Why is it taking so long?"

"The key wasn't at the estate, so—"

"Spence, was that you?" Waylon's sleep-heavy voice called.

Fletcher recognized the look in Jackie's eyes because she'd worn it herself when her name hadn't appeared on the Lydell invite list. *Betrayal.*

She knew what this must seem like to Jackie. Fletcher, a lying double agent. The key, probably already shoved in her pocket. Waylon, about to take Jackie's spot on the escape boat.

"What is *he* doing here?" Jackie stalked forward as if to hunt Waylon down and skin him alive, just like she did Bertram.

"Don't!" Fletcher said. Instinct took over, and she grabbed Jackie's arm. "He's with me."

"That much is obvious." Jackie's gun found its way back to Fletcher's temple. Lovely. "I thought we had an agreement, Miss Spence."

A few gulps of air and Fletcher regained her composure. She was Fletcher Spence. Competent, capable Fletcher. Always in control. She could handle this. Even if *this* was a head shot away from being vulture breakfast.

"We do. I'm working with—I'm *using* him."

Few things in this life did Jackie Caldera love more than using people to get what she wanted. The buzzword worked like Fletcher hoped—Jackie paused. A curious if disbelieving look crossed her face. Mouth pinched, eyebrows drawn, head tilted. "Using him?"

"He knows where the key is, so he's guiding me to it but won't tell me where it is. I need him on my side until I have the key in hand, so I told him he could leave with me. I know, I know. But it had to be done. So, *he*"—Fletcher pointed over her shoulder—"can't know about *us*. And *you* can't shoot him. I need him in one piece."

Jackie's frown grew deeper by the second. "A pity. I thought you had what it takes to get ahead."

Ambition was Jackie's greatest weapon. The youngest editor in chief in *Jet-Setter* history wasn't a title easily earned. There was nothing she wouldn't do—no one she wouldn't kill—to get what she wanted.

The alliance they'd forged was the only thing keeping Fletcher's brain inside her skull.

"I do. I swear I do. I'll get you your key." Fletcher's stomach settled. She'd told so many half-truths that the whole truth came easily. "I want that promotion, Jackie. It's all I've ever wanted. He thinks I'm on his side, and he has to *believe* it."

Judging by the way the gun bit into Fletcher's skin, Jackie had never believed a person less. But she didn't have a choice. For once, everyone was playing by Fletcher's rules.

Beyond them, Waylon's sleeping bag crinkled. He yawned, so loud against the quiet morning Fletcher felt it in her teeth.

"Leaving without me?" he asked, and Fletcher imagined him rubbing at his eyes, his sharp features softened with sleep.

"You have to go," she urged Jackie. "Don't let him see you."

Jackie didn't budge, her trigger finger all too ready. "You've got one day left. Get me that boat key, whatever the cost, and get rid of

Waylon. If you don't kill him, I will. And if you try to pull anything, you'll be next."

Fletcher's mouth went so dry she could sand walls with her tongue. Whatever makeshift truce she and Waylon had come to, Jackie didn't need to know about it. "Understood."

The pressure of Jackie's gun vanished, and so did she. A few moments later, the engine of her Jeep rumbled to life, headlights streaking through the grasses and steering into the depths of the jungle. No doubt off to beat Fletcher to the marina to make sure she didn't go back on her word.

And she wouldn't.

It wasn't like she and Waylon were going to see each other ever again after this godforsaken company trip ended. He didn't deserve to die here, but he wouldn't. The rescue crew would come. She'd step off the boat ramp with a wave or maybe skip goodbyes altogether, knowing they'd stay on their separate sides of the Hudson.

Although, he was helping her, and maybe she could repay the favor by figuring out how to vouch for his asylum once she had the key—and some leverage.

"Don't steal my covers, Spence," Waylon said, drowsy and slurred as Fletcher broke through the brush.

Where she promptly froze in her tracks.

Waylon wasn't alone. He'd rolled over onto his back, and squatting on his belly was a . . . rat monkey?

The creature was mostly eyeballs and fur. It had toppled over their bag of fruit, feasted efficiently but thoroughly, judging by the bite marks in the strawberries, and now crouched on Waylon's torso, a hunk of tangerine in its paws. Claws? Rat monkey fingers.

"Waylon, I need you to not freak out," Fletcher said, sounding admittedly freaked-out.

A drop of juice dribbled onto Waylon's cheek, and he swiped it away. Eyelids heavy, still stirring, then snapping open at once.

He screamed at eardrum-bursting decibels, louder than Fletcher when held at gunpoint. At first, he tried to stand, but his legs got trapped in the sleeping bag, and he toppled over. The furry invader took the opportunity to cram a chunk of fruit in its cheeks before tearing off another from their wine cellar spoils.

What *was* that thing? Fletcher scrambled through her mental backlog of *Nat Geo*, trying to find any recollection of a creature like this.

The blob of fur skittered up Waylon's pants, his shirt, and onto his shoulder. More primate than rodent, actually. Long tail, saucer-wide eyes, a ball of brown-gray fluff . . .

"I think it's a bush baby," she said.

Waylon scowled as he tried—and failed—to shrug off the creature now eating citrus on his head. "Don't call me baby when I'm being attacked."

Fletcher flushed. "Not *you*. The tiny monkey. It's called a bush baby."

"I don't care what it's called—ow, ow, *ow!*" The bush baby dug its little critter hands into Waylon's scalp, holding on for dear life. "Get rid of it."

As she stepped closer, the bush baby crouched, half its body beneath Waylon's curls and its tail dripping down the back of his neck. With little warning, a warbling screech erupted from the animal. Its head twisted and kept twisting until its eyes were where its chin was supposed to be.

"Oh my god, and it's possessed," she whispered, trying to clamp down on her own panic. There was enough radiating off Waylon for the both of them.

What Waylon should have done was remain perfectly still and let Fletcher reach up on her tiptoes and remove the unwanted mammal.

What Waylon actually did was hop around like he was actively being overtaken by a violent, if affable, poltergeist who died in a heavy metal mosh pit. Head banging wasn't enough to fling the primate away from him. The bush baby stayed put, alternating between ear-piercing howls and unfazed chewing.

Fletcher needed holy water. Stat.

"Calm down, you're going to alert the whole island."

Waylon ceased thrashing only long enough to glare. "Me? Try taking that up with the car alarm on my head."

Fletcher caught Waylon by the cheeks, palms pressed to each side of his face. "Listen to me. I need you to bend your knees."

He did.

His eyes were replaced by two orange orbs, reflecting the first drops of pale sunrise.

"Hi, there," Fletcher said to the bush baby.

"*Oo-oo-oo*," the bush baby responded.

"Is that so?"

"Stop trying to befriend the damn thing and get it off me, Spence," Waylon growled.

Right. Fletcher scooped the bush baby up with fingers wrapping around its middle and tried not to think about how most primates were omnivores, which meant that as much as he was enjoying his contraband fruit salad, he probably wouldn't mind a piece of Fletcher Steak.

Before it could try to eat her or give her rabies or both, she lobbed it toward the acacia trunk. The primate leaped toward the branches with a full belly and a hell of a story to tell its weird monkey friends.

Arms spread wide, Waylon crashed into Fletcher with renewed force. With her face smooshed up against his chest, she could feel the riotous rhythm of his heart. Gone was the lingering scent of the manor's cedarwood-and-amber soap. Instead, he was earth and salt and the charcoal deodorant she saw him swipe on after their river water baptism.

"Are you hugging me?" Fletcher asked, muffled against his shirt.

Yes. The answer was *yes*. His arms coiled around her back, their bellies pressed together, and his cheek rested on top of her head. It was, by definition, a hug.

And she . . . didn't hate it.

It was so Waylon. The confident way his hand came to rest on the back of her head, nudging her closer to his collarbone. His grip firm and self-assured as warmth seeped from his skin to hers and the *thump-thump* of his heartbeat as it slowed, steadied.

But at her question, Waylon arched back, as if only then realizing what he'd done. His arms fell away from her sides. She shivered in their absence. Around them, morning dawned pastel pink, and the same hue flared across his cheeks, though he tamped it down as quickly as it rose.

"Did I hear you scream earlier?" he asked. His usual gruff tone returned, but this time it wasn't at her expense. It was *for* her. Concern etched into his brows on her behalf.

"Oh, I—" What? Had a predawn stand-up with Jackie Caldera to discuss some urgent agenda items? "Yeah. About the bush baby. Terrifying creature. We should get out of here before it comes back with friends."

Waylon practically ran. "Way ahead of you."

17

In hindsight, Fletcher should have packed sneakers. The whole outfit was wrong: the poly-blend skirt, the buttoned shirt, the strappy flats. They were designed for standing near someone more important than her and handing them a stack of neatly stapled documents—ledgers, expense reports, vague threats from Sales about a mutiny. Not trekking through Rhodes grass so tall it tickled her chin.

She missed the overly air-conditioned skyscraper with the drooping monstera on the sixty-fourth floor that refused to perk up no matter how many times she watered it.

She missed gossiping with Ford over piles of mediocre noodles and new *Jet-Setter* editions, their talking points ranging from worthless celebrity drama to in-house scandals seeded from the mouth of Molly Bradhampton herself.

At this rate, she even missed the estate. Sure, they had been surrounded by people who wanted them dead—and the bodies of colleagues already killed—but at least back there, Fletcher could perform basic hygiene tasks. Flush a toilet. Wash her hands. It had barely been twelve hours since their escape and her scented travel hand sanitizer already wheezed with every squirt.

She and Waylon had walked until the sun burned off the morning dew, but the jungle wasn't getting any closer. Meanwhile, clouds that yesterday clung to the edge of the horizon now nipped at the island's shores. Those roiling black thunderheads cast darkness over the plains, threatening rain.

Fletcher didn't walk any faster despite it. Between her heels blistering and her thighs chafing, she couldn't.

"What's that thing people sometimes use to clear paths in the wilderness?" In the midmorning heat, she'd folded up her sleeves, but now her elbows had rug burn from forcing through the grass stalks. A particularly unruly brush smacked the side of her face in retaliation.

"Spence," Waylon clipped.

"Oh, right. A machete."

Maybe it was the way exhaustion scratched at the back of her retinas like steel wool or Jackie's descent into supervillain territory or how she'd been forced to share her breakfast with a monkey, but the fight was picking itself.

Waylon groaned, back to his usual demeanor, floating somewhere between purposefully nettling and naturally on edge. "We're almost to the jungle."

"Are we? Because it looks like—" A fringed piece of grass thwacked her, some of its frilly seeds sticking to her lips. She spat it out. *Mmm, whole grains.* "It looks like we're lost."

For the first time in hours, Waylon glanced down at Fletcher. He'd spent most of the morning plunging deeper into the savanna without ever once asking Fletcher for directions. Or talking to her. Or acknowledging her existence at all, really, aside from the back of his hand brushing against hers every few steps, close enough to say

I'm right here without crossing any uncharted territory after The Hug™.

It riled her up. The Hug™ and this, now, whatever it was.

Their physical contact had been limited solely to life-or-death situations, but this was just a hike. And Fletcher hated hiking. No road rules, no structure, no lines to stay inside. Every step unmapped, undefined. Anything could happen.

The sooner they made it to the jungle, the sooner they'd find Carlotta's key in the staff building, and the sooner she could make it to the marina on the other side of the island and—hopefully—out of here alive.

Before long, she'd get back to the city where everything was gridded streets and dollar pizza and mystery steam wafting from subway grates. The constant hum. The reliable chaos.

Occasionally, Waylon would shake out his arms or flex the muscle of his jaw, a divot forming on his forehead. A few times, he pivoted their direction so dramatically she grew fairly certain they were heading the same way they started.

And every time his touch grazed her hand, she inched closer to an unknown cliff, not fully understanding what mountain she was climbing or why Waylon made her feel like she could jump without crashing.

Now he cast a glance back at her, the wrinkle between his brows relaxing and then fading altogether. A slow smile spread across his face. Unfiltered and indulgent. His gaze roved over her, like he enjoyed the pointed crest of her nose, the sun-inflicted freckles on her already-burned cheeks, the irritated slope of her lips.

Reaching, he plucked and discarded a clump of grass from her hair. Then another, tucking a strand of copper behind her ear when he was finished.

His eyes lowered.

A third, he swiped off the corner of her mouth. His thumb lingered there, gentle against her full bottom lip. Fletcher's blood raced readily through her veins, like it had been crouched at the starting line waiting for the flare to fire.

Her skin thrummed beneath his touch. Some part of her wondered if she'd remembered to drink enough water or if this was a dehydration hallucination and, if it was, she really needed to have a stern talk with her subconscious mind for conjuring Waylon as the protagonist of her fever dreams.

"You can't see shit, can you?" he asked.

"Nope."

"Get on."

Fletcher blinked. "On?"

"Me."

Again. "What?"

"My shoulders." Waylon scrubbed his knuckles through his hair. In the sun, it was blonder than usual, coils of molten gold and alabaster white. "Get on my shoulders so you can see."

She didn't have time to argue before he ducked down in front of her, hands poised to lock around her calves like a Nebraska state fair carnival ride. Admittedly, she felt surer of her fate on the Tilt-o-Matic 3000 than she did with skin-to-skin contact. Her right leg heaved over his shoulder before she could muster a good enough reason not to, and the left leg followed.

Waylon's palms roughed against her calves, then slid higher. Kneecaps. Higher. His fingers brushed the hem of her skirt, hiked perilously high around her thighs, and she felt the echo of his touch in her hip creases.

She squashed a yelp as he stood without warning, and his shoulders shook with a restrained chuckle, clearly amusing himself. All her indignation subsided as soon as he rose to full height.

"Wow, you live like this?"

Waylon hummed, and the vibrations coursed straight to her bone marrow.

"You can see *everything*." Fletcher considered herself firmly of average height, creeping into the upper middle class of the height economy when she wore her work heels. This was the 1 percent.

"Including?" Waylon asked. Bait. Her stubborn lips stayed superglued shut. "The jungle. Right where I said it was."

Fletcher huffed. Okay, fine. Somehow, he'd navigated them toward the jungle without getting them irrevocably lost. Without thinking, she touched the curve of his finger where a handkerchief hid a jagged red line carving knuckle to knuckle. "Why'd you fistfight the map case if you have such an aversion to longitudinal lines? You clearly know this island inside out."

"You wanted it."

Her cheeks burned. She really should have reapplied her SPF before running for her life. "I didn't ask you to do that."

"I know." Haughty. Arrogant. And yet. "One day you'll figure out how to ask for what you want."

A breeze lifted Fletcher's hair, looser than usual in a haphazard bun, save the few strands around her face. Here, the sun's unimpeded glow tested the limits of Fletcher's ability to avoid a sweaty upper lip, but the breeze hadn't gotten the memo. It smelled like petrichor and soot. Like a snuffed candle.

Twisting, Fletcher peeked behind them, following the path they trod away from the cliffs. A storm blotted out the estate fire. The manor's foreboding walls still stood tall, if a bit charred, but a few petulant embers splashed the gardens orange.

"Have you seen anyone else since we left the manor?" Fletcher asked instead of what she really wanted to know: *Did you hear Jackie last night? Is anyone else following us?*

Waylon shook his head, and she felt it between her thighs. Which was not a situation she ever expected to be in. Her body was not adequately prepared, limbs turning a little too gooey given the topic at hand. "No. Who's left?"

She'd obsessed far too much over her mental checklist in the dawn-dim savanna, committing the remaining players to memory. "You and me, obviously. Most of Sales: Opal and Sheila and Asshole Rick."

"Oh, is that what Rick is short for?" A smile tilted his words.

"Most people assume Richard, but most people are wrong."

Waylon laughed, and Fletcher lapped up the sound, the honesty of it. No barbed fence, no alligator moat keeping her out. Just laughter: deep and resonating. When he wasn't too busy playing the spoiled, rich, estranged slash prodigal son, his company wasn't *that* bad.

Or maybe her standards for companionship were lowering to *anyone who hasn't actively tried to mutilate me in the last twenty-four hours.*

"Who else?" he asked. "The C-suite? Deepti and Jackie and Melv and Bertram."

"No, Bertram's dead."

Waylon's voice pitched up. "Is he?"

"I . . ." *Shit.* "I saw his tie floating down the river this morning. Bloody."

"And you hate blood."

"Does anyone really *love* blood?"

His hand left her leg only long enough to scratch at his jawline. "Phlebotomists. Vampires. Cult leaders."

"Yes, I'm of the belief that blood objectively belongs inside the body." Fletcher ruffled Waylon's curls. Surprisingly soft. Did he use a leave-in conditioner? She wouldn't put it past him. "So, that leaves eight. Give or take a pride of lions, a well-fed bush baby, and whatever other *Jumanji* horrors the island wants to throw at us."

Buried in the brush, something growled.

"Like," she added with a gulp, "whatever that was."

"Do you see anything?" he asked.

Trees dotted the grassland, giraffes grazing at a few of them. Squawking birds flitted from branch to branch, migrating closer to the jungle's shelter as the clouds crept in. Other than that, the savanna had quieted.

"There!" She pointed.

Something a few yards out zigged through the grasses, then zagged, then zigged again—she just couldn't see what. Whatever it was hulked toward them, crouched low. The noise ramped up, stuck between a rattle and a deep-bellied roar. Louder this time. Closer.

"Get me down. Get me down. *Getmedown*." She smacked Waylon's hands. "Now. *Now*."

"What was it?" he asked as he lowered her.

No sooner than her feet hit the dirt did Fletcher power forward. Stalks razed down her arms, her legs, leaving her skin red and raw. "It sounds like a lion had a baby with a super venomous snake."

Waylon stayed close on her heels, a hand on the small of her back propelling her forward. "That's biologically improbable."

Fletcher sighed. "Okay, Steve Irwin. What do you think it is?"

The grass growled again, and he pressed closer to her. "Maybe a lion or a snake, but not both."

She had her mouth open to argue that after everything they'd witnessed this week, a lion-snake hybrid hardly seemed outrageous. There was a whole rebuttal on the tip of her tongue about how his dad could have very well hired private zoological geneticists to create the first mammal-reptilian crossover species. A useless vanity project for the sake of playing god. The Tesla Cybertruck of predators. A slion.

But then, Waylon gripped her shoulder, jerking her to a halt. He roped her against his chest, arms looped around her shoulders.

"Using me as a human shield is a new low, Cartwright," Fletcher whispered.

He exhaled. Almost a laugh. His breath brushed against her ear, still minty from their riverside freshening-up this morning. "You really don't get it, do you?"

A hiss raised goose bumps up Fletcher's skin. She didn't imagine the way Waylon's fingers flexed, the way he shifted her into him, the way their hearts pounded in sync. There was nowhere else to run. When the grass parted, they'd meet the slion's fanged maw, and it would sink its teeth into—

An ostrich barked at them.

A beaky thing the size of a lesser dinosaur with black beads for eyes broke through the brush. It made that sound—the slion sound. She'd hardly call herself an ostrich connoisseur, but she knew the universal noise for pissed off. The ostrich poked its head over the grass, peeked behind it, and then ducked back down.

When it charged, Fletcher gasped. It wasn't running toward them. It was running *away* from *something else*.

The something in question shouted, "Come back, birdbrain. I'm trying to ride you!"

Fletcher and Waylon turned to each other and, in unison, said, "Deepti."

An evil ostrich was one thing but a CFO riding an ostrich was the thing of Fletcher's nightmares.

Without someone to tether herself to, Deepti had gone fully rogue. Dirt smudged her polka-dot blouse, the hem torn, and her elbow-patched blazer had been tied around the waist of her knee-length skirt. No Prada loafers deserved to be slathered in mud like hers were.

Unfortunately, she had her briefcase hitched high, as if to bore the ostrich into submission with payroll, and Fletcher and Waylon were in her warpath.

They sprinted, shooting off through the brush, sandwiched between the ostrich and Deepti.

"Look who's back," the CFO snapped. "Get out of my way."

"Okay, okay! We're getting!" Fletcher called. Her fingers laced through Waylon's, and she tugged him hard to the right.

The momentum threw them off-balance, sending them toppling *down*ward instead of *for*ward. Their limbs tangled, so much that Fletcher couldn't tell where her elbow ended and Waylon's arm began. When her world stopped spinning, Fletcher looked down at Waylon where he sprawled across her belly.

Being around Waylon was proving to be a risk to her physical well-being. This much heart pounding, breath holding, stomach clenching couldn't be good for a woman.

And it didn't help that during their tumble, Deepti had managed to wrangle the ostrich and mount it. Now she charged toward them.

She rode sidesaddle. Of course. Deepti was a lady. She'd grown up near the city, her family members of the polo club. One arm wound around the ostrich's neck, and the other snaked around her briefcase handle like a mallet, poised to pummel them to death.

"My two least favorite people," she said. Then her eyebrows shifted. "Actually, second and third. My first least favorite is Raul's wife."

"Have you ever considered that maybe the problem is the person doing the cheating and not the person they're cheating on?" Fletcher asked, breathless beneath Waylon's body.

Deepti's eyes narrowed. She was *also* cheating on her husband, so no, Fletcher suspected she had not considered that.

"Peck their eyes out," Deepti stage-whispered into the bird's ear. (Did birds even *have* ears?)

Waylon scrambled up first and hauled Fletcher up by the forearm. "Run now," he said. "Plan later."

Here, the grass was shorter, knee-high in some places and nothing but dirt in others, like the earth had alopecia. It made it easier for Fletcher to see the deranged look on Deepti's face as she chased after them.

New rule: No more looking back.

Waylon's strides were twice as long as hers, but he kept a firm grip on her arm. Every three or four steps, Fletcher wobbled, toes blistered from gripping the soles of her flats for dear life.

Ostriches ran faster than either of them. Deepti appeared to their right in a flash. Her heels dug into the ostrich's sides, spurring it forward, but instead of rushing toward them, it hesitated with a squawk. Again, she kicked him. Her ostrich thrashed his neck, bucking Deepti off its back.

She lay there, unmoving, as the ostrich sent dust flying and beelined back toward the tallest grasses.

Deepti laughed, a hollow sound.

No, not Deepti.

Deepti was righting herself, a hand to her sore scalp, but she froze suddenly in her tracks. Waylon skidded to a stop, Fletcher following suit with an alarmed inhale.

Hyenas. Eight of them.

Whatever she thought hyenas looked like based off *The Lion King*, she was wrong. These were spotted like cheetahs but twice as bulky. Fifty-five percent muscle fiber, forty-five percent sharp teeth, bared and ready to bite.

The CFO's head swiveled between Fletcher and Waylon and the hyenas. Fear burned in her gaze. Her eyes flared with an unspoken question. *Truce?* As if thirty seconds ago, she hadn't instructed her temperamental pet ostrich to blind them.

Deepti readily subscribed to the Denis Bertram School of Thought that Fletcher was overambitious and underqualified for a Lydell invite, but a clan of hyenas really evened the playing field. Hyenas didn't care about corporate politics or the socioeconomic leverage Dyer used to pit everyone against one another. They weren't here under the guise of promotions: They just wanted blood.

Eight pairs of eyes flashed at them, searching for the tastiest dinner.

Personally, Fletcher's money was on Waylon. He had more muscle on him than Fletcher and Deepti combined—and Deepti kept a Peloton in her office.

Waylon laughed—one stiff, bemused huff. There was no time for truces. In the wild, everything moved at the speed of survival. (Especially less than twenty-four hours after being Tased.)

One of the hyenas yipped, and it set the three of them off.

Every inch of Fletcher ached as she ran. Arms pumping. Quads searing.

The first chance she had, Deepti yanked Fletcher by the shoulder and threw her behind her, which was the exact reason Fletcher had hesitated in entering a truce with the CFO. Ordinarily, Fletcher was happy to root for a give-no-fucks mentality from women in a male-dominated workspace, but this time, just this once, it would have been nice for a singular fuck to have been given on her behalf.

One of the hyenas, the pack leader maybe, smacked its teeth in the general vicinity of Fletcher's leg. Rather fond of her left ankle, Fletcher made a fast break for it.

Waylon cut a hard right. Then he cut back to the left. Each time they crisscrossed, there was a little more distance between Fletcher and the hyenas.

On their third cross (or was it a criss?), he called out, "Hyenas can't swim very well, and they climb worse. We have to make it to the jungle."

The rapidly approaching jungle suddenly felt five hundred miles away. Fletcher's shirt was soaked with sweat. She wouldn't make it five hundred miles. She might not even make it one mile. Especially not with the way Deepti kept trying to trip her.

"Could you maybe stop trying to use me as a human sacrifice?" Fletcher asked.

Deepti frowned. "Why? So you can use me as one?"

"Believe it or not, I'd rather not see you get mauled by a bunch of hyenas." Fletcher found herself slowing her pace to keep in stride with Deepti, even if just to look the CFO in the eye as she said, "We can both survive this."

A cold laugh shook Deepti's shoulders. "We both know we can't. You want Dyer's money as much as the rest of us."

"I don't," Fletcher panted. Why couldn't they have had this conversation over coffees?

"Why else would you have been so adamant to come? You know, when I saw you at the airport, I assumed Dyer forgot his reading glasses."

He had, actually. Fletcher had stashed them in the bottom of her bag after she found them neglected on his desk beneath a stack of paperwork Melv dropped off the night before. Paperwork that, in hindsight, she probably should have paid more attention to.

That was beside the point. The point was—

"We don't have to watch each other die, Deepti. I like you." Well, enough to not want to murder her, at least.

The smooth skin around Deepti's eyes crinkled. Not quite laugh lines but something close. She wasn't much older than forty, but suddenly Fletcher wasn't sure she'd ever seen her truly happy. Controlling the finances of a billion-dollar corporation probably didn't lend itself to smiling much. (Not that she should have to smile at work, anyway. That's an inherently sexist ask.)

"Yeah? What does Fletcher Spence like about Deepti Kaur?"

It wasn't a trick question, but the words suddenly felt hard to reach. Could be the runner's cramp scraping down Fletcher's abdomen. "I really admire how you present yourself in meetings. Remember that time Bertram interrupted you, and you waited until he'd finished talking to apologize to the board for his inconsideration. Badass."

Deepti brightened. "I didn't know anyone noticed that."

"As much as I love all the team building happening back there, is now really the time?" Waylon asked. Fletcher's side protested with lactic acid, but he hadn't even broken a sweat. How much casual cardio did this guy do?

One of the hyenas giggled, and the rest followed suit. Answering his question with a resounding: No, now was not the time. They weren't slowing down.

Water shimmered at the edge of the jungle where the savanna grasses gave way to waxy leaves and weeping vines. Mirage or not, it was their only chance. She couldn't keep running much longer.

"This way!" Fletcher called. The sudden change of direction bought them a little extra time as the hyenas regrouped, but not much.

Fletcher splashed into the water, more toddler with a soggy diaper than *Baywatch*. Waylon and Deepti rushed in behind her, Deepti less than enthusiastically. Unlike the river's clear, cool blues, the watering hole was like wading in the Manhattan sewer line. The water left a brown slime on everything it touched.

Still better than being lunch.

The hyenas stalled at the water's edge. A couple of them dipped their paws in but backtracked with growls. Fletcher's lungs ached with relief, or maybe just exertion, as she paddled out deeper.

Any semblance of relief vanished when Deepti grabbed Fletcher's ankle and jerked her back.

Hands pressed against Fletcher's shoulders, dunking her under. Her eyes flung open in surprise despite the stinging silt. It made little difference. The soupy brown water was nearly impossible to sift through. Up was down and left was right.

She kicked and clawed, gasping when her head finally broke the surface.

"What is wrong with you?" Fletcher asked, breathless as she grabbed hold of a sturdy rock outcropping and spat out a mouth of mud-water.

Waylon appeared next to Fletcher, a firm hand against her waist. He said her name like a warning. "Fletcher, we have to keep moving."

"Don't—" Deepti bubbled, barely breaking the surface.

It hit Fletcher like a NYC heat wave. Deepti couldn't swim. She didn't step within eight feet of the infinity pool at the estate, and her stories from the Maldives involved beachcombing and basting herself in tanning lotion.

The CFO bobbed in the center of the watering hole, panic seizing her limbs. There was no coordination in her movement. Desperate, weary motions that turned knives in Fletcher's stomach.

"She's going to drown," Fletcher said, but Waylon only tugged harder.

"We have to *go*." His knuckles caught the fabric of her shirt and hauled her back. "Now."

Fletcher's fingers tightened around the rock. Obviously, Waylon didn't kiss the ground upper management walked on, but she didn't think he'd actively endorse leaving someone for dead.

That was, until the rock . . . blinked?

Very much not a rock at all, actually.

A hippopotamus reared out of the water with a wide-open mouth. Waylon reeled Fletcher against his chest, dragging her to the far shore. Deepti flailed, too busy fighting for her next breath to escape, and the hippo's massive jaw clamped down around her. Her torso disappeared into its mouth.

Fletcher scrambled up the grassy bank, terror weighing down her bones. Wet and shaky, she flopped onto her back while the hippo was preoccupied with spitting out Deepti's legs. Her dismembered body parts floated around the pond. It clearly wasn't interested in eating her, just territorial.

Distantly, Fletcher was aware of Waylon settling down next to her. Both of their chests heaved in uneven tempos. Waylon smoothed the hair away from her face. "You okay?"

An auto-response *yes* crawled toward her lips. But then, the wheeze of the hippo, the splash as it sank into the watering hole, and the chilling silence that followed held her words captive.

Even if they didn't kill each other, the island would do the honors.

18

Fletcher was thirteen the first time she held a camera. She'd been bored out of her skull while her dad and brothers fussed with one of the tractor engines, and her mom handed it to her to keep her busy. Fletcher gladly accepted the offer. Anything to avoid spending the afternoon as a half-inch drive socket conveyor belt.

It wasn't *nice* by any means. A slim silver point-and-shoot that made a god-awful groaning noise every time Fletcher zoomed in. It stamped the date in little yellow numbers on the corner of all her photos, which was how she remembered that August 12, her life changed.

A series of flash photos captured snapshots of her redheaded family craning their necks over the engine block, followed by a blur of her oldest brother plucking the camera out of her hands, and then one of a pre-braces Fletcher stuck in a sweaty headlock. Those photos lived in a scrapbook gathering dust on the mantel, only brought down at Thanksgivings for reminiscing over sweet potato pie. The first photos of many.

It went with her everywhere, that camera.

Grainy snapshots of the drought-ridden football field during her brothers' games. Dewy early mornings on the farm. The Manhattan skyline from the back seat of her dad's beat-up F-150, so out of place as they crossed the Jersey turnpike. Her camera was her security blanket. It made looking at the world a little less scary.

Which would have been really freaking helpful right about now.

Next to her, Waylon's downturned gaze paid entirely too much attention to her and not nearly enough to the unfamiliar jungle terrain. The earth was denser here, stodgy with moss and mud, sticking to Fletcher's shoes as if saying, *Stay away.*

Every snapping branch sounded sinister, every animal a predator.

Their first half hour in the jungle involved encounters with a curious orangutan dribbling leaf tannins on Waylon's head, a slug the kind of putrid green that could only mean poison, and a boa constrictor squeezing Fletcher within an inch of her life until Waylon looped the leather cord of his compass around its jaw and forced it off.

Now, as they walked, the only thing keeping Fletcher from teetering over into full-blown panic was imagining how she'd frame this moment through her 55 mm lens.

Jungle greens shawled Waylon's shoulders, and his face craned toward her so she could see the sharp outline of his profile. His mouth slanting. The humidity wiping a sheen over his cheekbones. She'd position him just off-center enough to capture the curve of the river they walked alongside, darker here, and the low-hanging branch behind him where two toucans huddled. If only he'd scoot a little bit to the—

"Why are you looking at me like that?" he asked.

Fletcher chucked her mental Canon back into its imaginary camera bag. A hot flush crawled up her neck like a millipede. "Like what?"

"Like . . ." His hand rose, like he might smooth the crease between her brows with his thumb but thought better of it. Instead, he brushed his knuckles against the stubble on his jaw. "Like I just jammed your copy machine with bologna."

"A workplace hazard. You'd be surprised at the dangers deli meats pose to the future of periodicals." She ducked beneath a branch boasting bloated purple blooms. After their dip in the watering hole, their backpacks were thoroughly soaked. Now the soggy extra weight threw her off-balance. Or maybe that was the way Waylon looked at her. "I was wishing I had my camera."

Waylon immediately pursed his lips like he was auditioning for *Zoolander 3*. "You like what you see?"

"Grow up," she said, burying the rise of sparkles through her body, like her blood was carbonated. She heaved her shoulders, adjusting the weight of her dripping backpack and the weight of it all, really. "There's so much about this week that is horrifying and ugly and imperfect and flat-out scary, but looking at it through a lens would make me a little less . . . afraid."

Waylon considered this with a hum. Did guys like him have security blankets? Or was it security leather jackets and security ribbed condoms?

"And I guess I should thank you," Fletcher said, surprising even herself at how quiet it came out. "For, you know, not letting me get eaten by a hippopotamus."

"Thank you for saving me from the indomitable bush baby." Waylon's chin turned, the hint of a smile on that inscrutable slope of a mouth. "What photo would you take now?"

A flashbulb lit in Fletcher's chest. She didn't have to see her reflection in the river water to know she was glowing. Once, Waylon was the only person who knew why she clung so hard to her job at Cartwright Media. The only person who believed she could be more than an executive assistant.

"I'd want you in the foreground. Stand there and turn your head toward the river." She took a step backward, then another, then one to the left. Her heels indented the soft dirt at the river's edge, a steep drop-off into the glassy water. Neither of them had fully dried since their last water-feature encounter—Waylon's damp shirt draped around his shoulders, contouring around the divot of his triceps, the banks of his shoulder blades. She pinched one eye closed and formed a rectangle with her hands, imitating a viewfinder. "A little more, stop. I'd want your face to look like you, *not* a low-budget Ben Stiller impersonator."

"Low-budget," he scoffed under his breath. "Okay. How do I look to you, honey?"

While ordinarily more petulant than pet name, this *honey* melted in his mouth.

That prickly feeling returned. The usual avalanche of derogatory adjectives she associated with Waylon thawed. They were probably going to die here anyway, so what did it matter if she let her hard resolve to hate him melt away?

"You look rough around the edges on purpose. To prove a point, probably. But like you have a four-, maybe six-step skincare routine and try not to tell anyone because it would ruin your Cool Guy image."

"How'd you know?" He cracked a smile, a real one and not just the imitation he put on for show.

And he was, wasn't he? Putting on a show? Waylon Cartwright was the billionaire's castaway kid, a playboy and a problem child. Too smart for his own good, too stubborn to do the smart thing. But Waylon—this Waylon—had screamed in the face of a pocket-size primate and hand-fed her grapes and carried her on his shoulders when she couldn't see. Different from the version of him that had lived in her head the last three years.

She inched forward a hair, repositioning him in her finger frame.

"Curls expertly mussed. Eyes narrowed like you're always up to something mischievous. Deviously sparkling. Do you use special eye drops for that?"

His eyes flashed, then darkened as she paced toward him, trying to find just the right angle. Not the facade the tabloids or the creepy Reddit pages would see—but the version of him beneath the veneer. When was the last time someone actually saw him? Waylon sans Cartwright.

"A little tired." Closer still. "A little lonely."

"Fletcher." A whisper parted his lips.

The unguarded way he studied her robbed her legs of all structural integrity. She could lean into him so easily. Let his hands tangle in her hair. Let him kiss her until her lips were swollen, until her head spun, until she forgot why she was ever mad at him to begin with.

Her hands fell away from her eye, the gap between them reduced to inches, a few ferns between their toes. "*Click*. That's the one."

Fingertips brushed across her wrist, a tug to come closer. His head crooked, hers tilted. This was it. The moment she finally kissed Waylon Cartwright.

Waylon's hands slid around her waist, then tightened as his gaze flitted over her shoulder. "Fletcher," he said, this time with a severity that didn't quite align with what she thought he'd sound like when she imagined him kissing her. "I need you to trust me."

Her eyes fluttered shut. Dreamy. Dazed. What had gotten into her? Heatstroke was a hell of a drug. But she did trust him, much to her dismay. "Okay."

Behind her, thunder rumbled. Sun still filtered through the canopy, the air stifling without the savanna breeze. It didn't smell like rain—just earthy botanicals on the heady side of indulgent, a hint of copper, a touch of salt.

All too easily, she could picture this moment in a snapshot framed by the tropical blooms and waxy leaves. Her hand on Waylon's chest, his fingers tight against her waistline, him about to—

Waylon wasn't kissing her.

Why wasn't he kissing her?

Fletcher pried open one eye a smidge. Waylon's dagger-sharp eyes focused over her shoulder. "Naya."

Fletcher squinted. "Who's Naya?"

She followed his gaze. The magic spell severed.

Because it wasn't thunder at all. A shadow lurked in the brush, black fur with two yellow eyes. White teeth bared, then snapped. A growl swelled, emanating from the darkness.

"Tell me that's not a jaguar," Fletcher said as if it weren't Very Obviously a Jaguar.

A black cat trigintuple the size of barnyard kittens stalked out of the undergrowth. Naya peeled her ears back and crouched on her haunches, ready to pounce. Her body was pure muscle. Lean but powerful. Poised to strike.

"Get behind me." Waylon's voice was stern. Commanding. Sexy? No, now was not the time for sexy.

Fletcher moved as told, only barely refraining from gripping the back of Waylon's shirt. And she was glad she hadn't because Naya's hunting gaze followed her every motion. Protective and territorial. Eager to sink her teeth into Fletcher's skin. Fletcher was, admittedly, already more of a dog person to begin with, but getting ripped to shreds by a jaguar would really seal the deal.

Impressively, Waylon stood his ground. Not a single bead of sweat trickled down his neck. (Shocking, given the moisture pooling against the underwire of Fletcher's bra.)

Her thoughts scrambled like Times Square tourists. There had to be a way out of this. Trees? No, cats could climb better than Fletcher, and there was no hot firefighter to rescue her when she inevitably got stuck. The river, then. Cats hated water, right?

"Come on, we have to go—"

Before Fletcher could make a break for it, let alone finish her sentence, Naya's teeth flashed in warning. Waylon wedged himself between them, one hand outstretched toward Naya, the other shoving Fletcher farther behind him. That cat was going to tear him limb from limb. And then her. And then, their respective limbs would be left there in such a haphazard heap that thousands of years from now, archaeologists would hypothesize that Lydell Island had been so biologically isolated that a subclass of four-armed humans had evolved.

Naya lunged.

All Fletcher could do was shield her eyes. She'd seen enough blood for a lifetime. Which made sense since her lifetime was about to be over as soon as Naya's teeth ripped out their jugulars.

Except Waylon wasn't screaming.

Slowly, Fletcher pried her hands away from her eyes. Naya wasn't gnawing at his leg, licking her lips. Her massive head nudged into Waylon's open palm. And she was . . .

Purring.

The cat lifted onto her legs, front paws resting on Waylon's shoulder as she nuzzled into his neck, her nose running over the last reaches of his scruff. Like a house cat. A giant, saber-toothed house cat.

Cold flooded Fletcher's system. Relief and confusion and a secret third thing that felt an awful lot like affection. A nervous laugh bubbled out of her. Whether it was from the close encounter with the jungle cat or the loving way Waylon scratched at Naya's chin, she couldn't tell.

"Is this *your* cat?" she asked.

Naya's purrs halted. For two blissful, uneaten seconds, the cat had forgotten Fletcher existed.

That was over now.

Naya glared like Fletcher posed an imminent threat to Waylon's safety, despite the fact he could bench-press her with two fingers.

"Easy, easy." Waylon guided the feline back down onto all fours. He patted her head as if she were nothing more than an ornery tomcat. "I think it's more like I'm her person."

Judging by the way Naya's claws extended when she refocused on Fletcher, she clearly took her role as Guard Jag seriously.

"When I was seventeen, my dad brought his buddies out here, and I tagged along. Didn't know what I was getting myself into. He handed me a gun, told me to hunt. I am a man of many talents, but hunting is not one of them." A soft, sad little grin rose to Waylon's lips as he ran his thumb along Naya's jaw. "Naya found me before I knew she was there."

"And didn't eat you?"

"I'm sure she would have tried if she'd weighed more than a couple pounds," he said with a laugh. "She was just a cub. One of my dad's friends had poached her mom already."

Fletcher realized. "Right. The jaguar room."

"Naya knew how to be a cat about as well as I knew how to hunt one."

He didn't finish his story, but Fletcher filled in the blanks. A peach-fuzzed Waylon with a tiny shadow that turned into a much-less-tiny shadow. A protective friendship that went both ways.

"Pretty brave for a guy afraid of a bush baby."

"First of all, I was sneak attacked. And secondly, animals with opposable thumbs are objectively terrifying. Ask anyone."

"Thumbs?" Fletcher laughed.

"They're too powerful."

The jungle cat hummed unhappily.

"See? Naya agrees." A proud smile lit his face. "Here, you can pet her."

Before she could argue that that definitely wasn't a good idea, Waylon captured Fletcher's wrist. Naya watched them with anticipation, her stomach definitely already growling. In the back of her mind, Fletcher wondered if cats could smell fear. Waylon wove his fingers through Fletcher's and steered her hand toward the bridge of Naya's nose.

A deep-bellied grumble rose out of Naya but Waylon batted it away with a *tsk*. To Fletcher's immense surprise, it worked. Naya bowed her head and brushed her coat against Fletcher's fingertips.

"She's so . . ." Fletcher's words faded out, unsure which could accurately describe this moment. When she thought about traveling the world with *Jet-Setter*, these were the things she dreamed of. Unexpected encounters. Breathtaking scenery. The kinds of experiences Lincoln County locals would only ever see on glossy magazine pages.

Waylon craned his nose toward her. His open hand found Fletcher's waist, flattening against her stomach and pulling her closer. "Beautiful?"

Fletcher turned, too. Her nose brushed his. Much closer than two not-coworkers on a not-work retreat should have ever been. Much, *much* closer to Waylon than Fletcher ever thought she'd be again, barring a few extenuating circumstances she imagined might have included an expertly wielded paper cutter and an off-key rendition of "Cell Block Tango."

"I bet that works on all the ladies," Fletcher whispered.

"I don't know," Waylon said with a lopsided smile. "You tell me."

With absolutely no warning, Naya shifted back into a predator. This time, her instant animosity wasn't directed toward Fletcher, thank god. The cat's oblong pupils widened into blown-out spheres, searching through the depths of the jungle. For what? Not even the leaves dared to rustle in Naya's presence.

The cat prowled forward, low and slow. Waylon followed, his hand still wrapped around Fletcher's, and against her better judgment, she followed, too. While Naya crept silently, Fletcher and Waylon fumbled along behind her, and Fletcher was fairly certain she hadn't imagined the annoyed way Naya peeked over her shoulder after Fletcher tripped over a particularly unruly root system.

When Naya slowed, so did they.

She'd led them toward the main road, where the branches had been snipped and shaped to create a tunnel. Twin dirt tracks carved toward the center of the island, toward the landing strip and the staff building.

They weren't alone.

Two figures hobbled down the path, heading toward them. Sheila, one heel on and one dangling from her fingers, babbled about something Fletcher couldn't quite make out. Next to her, Opal crossed her arms against her chest. Soot smudged her otherwise pristine silk blouse.

Even if Fletcher wanted to sic Naya on them, she couldn't. The jaguar had vanished like an apparition.

"Are you sure we're going the right way?" Sheila whined as they marched closer.

Opal grimaced. "Ask me one more time."

"Are you sure we're—"

"Yes, Sheila!" Opal's oversize sunglasses masked what was certainly the death stare to end all death stares. "I'm sure. Now, I'm begging you to shut up and help me look for more of these business cards."

Fletcher raised her eyebrows toward Waylon, signaling for him to follow her, and then crept through the dense foliage, close enough to keep tabs on Opal and Sheila's conversation. Every few steps, Opal scooped up another little paper rectangle. Pocketed it. And mapped toward the next, several feet ahead.

Slinking behind them, Fletcher pried up a card they'd missed. Matte black and embossed with RICK EVANSTON in bold type. His phone and company email squished into the corner. Dirtbaggy even in business card form.

Sheila bobbled on her single stiletto. Her shutting-up was short-lived. "Why couldn't he have picked a hiding spot that wasn't a million miles away?"

"I've seen you Citi Bike in heels twice that high. Don't act like this is hard for you." Opal flipped her sunglasses onto her head, reassessing their path. "Besides, when has Rick ever put the needs of others first?"

"Is that, like, a trick question?"

"Obviously. If I can't convince you to let me walk in peace, at least tell me again what you heard yesterday."

Fletcher's boob-sweat situation multiplied rapidly. Could Sheila have listened in on her conversation with Jackie on the pool deck?

"It was this DJ mix of top songs from the dark ages, like 2005," Sheila said sagely.

"I meant about Jackie. God, do you even have a brain in there?"

No. *No.* No way was Sheila blowing her cover right now. Not when Fletcher wouldn't have a chance to explain herself to Waylon. If they spilled the beans, her feeble truce with Waylon would disappear faster than a happy hour martini.

Fletcher's body moved before her brain caught up. One leg jutted out—hard—in front of Waylon, and he tripped over it. The two of them tumbled into the brush with matching *thud*s. Her knees and palms screamed as they skidded against the earth. A stiff breath through Waylon's nose was his only external reaction, but the look he gave her could fill libraries.

Sorry, Fletcher mouthed.

"Was that . . ." Opal trailed off into an unsettling quiet until, finally, she said: "Forget it. Let's just find Rick before somebody finds us."

When they finally peeled themselves off the forest floor to follow Opal and Sheila, Fletcher gave the saleswomen a wider berth, just in case. Their voices grew faint. Any gossip blessedly unheard.

Dread gathered behind Fletcher's ribs as they paraded onward. Every step charted toward the staff building's little charcoal dot on the map. What should have been a quick in-and-out to grab the master key was proving to be anything but.

Summoned, the building rose out of the jungle in front of them, all stone walls with terra-cotta shingles. Large windows had been framed with dark wood shutters, watching them. Waiting for them. The jungle encroached on its territory with drooping branches and strangling vines. Bright red blossoms dolloped the stone exterior, the hand-carved doorways. Everything smelled sweet in a way that made Fletcher sick to her stomach, like overripe fruit forgotten in the sun.

Welcoming them with a gunshot salute was Asshole Rick.

19

Staked in front of the staff building was a hand-painted trifold board that read KEEP OUT JERK-OFFS ONLY SALES ALLOWED.

Respectfully, it could have used a little more punctuation for clarity. Was it *Keep out, Jerk-offs*, or *Jerk-offs only*? Inquiring minds longed to know.

Rick paced out front, cosplaying Chuck Norris. If Chuck Norris had spent the last decade in a cubicle. Mud and moss clung to the hem of his belted trousers. The sleeves of his pin-striped dress shirt had been torn off. His five-o'clock shadow had five-o'clock shadow.

Strapped around his chest was a horribly concocted weapon of mass destruction—a spear tied to the end of a sawed-off shotgun. The salesman slung the abomination over his shoulder and greeted Opal and Sheila with varying degrees of success. Opal went for a handshake when Rick opted for a hug, so they landed somewhere awkwardly in the middle before he turned to the intern. Meanwhile, Sheila barely acknowledged him at all, breezing in through the open front door and saying something about a Jacuzzi bathtub.

And somewhere inside, they'd find the master key.

"What's the plan, chief?" Waylon whispered.

She had one, but right now the only thing that came to mind was: *I should have listened to Bertram.*

He'd initially tried to ice her out, exile her to the jungle to sleep in the staff building, and Fletcher had the gall to be offended. But this villa was hardly a downgrade from the main manor. She could have traded every traumatic event from the last forty-eight hours for relaxing in the porch hammock. At least until Asshole Rick showed up and started man-caving the place.

Bandannas had been strung like pennant banners across the porch, marking his territory. A few lopsided spears like the one tied to his rifle had been staked in front of the entry stairs, sparkling clean and unused. He'd probably survived on Keurig coffee and break room snacks, but she had to appreciate the dedication to the bit.

When Opal joined Sheila inside, Rick resumed his patrol. He strode a wide path, eyes glued to the horizon for any oncoming threats. So, the front door was off-limits. This wasn't going to be the Central Park stroll Fletcher hoped it'd be.

A balcony jutted off the second floor, tempting. But the thought of clinging to a tangle of vines ten feet off the ground while Rick took shots at them sounded worse than sitting through one of Finance's budget-review meetings.

There had to be windows facing the back, maybe a door if they were lucky. They had options.

Fletcher nodded her head to the left as an unspoken answer to Waylon's question. Even with her plan in this nebulous state, she knew it could not commence here. One stray glance away from the worn path, and they'd face off with Rick's makeshift bayonet.

They crept, crouching, and Fletcher guided them toward the

flanks of the building where the ceilings sloped lower, the jungle's presence grew thicker, and their chances of imminent death decreased by at least 20 percent.

"What's the floor plan like in there?" she asked. Which was code for *On a scale of one to ten, how screwed are we, because the number feels high?*

"Everyone's got bedrooms, shared bathrooms. Garages, laundry, and kitchen are off the back. The third floor's Carlotta's suite, but the main stairwell off the foyer will take us straight to it if we can make it there."

Rick about-faced, and in unison, Fletcher and Waylon slammed to the earth.

"Emphasis on the *if*," Fletcher muttered after spitting out a mouthful of leafy greens.

They waited until he pivoted again to hop back to their feet. Her body groaned in protest with every cautious step. Waylon, however, clearly hadn't gotten the memo on *sneaking*. He trailed behind her, footsteps noisy in the underbrush.

"You could at least try to be quiet."

He huffed. "I am being quiet."

Another crunch. And another.

"Try harder," she said between her teeth. Fletcher ducked beneath a branch as they rounded the corner of the building, nearly out of Rick's line of sight.

This time, a rustle.

She skidded to a stop, spinning on her heels. "Waylon, I swear to—"

Fletcher's whole body tensed.

Behind Waylon stood a chimpanzee. Inky black eyes, coarse hair, human enough that, given a briefcase and an ego problem, it could have been Dyer's four o'clock meeting. It mimicked their every move. When they stepped, it stepped. When they crouched, it crouched.

And Waylon hadn't seen it yet.

Without thinking, Fletcher slapped her hand over Waylon's mouth because frankly after the bush baby debacle, she didn't trust him not to scream. His eyes flew open wide, and as delicately as she could, she said, "Do *not* look at its thumbs."

His mouth moved beneath her hand. When she peeled back her fingers, he said, "Whose thumbs?"

"Um, his." Fletcher pointed.

With only a peek over his shoulder, Waylon jolted, hands coming up next to his face, ready to go three rounds in the ring. Miraculously, he kept his voice to a hoarse hush. "God, no. No! Why is it here?"

"It's trying to—"

The chimp craned its neck back toward the front of the estate, where the tip of Rick's spear edged out. It started to hoot, trying to communicate with them, but all Fletcher could see in her mind's eye was a very near future where Rick paid homage to Dyer's creepy decor and had them all stuffed and turned into a real-life depiction of the evolution of man.

Fletcher planted her hands on the chimp's shoulders and dragged it down into a crouch. Rick's shadow faded back behind the building, still pacing, unaware of their presence. *Phew.*

With a shush from her, the chimp smiled, toothy, before making a big show of closing its mouth tight. Then, checking over its hairy shoulder for Rick, it took off toward the back of the house.

"I think it's trying to help," Fletcher finished.

Waylon muttered, "I think it's trying to lure us into a trap where it can ax-murder us."

When they didn't immediately follow, the chimp hesitated, mouth forming a confused O. Fletcher reached for Waylon's hand, hauling him forward. "Come on. If it gets any dicey ideas about ax-murdering, I'll volunteer to go first so you can say 'I told you so.'"

Fletcher didn't mention that she was markedly less concerned about ape-related murder schemes compared to human-related ones. Especially as they lurked past windows revealing Opal and Sheila running rampant through the staff building.

Besides, when a knobby branch swung back, nearly slapping Fletcher in the face, the chimp stopped it. (Thank you, opposable thumbs.)

Even Waylon, who kept an impossibly wide distance, owed the chimp his life when it plucked a centipede the size of a hoagie off his back and flung it into the forest. Fletcher had been so terrified by the insect's Entirely Too Many Legs to do anything besides breathe heavily and mentally plan a lovely funeral service for Waylon.

By the time they made it around the back edge of the property, the chimp had solidified itself as part of the crew.

And then Fletcher's worst nightmare came true.

Bananas.

A whole crate of them. It teetered next to the edge of the building, near a door that must have led to the kitchen. And it wasn't alone—there were mangoes and kiwis and dragon fruit, pineapple by the bushel, citrus as far as the eye could see.

The chimpanzee howled. All sense of preservation soared out the window. It broke free from the jungle and loped toward the treasure trove of fruit.

Fletcher waited, muscles seized, for someone to apprehend the chimp. She could practically taste the gunpowder in the air already.

One second passed. Then another. No one came. No Sheila shriek, no shotgun blast.

Because no one questions a chimpanzee in a jungle.

Of course! How hadn't she thought of it before?

Fletcher swallowed her pride. Took a deep breath.

And whooped like a monkey.

"What do you think you're *doing*?" Waylon hissed. "Is this the plan, Spence? Really?"

She bent her legs, imitating the monkey's gait as she crossed the clearing. The chimp hooted, and so did she. Her eyes met Waylon's, her lips finding a smiling curve. Daring him.

Waylon's head hung toward his chest, shoulders shaking with silent laughter. When he looked back up at her, his gaze dripped with enough affection Fletcher could have drowned in it. It pooled in every nook, every cranny. The bottom of her rib cage, the pit of her stomach.

Three howls later, she'd lured Waylon out of the trees.

Unlike Fletcher, who was plagued by constant scruples, Waylon had none. Totally, blissfully unscrupulous. There were a lot of things Fletcher could say about Waylon, but accusing him of not giving his all wasn't one of them. For as long as she'd known him, he had been unapologetically himself, inviting anyone and everyone to fuck off if they didn't like it.

She did. Like it.

Another horrifying realization to add to the multitude of horrors she'd faced this week.

He crouched low, taking broad steps to catch up with her. Lifting his face to the sky, he let out three wild cries. His fists beat against his chest, and Fletcher fought the blush that crept up her neck at the mere thought of his pectoral muscles.

Normally, Fletcher would have worried about the way her skirt wrinkled, about dirt beneath her fingernails, about being seen as anything less than perfect and proper and prepared.

But here she was, stranded on a private island in the Indian Ocean and impersonating an ape with the bane of her mortal existence who turned out to not actually be that baneful. Normal was a long-forgotten concept.

"What the hell is going on out there?" Opal asked from inside.

Adrenaline lanced through Fletcher, hot and sharp. Fun over. Waylon's arm soccer-mommed against her middle and dragged her against the wall behind the crates of drupes and bromeliads. Fletcher was almost preoccupied enough by trying not to die that she barely registered this was technically the first time he'd ever touched her breasts. Almost.

Above Fletcher and Waylon, Opal's head jutted through the open second-floor window, surveying the clearing and the gnarled greenery beyond.

Fletcher had never wished to be smaller. Not when the Fi-Douches manspread on the 6 train and invaded her personal space. Or that time Ford had been so enraptured with the ass of a biker with a bottom-lip tattoo that he'd forgotten they'd split the Uber. Or even July Fourth as Kent bent to one knee in front of the entire Spence clan, a horde of barefoot redheads about to fight their new brother-in-law with bottle rockets.

All it would take was one look down, and they'd be finished.

Or one look at the chimpanzee delightfully waving a banana peel in their direction, the insides shoved messily into its mouth. Whichever came first.

Waylon side-eyed her hard. *I told you not to trust it. Or its thumbs.*

Fletcher's narrowed eyes didn't have time to form a silent rebuttal because Opal *did* glance in their direction. Waylon and Fletcher shrank behind the crates. His arms crossed over her stomach, pulling her into his lap.

Opal looked, unseeing. Squinted. A million years later, she shook her head and any thought of intruders away, returning her attention to the chimp—now juggling papayas. Only then did Fletcher let her shoulders lower with relief.

"Get out of here," Opal called, annoyance threading her words.

The monkey barked back, equally annoyed.

And then, it lobbed a papaya straight toward Opal's head. The ripened fruit splattered against the side of the building in a pulpy explosion. Papaya gunk dripped toward Fletcher and Waylon, but it wasn't nearly as bad as the goop clinging to Opal's cheek.

Opal swiped it off with a finger, disgust on her face. "Ohhhhh. You. Are. *So*. Dead."

Her head vanished from the windowpane. Faint footsteps thundered through the house, growing louder and closer as Opal ran.

Thankfully, Fletcher's crisis response kicked into gear. Instead of obstacles, she saw only solutions.

First, she rolled a handful of kiwi far enough past the chimpanzee that it turned, abandoning them to hunt seemingly sentient fruit. Hopefully, it would dart off into the jungle and never look back.

Waylon moved toward the cracked kitchen door, but Fletcher stopped him with a hand to his bicep. The back door would inevitably be Opal's first destination on her manhunt. (Well, chimp-hunt.)

Windows, on the other hand . . .

Fletcher shimmied down the length of the building to the farthest window.

A cursory glance inside proved it was the laundry room like Waylon said—and empty, except for a few stacked washer-dryer combos and an ironing board. No one was waiting to decapitate them, so Fletcher flung herself into the laundry room headfirst. It was less secret-agent-tuck-and-roll and more trying-not-to-flash-her-coochie.

Waylon, on the other hand, clearly led a second life as a spy. His entry was graceful, soundless. He whipped a hand through his goldenrod curls, brushing them out of his face. A hell of a lot of confidence for a guy who quaked in the presence of a monkey ten short minutes ago.

When Fletcher eased the laundry room door open, she could hear Sheila babbling a couple floors up and the remnants of Opal's clipped responses, shouting as she slammed the back door shut. The ceilings stretched ten, maybe twelve feet, making everything echo. A hallway with alabaster walls and dotted with woven-cane chandeliers stretched out in front of them, a few doors on either side and a staircase in the center.

A flustered, slimy Opal stomped across the hallway and up the stairs. "Don't you dare hog all the hot water."

"No promises," Sheila said. "There's dirt *everywhere*."

"I'm serious, Sheila."

Fletcher plodded toward the staircase on quiet feet. Part home, part office, the rooms were a mix of comfort and utility: supply closets, bedrooms, a living room with rattan furniture. Nice, but not *nice* nice. A far cry from the manor's top-of-the-line furnishings. Frames with faded black-and-white photos lined the walls, vintage snapshots of the island. Less polished, more wild.

"Yuck. This terry cloth is so scratchy," Sheila bitched. She flitted across the second-floor landing, adjusting the shoulders of a robe the color of a prickly pear—and apparently the texture of one, too.

Waylon hovered at Fletcher's back as they crowded near the banister. A protective hand snaked around her waist, like he was ready to fling her behind him if one of the Sales girls decided to attack. The other pointed a finger upward. The stairs stacked on top of each other, wrapping around to the third floor. If they skirted past the landing, they could theoretically sneak up to Carlotta's suite before anyone knew they were there.

Theoretically being the operative word.

Clouds followed Opal as she stormed the hall, blotting out the sun and dimming everything. "God, I need to smoke."

"Relax," Sheila said, "there's, like, four other bathrooms here."

"Sorry I'm finding it hard to relax with rotted fruit on my face," Opal seethed.

"I'll be thirty minutes. Forty-five tops," Sheila said as she snuck past Opal in the doorway. "You know, this reminds me of the time—"

"I don't care!" Opal shouted.

Recognition flared at the crack of emotion in Opal's voice. It was the same Fletcher heard in Jackie's, in Molly's. The slide into hysteria. The splash into the deep end.

"I don't care about your friend Penelope's clairvoyant Chihuahua or how you almost made out with Timothée Chalamet on a yacht or how the robe is a teensy bit scratchy! I don't care about any of it! I just got physically assaulted by some idiotic monkey, but do you hear me complaining?"

"Uh, yeah. You're literally complaining."

"And you're an insufferable little brat."

"I'm just a girl." Sheila's nasally voice drifted down the hall, presumably toward the bathtub. There was the sound of a faucet twisting, water running. "You know, Stavros—the hairstylist I told you about who does the Reiki sessions—said that stress shrinks your hair follicles, so if you don't chill out, they could just close up, and then you'd go bald."

The bathroom door shut with finality.

Opal huffed so loudly the whole house shook. "I'll show you bald."

Opal darted past the landing, holding a hair dryer. She marched inside the bathroom, not bothering to knock.

Completely unfazed by her sudden entry, Sheila's voice carried on without pause. "Whatever you do, do not try one of these bath bombs. Opposite of relaxing. There's going to be glitter in my—"

A snap of electricity. A sigh of relief.

Opal exited the bathroom, massaging the tension out of her temples. "There," she said to only herself, "no more stress."

Fletcher's heart sank, squeezed. Beside her, Waylon tensed, bracing. Under his breath, he muttered, "*Fuck.*"

Fuck, indeed. Sheila was a slacker and a thief and an out-of-touch, privileged nineteen-year-old kid. *Was.* Now? Her only qualifier was *dead.* Fletcher didn't have to see it to know Sheila had been successfully deep-fried. Her nose wrinkled against the scent of burnt hair, charbroiled skin.

Finding Waylon's hand, she clenched her fingers tighter around his in three simple pulses. *I'm right here.* He pulsed right back. His presence kept her steady on her feet as they climbed the first set of stairs.

Distracted by the distant sizzling, they'd failed to remember how vulnerable the open stairwell was. Opal paced back out onto the landing, eyes locking onto Fletcher's. Surprised, then darkening.

At that moment, a white-hot flash burst through the seams of the shutters, followed instantly by whip-crack thunder that buzzed in Fletcher's teeth. The electricity flickered. Faded. Shadows flooded the staff building as rain hammered down.

For a harrowing second, the three of them stood in a saloon shoot-out. The part before everybody draws their guns, where they're just mean-mugging one another and wondering which of their life choices landed them in this situation.

Then Opal sprinted toward them, a woman possessed.

"Get upstairs," Waylon said, voice low. Shielding Fletcher from Opal's catlike claws, he thrust her toward the next staircase, and Fletcher didn't have to be told twice.

As she pawed clumsily through the darkness, the third-floor suite revealed itself in bursts and flashes each time lightning struck. A kitchenette, a bedroom with an en suite, and a final door that opened to an office with a vaguely wilted potted orchid, a few crowded filing cabinets, and a cluttered desk.

Fletcher knew Carlotta only in email chains and long-distance calls. Her habits, her quirks—those were mysteries. Where would the groundskeeper hide the master key?

A crash boomed through the building. Not thunder. More like someone getting body-slammed. Peering through the dark doorway, all Fletcher could make out were Opal's and Waylon's sparring silhouettes, but by the sound of it, Opal was winning. She needed to look faster.

Where where where?

Plain sight made sense given their location. But the desk, while tacked with sticky notes and scribbled reminders, was devoid of keys.

Cabinets? Filled with paperwork, a pile of books, a framed photograph of Carlotta and her son. No key.

Drawers? Snacks Fletcher pilfered and swore to repay Carlotta for, a pair of scissors, pens and pencils. Also, no key.

Inside the decorative vases? No. Freaking. Key.

A flurry of elbows and knees tumbled into the office. Unlike the Brians with their reliance on machinery or Bertram's intimidation factors, Opal's fast reactions made her slippery. Every time it looked like Waylon had everything under control, she slithered out of his grasp.

"Chair me," Waylon said.

Fletcher swiveled, slamming the useless drawer shut, and pivoted toward a green roller chair. "Yes, Chef."

The chair sailed across uneven floors, bumping over a crooked board in the middle. Waylon stripped the phone off the desk and lassoed Opal with the curlicue landline cord, reeling her into the seat. Teeth clacking, she gnawed at his arms as he roped the phone line around her shoulders.

"We don't have to hurt each other," Fletcher said.

"Yeah, right," Opal bit back. "I saw what you did to Molly."

"*Molly?* Who tried to stab me relentlessly and only stopped because she impaled herself after getting tranquilized by someone who was *not me*?"

Opal breezed right past rational. "For all I know, you probably whispered in Dyer's ear, orchestrating this whole thing."

The storm raged on outside and in Fletcher's chest. "Opal. Do you hear yourself? What makes you think I would *ever* want this? All I'm guilty of is wanting to earn a living wage. I came here as completely unaware as you, and you—*you* just killed Sheila. With a Dyson. Who does that?"

It was hard to tell in the dark, but Fletcher was pretty sure Opal rolled her eyes. "Does Dyer's little lapdog ever quit barking?"

"I'm a nervous chatterer!"

Waylon tied a knot in the phone line, spinning Opal to face him. "That's enough out of you."

"You know, Waylon, I'm glad Eliza left you," Opal snarked. Fletcher's stomach clenched like she'd been the one hit. Eliza. Left *him*? "Without Daddy's money, you're just an arrogant son of a bitch with an attitude problem. Makes me feel less bad for wanting you dead. Wait until I get Rick in here. Rick! Ri—"

Fletcher slapped a piece of packing tape over Opal's mouth. The saleswoman fumed with muffled arguments.

Waylon's protective devil-may-care grin seeped into his words. The sound of walls going back up. "A pleasure, as always."

Without another word, he wheeled Opal out the doorway and sent her spinning toward Carlotta's bedroom.

Aaaaand, still no key.

"You check the bookcases, and I'll look in the armoire," Waylon said, leaving no time for sympathies.

Fletcher tugged down book after book, each coughing up dust. None of them even had holes cut out in the middle to hide things in. *Damn it.*

They'd exhausted all the office hiding spots, but they hadn't scoured the bedroom or the rest of the building. Rick could wander in at any moment, and then they'd be at the mercy of his hillbilly harpoon. But . . . what if the master key wasn't here at all? What would have stopped Carlotta from taking her keys with her when she fled the island?

Pacing, Fletcher kneaded the puzzle in her head. Carlotta wouldn't have taken it—it wasn't *her* key; it was Dyer's, and Dyer knew he was bequeathing the island to Waylon. He'd have instructed her to keep it here, keep it safe. Somewhere only he could find it.

Something scratched at the back of her mind, like a splinter working itself to the top of the skin. Fletcher's gaze wandered toward the middle of the room. Toward the bump in the floorboards.

"He wouldn't . . ." she whispered, but Dyer would.

Bending to the floor, Fletcher dug her fingers in, shifting her weight to pry up the board, but it didn't budge. A breath out. A breath in. She tried again with aching knuckles. The floor was definitely fighting back.

With arms around her waist, Waylon heaved Fletcher out of the way. Slamming his bandaged hand into the board, the nails shifted loose, and he peeled it up with two fingers.

"I loosened it," Fletcher huffed, shaking out her fingers. "And tell your eyebrows to shut up."

"Whatever you say, honey."

Reaching past the floorboards, Fletcher's hands brushed a small cold metal box. No, a safe the size of a jewelry box. This *had* to be it. Her fingers flew over the padlock, spinning numbered wheels into combinations that would have meant something to Dyer. The last four of his phone number. The date of the first *Jet-Setter* issue. Waylon's birthday. Nothing.

Waylon slipped the safe out of her hands. "Let me try."

He worked through the numbers, waiting for something to catch. A film of worry layered her gut. They needed to get out of this place before Rick swept inside to host a Sales scrum.

Suddenly, Fletcher couldn't breathe.

It wasn't just anxiety. A thin, plastic stripe wrapped around her throat—tighter, tighter. Her last breath had been thick with the woodsy notes of Baccarat Rouge.

Opal Meena was *strangling her.* And a few feet away, Waylon worked through the safe's combinations with his back turned to her. She couldn't even call for help. Because of the aforementioned strangling.

A haughty little laugh met the curve of her ear. Opal didn't speak and risk blowing her cover, but Fletcher suspected the laugh was code for, *Gotcha, bitch! Told you the jig was up.*

As black wormed into the corners of Fletcher's vision, she wiggled her fingers toward the desk. If she could just reach a *little* farther . . .

In one quick movement, she slid open the top drawer and snagged the pair of scissors. And—*squelch.* The blades pierced Opal's thigh, metal against muscle. Opal staggered, a string of incoherent insults ripping out of her.

Air—beautiful, breathable air—sucked deep into Fletcher's chest. Could your trachea get bruised? Hers certainly was. Every breath was knives, cutting down her throat. She would never take her lungs for granted again.

"This thing is imposs—" Waylon spun, eyes wide. They grew wider at the shears protruding from Opal's quad. Blood gushed down her leg, seeping into the leather straps of her sandals. "What'd I miss?"

"Doesn't matter. Bring the whole box. We've got to go," Fletcher rasped. Grabbing his arm, she tugged him toward the landing.

Opal bobbed after them on uneven legs, slow down the stairs but angry as hell. Fletcher's feet had almost hit the first-floor landing when a pair of evenly tanned legs wrapped around her middle. Opal had catapulted onto Fletcher's back—hands dug into her hair, nails into her scalp.

Oh no. The ground rushed up to meet them. Pain seared through Fletcher's shoulder as it slammed onto the hardwoods in the foyer.

So much for being sneaky.

"Get off of me," Fletcher gritted through her teeth. Everywhere stung. Opal clawed perfect acrylic nails into Fletcher's skin, merciless.

In an instant, Waylon gripped Opal's shoulders, trying to tear her off, but Opal must have jabbed an elbow hard against his diaphragm because he jolted back with a gasp. Or something. The details were fuzzy from Fletcher's perspective, face planted into the ground.

Something boomed outside, interrupting them. As the door slammed open, Fletcher expected Rick, a shotgun blast to the forehead, and a swift end to her suffering.

"Naya!" Waylon greeted, hoarse but relieved.

The jaguar bounded into the foyer with a roar. All teeth, Naya tore Opal off Fletcher's back. Maybe Fletcher could be convinced to become a cat person after all.

The saleswoman scrambled back, scared stutters falling from her lips. Too slow. Fury glowed in the cat's yellow eyes as she stalked toward Opal. A growl rumbled deep in Naya's chest.

Fletcher wouldn't watch as Naya's incisors sank in, couldn't listen as Opal's screams started, then silenced.

"Let's get out of here," Waylon said, tucking the safe into his backpack and Fletcher under his arm as they plunged into the raging tempest outside.

20

Rick either didn't know they'd been inside or didn't expect them to live long enough to escape.

As Fletcher and Waylon rushed into the belly of the storm, Rick hesitated, startled, before bringing his ridiculous Mad Max gun to his shoulder. Aiming. "You aren't welcome here," he shouted. "Are you illiterate? The sign was right there."

"Just leaving!" Fletcher called back.

A malevolent wind thrashed as Fletcher and Waylon bypassed Rick, diving beneath the jungle canopy. Gunpowder swirled through the petrichor as a few blasts fired. Missing them. Badly. A couple disgruntled toucans flapped through the treetops. One even let out a little nervous squawk.

Waylon shot ahead. "This way. I know a place where we can wait out the storm."

"Please tell me it's bulletproof," prayed Fletcher.

On cue, another stray bullet whizzed past them, too far left to do any bodily damage, but it still managed to crack a tree limb overhead. The branch splintered, cracked. Above, a pair of macaws bristled, darting after the toucans as the branch broke away from the trunk.

Waylon leaped forward, but Fletcher startled back, seconds away from blunt force trauma. *Slam!* The bough crashed against the wet earth. Cold mud splashed up her calves, her thighs, over the threads of her skirt. Everywhere. With Rick trekking after them, a stain was hardly the gravest of her worries.

Fingers lacing around her hips, Waylon hoisted her up and over the branch. If they weren't running for their lives, she might have registered the flutter of endearment at his touch. The way his nearness no longer repulsed her. They raced forward, never straying too far from the other. Always within reach. Close enough to catch.

Being that Kent had monopolized Fletcher's romantic life for the last decade, she had never been exposed to the horrors of New York's dating culture. Didn't know the terrors of swiping right on a cute guy only to get stood up in the pouring rain outside a restaurant she never could have afforded. All she had were Ford's stories, and he wasn't exactly a reliable narrator. But as Waylon set her down gently, she wondered what it might have been like to get to know him under ordinary circumstances. Dinner. Drinks. The downtown lights illuminating everything around them.

Wanting that from Waylon used to be so far off the table, it splattered on the floor.

But now? Would it be so bad to admit she did—that she always had wanted it? To be with someone who actually saw *her* when he looked at her, and not whatever manic pixie farm girl Kent wanted her to be? Even if that someone was the last person on earth she ever expected.

It didn't matter.

In the city, Waylon had only ever been an enemy, and they

weren't splitting an overpriced appetizer right now. Rick had been only momentarily deterred by the consequences of his terrible aim. His mud-wet footsteps thundered behind them, and with a peek over her shoulder, Fletcher watched as he planted a hand on the fallen limb and heaved himself over.

Rage contorted Rick's face. A sneer, a snarl. The same bloodred hunger she'd seen in his eyes in the sitting room before he shot his manager, but this time Fletcher recognized it as greed.

Right now, Fletcher and Waylon were just obstacles between him and a billion-dollar company.

"What Opal said about Eliza," Fletcher started as she pumped her arms to keep up with Waylon. The words scraped up her throat, both from the fear of knowing and the Usain Bolt pace she was trying to keep. "Is it true?"

"Is now the best time for an oral history?" Waylon asked. Another shotgun blast shook through the canopy.

Fletcher ignored him. "Is it true?"

Waylon made a noise that was half scoff, half self-deprecating laugh. The truth was buried in it. "What, that she dumped me? Or that she only wanted to marry me for my father's name and my father's money and my father's influence?"

Fletcher's stomach pitted.

"That I was young and in love?" When Fletcher didn't immediately respond, he asked, voice deep with vulnerability, "Or that I had a heart to break?"

They ducked beneath a wiry limb, green with new growth, and Waylon dragged it with them. When he let go, the branch slingshotted back, lashing toward Rick with an angry *whack*. It slowed the rabid salesman, but it didn't stop him.

Fingerling branches swiped at Fletcher's skin, cuts stinging in the rain. Finally, when they met the murky waters of the river, she asked, "What happened?"

"We'd been together for six months, engaged for three. My dad wanted me to move through the company ranks, but it was really just his way of keeping me under his control." The storm winds blew faster, as if spun by Dyer's undead hand. Still mad postmortem that he hadn't gotten his way. "I wanted out."

"But she wanted in," Fletcher finished.

"When I turned down the chief marketing officer job because I wanted to do my own thing, Eliza told me she didn't think it was going to work out between us."

Thunder boomed, close enough to rattle Fletcher's single, shameful cavity.

"When?" Fletcher's voice caught. "When did she break it off?"

The timeline scrolled behind her eyes, all the ticks lining up. Some part of her already knew the answer, but she had to hear him say it.

"Right before the charity gala. The night we met."

That version of Waylon transposed over the one standing in front of her. Disheveled and devilish, a chilled glass in hand. Heartbroken? She hadn't seen it then for what it was, but now it was all too obvious.

And Fletcher, stressed out and sad and ashamed of the way he made her feel, she'd rubbed his family name in his face. Accused him of being nothing without it.

A sheet of rain pummeled down from the heavens, heavier than before.

They needed to keep moving.

Fletcher picked up her pace, elbowing through the knotted lianas at the river's edge. Behind them, Rick fussed with loading another round. *Excellent.*

"Keep running," Rick called. "I love the chase."

A bullet strayed a yard or so wide of them. A yard or so too close.

"A little to your left next time," Waylon shouted.

Rick happily obliged. Although this shot veered way too far left, missing them by several tree trunks. Waylon skidded to a stop, spraying dirt up with his heels. In the slick mud, Fletcher only barely caught herself before plummeting into the river.

Fletcher seethed, "Are you trying to get us killed?"

A serious hand landed on her arm as Waylon turned her toward him. Droplets clung to his hair, his eyelashes, the tip of his nose. "I would never let anyone hurt you."

Despite everything—or, maybe, because of everything—she knew he wasn't lying. For better or worse, Waylon was a man of his word. Never said anything he didn't mean. Never meant anything he didn't say.

It helped that her only other option was to have Asshole Rick be the last thing she saw while trapped in this mortal coil.

"Okay."

Which was all the answer Waylon needed to hoop an arm around her waist, drawing Fletcher to his chest. His other arm reached overhead and dragged down a vine as thick as his bicep. "Grab on."

She didn't exactly have much of a choice. As soon as she did, Waylon kicked off the ledge of the bank and swung them out over the water.

Water where, for the record, a couple hungry-looking crocodiles slithered.

Fletcher pinched her eyes closed, sinking into the soft folds of Waylon's rain-drenched shirt. Focusing on the way the crook of his neck smelled like salt and sun and the estate's cedar soap. How the hurried beat of his heart matched hers. She braced for a crash landing on the opposite bank, the scrape of earth against skin.

When she peeled her eyes back open, they hadn't moved.

Instead of *George of the Jungle*-ing them to the other side, Waylon had stranded them over the river's middle.

Her fingertips ached around the vine, knuckles white from the strain. Regret simmered in her blood. "I thought you had a plan. *This* was your brilliant idea?"

"Yes," he said proudly.

They were nothing better than live bait.

Something sparkled in Waylon's eyes. Something that made Fletcher keenly aware of how close they were. "Have a little faith, honey."

Rain knifed across Fletcher's cheeks. Metal coated her tongue, ringing through the enamel of her teeth. Out of the underbrush, Rick's shape emerged, gun in hand.

Behind the barrel, the blacks of Rick's eyes had blown so wide, there was hardly any color left. Black hair dripped over his face, his forehead peeling and cheeks pink from days in the Lydell sun.

A cruel smile stretched to the corners of his mouth. "I'd say I'm sorry, but I'm really not. When you see your dad, tell him I say, 'Thanks for nothing, you old fuck.'"

Adrenaline pounded through Fletcher's head, thick and potent. Her heart slammed against her ribs, trying to break free, but there was nowhere to go. Waylon's arm clutched her tighter. Beneath their feet, the reptiles circled.

Rick raised the shotgun to his shoulder, that absurd spear gleaming off the end.

Electricity prickled the back of Fletcher's neck, and she made the mistake of looking up. The trees parted for the river, leaving a gunmetal stripe of exposed sky.

A blue bolt of lightning zapped down and latched on to Rick's bayonet.

Fletcher shielded her eyes against the flash, but there was no hiding from the incinerating heat. The instant ricochet of thunder, so loud it left her ears squealing. The pungent stench of charred flesh. The unthinkable *thud* as Rick rag-dolled to the earth.

"Where did you say we're going?" Fletcher asked when her lungs remembered how to breathe.

After a coordinated effort, they managed to swing themselves to the far edge of the river, narrowly avoiding the crocodiles' serrated grins. All of their limbs were blessedly still attached. Somehow.

Their map, however, hadn't survived unscathed. The rain was unrelenting, soaking through the canvas of their bags, and reducing the map to a papier-mâché pulp. It crumbled in her hands, but that didn't stop Fletcher from trying.

"I didn't," Waylon said without looking back. Still self-satisfied from his grand escape. Fletcher refrained from reminding him that his plan primarily worked because Rick got barbecued in an act of divine intervention. His ego was big enough as it was.

Fletcher's waterlogged backpack dangled from his fingers. It weighed about a trillion pounds, and although Fletcher hadn't complained, Waylon slipped it off her shoulders with just as little verbal recognition.

On the edge of the map's last remaining legible strip, there was a smudge. If she squinted, maybe it looked like the marina. "Is this west? I thought we were supposed to be going west."

"Can't say." His voice lilted unexpectedly. After an afternoon of getting strangled, becoming Rick's target practice, and having her ankles nipped at by crocodiles, Fletcher's nerves were already plenty frayed. This fully unraveled them.

"You're enjoying this," Fletcher said pointedly.

"A bit." A smile. "When's the last time Fletcher Spence went with the flow?"

Fletcher huffed. Never. She'd much prefer it if the flow went with her.

There was no end to the jungle. Green webbed in every direction. They could be heading straight back to the ruins of the estate, and Fletcher wouldn't have been able to tell.

Despite the relentless onslaught of rain, Waylon forged confidently ahead, bending branches out of Fletcher's way and offering her a steadying hand anytime they crossed a patch of dense roots. They didn't say anything else, the silence falling between them cut by the constant drum of rain against soaked soil and the babbling of a brook too small for piranhas or anacondas or any other evil aquatic animals Dyer may have imported for his own sick amusement. The hike had rubbed Fletcher's feet raw, and the water soothed her chafed skin as they crossed into a clearing.

"Almost there," said Waylon.

One tree dominated the landscape. The shadows were denser here, and buttress roots braided together, wide and well-fed, leaving only enough light and nutrients for stubborn ferns and a patchwork of pink begonias. Even the rain softened.

Too late, she realized she'd let her guard down.

Waylon tugged her hand and spun her into his chest. Which could have almost been romantic if he hadn't also shucked off his backpack and unsheathed a knife he'd smuggled from the kitchen.

"There's just one catch," he said with a voice like amber whiskey.

With her back pressed against him, she knew he felt the shake of her inhale, the purposeful way she blew her breath out through her mouth. Trying to quell a rising tide of panic. "What's that?"

"I want to trust you." His voice held firm.

"Then trust me."

"But how do I know you won't betray me?"

Tension lanced down her spine as he brought the blade to her neck. He couldn't know. Could he? She'd covered her tracks. The deal she'd struck. The risk she'd taken forming an agreement with Jackie. The way she'd hedged her bets by circling back to create an alliance of her own with Waylon. It was wrong, she knew. All of it. Wrong, but necessary.

He'd do the same. Every trick she played, she'd learned from his father.

Fletcher bit her bottom lip. "I could ask you the same thing."

"The difference is," he said, measuring his words carefully, taking his time with each syllable. The blade's cold bite against her pulse didn't budge. "I've got nothing left to hide."

Her mind raced. This was Waylon. The same man who doubled back when he could have abandoned her at the manor. Who rescued her when she'd nearly run into an ambush. Who kept finding new ways to surprise her. Their past as sworn enemies had been set aside for a flimsy truce, but he was still a Cartwright, and she still had everything to lose.

And now—

She dared a glance down. His hand was steady. Not a tremor in his grip.

"What do you need?" she asked, keeping her voice level despite the fear rioting in her chest. "To convince you?"

Silence stretched between them, charged as storm clouds.

He craned his neck over her shoulder, eyes dark. Dissident heat rose between her thighs as his palm spread across her belly. The steel-sharp edge of his knife scraped the skin of her throat. In a voice softer than she expected, he murmured, "Tell me what you want, Spence, and I'll let you live."

Fletcher swallowed, her throat cording against the blade. "I want . . ."

She could almost see herself through his point of view: muddied and bleary-eyed, maybe, but still the quiet, rule-following assistant he'd met at the gala. A version of herself who had barely been brave enough to admit what she wanted, let alone chase it.

The only version of herself that existed for so long. Too long.

You could do it, Fletcher Spence.

Something changed the night they met. A seed buried in her chest, rooting around her ribs. Spiteful determination, yes. But also, a new kind of propulsive bravery, all because a dashing, dangerous stranger comforted and challenged her in the same breath.

Against all odds, they'd found their way back to each other. As much a surprise to him as it had been to her. Maybe this didn't have anything to do with Jackie.

Fletcher eased the knife far enough away from her jugular that she could spin to face Waylon without him slitting her throat. Sans high heels, her nose brushed the center of his chest. She planted her palms against him and rose onto the highest tips of her toes.

Before she could rationalize her way out of it, think of a hundred different backup plans, or talk herself back from whatever proverbial ledge she was about to throw herself off, Fletcher kissed Waylon Cartwright.

Shocked and then settling, he kissed her back. His mouth was firm, steady. Somehow both urgent and patient. Confident. Smug. Waylon, right down to the lips.

Need pooled in every erogenous zone that had been forgotten for the past ten years: the cave of Fletcher's collarbone, the crook of her elbow, the bend of her ear.

The hand that wasn't holding a steak knife trailed down her

waist, fingers tight against her hips. She arched into him, and he took the opportunity to deepen the kiss, teeth grazing. His tongue darted across her bottom lip, and her mouth parted in welcome. A noise—caught between a whimper and a plea—worked its way up her throat. Kissing Kent had always been quick, chaste. Another item on the long list of Fletcher's duties. This was . . . not that.

Waylon drank her like top-shelf liquor. Immediacy raced through every movement. Fletcher's fingertips toyed with the hem of his shirt, skimming the taut skin of his stomach.

His knife sank to the forest floor. Evidently, this was a two-handed task.

Waylon guided her back, back, back, until her skin met the roots of the kapok tree. Hands coming beneath her thighs, he lifted her onto a curve, the root ancient and unmoving beneath her. Her knees widened far enough for him to situate himself closer.

All that nervous energy she'd pushed down now snapped like a rubber band under too much force. There must have been enough epinephrine in her system to bring someone back to life.

Waylon pulled away first. Pupils blown out, lips swollen. "You have no idea how long I've waited to do that."

Fletcher caught a fistful of his shirt, suddenly wishing it were anywhere else. "I think I do."

He kissed her again, savoring it. Savoring her. Making up for three years of lost time, or maybe making amends for it. This thing between them, it wasn't just years of pent-up sexual frustration or a heat-induced delusion or the stress of survival.

Around him, she'd never been tasked with contorting herself into a box for his liking, shaping and molding herself into someone he expected her to be. She'd met him at her lowest, and he hadn't shied away. She was allowed to simply be whatever she was. Feel whatever she felt. Want whatever she wanted.

He pressed his palm to the back of her head, fingers weaving into the copper of her hair. Breathing? What was breathing? Fletcher barely remembered as his other hand traced the edge of her jaw, down the slope of her neck. He paused there, feeling the frantic skip of her heartbeat.

"I'm sorry I hated you for so long," she said. Barely more than a whisper.

"I'm sorry I made you."

His mouth latched on to the pulse point, lingering. She wanted more of him. More everything. Entirely too much wanting. So much it threatened to burn her to ash.

"Waylon," she said, but what she really meant was *yes* and *please* and *oh my god, are we actually doing this?*

When he drew back, his thumb touched the crease of her mouth.

"Okay," he said, as if convincing himself. To trust her. To give in to this thing between them. He leaned in for another kiss that left Fletcher's lips tingling and then rested his forehead against hers. "Come with me."

Around them, the chirp of the brush bugs had died, the birds had fallen silent. One monkey howled, and the branches above them shifted with the weight of them leaving until everything stilled.

As a general rule, anxious girlies should not trust gut feelings. Fletcher's gut frequently lied to her. *Everyone in this meeting is staring at your unsteamed blouse. Eat the cheese Danish—you're not* that *lactose intolerant. The restructuring meeting is at eleven, but if you don't have these memos stapled three hours early, you're first on the chopping block.*

Usually she kept those thoughts at bay with an antianxiety prescription, a bottle of Lactaid, and a color-coded Google calendar.

In the wild, there was only instinct.

And as her fingers laced with his, instinct told Fletcher that taking Waylon's hand might be the most dangerous thing she'd ever done.

21

If Fletcher hadn't been so distracted, she would have noticed the tree house. It wasn't some boyish construction with mismatched edges. *Tree house* surely wasn't even the correct terminology. This was an arboreal chalet. A timber mansion.

The wood-slat exterior had been stained and weather-sealed a rich brown, and the roof shingled with flat green slate. From way down here, it was impossible to discern its floor plan, only that it *had one*, which was more than her apartment could say.

Climbing the roots as pathways up the trunk, Waylon swung himself up onto the lowest branch and used the knife for its true purpose—to cut a rope that had been knotted around the base of the tree. A ladder loosed itself from the canopy, made of uneven rungs and frayed knots. Real reassuring.

Fletcher obviously let Waylon climb it first. At the top, he nudged open a hatch. You couldn't be afraid of heights when you worked on the sixty-fifth floor, but Fletcher's arms didn't get the memo. They shook all the way up.

Inside, Fletcher fought gravity as her jaw threatened to drop.

Unlike the estate with its gaudy grandeur or the staff building, which felt more like a Hilton than a home, the tree house conjured a whole suite of adjectives Fletcher never imagined she'd find on the island. Cozy, inviting, and sunny somehow, despite the ongoing storm.

"One of my grandfathers built this as a hunting cabin, I think. My dad never bothered with it, so my mom used it occasionally as her studio." He ruffled the damp curls at the back of his head. Bashful, almost. Another adjective she hadn't expected ever needing to deploy in Waylon's presence.

This wasn't just a tree house. It was a hideaway, a sanctuary. A priceless reprieve from the dangers awaiting them beyond the four walls, and he'd been willing to share it with her. The intimacy stuck to the back of Fletcher's throat and made it harder to breathe.

"All right, *MTV Cribs*," she said, an elbow ribbing him, anything to touch him again. "Give me the tour."

Most of the tree house was one room: an open-concept kitchen, dining, and living space. Windows mapped across the far wall, right up to the pointed roof, offering an unimpeded view of the canopy. There was a sunroom off to one side, where an easel and some dried-up watercolors had been forgotten, and a glass door walked out to the wraparound balcony. On the other side, a spiral staircase wound to a loft where she imagined a bed. (Wrapped in Egyptian cotton sheets, she hoped longingly. One night of glamping was plenty to satiate her morbid curiosity.)

Waylon walked her through the amenities, a hand tethering to the small of her back the whole time. The kitchen taunted a propane stove squished between the cabinets. A solar-powered generator fed lamps Waylon flicked on as they went, avoiding the Big Light altogether. Best of all? A rain catcher and a filtration system meant that—

"Holy shit, is there a bathroom?"

Waylon laughed, buttery. "There very much is."

A tiny yolk-yellow attempt at a bathroom, but a bathroom nonetheless. Fletcher would never look a gift shower-tub combo in the mouth.

As Waylon padded off to hunt down linens, Fletcher was forced to face the reality of her reflection. She didn't know where to start: the tangles in her hair, the hollow look in her eyes, or the way her lips were still plump with the aftertaste of Waylon.

Desire threaded through her skin at the thought, her fingers lifting to her lips like she might still feel him there, but it dissipated at the sight of the dirt caking her nails. Tiny lacerations marred her arms from the jungle. A ring of purple laced around her throat, bruised from the telephone cord.

Her clothes hadn't fared any better. Blood—hers, others, it was hard to keep up—crusted the fabric. Mud stained her shirt within an inch of its life. Grass and twigs and those prickly seedpods burrowed in the weave of her skirt. No washing machine in the world would be able to salvage it.

The thought of scrubbing her skin within an inch of its life under scalding hot water and then sliding back into her grimy clothes was horrifying enough to keep her awake for weeks.

This was who Waylon had kissed?

In the end, it wouldn't be one of her rabid colleagues or a dangerous wild animal that would keel her over. Mortification would do the trick.

Fletcher yelled, "I have to get out of these clothes immediately. Do you mind if I—" Waylon appeared back in the doorframe, entirely too close for her to be yelling about nudity this loudly. A cough, clearing her throat and dropping her voice. "Um, do you mind if I hop in the shower?"

"Ladies first." Waylon set a stack of things on the counter—a couple towels and washcloths, a T-shirt, some boxers, and a pair of khaki pants. "Faucet's a little tough. Let me help."

Nervous hands fidgeted with Fletcher's shirt buttons as Waylon twisted the shower knobs until water gurgled out of the fixtures. Slow at first, then with water pressure that put her apartment to shame.

She'd managed a whole two of six buttons by the time Waylon turned his attention away from the shower. His lips flicked upward into a faint smile. Being in such close quarters with him couldn't possibly be good for her cardiovascular health. Her heart thumped and thudded. Stopped altogether.

"Should be all set." Two confident steps brought Waylon in front of her, pulled by a magnetic force. Waylon's fingers found the buttons she fumbled with. "Sorry there's no silk robes here."

"How will I ever survive?" Fletcher asked, and it occurred to her again, in the milky light of the too-yellow bathroom that she might not. That this moment could be the last of hers before falling prey to a biting blade, a wayward bullet, or any number of wild beasts.

"It'll be hard, but I'm sure you'll find a way." Button by button, Waylon worked toward the shoulders of her shirt. Only one remained. His eyebrows *thing*ed in silent question. Waiting for permission to make the next move.

After high school gym class, Fletcher used to change in the bathroom stalls. She didn't have sisters who wandered around in sports bras or best friends to share changing rooms with. This kind of closeness, this kind of casual vulnerability was uncharted water. Something that used to be reserved for Kent alone, and even then, sparingly.

But what part about this week had *been* charted?

Her heart a bubbling cauldron of anticipation, Fletcher cupped her hands around his, sliding the last button through its hole.

Damp fabric dripped down to her elbows, revealing the beige lace of her bra and the divot of her belly button. Fletcher's skin buzzed as he digested her, dissecting every slope, every line. Suddenly, she grew entirely too aware of each rounded curve of her body, the dimples and freckles she usually kept hidden beneath polyester blazers and secondhand linen.

"Is that another tricky zipper?" he asked, eyeing her skirt.

Electricity thrummed under Fletcher's skin. "One of the many plights of womanhood."

Spinning her to face the mirror, Waylon's knuckles grazed past the band of her bra, down the ridges of her vertebrae, until his fingers found the zipper of her skirt. Loosened, tweed spilled off her hips, lower and lower until it joined the fabric pooling on the pale tiles. Waylon's hands hovered near the trim of her seamless panties. Nude. Practical. On sale from Target. But severely lacking in the sex-appeal department.

It didn't seem to matter. Any embarrassment she'd felt before vanished. Waylon looked at her the way a drowning man looked at dry land. Eyes roaming and ravenous. How long they stood like that, she wasn't sure. Seconds? Minutes?

Finally, his Adam's apple bobbed with a swallow, throat working when he said, "You're gorgeous."

Fletcher fussed with her matted hair. Pretty sure there was a caterpillar in there somewhere. "Oh, I don't—"

"It's not up for debate." His eyes roved down the length of her once more, scanning her like a Xerox machine. Committing her to memory. When he looked up, their eyes met in the mirror. The blues of his, the greens of hers. A dangerous mix. "I've never wanted anyone the way I want you, Fletcher Spence."

Waylon kissed her once, hard, and then inched back. Leaving

Fletcher grasping, head pitched back to watch him watch her. He knew exactly what he was doing to her. And she hated him for it. She also didn't hate him even a little bit.

Tension rippled between them. As fog gathered at the edges of the mirror, Fletcher considered the proper etiquette for asking someone to ignore the fifty-two layers of grime on her skin and thoroughly ravish her. Instead, she stood dumbly, lips parted and pink.

At her silence, Waylon tucked his hands into his pockets with a nod. "Water's hot. Here's a towel. Change of clothes. Everything else should be in the shower. Carlotta usually kept this place stocked." His voice strained, trying to stay even and calibrated, and his lips thinned into a thoughtful line, something tucked unsaid just behind them.

The door closed. Latched. Leaving Fletcher alone, half naked and flushed. In the shower, steam rose in rivulets around her, and she let herself think about Waylon as she lathered, rinsed, and repeated.

I think people who order Manhattans are too afraid to ask for what they really want. That was what he'd said on the pool deck, days ago but also a lifetime ago.

Things were different now. *She* was different now. And she wasn't afraid anymore.

By the time they'd both finished showering, the rain had lulled to a drone. It patterned the windows in fat droplets, smudging the jungle beyond into an abstract idea. If she squinted, she could almost pretend they were perched in a Park Ave. penthouse, overlooking the greens of Central Park.

She met Waylon in the kitchen. Their picnic supplies had rapidly depleted, but he'd spread what was left of them across the island's quartz countertop. "Ooh, you know how I feel about a charcuterie board," she said, sliding one of the bruised tangerine slices into her mouth.

A tint of a smile touched Waylon's lips. Beneath it, a smolder. While the rain turned the afternoon into a soupy gray, the shaded lamps and scalloped sconces cast orbs of amber light. Gold dripped off the lines of his face, gilding him. He popped a couple yogurt-covered cranberries in his mouth. Chewed. His gaze soaking her up. Finally, he said, "You look good in my clothes."

Good wasn't the word she would have chosen. One of Waylon's three-sizes-too-big Subtext shirts hung loose on her limbs, a wet patch rapidly growing beneath her plait of washed hair, and his pants bunched at her ankles but fell loose around her hips. Her nipples forced her back into her bra. They had no trouble remembering the way he'd kissed her, touched her, left her trembling and needy in the bathroom. They pebbled against the fabric, sensitive and eager.

If he asked, she'd lie about how comfortable the soft knit of his shirt was, how she longed to submerge herself in the oud and amber notes of his cologne that lingered on the fabric. But for now, she slid on the painted-blue barstool and said, "Thanks for sharing."

He hummed, amused. "Anytime."

Another bite of fruit. "Let me know when you want to get stranded on an island together next. I'll clear my calendar."

She conveniently avoided the part where it took her a five-minute pep talk to convince herself to actually put his clothes on. Mortal enemies didn't kiss in the rain and share clothes. And slipping his bar's T-shirt over her head solidified that *mortal enemies* didn't quite fit them anymore.

He wasn't just her boss's super-entitled, vaguely evil son.

Somewhere along the line, Waylon stopped being someone to hate or even someone to tolerate but someone she actually enjoyed spending her time with. Someone she was glad to have by her side, despite being on a corporate retreat from hell.

She could have blamed it on the week they'd had. The temperature and the frequent ring of adrenaline through her veins. Or the way they were so far from anything that felt familiar or normal or reasonable, so far from the Fletcher she'd been in New York.

But she'd be lying.

It was Waylon, whose protection never veered possessive, who surprised her by prodding her to define herself, rather than filling in the blank with his own definition. It was how much time they'd wasted despising each other and how little time they might have left.

"I decided what I want," Fletcher said, and Waylon swallowed loudly. She took her time choosing her next bite if only to avoid the searing way his eyes bored into her still-damp skin. "I want to know you."

There was a fraction of a second—of a millisecond—where he hesitated. He adjusted his cup on the counter, silver rings glinting. Straightened his shoulders, centered himself. "Okay."

"It's not an interview, I swear," she said, laugh brittle. Some of his PR-trained posture whittled away. "I just—I know some things, obviously. Like your birthday and your alma mater. I know you snore like a freight train and own a jazz bar in Brooklyn, but I feel like I don't *know you.*"

"You can ask me anything you want." Fletcher opened her mouth to get started, but he stopped her with a finger. "*If* I get to ask a question back."

"Deal." Fletcher propped her chin on her hands. "Why Bubbles?"

"That's what you start with?" He blew out a breath. "I'm surprised you don't know. It started the night Eliza dumped me, after I inexplicably crashed into the champagne tower at the charity gala at the hands of someone who shall remain unnamed. Once my dad finished excommunicating me, Joplin stole a bottle of Dom from the back kitchen and met me outside. We drank it all the way to Park and Fifty-Eighth, when she made me laugh so hard champagne came out of my nose."

"It's cute. Bubbles," Fletcher said. "Way better than Fizzgerald."

Waylon laughed, tipping his head back. A sound Fletcher could get drunk on. "You know, you're funny when you're not so tightly wound."

A surprised scoff escaped. "I'm not—" But her arguments dried up, her jaw hanging loose. Visions of checklists and meticulously organized Gantt charts twirled through her mind. Okay, fine, maybe she was a *little* tightly wound.

But now that she thought about it, she hadn't itched to check her email or fought off intrusive thoughts about missed meetings for at least eighteen hours. It was a wonder the kind of perspective fighting for your life could give a girl.

All she could do was shake her head, a smile touching her lips, unraveling a little more. "Just ask your question."

Leaning onto his elbows so their eyes met level, Waylon asked, "If we make it out of here, are you getting back together with Kent?"

"Definitely not. We've run our course." She stared down at her freshly scrubbed cuticles as she asked, "Did you and Joplin ever . . . ?"

"No. She's been off and on with the same girl for years, but we are—fuck, *were*—good friends. My best, maybe." A beat of silence stretched between them, neither antsy to fill it up. When Waylon finally caught her eye again, he asked, "What do you do for fun?"

"Fun?" The word felt foreign on Fletcher's tongue. "Next question."

"Come on, Spence. There's got to be something fun you like to do."

"Like what? I'm definitely not going to the racquet club or brushing elbows at soirees or whatever else you're used to people answering this question with. I haven't taken PTO in three years, and when I'm not working, I'm taking photos so that I have a portfolio ready to try to convince everyone I've got what it takes to join *Jet-Setter*. Except your dad destroyed my camera, so that's off the table until I build my savings back up." Fletcher worried with the ends of her wet hair, somehow both amped up and exhausted. "Right now, my apartment doesn't even have an oven, and that's only until next week, when they kick everybody out to turn it into a department store, so sometimes, when I'm feeling really wild, I'll look at Zillow listings of homes with stoves."

Reaching across the counter, Waylon folded her palms in his. "You shouldn't have to make yourself miserable for a job. Or basic kitchen appliances."

"Easy for you to say," Fletcher said, reaching for levity but coming up empty. "You're a trust fund baby who had the luxury of disinheriting himself."

"You're right. The wealth-distribution system's fucked up."

"So fucked up." She rolled the tension out of her shoulders, squeezed his fingers. "Anyway. New question."

Waylon pulled away from the counter in favor of pacing. "What do you think Jackie's up to?"

The sudden topic change had Fletcher choking on her charcuterie, little cracker crumbs shooting to the back of her esophagus. Tears sprang to her eyes. With two hands she reached for Waylon's canteen, chugging it dry.

She swiped the back of her hand over her mouth, took a deep breath, and tried to remember how to function like a normal human being who didn't have a giant deadly secret. She'd much rather discuss her apartment's blatant lack of culinary equipment.

"What, um . . . What do you mean?"

It hardly sounded casual.

"Opal said Sheila knew something about her plan, but I haven't seen Jackie in days." Waylon scuffed his knuckles along the cliff of his jaw. "Do you think she's heading to the marina?"

The truth was nuclear codes. A big red button that said DO NOT PUSH. Telling him the truth was something she'd assumed she'd get around to eventually—most likely around the time the yacht's engine chugged to life. But that was before she'd kissed him. Before she'd learned how the slant of his mouth felt against hers. Before she realized Waylon was someone she could lose.

If the words left Fletcher's lips, she would never be able to take them back. This thing between them—whatever it was, whatever it might become—would be blasted to smithereens.

Like sending documents through a paper shredder, Fletcher tore apart the honest answer until it was indistinguishable. All the information still there but unreadable. "Probably, right? You did say it was going to be a bloodbath over there. We'll have to be careful."

Waylon considered this. Evidently satisfied, he said, "Your turn."

With all his attention on her, Fletcher's skin felt too snug on her bones, her lungs too tight. Tapping her fingers along the countertop, she reached past a half-squashed pear where a bottle of alpine water acted as a paperweight. "What's that?"

Clearly, she'd caught Waylon off guard. Rolling out his shoulders, Waylon took a moment to say, "That's . . . the letter my dad left me. The one from his bedside table."

Fletcher eyed it. Wrinkled, water-damaged, and woefully unopened. "I think he might have intended for you to, I don't know, read it."

"Maybe."

"Are you going to?"

"Maybe."

What it felt like, holding the last words your father would ever say to you, Fletcher couldn't imagine. Estranged as they became, Dyer and Waylon hadn't always been at such odds. Different men on different paths, sure. But how did you say goodbye to someone you had stopped speaking to for so long?

It wasn't her turn again yet, but Fletcher asked, "What happened between you two?"

Waylon's shoulders heaved with an Atlantean sigh. "We never saw eye to eye, but things really started going downhill after my mom passed. She was like our translator. I'd always say the wrong thing, or he'd piss me off, but she helped us understand each other better. Hard to believe it's been five years already."

He rubbed at an ache in his chest. A raw spot of grief this week had only agitated.

"After that, everything became about the business—his legacy. Every conversation we had was just some checklist his lawyers gave him about *preserving the company's image* or *maximizing shareholder returns* or whatever other bullshit thing they wanted to control me with. All my life I've been Waylon Cartwright, whether I wanted to be or not. People always think they know me. Think they can use me to get whatever they want. I was sick of it, especially after Eliza. The mold he wanted me to fit in, I refused. Eventually, I guess it became easier to cut me out entirely."

His shoulders sagged, brows creased. Fletcher itched to smooth the wrinkle, massage the tension from his muscles.

"He loved my mom. I know he did. I even used to think he might have loved me." Resentment lingered in his tone. "But never more than he loved Cartwright Media."

Fletcher's feet hit the floor, the distance between them vanishing. Lifting her chin to meet his gaze, Fletcher could slather herself in SPF 50 and spend all day long swimming in those eyes. Want readily pooled beneath her navel. Guys like him really should come with a warning label. "Can I kiss you again?"

He towered over her, and a striking smile touched his lips. "I think I get to ask the next question."

"Maybe I'm tired of playing by other people's rules." Her fingers twisted into his shirt. She didn't want to think about how they got here, or what happened when the sun rose tomorrow and her time ran out. They were here. Now. Together.

"Won't this ruin your ten-year plan?"

"Yeah," Fletcher said, just a breath punctuated with a laugh. "But I think that plan went out the window a few days ago."

He grinned, a hand coming to rest against the dip of her waist. Desire bloomed in every corner of her body. "Sounds like a problem for us once we get off the island."

Us. The word rang through Fletcher, bright and clear as a knife against a champagne flute. "*If* we get off the island."

"If we get off the island," he conceded. His thumb traced the curve of her ear, down her jawline, until he caught her chin between his fingers. Waylon kissed her. Or maybe she kissed him. They met messily somewhere in the middle, kissing the same way they'd spent the last two days running: like their lives depended on it.

22

As long as their bodies pressed against each other, all lips and tongues and the occasional scrape of teeth, there was no one else on this island, no one out there waiting for them with ultimatums or expectations, or at least no one who could reach them. The tree house was a bubble, perfect and intimate and *theirs*.

He twisted his fingers through hers and dipped down so that his nose could trace the length of her neck. Shivers skated up her spine. When he spoke, his lips glanced across her skin. "Tell me what you want, honey."

"I want . . ." Fletcher gasped as he planted one kiss, two, against the hollow where her neck met her shoulder. Her stomach tied itself in knots. "I want you to kiss me again."

Waylon nipped at that familiar curve, then traced the spot with his tongue, working at the skin until she was certain she'd have a bruise. "That won't be an issue."

One hand drifted beneath her shirt, flattening against her rib cage and tugging her closer. Kissing her harder, deeper. His other palm wedged beneath her chin, holding her captive. As if she'd ever want to escape.

He broke away only long enough to ask, "And?"

Every nerve in her body was pure voltage. Snapping and sparking like an overloaded current. "And—I want you to touch me."

"Where?" he asked, dragging his nose toward her ear until he could suck her earlobe into his mouth, his teeth raking over it. "Where do you want me to touch you?"

Taking his hand in hers, she guided it over her borrowed shirt to her breast. He cupped, squeezed. Taunting her.

"Not, um—" Fletcher stuttered. Swallowed. Every synapse in her brain misfired as he pinched her nipple through her top. "Maybe underneath?"

His scruff scraped along her cheek as he pulled back, the reflecting pools of his eyes finding hers again. This time, they'd gone dark, deep as trenches. "Thought you'd never ask."

Fingertips trailed over her rib bones, outlining the swell of her breasts. Fletcher lifted her arms and snaked out of the fabric.

Waylon's hands hovered inches from her body. Like he wasn't sure where to put them first. "You're . . . I mean. Fuck, Fletcher. Look at you."

All she could see was the molten blue of Waylon's gaze, a blue so hot it burned. Greedy. His hand as it found its place again at her breast, kneading over her bra until Fletcher arched into his touch.

His other hand grasped the point of her hip bone, dragging her against the length of him and luring a throaty mewl from her lips. Some distant part of her subconsciousness that wasn't preoccupied with all the skin and friction wondered when the last time she wanted something this badly was. She only thought of Kent in contrast: of ways he hadn't held her, of things she hadn't felt.

"Yours needs to go, too," she said, feathery. Her fingers looped beneath the hem of his shirt, and she lifted it up and over his head. The Lydell sun had left an olive tan around his neck and forearms but missed the continental expanse of his chest, leaving it a shade lighter.

Waylon's touch glanced back up her sides, fingers dancing beneath her bra straps. "And this?"

"Gone," Fletcher breathed.

She'd never been this forward, this confident. But Waylon made her feel powerful. Like there was nothing she could ask for that she couldn't have.

On her command, he unclasped it, and Waylon inhaled unsteadily. His gaze glazed over, round and unblinking, like he'd never seen a pair of tits before. Hers were full, nipples peaked. He ran his tongue over his bottom lip, and her name slipped out of his mouth.

The calluses of his palms circled her stomach, her chest. Fletcher let her eyes flutter closed, even as she knew Waylon's stayed open, watching her turn supple and pliant in his grasp. Her touch wandered, feeling for his thighs, trying to inch toward his erection, but one of his hands captured her wrist.

"This part isn't about me," he said before his mouth met hers once more, and in the soft light of the kitchen, the trail of his lips cooling against her skin, Fletcher was writhing and craving. Kissing him like there would never be enough.

"Three years, I've wondered what it would be like to have you." Waylon shifted his attention to her collarbone. "And you've been someone else's the whole time."

Fletcher sighed. "I could be yours."

A satisfied hum resonated from his chest. The sound—so pleased, so Waylon—coiled a spring deep in Fletcher's core, and she clenched her thighs tighter. Reading her body language, Waylon adjusted, slotting a thigh between her legs.

"That's my girl," he whispered into her freshly showered skin.

Goose bumps rose against his breath, eliciting a noise from deep in her chest, every inch of her on edge as she settled onto him.

Fletcher circled her hips, relishing the scrape of his jeans against her core. Wishing her pants had been discarded on the floor with the rest of her clothes. Building and building. Nothing had ever felt this good before. Not even a fully checked-off to-do list.

Waylon's fingers skidded once past her hips, between her legs. Curse these stupid khakis. Business casual attire or not, there was no denying the slickness there. Pressure gathered, corkscrewing up her spine until her head tipped back, leaving the wide spill of her neck open for Waylon's mouth.

Drawing away from her, his fingertips dusted up the front of her, past her navel, her sternum, her throat, until his thumb touched the pout on her lips. "Tell me what else you want."

"We should go upstairs." Her voice was coarsely ground. It was like she hadn't had a drink in days. Parched. Desperate. Thoughts were a distant memory. All she knew was want, need. Primal lust that craved anything he had to give.

He pulled back just enough to look at her beneath his lashes, noses grazing. "Are you sure?"

Together, they had outlasted almost everyone. So few of them remained on the island that Fletcher couldn't stop hope from sprouting. Maybe they actually *could* make it off Lydell alive. She'd thought that if—when—they did, Waylon would go back to Brooklyn, and Fletcher would cross the East River. That their lives would go more or less back to normal, give or take a few extra therapy sessions.

But this was a bridge they couldn't uncross. She couldn't *unfuck* Waylon any more than her colleagues could be *unkilled*.

Fletcher nodded. "Never surer. Are you?"

He made a noise at the back of his throat. "I'm happy to show you how certain I am."

With her legs wrapped around his waist, he carried her up the spiral staircase to the loft and eased her onto the mattress, the sheets devastatingly soft against her back. Egyptian cotton, for sure. *Hallelujah.*

He caged her, hands splayed on either side of her head, the feel of his *certainty* undeniable between them. Fletcher was going to have sex with Waylon Cartwright. Likely very, *very* good sex. Her experience was comparatively limited, but the half-lidded way he looked at her stoked a fire in her belly. Made her feel confident and capable. Like just being *her* was enough.

Waylon kissed the tender skin between her breasts as his hands mapped up her body. Fingertips trailed up her legs, flush against the borrowed fabric. His palm glided between her thighs toward the center of her, and he pressed against her aching pulse point. Fletcher raked her fingers through his curls as he circled, her nerves arcing with each revolution. She'd never hated a pair of khakis more than she did right now.

His other hand slid past her loose waistband, curving against her ass, fingertips expecting to meet a pair of underwear but . . . not.

"I decided to wash mine and let them air-dry," she said, relishing the surprise on his face as his fingers met her bare skin. "But I appreciate the offer."

His mouth hung open, a devious smile lifting the corners. "Fletcher Spence, you are full of surprises."

She unbuttoned the trousers and kicked them off, eager to feel his touch at the apex of her thighs, and he obliged with one finger, then two. Waylon's lips found hers again—firm, needing. It worked her into a sweat, the heel of his palm, the rhythm of his fingers.

"You like that, honey?" he asked.

The words for *I'm not sure I've ever liked something quite as* much *as I like this* felt too far away, so she settled for a breathy "Yes," and a reedy, "Whatever you do, don't stop."

"Anything you want."

Fletcher believed that he meant it. Pleasure pulsed, hot and tingling, through her. She'd sustained herself for the last several years on touching herself in the shower and compulsory sex with a man she didn't truly love. It was like a vampire drinking only from squirrels. Survivable, but barely.

She'd told herself for so long that it was fine, that everything was fine. That being with someone who wanted only things she couldn't give was par for the course. That chasing her dream life meant living in a nightmare sometimes. That getting what she wanted might always be out of reach.

But here was Waylon, finger-banging her to her heart's content like he didn't have his own burgeoning need for release. Smiling into their kiss like he didn't mind the wait. Sharing his clothes. Saving her life. Maybe in more ways than one.

Even when she reached her peak, it wasn't enough. She needed more of him. Waylon may have majored in business, but he must have minored in telepathy because as soon as the thought crossed Fletcher's mind, he leaned back, reaching for his own waistband.

Adrenaline coursed through her body as he unzipped his pants. Beneath his boxers, the length of him was already bulging. Then, the boxers were gone, too. Fletcher reached out to feel him, all of him, and Waylon sucked a breath through his teeth.

His head dropped forward, eyes pinched closed. Gathering himself. "Fuck. Two seconds," he whispered, and his weight shifted off the bed.

Rising onto her elbows, Fletcher tracked his movements as he pawed clunkily through his backpack at the foot of the bed. A metallic square manifested in his fingers.

"You packed *condoms*? What else did you find time to grab? The

Oxford English Dictionary? A Jet Ski with a satellite GPS and a full tank of gas?"

"Condoms are very small, Fletcher," he laughed, rasped.

"I'm not complaining. Look at you, being all prepared."

Waylon's thigh warmed under her touch as he sheathed himself in whatever brand of condom billionaire heirs preferred. "I learned from the best."

"Personally, I was more concerned with not getting killed by Asshole Rick or Deepti or the Brians but—" The sentence died in Fletcher's throat as Waylon pressed into her. "Oh."

He smirked, and if her heart hadn't already been hammering, it would have lurched. "The only name I want to hear out of your pretty little mouth tonight is mine."

Her hips drew wide, making more room for him. There was a shuffle as they found the right shape. Him lowering, her rising to meet him. Then: a moan. Hers or his? Both, maybe.

Hooking a hand beneath Fletcher's knee, Waylon hiked her leg up, allowing him to work his way deeper. A groan slipped past her lips, and she clawed at his back, desperate for purchase. He pulsed again and again, each stroke carrying Fletcher closer and closer to dizzying bliss.

They stayed there, tangled in the sheets and each other, until the storm cleared and the clouds shifted and all Fletcher saw were stars.

23

When Fletcher stirred awake, she'd been trapped. Waylon's sleep-heavy arm slung around her waist. The tree house mattress molded around them, as if they were one entity, and she allowed herself the small pleasure of nuzzling in tighter. She could've stayed in this dreamy microcosm for the rest of eternity—just them, the melting shadows and honeyed daybreak, the feel of his bare skin against hers.

Wanted to. But she knew that she couldn't.

Jackie was their biggest remaining threat. Waylon would never forgive her if he found out she'd lied to him to take advantage of his Lydell knowledge. And, sure, this fit firmly in the *desperate times, desperate measures* category, but that wasn't how the heart kept score. She'd used him. Pressed the same purpled bruise left by everyone else who treated Waylon like a chessboard pawn.

But if Fletcher went back on her word to Jackie, it wouldn't just be the Cartwright Media gig she'd lose. Revenge was a seven-letter word Jackie knew well, and as one of the industry's most well-respected editors, one email to anyone in her contact list would blacklist Fletcher from every major publication. That was, if she didn't kill her first.

"Waylon?" Fletcher whispered.

He groaned. His mouth brushed against her neck with some unintelligible assortment of consonants and vowels.

"We need to get to the marina."

Waylon shushed her with his lips against her shoulder, and it worked, because every argument on Fletcher's tongue dissolved like spun sugar. "Too early," he muttered, groggy and slow. "Five more minutes."

"You know we should—"

Wriggling around to face him, Fletcher knew her mistake immediately. One look at the relaxed planes of his face, and her treasonous heart squeezed with a twinge of emotion she couldn't name or didn't want to.

Half-lidded eyes batted, embers still burning from the fire they'd stoked the night before. He ran his tongue over his bottom lip and peeled his mouth into a grin. Peaceful, unbothered, satisfied.

"What's the rush? I love seeing you undone." Waylon pulled Fletcher flush with his chest, pinning her so there was nowhere to run. "Why don't we just stay? The rescue crew is coming. And if I'm lucky, so are you."

This side of him, unreserved and flirty, made lying to him so much worse.

Fletcher buried her face against his skin, never so grateful he couldn't see the expression she made. She swallowed evenly. Breathed evenly. But her heart stirred around her chest, nervous and off-kilter. He must have felt it. He could probably read her heart's rhythm like Morse code, decrypt her secrets like they were plain text.

The second they left this treetop perch and their feet hit solid ground, everything would change. The bubble would pop.

Maybe it didn't have to.

Waylon's reluctance to reach the marina was hard to argue with, especially wrapped in his cedar-and-amber scent, blissfully exhausted. No one would find them here. Even if they did, with neither of them vying for the company, no one should feel threatened by their presence once the rescue crew arrived.

Besides, once Jackie got the island out of her system, she'd come to her senses. Return to the polished, pristine woman Fletcher knew in New York. And, if Fletcher got really lucky, keep her word about offering Fletcher a position on the *Jet-Setter* staff.

Waylon would never have to know she'd gone behind his back.

When she didn't immediately answer, his fingers trailed against the delicate skin behind her knee, scuttled toward her thigh. A touch so faint she thought at first she'd imagined it. The higher it inched, the more obvious it became. Playing dirty.

"Okay, okay. We can stay here while we wait for the rescue crew." She squirmed in his grip, biting down a laugh. "That tickles."

"What does?"

"Your hand on my leg."

Except both of Waylon's hands curled around her shoulders. So unless he'd grown a third arm in the last thirty seconds . . .

Fletcher flung the blankets off in one big ripple, and then her heart stopped beating entirely. A spider the size of a silver platter crawled up her thigh.

"Oh my god!" she yelled, at the same time that Waylon shouted, "Don't scream!"

Easy for him to say. He didn't have Shelob scuttling up his bare leg. Her arms flailed, one of her hands hitting the spider's meaty legs, and it lost its grip. Its giant, fuzzy grip.

The spider plummeted to the floor and righted itself, rearing back for another deadly attack.

"It's just Arnold Schwarzenegger," Waylon said, way calmer than any single naked person should sound in the presence of a creature that unholy.

Fletcher swore Arnold shot her a judgy look. Her chest heaved. "What do you mean *just* Arnold Schwarzenegger? You *named the tarantula*?"

"Technically, I think he's a huntsman spider." Waylon flipped a wicker basket over and contained the spider. Barely. The basket shuffled toward Fletcher with a vendetta. This was a million times worse than the bush baby. This spider ate bush babies for breakfast.

She hopped on the bed, though it hardly seemed safe now, and shook out one of the blankets before swaddling herself in it, just to be sure Arnold didn't bring any body-building friends. "I'm sorry. Just so I'm clear. When did you and Mr. Schwarzenegger become so well acquainted?"

"Twelve hours ago, give or take. We made introductions while you were in the shower." *Made introductions*. Like they met for coffee to discuss next quarter's stretch goals. "I trapped him under the basket last night, but I guess he got out."

"You *guess*?"

The basket lurched on cue. Fletcher inched back toward the headboard, determined to put as much distance as possible between her and Arnold, in case he decided to reprise his role as the Terminator.

"I am not nearly clothed enough for this," she said before unceremoniously yanking the heap of khaki off the floor and marching downstairs, wearing the blanket like a royal cape. Waylon's amused laugh followed after her.

Fletcher took advantage of hot running water with another shower. She dressed quickly, back in Waylon's shirt and a clean pair of too-loose trousers but this time with a typical number of undergarments, much to Waylon's dismay.

She hadn't meant to wander into Tiffany's office, but curiosity got the best of her. Curiosity, and a leather case on the painted desk in a familiar shape. Fletcher couldn't help the way her breath lodged at the back of her throat, hope sprouting between her ribs.

With careful fingers, she unlatched the buckle and opened the lid, revealing the sleek black-and-silver body of a Leica camera. In one of the pockets there was a roll of film Fletcher uncapped and slotted in with shaking fingers. (This camera was easily worth two months of rent.)

She clipped a leather strap to the camera and hung it around her neck, feeling like gravity had returned for the first time since she left New York.

Peeling the viewfinder up to her eye, Fletcher saw the studio in a new light. The way the sun rays filtered through the arched window, how the jungle tapped against the pane, asking to be let in. For a moment, everything else disappeared.

This. This was why she wanted to be a photographer.

As the lens came into focus, so did Fletcher's resolve. Her future as a photographer couldn't be collateral damage from this hellish company retreat. One way or another, she'd find her footing in the industry.

When a blanched Waylon halted in the doorway, dressed in a fresh T-shirt and black pants, Fletcher clutched the camera to her chest, caught. A reticent pink seeped into her cheeks. "I should have asked. Do you mind . . . ?"

But Waylon didn't answer. He'd gone totally catatonic. The envelope from Dyer dripped from his fingertips, plucked from where they'd forgotten it on the counter last night.

"Waylon?" Her mouth gave his name too many syllables. Dragged out the *Way*, drifted off with the *lon*. "What is it?"

"There is no rescue crew."

"What?"

Once more: "There is no rescue crew."

Fletcher's heart got the memo, pulse skipping and blood pressure rising, but her brain couldn't catch up. "What do you mean?"

"There *is* no rescue crew, Fletcher."

She stepped closer. "What'd the letter say?"

He shifted his weight onto the doorframe. Defeat dragged down his shoulders, his spine. Limply, he raised the envelope to her.

Waylon hadn't opened it neatly. Toothy paper snags rimmed the seam, and Fletcher unfolded the single piece of paper that had been tucked inside. There was nothing personal about it. Typed on company letterhead and signed with crisp blue ink, the way all Dyer Cartwright correspondences were.

Waylon,

By now I'm gone, and Cartwright Media's fate rests in your hands as we always knew it would someday. I apologize that someday came sooner than either of us hoped.

On the flash drive, you'll find my last will and testament along with a video I've recorded for everyone. Everything I say is true, unless you count lying by omission as a falsehood. The whole truth is this: I've made more mistakes than I can count. My trusted confidants proved untrustworthy. I was made to believe you were unsuitable to lead and told that the company would fail if I let you inherit it.

I never quite liked being told what to do. We have that in common.

This trip is a necessary loophole. A way to reinstate your legitimacy as my heir without stirring suspicion before it's too late. Unfortunately, there's a traitor among you, a bad seed poisoning the crop. I could not allow them to fall into power. There is no rescue crew coming. While the others argue among themselves, leave. Find Tiffany and call for everyone else's rescue once you've finished the paperwork. My legacy has always belonged to you.

Sincerely,
Dyer Cartwright

Shadows bled into the edges of Fletcher's vision. Beneath her feet, the ground shifted. She was suddenly too hot and too cold at once. Her palms sweated, but goose bumps trailed down her arms.

"This is . . ."

"A worthless excuse for an apology," Waylon seethed. "Unbelievable. When he invited me on this trip, I thought things between us actually stood a chance at getting better. But he—he stranded us here, as good as dead. And this is how he justified it to himself? *A bad seed?*"

Knots tangled in Fletcher's stomach. Unfortunately, she had a hunch she knew exactly who the bad seed was. Jackie's wild eyes flashed through her mind. The editor in chief had never once been shy about her distaste for Waylon or her unquenchable ambition.

Fletcher tried to think back to the tarmac, tried to remember exactly what was said and in precisely what order. Dyer had appeared out of a jet-black SUV, his silver hair slicked back, curls gathering at the base of his neck, looking in her memory less like her demanding boss and more like a comic book supervillain. She recalled the way his cane rapped against the airstrip, the way he chatted with the C-suite. Their first tour of the manor. His retirement speech.

And always at his side: *Jackie.*

She'd looped her arm through Dyer's as they approached the plane with sunglasses jammed up the bridge of her nose despite the bleak November clouds. She'd patted Dyer's hand as he spoke fondly of his late wife. After the will reading, Jackie had been the first to suggest hunting one another for sport.

All of it carefully orchestrated. None of it a coincidence.

Fear and frustration that matched how Fletcher felt splashed across Waylon's face. The color returned to his cheeks, splotched and red-hot. He crumpled the letter in his fist. "Why didn't I read this earlier?"

"You didn't know. You couldn't have known." Fletcher tucked her arms around Waylon's middle, hearing the rapid patter of his heart. "I mean, Waylon, this is . . . Are you sure? Maybe we're missing something."

"We aren't. This is exactly the kind of psychotic bullshit my dad loved."

"Okay . . . There's no rescue crew coming," Fletcher parroted as the truth sank in. Dyer brought them here, stranded them, and orchestrated a cockfight, well aware that Jackie was out for blood. The promise of rescue had been a distraction at best. At worst, the last nail in the coffin. "Oh my god, Waylon. We have to get to the marina before someone else does."

Any foolhardy dream of waiting out the worst in their tree house bubble was dashed. If they stayed here, they'd die. Starvation, dehydration, any of the other terrible -ations. Not a matter of how, but when.

To live, they had to escape. There was only one way off the island, and Fletcher had unknowingly led Jackie directly to it. Jackie, who had manipulated her colleagues into participating in a killing spree. She would stop at nothing to secure the inheritance.

"The marina. Of course." Waylon pinched his eyes closed. "I don't know why I didn't think of it before. Tiffany."

Fletcher dug through the scrambled eggs formerly known as her brain. What *exactly* had Dyer said in his farewell video? The memory was fuzzy with adrenaline, darkened with panic.

To my son, Waylon Cartwright, I leave Lydell Island, its animal inhabitants, as well as all of its structures and assets. It's what your mother would have wanted, and you know I've never trusted anyone more than Tiffany to protect what I love most.

At dinner, Dyer had given a speech about how he and his wife loved coming to Lydell—enough that he'd buried her here somewhere.

"Are we . . . becoming gravediggers?"

"No, my mother was cremated, and we spread her ashes in the sea. But that's it. The sea. *Tiffany.* My dad's boat. He named it after her. God, he even said as much in the video, but I just didn't know I needed to be a fucking detective." Waylon disappeared, calling over his shoulder, "Start packing."

Any satisfaction Fletcher might have gleaned from correctly assuming Dyer wasn't unhinged enough to abandon his son on this island without a getaway plan washed away with a swell of petrifying awareness. They needed to get to the marina ASAP.

Their things had somehow exploded around the tree house, and Fletcher quickly consolidated their semidry backpacks into one: a freshly filled canteen, an array of mildly expired granola bars they'd found in the cabinet, the scraps of a map, and her capybara room key.

Before cramming her phone into the backpack's inner pocket,

she fired off a string of new texts to Ford. Just in case she never made it off the island, at least there would be written proof that she'd had the best sex of her life. And, oh yeah, her boss was a maniac.

Waylon met her back in the studio, cradling the safe. He thumbed a few numbers into the lock. A *click*, and it opened. "My parents' anniversary."

She expected his hand to unfurl, revealing a slim metal key against his palm. That didn't happen. Instead, his fingers opened up to a brilliant heirloom diamond—an Asscher cut with too many carats for Fletcher to count on one hand. His mother's, no doubt.

"It's beautiful." Staring at the ring was like looking in a kaleidoscope. Mesmerized, Fletcher muttered, "But I don't understand."

"The date they got married. *That's* the master key. It's how we'll access the lockbox."

Fletcher smiled, something small and a little sad. Dyer always did call Tiffany his safe place. "Then let's get out of here before—"

A gunshot rang through the canopy.

24

Heart meet throat. Fletcher's pulse jumped around her jugular as she and Waylon crouched beneath the windowsill. *Don't be Jackie, don't be Jackie, don't be Jackie.* Fletcher dared a peek below. "Um, is this a stress hallucination, or do you see the Ghost of Salesmen Past, too?"

"You're joking." Waylon inched up. Looked. Shook his head. "Not unless we're both hallucinating."

Asshole Rick stood at the base of the kapok tree. Alive, but stretching the definition.

With him wafted the undeniable stench of fried flesh. An angry pink blister formed over half his face, and the other half scowled. Black, bubbled skin covered his arms, one hand hanging limp at the side and the other clutching the lightning rod bayonet that got him electrocuted in the first place.

How the gun still worked was beyond Fletcher, but he'd strapped a bandolier across his chest, stuffed with shells. He wore a wicked grin, although his lips had been burned off, so it was mostly skeletal teeth with very little gums.

"You thought you could outrun me?" Rick slurred. At this point, even a sloth could outrun him. Clearly, he was operating off fumes of pent-up rage and very little else. When Fletcher squinted, she swore steam still radiated off him.

Then, Fletcher noticed the ATV. He'd parked it behind the roots, the engine still humming. Once the idea sparked, there was little Fletcher could do to snuff it out. They'd make it to the marina *way* faster if they had a ride.

While Rick wasted his breath shouting at the sky, Fletcher pointed toward the ATV. "What's a little grand theft auto when you're already an accessory to, like, ten murders?"

"Probably ten to twelve years," Waylon muttered. It really wasn't much of an argument, considering their other option was serving a life sentence on a deserted island.

"We need to throw him off. If we try to waltz down there now, we're definitely getting shot." Fletcher tucked her camera into the rucksack before Waylon hauled it over his shoulder. They didn't have much time to spare. An eight-legged rustling upstairs hatched an exit plan. "Arnold!"

No ordinary paper in the world had the heft required to support Arnie's leviathan leg span, so Waylon wedged one of his mom's left-over canvases beneath the basket and carted the spider downstairs.

"Three, two, one . . ." Fletcher counted. On "go," she shoved the balcony door open, and Waylon shuffled out far enough to hurl Ar-nold over the railing.

Ambient screaming signaled the Austrian Oak made impact.

Shooting back inside, Waylon said brusquely, "That's our cue."

The tree house's ladder unraveled back toward the forest floor, and they wasted no time sliding down the rungs, moving too fast for the fear to set in. A glance sideways proved Rick still wrestled with the heavyweight champ.

But when they were mere inches from their getaway quad bike, Rick laughed, harsh and maniacal. Much, much too close for comfort. The barrel of his gun pointed at Waylon's back, and Arnold Schwarzenegger perched on his shoulder. *Traitor.*

"I don't think you're going anywhere," Rick spat.

Up close, his scorched wounds looked so much worse. Pus-filled, oozing. Puckered scar tissue already formed beneath the uneven terrain of his skin. The bayonet must have taken the brunt of the lightning bolt, but he hadn't fared much better.

Even Fletcher, who had never called out of work in her entire career, could admit he needed a sick day. Or three. Or three hundred. She may have hated his guts, but the man clearly required medical attention.

The empathetic part of her quickly shut up as he plodded forward, ramming the burnt end of his spear against Waylon's ribs with enough force Waylon sucked a stiff breath through his teeth.

"Look, Evanston, we're unarmed," Waylon rationalized. Not even Naya was prowling around, the undergrowth disappointingly undisturbed. "We don't have to fight."

"You got me struck by lightning." The air around Rick still smelled vaguely metallic. "And then threw a spider at me."

Hot exhaust made it hard to breathe. Harder to think. The clock was ticking, and Fletcher didn't like it. She'd seen how fast Rick's temper had snapped with Theo, how quickly blood could splatter and a body could drop.

They needed to act now, before Rick's rifle remembered it, too.

Fletcher stomped on Rick's foot, and his gun tipped downward, spear tearing through the fabric of Waylon's T-shirt but thankfully no deeper. With a curse, Rick's finger instinctively pulled the trigger, resulting in more cursing and a few of Rick's wayward toes spraying around the clearing.

No time for sorrys. Fletcher slung herself into the front seat, revving the engine. Waylon clambered on behind her, arms seat-belting across her middle. And they were off.

Rick's first bullet sliced past them as the jungle clamped its teeth around them. Instantly, saturation faded, shadows thickened. Tangled branches and wide, waxy leaves blotted out the sunlight she'd grown used to in the kapok clearing.

On foot, the rainforest's gnarled landscape was cumbersome, but on four wheels? Nightmare fuel. Fletcher drastically overestimated their speed. The extra horsepower couldn't compensate for claggy soil, spined thickets, and root-choked paths. Each jolt rattled Fletcher's bones.

As they sloshed through a mud slick, Waylon cupped his hands over her death grip on the handlebars. "Cut through here."

A quick jerk to the side narrowly avoided a web of needle palms.

Unfortunately, the sudden movement put them in Rick's direct line of sight.

Hobbling after them, Asshole Rick ranted about how *he* had given everything he had to Cartwright Media, and *he* deserved to inherit the Cartwright wealth, because *he* hadn't been able to take a trip to Ibiza with the boys last year and evidently it was a great inconvenience to him that required a multibillion-dollar reparation.

Fletcher didn't have the heart to turn back and tell him the blood loss would likely kill him long before he ever made it back to Manhattan.

Electrocution only hardened his resolve. Errant bullets spewed from Rick's shotgun, his aim expectedly worse than before. He'd more likely hit them by accident than on purpose.

Only then did Fletcher realize his aim trailed too low, a little too wide. Not aiming for them at all.

No sooner did she think it than one of the bullets hit its mark. The ATV's back tire popped. Rubber everywhere. Lurching forward, Fletcher and Waylon were bucked off the saddle. The world blurred. Fletcher clamped her eyes shut against the landing. She didn't need to see the impact to feel it.

"Get up." Waylon's voice floated over her.

"All of my bones are broken." Talking hurt. Everything hurt.

"If Rick the Zombie can run, so can you." His hands slid beneath her arms, peeling her upright despite her groaning protests. Fletcher wiped the dirt off her lips, her eyes, shaking the ache out of her limbs. Not broken, but sore.

Another round of shotgun shells spurred them into motion. Fletcher's too-big pants slid down her hips with every step, and she kept a finger through the front belt loop to keep from mooning anyone.

Arms pumping, lungs chafing. Rick's advances didn't slow—he'd never known when to take no for an answer. That kind of determination worked as well in the Sales bullpen as it did in the throng of wilderness. A few close calls had Fletcher gritting her teeth, ears ringing as his blasts got closer. Seriously, *how* was this guy still chasing them? His brain had to be entirely endorphins at this point.

Around them, the jungle sifted away slowly, trees thinning, brush clearing, until the island transformed into an expanse of sprinkler-fed green, smooth and manicured.

A . . . golf course.

No, an entire country club. Eighteen holes, tennis courts, swimming pool—the whole kit and caboodle. A sleek glass-and-steel building rose in the distance, and beyond it: a patch of fluffy white sand and a blue horizon with an enormous yacht bobbing at the docks.

Fletcher should have been watching her step instead of salivating at the thought of salvation because her foot slipped on the edge of a sand trap, and she tumbled into its banks. Grit coated her lips, her eyelids.

Another body slid down next to her. Fletcher was too busy scraping sand off her eyeballs and debating dunking her head in the nearest water hazard to dispute when Waylon hoisted her over his shoulder and hauled her back to the sod.

"I know everything," Rick shouted. "I heard them talking."

Fletcher cracked an eye open, ignoring the way the sand stung. From this angle, the world looked as off-axis as it felt. The salesman stood on a slant of green, and behind him, the jungle bowed and shook, something inside as angry as Rick looked.

"Jackie's little Faustian deal. The reason we're doing this whole fucking charade." Asshole Rick's bloodshot gaze shot toward Fletcher, where she dangled upside down. "You know exactly what I'm talking about, don't you?"

"No, Rick, I—" An engine rumbled. Close enough that Fletcher smelled gasoline on the breeze. Her hands beat against Waylon's back until he lowered her back to solid ground.

Weaving her fingers through Waylon's, she yanked him backward as a pair of high beams cut through the underbrush. A truck plowed out of the jungle and onto the fairway. Forward, forward, forward . . .

And right into Rick.

A horrible *snap* prefaced an equally horrible *wheeze*. Fletcher didn't have to look closely to know Rick's deep-fried tendons couldn't handle the hit. His body splayed disgustingly limp beneath the Jeep's monster truck tires, pitching it up unevenly. Blood seeped from his pile of loosely attached limbs, and Jackie stepped right into it. Unbothered by the red on her Louboutins.

"Look who it is," Jackie said by way of greeting. As if she hadn't just manslaughtered their colleague.

At some point, Jackie had commandeered a golf bag that now teetered in the back seat, clubs sticking out over the bumper. That thought alone ramped Fletcher's nerves up another notch. It meant Jackie had circled back. Looking for them.

"What are you doing here?" The words left Fletcher's lips with a bite. They had a deal. This wasn't part of it.

Flicking her wrist up, Jackie read her watch. "You're thirty-eight minutes late. When I assign deadlines to my staff, I expect them to be met."

The harsh curve of Waylon's mouth wrinkled in her periphery. "Fletcher, what—"

Jackie turned, as if only now noticing Waylon's presence. Which was statistically improbable given both his formidable height and the tsunami waves of hurt and confusion radiating off him. She grinned, flashing the vicious incisors of her too-white veneers. "I thought I told you to get rid of him."

The contents of Fletcher's stomach curdled. She pressed herself in front of Waylon, hardly a shield, given he neared twice her size. "And I thought I told you I'd meet you when I had . . . it."

"Had what?" asked Waylon.

The editor in chief giggled behind her hand like a schoolyard mean girl.

Sterner: "Had what, Fletcher?"

"A key to your dad's boat," Jackie answered when Fletcher couldn't. "So we can get out of here, and you can wait for whatever half-rate rescue crew is coming in a few days to ship you back home. If you live long enough."

Could you be strangled by your own guilt? Fletcher was about to find out.

Waylon closed the space between them, and no matter how outraged he was, Fletcher didn't flinch. Somewhere, deep down, some part of her knew Waylon Cartwright enough to know he wouldn't lay a hand on her she didn't ask for. "What is she talking about?"

"I told Jackie I'd help her get off the island, but I didn't know about . . ." Fletcher trailed off, lest she give Jackie an even better reason to maroon them. "If I helped her, she'd make me a photographer."

He'd understand. He *had* to. It was the one thing Fletcher wanted most in the world.

Instead, the muscles of Waylon's jaw twitched. "I thought we were a team."

"We were." The vulnerability stung. "We *are*."

But it wasn't enough. *We* didn't exist anymore. *We* was ancient history because she'd betrayed Waylon.

Waylon winced and recovered with a steely stare. "Was any of it real?"

Fletcher swallowed. He'd seen every part of her—every rough edge, every soft curve, every daydream, every nightmare. If what they had wasn't real, nothing ever would be.

"Yes," she admitted. Each word burred against her throat, snagging on its way out. "For me, it was."

There was a fraction of a second where a carousel of emotions flashed across Waylon's face—surprise, relief, hope—but it was gone as soon as it came. Tucked neatly beneath that hardened shell he always wore so well. Fletcher hadn't realized how nice it had been to see the real him until it was gone. It was worse to have to guess what was going on inside his head.

His breath was hot on her face when he said, "I would have saved you."

"I was trying to save myself." Fletcher swallowed hard, staring up at him. She wouldn't apologize for it.

He didn't ask her to. Just nodded and swiped a hand over his face. "And how'd that work out for you?"

Fletcher's gaze cut hard back to Jackie. When she answered, her voice was two steps lower, hushed but no less urgent. "She put a gun to my head. What did you want me to do?"

"I wanted you to tell me the truth, Fletcher." Waylon shook his head in disbelief. The distance between them reduced to inches but stretching miles. "But you couldn't do that because you were biding your time with me to get what you wanted, exactly like everyone else."

"I wasn't," Fletcher said, reaching toward him, but he shrugged her off. Slipped through her fingers.

"Oh, my mistake. I thought that was what it was called when you lie to someone, lead them on, and then turn around and stab them in the back. Is it not?" There was no answer except the truth. A truth Fletcher couldn't bring herself to say. He already knew, anyway.

The vein in Fletcher's forehead pulsed with a vengeance. "If anyone taught me to be selfish, it was you. You're exactly the Cartwright you never wanted to be."

"You used me." Something split wide open on Waylon's face. Hurt, raw as an open wound. "You're exactly like Eliza. Like all of them." His head tipped back, blue eyes skimming the sky. "What are you waiting for, honestly? Finish me off yourself."

Before Fletcher could say anything, a driving iron slammed over Waylon's head. He folded in on himself as bright red bloomed from a gash on his forehead.

"Don't mind if I do," said Jackie on the follow-through. She propped an elbow up on the edge of her club.

Waylon didn't move.

Was he *breathing*? Oh, god. Fletcher couldn't tell.

And if he wasn't breathing, what did that mean? He was *dead*? A wave of nausea brought her to her knees. She crawled toward Waylon, shifting his bleeding head into her lap. At the base of his neck, his pulse . . . existed. There was too much panic in her body to decide if it was a normal, healthy pulse or a tiny, fragile pulse.

The point was: He had one.

He also, most definitely, had a concussion. A minor inconvenience, given he hadn't died.

The editor in chief clicked her tongue against her teeth. "Stop groveling. I told you this business was cutthroat. You said you had what it takes."

Fletcher fought to find her words. Whatever manipulative, Machiavellian pieces built Jackie Caldera, Fletcher knew with sudden clarity she was not made of the same stuff. "And what is that, exactly?"

Jackie *click-click-click*ed her chipped nails along the driver's grip. "Ambition. Drive. Tenacity."

Gumption, she heard Dyer's echo say.

Those? Fletcher had. In spades.

But she knew better now. It wasn't *just* about being ambitious or driven or tenacious. Unspoken qualifiers attached to those values. Adjectives that tricked unsuspecting victims who simply wanted to succeed into selling their souls to corporations: ruthless ambition, merciless drive, and selfish tenacity. A willingness to put yourself before others. To push down your colleagues if it meant climbing higher faster.

Fletcher had let other people define her for so long. Kent, Dyer, and now Jackie. Look where that got her. She had acted as cold and calculated as the rest of them. Only looking out for herself in the end.

Now her brain veered straight into survival mode, like she had walked into the boardroom during a quarterly exec meeting. Jackie had said this was kill or be killed.

Fletcher really, *really* didn't want to be killed.

Luckily, if Fletcher's lasting legacy was going to be anything, it was that she always had a plan, a backup plan, and a backup to the backup plan.

So she sucked a breath into the deepest corners of her lungs, steeling the tender parts of her heart, and prayed Jackie believed her when she said, "I do. Have what it takes."

If Jackie's eyebrows hadn't been Botoxed within an inch of their life, one would have quirked up in disbelief.

"I'm here, aren't I?" said Fletcher.

Here, with Waylon's head in her lap, his eyes shut and forehead bleeding and his mouth still turned into a frustrated frown. Here, on this ridiculous private island, where greed gave her colleagues brain worms and convinced them to commit a little first-degree murder.

Jackie's lips pulled into a flat line, unimpressed and unconvinced. "What about the key?"

"It's in a lockbox at the marina."

"Fine. Hurry up," Jackie urged. "You've got a promotion to earn."

A promotion. As if Fletcher cared about that anymore. Right now, all she cared about was making it back to Manhattan—preferably not in a body bag.

"We can't leave Waylon." Then, to appease Jackie, who was already frowning with clear intent to do precisely that, she added: "The lockbox might be biometric or something. Dyer left the island to him, remember?"

Irritation worked through Jackie's shoulders. "If I'd known that, I would have used the putter."

Fletcher hefted one of Waylon's arms around her back, and Jackie grabbed the other side. Together, they *Weekend at Bernie's*-ed Waylon's limp body into the passenger seat of the Jeep.

While Jackie went around to the driver's side, a palm slamming on the hood for dramatic effect, Fletcher pressed her forehead against Waylon's. *Please wake up and don't hate me. Or wake up and* do *hate me. I'd deserve that. Whatever you do, wake up.*

Before Jackie could drive off without her, Fletcher flung herself over the back tire and into the back seat next to the club bag.

They sped across the driving range, the air tinged with sea spray and freshly cut grass. Jackie didn't bother swerving out of the way of the tennis court, and the net wrapped around the front bumper as she barreled toward the clubhouse with its gaping windows and oceanfront view.

Blessedly, Jackie cut the engine before crashing through the double doors, but only barely.

A quick sweep of the layout put the clubhouse with panoramic windows to their left, and the marina to their right. Farther out into the waters sat a fuel station and a floating concierge, where she envisioned staff members radioing to coordinate the arrival of megayachts. Most of the marina was empty, reserved for guests, but there, bobbing at the far slip, was one lone ship.

No one had ever been quite as happy to see a boat as Fletcher was at this moment, barring maybe the *Titanic* survivors, teeth chattering in their lifeboats.

Spinning back to Jackie, Fletcher said, "Help me get him inside."

"Is that how you speak to your soon-to-be manager?" Jackie asked.

The thought of joining Jackie's staff should have churned up some modicum of excitement. A week ago, it would have. Today, not so much. All she cared about now was getting her and Waylon off this island, whatever it took. And if that meant kissing Jackie's ass, so be it.

"Sorry," she grumbled. "Could you *please* help me get him inside?"

"Much better. We'll have to discuss communication styles at your first review."

Waylon was deadweight between them, head lolled against his chest. Glass doors wiped open automatically with a cloud of stiff air-conditioning that smelled like lemon disinfectant and aerosol deodorant.

Whoever designed the clubhouse deserved jail time.

There was not a single flat, soft surface in sight. Everything was polished black marble and sharp chrome edges, another gaudy chandelier dripping from the ceiling over a massive staircase that led to rows of expensive equipment, cable machines and stationary bikes and Pilates reformers.

The only two chaises in the lounge were carved from angular stone, clearly intended for looking at and not sitting on. *Great.*

A groan filtered through Waylon's lips, and Fletcher felt herself take a full breath for the first time in a trillion years. He'd wake up soon. Even if he hated her guts, they could work out their apologies over bagels and lox as soon as they got off this devil island.

"Almost there," she crooned, the same way her mother would address a scabbing knee, soft and fibbing. The nearest chaise would have to do, uncomfortable as it looked.

Finally, they heaped his body on it, propping him into a seated position, but the second Fletcher pulled her hands away, his clothes slipped against the polished granite and his spine settled into a zigzag line that would require serious massage therapy to iron out.

Fletcher slumped their backpack on the ground next to him, fishing through it to retrieve her canteen and take a long swig.

Jackie dusted off her hands on her blouse. She leaned on her golf club, and it might as well have been Dyer leaning on his grandfather's ivory cane, tapping the handle impatiently against the tile. "I'm going to tie up a few loose ends. Stop fussing with that brat and get me that boat key or neither one of you will live to see sunset."

Fletcher had no doubt Jackie meant it. Her eyes had gone dark, pupils blown out with untempered greed. Whatever borrowed time Fletcher was living on, the hourglass sand was running out, fast.

"I'll be right back," she told Waylon's unconscious body before creeping on quiet toes down a too-fluorescent hallway. Any key that warranted a lockbox wasn't going to be tucked inside one of the drawers at the waterfall reception desk

One of these rooms had to be the main office, ocean-facing so it had a clear view of oncoming ships. With each opened door, Fletcher's hope shriveled—a waterfront yoga studio, an infrared weight room, an indoor soccer field, and a smoothie bar. Then, the plaque on the last door kick-started her heart again.

CREW LOUNGE.

Inside, there was the typical stuff. Keurig. Television. A ten-foot swordfish mounted above an equally long dining table. At the back, a fogged glass door led to the manager's office, plainly decorated but the dark-wood cabinets could have been solid gold for the way Fletcher's pulse accelerated.

The middle cabinet swung open to reveal a gray metal panel with an electronic PIN pad. With shaking fingers, Fletcher thumbed in Dyer and Tiffany's wedding date. The numbers blinked. Red. Red. Red.

Green.

Fletcher tugged on the handle, the latch lifting with a mechanical *chug*, and she heard herself gasp with relief. There, dangling off a hook, was a slim silver glint.

Boat key. Singular.

Fletcher knew what she had to do. She had to be quick, and she had to be precise. It wouldn't be long before Jackie—

"I knew you wouldn't let me down," Jackie said behind her. She snatched the key into her palm. "And to think, Dyer tried to spare you all the fun of this week. He always spoke so highly of you and your ability to get a job done right. I'm not disappointed."

In the back of Fletcher's brain, an alarm flared. The key was in Jackie's hands. She'd finished her assignment. Why did she feel like she was going to throw up?

"You did it, Miss Spence. Congratulations on your new promotion!"

Something wasn't right.

Another wicked laugh bubbled out of Jackie. "You're *Jet-Setter*'s newest photographer."

Realization settled over Fletcher like a smothering pillow. This was all she had been promised. To live long enough to see her promotion.

"Jackie, please—"

Before she could change her fate, her skull snapped back with a sharp blow. The edges of her world frayed, split, cracked open into bleeding black nothing.

25

That bitch hit her with a golf club.

The way the crown of Fletcher's head throbbed confirmed it. Only distantly could she muster the strength to be thankful Jackie hadn't unsheathed her pistol and shot her right there in the crew lounge. The thought did nothing to quell the copper tang in her mouth. It meant only that whatever Jackie had planned for her was worse than a bullet to the chest.

A chill spread down her body. Wet, like she'd sweated her way through a night terror. But when Fletcher finally convinced her eyes to open . . . this wasn't a dream she could wake up from. And it was far from over.

Nylon mooring line burned against her skin. A knot wrenched her arms behind her back, one of the dock's support beams stiff against her spine. Cold salt water lapped at her chest. The tide wasn't merciful enough to be lowering—it was only a matter of time before it coaxed its way into her mouth, her lungs.

Fletcher jerked, tugged, stretched. Anything to break her bonds.

Now, she thought begrudgingly, *would have been the perfect time to have a machete.*

"You look like shark food."

The familiar tone shocked Fletcher's system. Two posts down, Waylon was trapped. Awake, but trapped. How the fuck Jackie managed to drag them down here was a case for the FBI. Fletcher was so relieved to hear the rasp of his voice that his words didn't connect. "Like what?"

"Shark food." His head nodded toward the cresting waves.

Below, circling along the sand, were shadows too big to ignore. Sharks (of a variety Fletcher had no intention of being close enough to discern) lurked with hungry anticipation. So, if she didn't drown, she'd be shark chum.

Was one a more preferable death? Drowning sounded bleak—the slide of water down her windpipe, a useless gasp for air—but sharks had *infinite teeth*.

Her thrashing stalled. Drowning it was.

And if she was going to drown, at the very least she'd do it with a clear conscience.

"You were right, you know," she said.

Waylon stewed, silent. But when she turned her head, his eyes bored into hers. His mouth pinched into a tight stripe, flat and unemotional. At least he was listening.

"I did use you. Just like Eliza, just like everyone. You're Waylon Cartwright, and I took advantage of that, and I'm sorry." A particularly rowdy wave crested over the breakwater and slammed into her. It took a second to find her breath, her bravery, again. "I think I've been using a lot of people for a very long time."

His eyebrows lifted, but his lips stayed shut.

Near-death experiences were either the best or worst time for self-reflection. The jury was still out on which.

"Using them as excuses mostly. Like Kent. He was constantly trying to get me to go home, and I . . . let him keep trying. I could have broken up with him a hundred times, but I never did. If I really couldn't cut it in New York, I knew he was right there waiting for me. The safe option. The backup plan." Salt water stung her eyes. That was why they teared up. Obviously. (The quiver in her voice, however, was not going to be addressed.) "The night I met you, it scared me how you saw straight through me. It had been so long since I had felt that way with Kent, but admitting that to myself . . . I couldn't. And when I learned who you were, well, I assumed the worst. It was wrong, and I'm sorry for that, too."

While she spoke, Fletcher worked at the rope, twisting her hands to earn as much slack as she could, until she caught the first knot between her fingers. *Thank you, company-sponsored self-defense classes.* A few more tugs, and the knot unraveled. A sigh parted her lips when the rope floated away. Next up: ankles.

In response, Waylon said nothing.

Lucky for him, Fletcher had always been a nervous talker. "And your dad said it himself. I'm an excellent executive assistant. It was way too easy to blame him for demanding so much of me, but I was the one who never set any professional boundaries. I tried so fucking hard all the time, and I was stuck in the same place I always had been. As long as there was always someone else to blame, I never had to admit to myself that I was so scared of failing that I'd never truly tried."

It was easier to be unhappy somewhere familiar than to strike out on her own. Even when that meant working seventy hours a week while her portfolio collected dust. If only she could have seen that three weeks ago.

A deliberating sound thrummed deep in his chest. A lot like *I told you so*. She deserved it. His mouth was still set in an uncompromising frown when he said, "You lied to me. Repeatedly."

"I did." She breathed. "It doesn't help that I wanted to tell you. I didn't, and I should have. When I offered to help Jackie escape in exchange for a job on the *Jet-Setter* staff, I thought getting off the island as soon as possible was a safer bet than waiting for the rescue crew. But this morning, when you asked me to stay, I meant it when I said yes. It doesn't—it doesn't undo what I did. I know. But it's the truth."

Waylon focused on the horizon, throat bobbing.

The waves battered Fletcher as she crunched herself into a ball, shimmying her bound feet up the beam until her fingertips could reach the mooring rope. She swore the sharks' eyes trailed her movement, and she picked up the pace for good measure.

"What happened up there?" Waylon changed the subject. "And why does my head hurt like a bitch?"

"That would probably be a traumatic brain injury. Say what you want about Jackie, but she's got a mean backswing. During a brief hostage situation, I found the lockbox, and she wasted no time stripping the key from my hands."

A breath rushed out of Waylon, like he'd been punched. "So, we're stranded?"

"Well, I—"

The knot around her ankles gave, and with one quick shift of the current, Fletcher sank beneath the waves. She spun. Lost. With too little oxygen. Until eventually, kicking, Fletcher broke the surface and spat out a mouthful of water.

"Come again?" Waylon asked.

The water hadn't lost its fight, towing Fletcher this way and that. Every time she opened her mouth, more ocean water snuck in. Her head bobbed beneath the surf once more.

Waylon shook out his hair, the drenched curls clinging to his cheeks. Enjoying this a little too much, if you asked Fletcher. "One more time."

Like Poseidon was playing a sick joke on her, another maverick wave crushed the jetty. Salt water stung in every crevice of her sinuses as Fletcher coiled her arms around the dock to keep from getting carried away.

"Seriously?" she asked anyone listening—Waylon, the sea, the slice of daytime moon hanging in the sky, controlling the tides and clearly laughing at her.

"Let me guess, another patented Fletcher Spence plan."

Was he smiling? Fletcher couldn't tell because another wave splashed into her face.

Fletcher huffed. Wiped the salt from her eyes. She opened her mouth to speak once more, expecting it to summon another jarring swell, but the ocean stilled, if only briefly. Fletcher took the opportunity to say, "Yes, I have a plan. Step one: dry land."

"Easier said than done," Waylon grumbled, still fighting the knots behind his back.

Swimming with smooth strokes, Fletcher muscled toward Waylon, careful not to stir up the wake. The loose folds of khaki around her hips dragged against the tide, weighing approximately ten thousand pounds.

Finally, she latched on to the beam behind him and muttered an apology as she anchored her legs around his thighs so she didn't drift off while untangling him.

"I know it sounds crazy when everything has been so horrible, but I'm kind of glad I came here." The skin of his neck pebbled against her words. Fletcher focused on the knot in the rope rather than the knot of nerves in her stomach. "I guess nothing gives you the perspective you need like thinking you might die at literally any second."

Waylon scoffed in disbelief. Fair. Dying wasn't off the table yet, anyway.

"I'm not afraid to go after what I want anymore. Well, I *am* afraid. Exceptionally afraid, really. But I've realized that some things are worth doing scared."

When she finally unleashed his hands, Fletcher swam around front, and Waylon's free arm caught her hip. She was close enough to feel his breath against her cheek.

"Like what?" he asked.

The odds that Waylon forgot she'd nearly handed him to Jackie on a silver platter in exchange for a job were slim, but even if he didn't, he deserved to know the truth. She knew what she wanted. If he didn't want the same thing, that would be okay. *She* would be okay. Falling was the risk you took to fly.

"I'm going to get us out of here," she told Waylon as she loosened the ties around his ankles. "You don't have to forgive me. You definitely don't have to say thank you, since I'm responsible for at least sixty percent of the fuckery we've encountered this afternoon alone. But I think I'm falling in love with you, so I'd really like for you to not die right now."

For a long moment, he watched her, eyes trained downward as she pried her fingernails between the coils of rope. In the blue of his stare, every fleck of emotion he buried deep swam to the surface. She would understand if he didn't believe how she felt, let alone if he didn't feel it back. The rational response would be leaving Fletcher for shark bait.

Waylon thought. Then said, "You know, I've been thinking about the company, about my dad's letter. Not much else to do when you're held hostage, I guess." A laugh trickled out, nervous. "I thought I would gladly live the rest of my life without another mind-numbing all-hands meeting about OKRs or ROIs or whatever acronym they're shoving down your throats this quarter."

"KPIs. End-of-year evals are coming up. Gotta keep an eye on your key performance indicators."

Waylon's eyes rolled back into his skull. "Exactly. I'm sure someone else will be a much better CEO than me. But, I don't know, I've been thinking, maybe I don't have to turn my back on everything entirely. I've been so hell-bent on pushing my dad away, but the company's the only real tie I have left to him. All I ever wanted was to make my own legacy, but maybe they're the same thing."

"You could do it," Fletcher whispered.

"Do what?"

"Get everything you want."

When the last snag in the rope came undone, she expected Waylon to swim for the shoreline.

He didn't.

Instead, he tipped her chin to his with a finger and pressed his mouth against hers. Fletcher's eyes fluttered closed, sinking into him. This kiss was a pull from a tequila bottle during one of her weeknight escapades with Ford, sweet and dizzying. The only thing getting her through the worst week of her life.

As they broke away, there was a fuzzy look in Waylon's eyes like maybe he was falling in love with her, too.

"Thanks for saving me."

Fletcher slid her nose against his. "We had a truce, remember? You don't kill me. I don't kill you."

It all would have been very romantic, if it weren't for the impending shark attack.

A snaggle-toothed gargantuan swam closer, curious about the public display of affection. It rose through the waters, corralling them in a figure eight.

"Up, up. Go up," Waylon ordered, and Fletcher was more than agreeable.

She scrambled higher, climbing the post like a rope. Barely flinched at the splinters digging under her skin. Her legs coiled tightly around the beam, Waylon's stacked beneath hers, high enough to be out of the chomping zone.

Except the shark reared its head out of the water, unconcerned with its inability to breathe air, and pried open its mouth, infinite teeth gleaming.

She was going to get eaten, and it wasn't even going to matter that she and Waylon had feelings for each other because they were going to die, and not even by drowning.

Then Waylon punched the shark in between the eyes.

Stunned, the shark stuttered. It sank back into the water, and then, when its brain kicked back into gear, it turned and went, clearly more interested in easy prey. Below, its friends got the hint and retreated.

"Oh my god, that actually worked. I thought shark-punching was an urban legend," Fletcher said, tinny and still shaking.

"How many city-dwelling sharks have you met?"

"I meant thank you."

His chest heaved. "I guess we're even."

"I guess we are."

If Fletcher closed her eyes, she could almost pretend that this weekend had gone the way it was supposed to. That this was nothing more than a tropical vacation. No hungry sharks, no evil coworkers, no battle royale.

But then, a week ago, Fletcher would have abided by her checklist, run point for Dyer at his beck and call, and drunk her fill of Manhattans with bourbon-soaked maraschino cherries while clinging dutifully to the sidelines. She never, *ever* would have let herself trust Waylon Cartwright.

Some things couldn't be planned.

Bringing her hand to Waylon's face, she smoothed the pad of her thumb along the ridge of his cheekbone, right beneath the dull purple of his blackened eye. "How about that patented Fletcher Spence plan?"

"Let's hear it."

Above them, the dock groaned with the weight of footsteps. Fletcher's whole body tensed, then relaxed. Jackie's red-bottomed heels weren't pacing above them. Instead, through the pinstripe gaps in the dock, Fletcher spotted a neon-green Croakie.

"Is that . . . Melv?" she asked.

She'd thought—

Well, frankly, Fletcher hadn't thought much of Melv at all in the last twenty-four hours. After he'd ushered them out of the burning estate, their paths hadn't crossed again. Any number of hideous deaths could have befallen the mild-mannered lawyer. Poisoned by a suspicious berry. Crushed in an elephant stampede. Golf-clubbed into oblivion by the editor in chief.

But he'd survived.

"Fletcher?" Melv asked, peering over the dock's edge. "Waylon? Is that you?"

Relief flooded Fletcher's system. Melv might have been the only person Fletcher trusted to talk sense into Jackie. He had the kind of levelheaded composure unshaken by the island. She hoped.

As Fletcher hauled herself up the ladder at the end of the dock, Melv offered her a hand. The sleeves of his blue oxford rolled up his suntanned arms. Not a single speck of dirt. Anywhere.

Hot sun silhouetted Melv, and Fletcher squinted. Down the

boardwalk, *Tiffany*, with her polished white decks and three-hundred-person capacity, waited. So close.

Stubborn and dripping, Waylon heaved himself onto the dock with no assistance. Water suctioned his shirt to the broad plane of his chest. "Couldn't have gotten here a few minutes sooner?"

Suspicion laced each word, but Melv was hardly a threat. Unless he decided to use his briefcase as a bludgeoning weapon.

"Don't mind him. He's in a bad mood because we almost got eaten by sharks." Melv's expression torqued toward confusion, but Fletcher barreled on: "You can't let Jackie see you, or—"

"Or what, Miss Spence?"

26

At some point during the week, Fletcher had stopped flinching every time someone pulled a gun on her. If she lived long enough to look for a new job, she'd have to remember to add this to her résumé.

The editor in chief stalked toward them, coming down from the yacht. Clearly preparing for her great escape. Jackie's—and her pistol's—sudden appearance had Waylon taking a step closer, his hand circling Fletcher's and pulsing three times. *I'm right here.*

Fletcher flitted her eyes toward Melv. Was this the right time to plead the Fifth? "Or . . . else?"

Jackie's clarion laughter cut across the docks. "Are you really in the position to be threatening anyone right now?"

Caged between gunmetal and shark-infested waters, she couldn't afford to be anything else. Without Jackie, none of them would be in this situation. None of them would be dead.

Like dropping a Mento into a bottle of Coke, rage bubbled behind Fletcher's sternum and spewed out her mouth. "I trusted you.

Hell, I wanted to *be* you, Jackie. You knew that, and you exploited it."

Dipping into her pocket, Jackie dangled the key. Baiting Fletcher's temper. Bad seed indeed.

Waylon hardened. "Enough is enough, Jackie. You're outnumbered."

A toothy grin. "Am I?"

Shoulder to shoulder, Melv and Jackie couldn't be more different. Melv was all crisp lines and neat slacks while blood stained the editor in chief's nail beds, and her blouse had been reduced to shreds. He was a statue, perfectly still, but every noise sent her twisting over her shoulder, antsy. The island had barely touched the lawyer's polished exterior, but only one artifact remained of the version of Jackie Fletcher once admired. A stripe of red lipstick, perfect save for one smudged corner of her bottom lip. Almost like she'd just been kissed.

It was exactly the same smudge Fletcher had seen three weeks ago in the Art and Design Lab after the C-suite's lunch meeting. That afternoon, she'd met with Melv. Innocuous at the time, barely a blip on Fletcher's radar. What had they been discussing?

An ownership dispute.

A knife of realization twisted in Fletcher's gut.

"You're together." The words flew out of Fletcher before she could think better of them. Not a question. Not even an accusation. The truth, out in the open.

When Jackie sidled up next to Melv, she was a moon entering orbit. Something in her razored gaze softened when she looked at him. Fletcher should've realized it before. How could she not have noticed?

Sudden, righteous anger slammed through her. "And you," she said to Melv. "Saving us from the fire? Don't tell me you only did that because you knew I owed Jackie the boat key."

He answered with a silent shrug that said *I don't recall the event in question*. Typical lawyer. But Fletcher knew she was right. What Rick had overheard on the pool deck wasn't Jackie and Fletcher—it was Jackie and Melv.

"What are you going to do? Tell HR?" Jackie snarked. "You made short work of Molly, didn't you, Fletcher?"

"She. Stabbed. *Herself*."

Jackie bulldozed on. "Semantics. It's not like either of you are making it off this island today anyway. Eleven innocent people have died. Why shouldn't you join them?"

Innocent was a stretch, in Fletcher's humble opinion. That still didn't mean they deserved to die. Fletcher might not have killed anyone this week, but she couldn't save anyone, either. Survivor's guilt was a sticky thing, congealing to the underside of her ribs, making it harder to breathe. If she closed her eyes, she could still see the blue of Joplin's lips, the red ringing Molly in the foyer.

When she met Jackie's gaze again, the editor's eyes were empty of contemplation, devoid of any mercy. Jackie didn't regret what she had done. Or what she was about to do.

"Do you hear yourself?" Fletcher steamed. Dyer was right about one thing. After all the shit she'd pulled, Jackie deserved to get stranded on this island. "If it weren't for you, the team would still be alive. You really think you're going to kill all of us and still claim the inheritance? How's that going to look to a judge when you cash in on the will?"

Smug, Jackie peered up toward Melv. "I think I'll be fine when it's all said and done."

All the puzzle pieces clicked into place. A mutual back-scratching. Melv got the protection of being on Jackie's good side, and Jackie got impunity. With the right lawyer, any misgiving could be erased. Any will could be reworked. Melv didn't get his job at Dyer's side by being anything less than the best.

Jackie barreled on, clearly enjoying her captive audience. "All of Dyer's remaining assets will be delivered to us, and since lonely, orphaned Waylon Cartwright was devastatingly lost in a plane crash with the rest of the invitees, Lydell Island will return to the corporation. Which will make it . . . Oh yeah. Ours."

Nothing to hide. No messes to clean up. This whole week reduced to a terrible accident.

"And since you didn't have the decency to feed the sharks," Jackie said, "the two of you are the only loose end."

Melv moved first, grappling Waylon's arms behind his back and lugging him to the opposite end of the boardwalk. Fletcher didn't have time to feel betrayed. Jackie lunged. Her arm snared Fletcher's neck, and the mouth of her gun kissed Fletcher's temple.

"Don't touch her," Waylon spat. A new fury burned in his gaze. "It's me you want."

Waylon broke Melv's grasp only long enough to slide-tackle Jackie. A wayward shot looped into the atmosphere, but the echoing *slam* as Jackie's back hit the boards sent the pistol scattering across the dock. Out of reach. Close to the edge, but not close enough to tip over into the blue deep and spare them from Jackie's violent power trip.

"That's where you're wrong," Melv said, thick with bloodlust. He wrestled Waylon back into a headlock, but Waylon showed no signs of tapping out. "I want it all."

Fletcher got one good look at Melv, as if only truly seeing him for the first time. Suntanned skin; a gel-slicked coil of black hair; long, easy breaths; and a relaxed slope to his shoulders. Smart, meticulous. The kind of person who didn't leave any box unchecked.

It all made sense. The extra meetings with Melv Fletcher had managed to squeeze into Dyer's packed calendar. The last-minute paperwork they needed to review before heading to Lydell. It wasn't intellectual property they were discussing in those copyright meetings.

It was the fate of Cartwright Media.

And Melv . . .

Melv had pulled the strings all along.

His unwrinkled shirt and shiny loafers. Unaffected by the island's elements. He'd bolted north toward the base of the mountain while the others had been driven south. All while someone had been planting seeds in everyone's mind and sowing them.

Jackie struck deals and made bargains. Jackie pinned a target on Fletcher, whispering in Bertram's ear, trying to keep him off her tracks. Jackie fought filthy fights and won, losing herself along the way. Jackie, Jackie, Jackie. A decoy, a diversion.

It had been so easy to overlook the truth.

"When did you start dating?" Fletcher asked suddenly, her eyes zipping between Jackie and Melv. Calendar pages ripped through her mind. Dyer's first visit with Dr. Hawks coinciding with an uptick of copyright liaisons. "February?"

As Jackie lifted onto her elbows, surprise manifested in the arch of her eyebrows, the wide moons of her brown eyes. A yes, then.

Before she could say anything else, Jackie launched upright and wrapped her hands around Fletcher's throat. Her head smacked against one of the dock beams with a *crack* that reverberated down her spine. The cogs in Fletcher's head spun, trying to get the math to add up. Basic arithmetic didn't usually evade her, but she also wasn't usually being strangled.

"Do you love Melv?" Fletcher asked, struggling beneath the weight of Jackie's hands. Each breath wheezed against the pinch of digging nails. The bruise from Opal's choke hold doubled the ache.

"Of course I do," Jackie said, and she took the opportunity to squeeze tighter.

Behind them, Waylon landed a punch against Melv's jaw that

sent him spinning. Fletcher only barely registered it. It seemed so far away.

Her voice was too thin, her lungs too empty. "Does he—love—you?"

Fletcher blinked away black Rorschach splotches. Szechuan's lo mein, an extra dry martini with too many olives, antique suitcases, and a slobbering giraffe. Her life before her eyes.

Air rushed into Fletcher's lungs as Waylon ripped Jackie off her back and flung the editor in chief to the planks. He pulled Fletcher to his chest, a protective hand palming her waist and the other weaving through her copper tangles. They staggered toward the yacht, Fletcher dragging him as far from Jackie and Melv as possible.

"Only one person can inherit the company, Jackie." The words rasped out of her, a cry and a warning. "*All other guests must forfeit.* That's what the will says. Melv knows. He wrote it."

Across the dock, Melv scooped the gun off the dock, eyes dark with greed. "She's right."

In the Drowning vs. Shark Attack debate, death by gunshot probably trumped them both. She only hoped Melv had the mercy to shoot her where it counted, rather than letting her bleed out.

It would have to be at least two shots. Her, then Waylon. Or Waylon, then her. Which was worse? To die, knowing she would be missed, or to have the last taste in her mouth be the bitter tang of grief?

Fletcher squeezed her eyes closed. Every late night and too-early morning revolving around Dyer's needs led her right here. To this marina where everything smelled like brine and pressure-treated wood. She had no hobbies, one best friend, and a mile-long to-do list that would never get done. God, that would haunt her in the afterlife. Her ghost would trail aimlessly around the Cartwright Media office, refilling the copy machine with paper and restocking the break room fridge.

What would her family be told? Who would send them flowers, if not her? Her replacement would be some hotter, younger version of her with a future twice as bright. She'd fare the same. This company would take everything she had to give: her nights and weekends; her hopes and dreams; her life, if she let it.

The pistol fired—a blast that rang in Fletcher's ears.

After deciding that ears probably didn't ring postmortem, she held tighter to Waylon, expecting his body to go limp as his life seeped out and his heart stalled. Her eyelids pinched tighter.

A *thump* vibrated the dock beneath her feet.

Waylon was still standing, his heart still beating.

Opening her eyes took some convincing. When she did . . .

Jackie splayed across the dock. A lovesick smile spread across her painted mouth, but a bullet wedged between her eyes. Fletcher's knees buckled at the sight.

"You're fine," Waylon gasped. His hands flattened against Fletcher's shoulders as he peeled her back to examine her and all her intact limbs. Tension carved grooves in his face, his jaw clenched as if still bracing for the blow that never came. "I thought—"

"I know." Her head rested against his chest. "I know, but I'm fine. We're fine."

His throat worked with a stiff swallow. "Our definitions of 'fine' are very different. He has a gun *and* the boat key."

Fletcher's attention snapped back to Melv, where, across the dock, he snaked the key from Jackie's pocket. Smoke wafted off the muzzle of the killing pistol. Catching Fletcher's eye, a proud smirk glazed over his lips. It sank a pit in her stomach.

They *had* to get on the yacht, and fast.

"It's okay, because—"

"Do you know how long I've worked with your father?" Melv asked, his voice way too relaxed for the circumstances.

Waylon fumbled, eyes flickering like he was searching his brain for the right information, but Fletcher aced this pop quiz because she'd written off an expensive-ass box of golden pears.

"Thirty years," she croaked.

Melv paced toward them. With each step, he popped open the magazine and dropped bullets one by one by one into the sea. Somehow, it felt more menacing than firing at their hearts. "Thirty years. Longer than little Waylon's been alive. Thirty years of loyalty apparently meant nothing in the end."

"But we sent you the pears."

He ignored Fletcher, which she wagered was the best thing he could be doing with regard to her at this precise moment. Much better than the expected massacre. His attention was locked onto Waylon alone.

"Your father wanted to leave you *everything*," said Melv, mouth warping into an ugly frown. Another ammunition shell splashed into the sea foam. "Luckily, I was his trusted adviser. I barely had to do any heavy lifting to convince him you weren't ready or willing to take over the company."

"You. This *whole* time, it was you." A vein ticked at the base of Waylon's neck. "Advising my dad to cut me out? The no-contact agreement?"

"You'd already done the hard part. The rift between you and Dyer broke his heart. After Tiffany died, you were all he had, and you wanted nothing to do with him. He offered you the job as an olive branch, and you snapped it in half."

"Shut up," Waylon gritted through clenched teeth.

"Don't be mad at me. It's not my fault your father's dead. When I suggested he go out in style, he was all too eager to agree. Coming here, forcing everyone to survive in the wild without chef-made meals or precious cell service while arguing over who became his successor—he truly believed it would be the catalyst Cartwright's next leader needed to rise to the occasion."

"He's not shooting us," Waylon whispered. "Why isn't he shooting us?"

"Shh, he's monologuing." Fletcher dragged Waylon back an inch, then another.

They reached the end of the dock where the slip jutted out. The yacht—a behemoth of white and chrome with pale blue script that read *Tiffany* etched on the side—must have been two hundred feet long. A wooden gangway had been drawn out at the end, connecting the boat to the dock for boarding.

All they had to do was get across the passerelle. If they made it on the boat, they'd be fine. All of this would be over.

Melv's soliloquy continued. "But Dyer always was too soft, down underneath it all. Wouldn't agree to the trip if we didn't invite you. He wanted me to make sure you inherited this scrap of useless land for some sentimental reason, but I didn't mind. Luring you out here only meant it was that much easier to get rid of you."

With a *click*, the pistol chamber snapped shut. Two bullets remained.

"So, this is where I leave you. On beautiful Lydell. Don't worry, I'll take the liberty of letting the rescue crew know their services will no longer be needed." A gleam shone in Melv's ink-dark eyes, like the drip of a fountain pen, already dry. He slid the gun across the dock, far out of reach. "A bullet for each of you. You can decide who gets killed and who has to kill themself. Fun, don't you think?" His other hand waved the key. Victorious. "And when you look up from hell, I'll be sitting in Dyer's penthouse office, staring longingly at all the zeros in my bank account."

Fletcher bristled with the knowledge of how many zeros were *already* in his bank account, given the kind of paychecks he received as general counsel. Melv could inherit the world, and it would never be enough.

Propelled by greed, Melv shoved past Waylon, nearly toppling him into the churning sea. Hooking his fingers around the dock post, Waylon barely stayed upright. Fletcher caught him by the front of his shirt.

"Are you okay?" she gasped.

"Don't let him leave us here," Waylon said as he took off running. "I'll grab the gun!"

Racing down the slip, Fletcher leaped onto the *Tiffany*'s extended gangway. Obviously, she'd never seen the captain's quarters of a gazillion-dollar megayacht with her own eyes, but she imagined a giant spoked wheel, some levers, maybe a big red button or two. Couldn't be *that* hard to miss.

Unfortunately, this boat was big enough to be a sovereign city-state. She didn't have time to waste getting lost.

Up ahead, Melv zipped across a deck splattered with cushioned chaises and striped umbrellas. Perfect. He'd lead her right where she needed to go.

With a glance behind, Melv's lip curled in a snarl when he spotted her. The lawyer broke into a run, all that marathon stamina making it look easy. Curse his runner's endurance. She lost sight of him as he veered through the glass doors of the saloon toward a spiral staircase to the upper decks.

Fletcher slowed, nursing the stitch in her side, when a very familiar canvas bag slumped against the saloon doors caught her eye. Jackie must have loaded it. Digging inside, she found the camera she'd stashed. Not that she really craved to remember this moment for the rest of her life, but at the very least, the flash might blind Melv momentarily.

Waylon found her as she looped the camera strap over her neck. Pistol in hand, he asked, "Where'd he go?"

"Up," Fletcher answered. "But Waylon, forget the key. We just need to find the bridge room."

"This way."

The endless spiraling steps and the threat of getting marooned on Lydell dueled to see which one could make Fletcher dizzier. Thankfully, they found Melv on the second-level deck, darting toward a narrow staircase labeled PERSONNEL ONLY.

Before Fletcher could stop him, Waylon sprang into action. He closed the gap between them and Melv, tearing a white-and-red lifesaver off the wall on his way. As he thrust the float around Melv's shoulders, the lawyer rocked back against the deck railing, arms pinched by his side.

Waylon easily pried the key out of Melv's fingers. "It's not polite to take what isn't yours."

In response, Melv headbutted Waylon's sternum.

A sympathy *whoosh* of air rocketed out of Fletcher's lungs.

Gasping, Waylon staggered into the wall while the lawyer shimmied out of his nautical trap and tossed the lifesaver overboard with a growl, still determined to stage a mutiny. "This ends now, Waylon."

"Couldn't agree more."

Waylon lowered his shoulder like a linebacker and plowed into Melv.

Melv bobbed, sinking against the rail, and his hand caught the banister at just the wrong angle. In slow motion, his wrist snapped, fingers prying open from the force. Sunlight caught the teeth of a bronze key as it arced over—and then into—the water.

The splash was too small for something so consequential.

Melv recoiled, first in shock, then in anger. "How could you?"

Sizzling with unbridled wrath, he muscled past Waylon and knocked Fletcher out of his way. Instead of heading up, Melv speared down the staircase that must have led him toward the aft deck.

"Stay here. I'm going to finish this," Waylon ordered.

"Don't." Fletcher stopped him with a firm hand against his forearm.

Years of hurt slashed through his features. Fists clenching and unclenching around the hilt of Jackie's gun. "He deserves it. Or worse."

"Listen to me." Fletcher repositioned herself in his path. "He might, but you don't."

Waylon barely heard her. "Don't you get it? I pinned my dad's headshot on the dartboard at the back of the bar one year on his birthday. I hated him. I still hate him. But he . . . Maybe my dad and I could have fixed things before he died—maybe we wouldn't have come here at all—if it weren't for Melv."

"Killing Melv won't bring your dad back from the dead. Nothing will. But Dyer wouldn't have wanted you to have to spend the rest of your life knowing you took someone else's. That's why he wrote you the letter and left you this boat. Because he loved you—in his own messed-up way. You don't have to forgive your dad for everything he's done, but if you kill Melv, you'll never forgive yourself." Fletcher cupped Waylon's cheeks in her hands. Forced him to look at her. "We can still save ourselves. But we need to get to the bridge room."

It took all of Fletcher's strength to usher him down the hall. Waylon wheezed with every step, a palm massaging the sore spot on his chest. He harped, "What good does that do us without Melv's key?"

Fletcher planted her hands against the solid expanse of his back. Even using all her body weight, Waylon barely budged. "We don't need it. Come *on*."

His gaze met hers with a hard cut. "What do you mean 'We don't need it'?"

"I've been trying to tell you. *We. Don't. Need. It.*" How could she make it more obvious? Fletcher glanced over her shoulder to make sure Melv was preoccupied with his descent toward the lower decks, probably going to try to retrieve the sinking key. As long as he wasn't anywhere near them, she didn't care where that miscreant slithered off to. "I've got the key we need."

The skin between Waylon's brows folded with frustration. "Did you miss the part where Jackie stole the boat key out of your hands, and then Melv shot her in the face and *he* stole the boat key, and then I hit him, and the boat key *flew into the ocean*?"

"No," Fletcher said calmly. She dipped into the pocket of her still-drenched khakis and pulled out a tag that read CAPYBARA. A little silver key dangled off the end. "Jackie stole *a* key out of my hands. *That* key gets her private access to my room at the manor. *This* key gets us home."

Fletcher barely had time to finish her sentence before Waylon kissed her. Well and truly kissed her. With enough urgency to knock her off-balance. His hand skimmed toward the small of her back, setting her straight again.

He tasted like salt spray and yellow sunlight. As her hands twisted into his shirt, Fletcher wished she never had to open her eyes, never had to be anywhere but here: wrapped in his arms, her heart beating against his.

"You're brilliant," he said, pressing his forehead to hers. His fingers twined in her hand, and she let him lead her through the saloon, up a coiled staircase, and down a hall toward an oval door studded with grommets.

A *locked* door.

Waylon, however, seemed prepared for this possibility. "Step back."

He aimed the pistol toward the lock and fired. One bullet down. The lock snapped, and the door swung open easily. Another thin staircase spat them out at the captain's bridge. The room, walled with panoramic windows, boasted a white-leather seat and a console with several dark screens.

Dipping into the captain's chair, Waylon stuck the key in the ignition. One turn, and lights flashed, radars beeped. The sight of a radio was enough to bring Fletcher to tears. Another turn, and Fletcher expected a revving start, but there was nothing. Once more, the engine tried to kick but failed with a sputter.

Waylon's hands slammed against the chart table. "Damn it. The generator's working, but something's wrong with the engine."

Dread pooled in Fletcher's chest, dripping all the way down to her knees. No way did she survive this long only to be thwarted by a faulty alternator or a slipped belt. She would never be sorry for leaving Kent, but she suddenly wished she'd paid more attention to his efforts around the shop or his droning conversations with her dad and brothers. Spark plug, this. Radiator, that.

A migraine pulsed at the base of Fletcher's skull. She'd seen a hundred tractor engines, if only in her periphery. "If I could get to the engine room, maybe we could figure it out?"

"There's no time for that," Melv said from the doorway, voice slick with rage. A wad of tubing dangled from his hand. The kind typically reserved for engine bays, if Fletcher had to guess. Sabotage. "No one's getting off this island but me."

When Waylon moved to disarm Melv, Fletcher dove for the radio. She pressed a button, and a green light flashed on the board. Her cue. "Mayday, Mayday. We've been marooned at Lydell Island. Map coordinates—"

Melv stripped the radio out of her hand, tearing the cable clean out of the mic. Goodbye, radio. Any resemblance to the levelheaded, handles-himself-well-under-pressure Melv they'd seen on the docks had vanished like a mirage. Now, his olive skin was tinted red with wrath, his usually coiffed hair was a mess of black waves, and his charming smile was reduced to a vicious flash of teeth.

Desperately, Fletcher wailed on the boat horn, and its bellows shook the yacht. The dead? Probably awake now.

"Didn't you hear me?" Melv raged. "I live. You die."

And when threats didn't work, he landed a jab against her cheek, and the sting shot tears to her eyes. The boat horn silenced as Fletcher stumbled, bringing a hand to her rapidly bruising face.

"There's no rescue crew coming." Fletcher relished the way the light in Melv's eyes dimmed. "So, actually, now we all die, asshat."

Grabbing Fletcher's hand, Waylon swept her back down the tight squeeze of a staircase. The bridge door slammed behind them, and footsteps hammered as Melv chased after them.

Everything blurred together—gold fixtures, granite counters, marble floors. Finally, a set of sliding doors opened, and a rush of sea air guided them back onto the main deck. Wind whipped the ocean crests into stiff white peaks. Almost like the island itself conspired to hold them hostage. Fletcher's gaze snagged on the horizon.

Waylon must have seen it, too. "Is that—"

"Hey!" Fletcher shouted, because *yes*. A boat cut through the choppy waters. Far enough out to be wholly unconcerned with Lydell, but a boat nonetheless. The most magnificent boat she'd ever seen. "Over here!"

Waylon tipped the pistol into the air and sent a bullet soaring. "This way!"

They screamed and screamed until their voices went hoarse. The boat floated on. Their one remaining chance at getting off this island without major bodily harm . . . and it didn't even slow down.

It was over. She couldn't stand the thought of looking into

Waylon's eyes and finding the same desperation reflected back at her, so Fletcher settled for leaning her head against the railing and waiting for death to take her.

A sound rumbled in the distance.

Faint, like an alarm clock fighting its way into REM sleep.

Then, again. A horn blasting in the distance.

Someone was coming to rescue them.

27

Celebrating didn't last long.

An elbow crashed against Waylon's shoulder. Melv stripped the gun out of his hands and grabbed Waylon by the arm, spinning him around so he could slam the pistol against the chest of the only living Cartwright.

"Enough," Waylon said. Blood dribbled from his nose, new bruises forming over every patch of skin, but his shoulders straightened with determination. "It's over, Melv."

An oily laugh seeped out. "For you."

A steady thumping pulsed across the waves as their rescuers sailed nearer. Morse code? No. It almost sounded like . . . trap music. They were coming, but not fast enough. Fletcher had to do something before Melv did.

She tapped on Melv's shoulder. "Say cheese!"

Her camera shutter clicked, capturing the moment in perfect clarity—Melv with a fistful of Waylon's shirt and ramming the gun into his sternum, Waylon with his hands spread wide on either side of his face in innocence.

Melv's interest in Waylon immediately waned. He twisted, arms extended with incredible form and his finger hovering over the trigger. Ready to kill. "You want to go first? That's fine."

Through the viewfinder of her camera, Fletcher centered the barrel of the gun. A twist of the lens, and Melv's face came into focus behind it. She set the aperture, shortened the depth of field. The kind of photo that belonged on front pages.

Melv's trigger sank.

A flashbulb popped.

The moment stretched, infinite almost, in that postflash haze as the gun still smoked from its last desperate shot. There was nothing but brine and gunpowder, iron and salt. There was nothing at all.

Then, a scream as Lil Jon's voice tore through the moment.

The rescue boat drifted toward the dock with each *thump* of an 808. Crunk had never sounded so good.

Fletcher lowered her camera. Smiled. "Great work, Melv. Has anyone ever told you how photogenic you are?"

A roar tore up Melv's throat. He pulled the trigger again and again. The gun exhaled soot and little else.

"You're all out of bullets." Waylon dragged Melv away from Fletcher and wrapped him in mooring line. "I'd say your plan backfired, but I guess it didn't actually fire at all."

Fletcher tied the last knot. "Stranding us with two bullets? Diabolical. Great for the theatrics, but a truthfully poor execution."

Melv tried to respond, but Waylon gagged him with a twist of rope. Wedged between the two of them and forced to listen to the worst performance review of his life, Melv floundered against his holds, likely trying to decide which of them to pummel first once he freed himself.

"Your complete disinterest in basic human decency served you well. You really nailed the comic book supervillain vibe," Fletcher ribbed. "I feel like you had us there for a minute. Those sharks got *pretty* close. Ultimately, your downfall was all your own. You had to have the last word."

"But now we get to have it," Waylon added, triumphant. "And the word I'd like to go with is 'goodbye.'"

All the trash-talking bought them enough time for their saviors to sail closer, coming alongside the docked yacht in the inner harbor. The closer the boat got, the easier it became to read the banner draped over the highest deck. In wide pink-and-green letters, it read: THE S.S. SHIP-FACED.

A party spanned both the ship's decks, each filled to the brim with writhing twentysomethings. The lower looked like a dance floor that boasted a preternatural glow—Fletcher squinted, trying to make it out. Ah, that would be a bar draped in rainbow string lights shaped like flip-flops. Upstairs, there must have been a pool because she glimpsed a few foam noodles, a ring floaty shaped like a sprinkled donut with a bite taken out of it, and someone catching some serious height off a diving board, only to belly flop with a tremendous splash.

A passerelle extended between the two boats. For the sake of her stomach, looking down wasn't an option. If she had, she knew she'd find the starved shark tracking beneath, hoping she lost her balance.

When they made it to the other side, a sunburned crew member in an airbrushed cutoff whooped, "What's up! You look like you need a drink!"

Understatement of the century.

The glass-bottomed boat teemed with partygoers. Half the guests wore crop tops painted with "I got Ship-faced," and the other half wore barely anything at all. Neon nylon and sunscreen-slicked skin swirled together. Everyone had a glass in their hand, well on their way to living up to the boat's name.

Fletcher had barely stepped off the gangway when she spotted a shock of bottle-blond hair atop an all-too-familiar wiry frame. Shirtless, wearing a Speedo, a fanny pack, and an ungodly amount of glitter. Only one person on planet Earth possessed that much self-confidence.

"Ford?" she barely heard herself say over the blaring early-2000s hits.

"Look what the tide washed up!" Ford crooned. He wrapped her in a massive hug, lifting her feet off the ground and spinning her in a circle. Coconut-scented suntan oil smeared across her cheek. With her feet solidly back on the deck, he scanned her top to bottom. "You look like trash."

In the name of friendship, she would be ignoring that. "What are you doing here?"

"Day drinking. Seychelles, baby!" He slurped through a loopty-loop straw to really drive home his point. "Plus, I got your texts. You have some explaining to do."

If Fletcher's brain hadn't been so busy figuring out how Ford had gotten her middle-of-the-safari panic texts, she would have been mortified by the knowing look he gave Waylon over her shoulder.

"You . . . got my texts?"

Ford wiggled his phone out of the highlighter-yellow fanny pack. "Yeah. I was, in fact, taking body shots. You know me so well." He thumbed to their text thread, where Fletcher's stream of disjointed thoughts bubbled up one after the other. "If you were—and I quote—going to spend the rest of your short life daydreaming about Waylon's body, I knew there had to be *something* going on."

Waylon snorted. "I gave the DJ a lap dance as a bribe to get him to swing this way."

"The DJ?"

"The DJ is also the captain."

Duh.

"The yacht has Wi-Fi," Waylon said. A smile curved his lips. A little teasing, a little too proud for his own good. "The generator must have powered up the router, so your texts could be sent." He pivoted to Ford. "Can I see these messages?"

"No!" Fletcher shouted. But then, she couldn't help it. She giggled. Despite everything, laughter fizzed up her throat, giddy and light. She'd never been so glad to have a doomscrolling addiction and friendship-separation anxiety. "Ford, I love you, you little heathen. I'll buy you lunch for a month. Three months. The rest of your life, I don't care."

She smashed her face against his bare chest again, squeezing him tight. Ford's slurred laugh vibrated through her cheek. "Does that mean you got the promotion?"

"Something like that," Waylon said.

A petrified screech severed their conversation. Stalking through the crowd of undulating bodies was Melv.

Stomping, spitting mad, and . . . dripping wet? A party foul had clearly been had. The brown stain of a spilled Jack and Coke ruined the front of his ironed shirt, and he'd apparently been hit by a confetti cannon, because he sparkled in the midday sun.

"Is that *Melvin*?" Ford asked, a little too loudly and a lot too drunk.

Melv's face burned red. "This isn't over."

He looked ready to pounce on them, but then Captain DJ's omniscient voice crackled through the speakers. "Cannonball contest starts on the upper deck in five minutes. Wet T-shirt contest to follow. Get up there, folks!"

"Let's go!" one of the partiers shouted. She daisy-chained herself to six other girls in matching Technicolor bikinis. The last of them carried a massive foam floaty under her arm, barely managing to control it.

With a slap, her pool noodle smacked Melv in the chest.

He stretched for the railing, but it must have been slippery from the last cannonball splash, and his fingers slid off. Bobbling, Melv flipped over the edge, disappearing into the deep.

Ford hissed a breath through his teeth. "Should we help him?"

At once, Waylon and Fletcher said, "No."

After everything he'd done, all the pain he'd caused, Fletcher didn't mind letting him sleep with the literal fishes.

For a half second, Ford contemplated this. Then he shrugged. "Cannonball time!"

With as much liquor as he'd clearly consumed, Melv's interruption would be blacked out of Ford's memory by morning.

He trailed after the stampede upstairs, leaving Waylon and Fletcher to mull around the rapidly emptying dance floor. Through the glass bottom, the center of the boat windowed into the ocean as they routed away from the marina and back out to open sea.

Schools of vibrant fish parted, revealing a raging attorney, tangled in the kelp. As if sensing her gaze, Melv craned his neck toward the surface. A stream of bubbles left his mouth with what Fletcher could only assume was a deeply unpleasant combination of profanities. He raised his middle finger. Wicked to the very last breath.

"Can I get you something to drink?" the bartender called. He looked like Waylon's party boat alter ego—sun-bleached hair grown long enough to wrap in a bun, a beard that hadn't been trimmed in god only knew how long, and a stripe of zinc down his nose.

Waylon cracked the faintest hint of a smile. "Oh, she'll have a—"

"Actually." Fletcher tapped her nails against the counter, perusing the shelves behind his head. With a thoughtful hum, she said, "I want to try something new. What's your special?"

The bartender sliced a pineapple. "That's the Dramarama Bahama Step-Mama."

"What's the dramarama?" Waylon asked, his eyebrows doing that wiggly thing again. Uncertain but intrigued.

Pouring as he went, the bartender said, "Five types of rum: dark rum, aged rum, banana rum, coconut rum, and spiced rum."

Fletcher hesitated. "What part is the . . . step-mama?"

"It's strong enough to make you forget your old life," the bartender deadpanned.

"Incredible," Fletcher beamed. "We'll take two."

An umbrella poked out of each of their frozen drinks, skewering a slice of pineapple, a plump cherry, and an orange wedge. Nary an olive in sight. Fletcher and Waylon elbowed through the throng to find a quiet corner by the rail where the pulsating kick drum faded out, leaving only the hypnotic wash of the ocean.

"I propose a toast." Fletcher lifted her pink plastic cup.

Waylon lassoed her closer with a hand skimming beneath her loose shirt. "What to?"

"To defining ourselves and exploring new horizons. Together."

"Together," he echoed. His gaze sparkled like sunlight glistening against the sea. "I could get used to together."

Fletcher inched onto her toes and pressed a kiss to his lips. "The feeling's mutual."

As they tipped their cups together, a wave crested over the top deck and soaked them with pool water. Above, the announcer shouted, "Ten points for Foooord Jepson!"

Fletcher sputtered, lips slick with chlorine. Waylon hadn't fared any better. And when they laughed, it almost erased all the bad parts of this week from her memory. Almost.

She craned her head against Waylon's soaking-wet chest as the tide carried them away. They stood like that until the ice in their drinks melted, until Lydell grew speck-small in the distance, until all that remained was the churning blue sea, the whipped white clouds, and the wind in Fletcher's hair.

28

Six months later

The shutter of Fletcher's camera snapped. Peeling the viewfinder away, she looked up at all sixty-five stories of the Cartwright Media building. A limestone monolith, its windows were capped with art deco flourishes, and the golden revolving doors spun into a marbled lobby.

Some part of her brain wondered when she started looking at this building like an interesting piece of architecture and not a place that gave her heart palpitations.

May had blossomed, drenching the city in color. Around her, New York danced to a symphony all its own—one of taxicabs and squealing train brakes and jaywalkers shouting about having the right of way—and Fletcher found a new rhythm that didn't involve panicked dry-cleaning runs or copying memos. She'd strolled Central Park. She'd consumed enough bagels to last a lifetime. She'd even stopped waking up from night terrors about sleeping through her midyear review.

Still, her palms grew slick with condensation as she watched her former coworkers come and go through the gilded doorway. That was mostly the coffee's fault. She was halfway through her vanilla latte when Waylon ambled onto the sidewalk.

"I came all the way from Brooklyn, and somehow you're the one who's late," she said as she lifted his iced Americano out of the cardboard drink carrier.

His smiles came easier these days. Each one belonged singularly to Fletcher, like she'd been the spark that lit him up again. "That's a weird way to say 'I love you.'"

"I do love you," Fletcher said warmly, "*and* you're late."

He pressed a kiss to her temple, loosening his tie with one hand. Waylon Cartwright in a three-piece was already a sight to behold, but a loose tie? Alert the press. "The board meeting ran a little over, but we finally secured funding for that wildlife conservation project."

"What convinced them? Was it the taxidermied lion? Or the taxidermied zebra. Don't tell me it was the taxidermied capybara."

"Funny enough, it was actually the sustainability models and the carbon-offsetting ROI analysis."

Fletcher cocked her head, a sly grin working over her lips. "Look at you and your three-letter acronyms."

Waylon scrunched his face up in mock distaste.

In the months after returning from Lydell, they'd worked to clean up the mess Dyer left behind.

To start, they had developed the long-expired film from Fletcher's borrowed camera, and even with a timeworn grain and a few faded sunspots, the image of Melv holding Waylon at gunpoint had been damning enough evidence to pin the crime on the late lawyer. Rightfully so. Melv got what he wanted in the end: notoriety and a lasting legacy built on a stolen inheritance.

Generous bereavement packages were extended to the families of those lost on Lydell. It wasn't enough, but shy of searching the earth for the Fountain of Youth or a necromancer's potion, they did everything they could.

The island's animal population was being carefully reintegrated to their natural habitats. (Although the stuffed ones were a bit more challenging to rehome. Eclectic billionaire decor taste wasn't exactly universal, and there were only so many natural history museums.)

Mounds of paperwork had to be reviewed, reverting Dyer's will to the most recent iteration prior to Melv's meddling, but ultimately all of the Cartwright assets were peacefully transferred to Waylon.

He still moonlighted at Subtext, but he'd hired a general manager to take over the day-to-day so that he could have his mornings and afternoons free for meetings like these. While he hadn't stepped in as Cartwright Media's CEO, he'd assumed a position on the board of directors, helping guide the company in a new direction. One that looked forward instead of back and watched out for others rather than only itself.

Waylon checked his watch. "Where's Jepson?"

On cue, *Jet-Setter*'s new senior designer bustled through the doors. Ford greeted them with grabby hands, and Fletcher ushered a coffee into his open fists. Ford took a sip. Sighed. "Remind me how I survive when you're traveling?"

"Miserably and much less caffeinated," Fletcher said with a laugh.

Her recent endeavors had whisked her away from New York for weeks at a time, her passport filling up with stamps. She was her own boss now as a freelance travel photographer. The eviction notice on her door hadn't vanished while she was on Lydell, but even though her tiny studio apartment got Saksified, she could now work from anywhere in the world. (Plus, Waylon's Brooklyn loft had plenty of natural light, and after surviving on Lydell together, cohabiting was a breeze in comparison.)

Ford dry-heaved. "A terrible existence, honestly. Are you sure you don't want to come upstairs? I could show you the plans for the summer issues. I think we've got a couple assignments for you."

"Respectfully," Fletcher said, "I am never stepping foot in that office again. It's called boundaries. Say it with me. *Bound-a-ries.*"

"Okay, okay. Fair enough. In that case, this should suffice." He pulled open a manila folder to a stunning proof of the June edition of *Jet-Setter.*

Fletcher skimmed through the early edition on luxury seaside escapes, past titles like "What to Pack for Your Coastal Getaway" and "Côte d'Azur's Best-Kept Culinary Secrets" until she found the featured article on the Ligurian coast's historic villages.

The lead image rendered Cinque Terre in stunning clarity. Coastal blues made the pastel stucco buildings pop. The foreground boasted a balcony railing and the stripes of linen curtains billowing in the open doorway. Fletcher could still taste the air's sharp citrus, feel the Aperol buzzing through her veins.

Waylon leaned close, reading over her shoulder. His hands settled around her waist as Fletcher scanned the page. Her breath hitched. There, in the corner, printed in little white letters read, *Photo by Fletcher Spence.*

ACKNOWLEDGMENTS

Safari Murder Party is a book about bravery. Yes, if you got stranded on a remote island with a gaggle of murderous colleagues, you'd need to be brave. But beyond that, it was Fletcher who found me working a life-draining job. Whose voice I heard during my regularly scheduled eleven a.m. mental breakdowns, chanting: *You shouldn't have to kill yourself for your job.* Who asked me to be brave enough to try something new, something daring, something scary.

I'm so thankful I did.

If you've found a piece of yourself in Fletcher, in someone desperately hanging on by a thread at a job that takes more than it gives, I mean it when I say: Take a break; feel the sun; choose yourself.

When I told my mom this book would be published by Berkley, she said, "No shit!" Honestly, she took the words right out of my mouth. To my editors, Lisa Bonvissuto and Carly James: I can't say thank you enough. You're the dream team. You chiseled away at Fletcher and Waylon's story like expert sculptors. What's left is exactly the book I hoped it would be: punchy and horrifying and surprisingly romantic. To everyone at Berkley whose hands helped make this book possible—I owe you a lifetime of gratitude. No shit!

Claire Friedman, agent extraordinaire, thank you from the bottom of my heart for everything, from believing in this book when it was nothing more than a wackadoodle title to being probably the world's fastest emailer. You fearlessly chart the way through unexplored waters, and I don't know where I would have ended up without you.

I owe a special thanks to the copycats and, specifically, to Taylor Gates, who, for so many reasons, this book could have never been written without—both for being such an inspiration with your passion for storytelling and for being one of my favorite coworkers ever.

To Kara Kennedy and Mackenzie Reed, I can't remember a version of reality before we were attached at the hip, and I hope I never have to. I wouldn't be half the writer—or woman—I am today without your influence in my life. ILYSM, breads.

Olivia Nash, I could tell you for twelve hours straight exactly how thankful I am for your friendship, your creative input, and your hash-brown casserole. (You were right about the tree house scene.)

Taylor, Liz, Sarah, and Kelsey: Thank you for helping make the Lydell deaths deathier. I apologize to every coffee shop bystander who overheard the many ways we considered murdering Cartwright Media employees.

Barb, Brit, Crystal, Darcy, Holly, Juju, Kahlan, Kalla, Kat, Lindsey, Maria, Marina, Morgan, Olivia, Phoebe, Sam, Shay, Skyla, and Wajudah—thank you for being the first people to hear this idea (six?! years ago) and never trying to dissuade me from writing something so shockingly different from anything else I'd ever worked on.

I've completely lost count of how many times Kaleigh has read this book or how many texts I've sent saying, "Just kidding! Read this version instead!" Thank you for reading every iteration just as enthusiastically as the last.

To Mom, Dad, Tyler, and Alex, it's you I have to thank for inspiring me to dream boldly and take chances, knowing I always have a safe place to land.

And to Christopher, I never know how to distill everything you mean to me into a few simple sentences. Our love story is one I'll spend the rest of my life writing. But the short version is this: We're sitting together on the porch, drinking lemonade, while the world around us is in full bloom, and that is how every day feels with you.